Family Business 7

FAMILY BUSINESS 7

NEW ORLEANS

CARL WEBER
WITH
C. N. PHILLIPS

THORNDIKE PRESS
A part of Gale, a Cengage Company

GALE
A Cengage Company

GALE
A Cengage Company

Family Business Series.
Thorndike Press, a part of Gale, a Cengage Company.

Thorndike Press® Large Print Black Voices.
The text of this Large Print edition is unabridged.
Other aspects of the book may vary from the original edition.
Set in 16 pt. Plantin.

LIBRARY OF CONGRESS CIP DATA ON FILE.
CATALOGUING IN PUBLICATION FOR THIS BOOK
IS AVAILABLE FROM THE LIBRARY OF CONGRESS.

ISBN-13: 979-8-88579-834-1 (hardcover alk. paper)

Published in 2024 by arrangement with Kensington Books, an imprint of Kensington Publishing Corp.

Print Number: 1 Print Year: 2025
Printed in Mexico

Family Business 7

Prologue

It was some time after midnight when the faint sound of a jazz band began to warm Skunk's ears as he made his way off the rural Louisiana two-lane highway just outside of New Orleans' city limits. He entered Gator Lake Parish on a dirt road that most people might have missed if it weren't for the billboard with its purple background and green lettering that read: MIDNIGHT BLUES. Underneath the letters was a large yellow arrow that pointed the way.

Skunk followed the road for about a quarter of a mile before he was greeted by the white lights that hung from the magnificent trees bordering either side of the road. The old, majestic mansion, with its huge columns and wraparound porch, came into view. Once one of the largest slave plantations in the South, it had been transformed a century ago into the club and gambling spot known as Midnight Blues. Skunk and the rest of the locals simply called it the Blues.

As Skunk parked his car and stepped inside the Blues, his senses were overwhelmed by the sounds of the jazz band, the slot machines, and the action at the craps tables, as well as the sight of all the flashy clothing and sparkling jewelry worn by the patrons in the bustling crowd. This was clearly a very profitable night. He headed right up to his favorite room to watch the big boys gambling the big money.

Monique Cartwright, the no-nonsense floor supervisor, watched everything and everybody intensely. It was her job to foresee any problems, and she was damn good at it. She was dressed conservatively in a designer black dress, medium heels, and very expensive yet not ostentatious jewelry. She yawned as she casually surveyed the surprisingly large casino floor, concentrating on the activity at the craps table. The shooter had been betting high and had the dice for almost an hour, which she thought was on the verge of being a little more than luck. She relaxed when he crapped out, losing a substantial amount of chips.

Her phone rang.

"Hello?" she answered as she walked around the craps table.

"You might wanna come up here." It was the deep voice of Dice, the head of security.

"What's going on?"

"The pot in the high stakes hold-em poker game just went over a hundred K pre-flop," Dice replied.

"I'll be right there." Monique calmly hung up and headed toward the step to the second floor, where the private parlor rooms and high stakes gambling took place.

Monique entered the poker room quietly, so as not to disturb the game. She took note of each player at the table and the stacks of chips in front of them, along with the large pile of chips and cash sitting in front of Tom, the dealer, who was dressed in a white shirt and gold vest. Laid out next to the poker chips and cash were four cards: the ace of spades, king of diamonds, a three of diamonds, and seven of clubs. Across the room, Monique made eye contact with Dice, who had positioned himself out of the way in a corner but close enough to see and stop any sort of problem.

Tom looked from his left to his right at Todd, Eric, and Fred, three regular high stakes players at the Blues. They were joined at the table by Billy Bob, a thin, middle-aged cowboy with a deep Southern drawl and very deep pockets. Tom's eyes finally landed on Pierre LeBlanc, a handsome man who frequented the high stakes rooms, draped in expensive designer clothing and enough gold to rival Mr. T.

"The bet is on you, Mr. LeBlanc," Tom said politely.

Pierre lifted his head and smiled, revealing his gold front tooth, as he stared at the money sitting in front of him. "That's a lot of money in that pot."

"A whole lot of money," Billy Bob added. "Now, you gonna bet, or get out the way so the rest of us can have a chance at that money? You been talking a lot of shit, and where I come from, shit talkers don't have the stomach for where this game is about to go."

Pierre glanced over at Billy Bob with a brief flash of anger, but he reigned it back in and playfully wagged a finger at Billy Bob. "You're tryin' to throw me off my game. That shit ain't happening."

Billy Bob shrugged. "It was worth a try. So what you gonna do?"

"Don't rush me. I'm thinking."

"Well, don't hurt yourself. We know how painful that is for you." Billy Bob laughed, and the rest of the room joined in. He even got a smirk out of Monique.

Pierre ignored them, looking down at his two hold cards, lifting them so that only he could see the two aces he had hidden. With the third ace on the board, he had what you might call an unbeatable hand.

"Y'all think shit's funny, right?" He looked up, grinning at everyone at the table, but mostly Billy Bob. "Let's see if you think this shit is funny." He placed his cards down and without hesitation, pushed his sizable pile of chips into the center of the table. "I'm all in."

There was surprise on the faces of all the other players, and Eric, Todd, and Fred quickly surrendered their cards, folding in a sign of defeat. The only person left was Billy Bob, who finished off his drink in one long gulp.

"Woooo-weeee," Billy Bob snorted. "I didn't mean to get your panties all in a bunch, Pierre."

Pierre ignored the taunting. "Now, what *you* gonna do?"

Billy Bob sat in silence for a moment, then looked down at his two hidden cards. He turned to his opponent and studied his face, as if he could read Pierre's cards on there.

The dealer broke the silence in the room. "On you, Mr. Billy Bob, sir."

"Yeah, yeah, I'm thinking," Billy Bob snapped, looking down at his cards once again.

There was nervous laughter from some of the observers at the table. They understood the tension that Billy Bob must be feeling at this moment.

After a bit more hesitation, Billy Bob finally pushed all his chips in the center with a big sigh. "Fuck it. I call," he replied, sounding not at all confident.

The mood in the room was tense as all eyes fell to the dealer, who bumped his hand on the table twice and turned over the last and final card: a king of hearts. Pierre froze and stared as if he couldn't believe what had transpired in front of his eyes. Oh, the gods were shining on him today.

"Full house, motherfuckers!" Elated, Pierre leapt up from his chair, threw his cards down, and started doing a victory dance.

"Three aces and two kings. Mr. LeBlanc has a full house with aces high," Tom announced. Then he turned to Billy Bob and said, "On you, sir."

"Good hand, Pierre," Billy Bob said humbly, raising his arms as if in surrender.

"Damn right." Pierre couldn't hold back his smug grin as he reached for the huge pile of chips and cash in the center of the table.

Suddenly, Billy Bob's arms came down and halted him. "Yep, good hand. But not good enough." He turned his cards over for everyone to see two kings.

"Four of a kind!" Tom sounded surprised as he said it. "The pot is yours, sir."

Pierre, still standing, looked dumbfounded as he watched Billy Bob rake in his chips. "You gotta be fucking kidding me." It took a moment for reality to set in, but then Pierre became indignant. How the hell had fate turned against him so quickly? That was supposed to be his victory.

He turned to his fellow players. "We sure this dude ain't cheating? Nobody is this fucking lucky!"

"The only cheating around here was when God handed out brains and cheated you out of one," Billy Bob jeered, and the rest of the room laughed at the insult.

Pierre lost control at that point. He stepped around Todd and headed toward Billy Bob, thinking about wringing his neck. Things were about to explode in this room.

"Don't even try it, Pierre." Dice stepped out of the shadows of his corner to end the fight before it could start. Monique came up beside him.

"This motherfucker cheated!" Pierre declared.

"Fuck you," Billy Bob snapped.

Pierre tried to lunge for him, but Monique stepped in between, as if Pierre's being a foot taller than her meant absolutely nothing. "Stop it right now, Pierre!" she shouted. "You know we run a clean game here at the Blues. This ain't the first time you lost, and it won't be the last. Now, take a walk, go smoke a cigarette, or take your ass home. I don't care, but I'll tell you what you're not going to do, and that's start some shit in my club."

Pierre stood there, glaring at her and breathing heavily. He was obviously still itching for a fight.

"Go on," Monique said. "Take a walk. Or would you rather be barred from here for life?"

Pierre looked at Billy Bob, who had started raking up the pile of chips. "This ain't right. Y'all know he cheated me."

"We know nothing of the sort. Now, git outta here with that mess. Git!" Monique demanded.

Dice moved toward Pierre, prepared to carry him out of here if it got to that point.

Pierre was pissed off, but he wasn't stupid. Having to be carried out by Dice would add even more humiliation to this terrible night. So, he reluctantly headed for the exit, his hands and pockets empty. Before he walked out the door, he turned back to Billy Bob and pointed a finger at him. “This ain’t over.”

“Sure it is. It was over when I turned over those two kings.”

Pierre heard the mocking laughter of all the other players coming from behind him as he hung his head and walked away in defeat.

Chapter 1
Marquis Duncan

"Damn, Marquis! Nobody fucks me like you, baby. Nobody!"

Maybe Antoinette was gassing me up, but her choice of words, along with her sexy-ass Cajun accent, brought a confident smile to my face as I slid deep inside her again and again from the back. The two of us had been going at it damn near since we'd hit my door twenty minutes ago. How we even made it to the bedroom was a mystery.

"Oh, shit, babe, I'm cummin'. I'm cummin', daddy!" she purred as her back arched and her phat ass clapped back at me. God damn, that pussy was good, and the way she was squirming around like I was the best she'd ever had just made me pump away harder. I'll say one thing about her: if she was faking, she deserved an Academy Award, because she had me open.

After what seemed like an eternity of uncontrollable spasms, accompanied by some of the sexiest moans and groans I'd ever heard, Antoinette finally collapsed on the bed. Despite all that, she wasn't done yet, and neither was I. I continued to slide myself in and out as she squeezed her muscles around me.

"Damn, baby, that was some of the best dick I've ever had. I'm so glad you finally gave in."

"Me too," I replied, trying to control the raging orgasm building inside me.

We'd been resisting this moment for almost a year, but today, I'd finally relented when she asked for a ride home from work. I could not help myself. I liked what I liked, and I loved me a ghetto-ass woman with an Instagram face and porn-star body. Her being from the Fifth Ward, one of the rougher sides of town, just made things even more exciting. We both knew we shouldn't be doing this.

"Now, turn me over, daddy, so I can return the favor. I wanna see your pretty face when you cum for me."

Her words were like angels singing to me. I turned her over on her back, staring down at her sandy brown face for a moment. She was beautiful. There was no doubt about that, with her long, fake eyelashes highlighting her large, almond-shaped eyes, full succulent lips that she knew how to use, and a cute nose highlighted by a large diamond stud. I moved a strand of hair from her face, and she smiled up at me as our lips and tongues met. I positioned myself between her thick, healthy thighs, sliding myself inside her warmth as she took a sharp breath. I instantly felt the pleasing pain of her long, talonlike fingernails in my back as she pulled me in deeper.

"Don't play with it, baby. I won't break. Just fuck the hell outta me," she shouted, digging her claws into my skin and wrapping her legs around my lower back so I couldn't get away. She began gyrating her hips and bucking up and down until we were moving the bed halfway across the room. "Fuck me! Fuck me harder, Marquis!"

She was scratching and humping me so hard I was sure she drew blood, but I didn't give a shit. That just turned me on more, and I was on the verge of an orgasm of my own. It was only going to take a few more strokes to send me over the edge, although I was trying to prolong the moment.

Suddenly, Antoinette's body froze like a deer caught in headlights.

"What happened? Why'd you stop?" I looked down at her face incredulously and saw what could only be described as a look of horror. "What's the matter?"

She didn't answer with words, but her body language told me someone was behind me, and whoever it was had her scared shitless. There weren't many people who could scare a girl like Antoinette, so the first person who came to my mind was her husband. Yes, she was married, and up until now, he and his crazy-ass fucking reputation for being over-the-top jealous were the main reasons I'd been resisting her so long.

"Fuck," I mumbled under my breath, swallowing hard. That's when things got even worse, and I heard the click of a gun being cocked.

My momma had always told me that pussy was going to be the death of me. I had always thought she meant I was going to die by some type of horrible STD, but now it seemed that pussy was going to get me shot in the back. It took me a moment to gather myself before I rolled off Antoinette to face what I was sure would be my demise.

"I know how this looks, but —" I raised my hands to see someone far worse than Antoinette's husband pointing a .44 Magnum at us.

"Nigga, I been calling your ass for the better part of an hour. I know you ain't ignoring my calls 'cause you got Antoinette laid up my house." The beautiful thick woman sneered angrily, pointing the gun directly at Antoinette, who quickly tried to cover up. Not that it mattered. By this time, she had seen all she needed to see. "Him I can almost understand. He ain't nothing but a man. His little head always going to be thinking for his big one, but you? How dare you fuck him in my house! After I took you in and gave you a job."

"Shirley, it's not what it looks like," Antoinette pleaded. I could feel her shrinking beside me, but there wasn't much I could do for her. It was only a matter of time before I got my ass chewed out myself.

"Oh, no? 'Cause it looks like you're fucking my son behind your husband's back. And that's *Mrs. Duncan* to you," my momma growled angrily, glaring at Antoinette as if she were the devil himself. "Now get the fuck out my house." My momma pointed at the door with an angry scowl across her face.

When my momma got like that, there was no talking to her, and I think Antoinette sensed it, because she shamelessly slipped out of bed without covering up. She retrieved her clothes and headed for the door without making eye contact with either me or Momma.

"I'm going to need a ride home."

"Why don't you call your husband?" Momma sneered behind her. "You little tramp."

"Momma!" I exclaimed.

"Don't you 'Momma' me! Do you know what the hell you've done?" She gave me a look of disappointment, but I'd take that any day over the look of distaste she'd given Antoinette. "Her husband will kill you."

I wrapped the sheets around my waist to retrieve my clothes, which were strewn around the room. I shook my head. "It was only a one-time thing. First and last. No big deal."

"I hope so, because that girl is trouble with a capital T." She sat down in a chair across from my bed as I got dressed. "I'm guessing you were too preoccupied screwing her to answer any of my calls."

"You been calling me? I ain't hear my phone." I glanced around the room for my phone, patting my pants. "Damn. I must have left it in the car. What's going on?"

I looked at the seriousness on her face, and I could tell she wasn't as upset about catching me and Antoinette together as I thought. Something else was on her mind.

She reached into the black Chanel dangling from her wrist and pulled out a gun, then handed it to me. "Finish getting dressed and get your ass down to the Blues. We've got problems."

"What's going on?" I stared down at the gun in my hand and exhaled. Whatever was going on had to be big.

"I got a call from Monique. Something went down at the Blues tonight. Something that could have real implications down the road."

"Shit. We got robbed?"

"Worse, baby. Much worse," she said sadly.

"Momma, what could be worse than us getting robbed?"

"A body."

"Fuck." I felt my heart rate increase with this bad news.

The Midnight Blues, or the Blues, as we called it, was a unique and popular casino and after-hours club that my family had owned and operated for more than a hundred years. It was one of those places that was always filled with tourists and regulars. Outside of gambling and partying your night away, it was just a place where you could kick back and listen to some of that good ole jazz music. That was the brighter side of our business.

The darker side was our parlor rooms, where backroom deals of all sorts took place over high stakes gambling with no questions asked. I felt fairly certain that those parlor rooms were where this body was found.

"Who?" I asked and watched a look of distress cross her face. "Who, Momma?"

Her hesitance made me imagine the worst. "Not Uncle Floyd?"

She shook her head. "No, him and Monique are fine."

"Then who?"

"Pierre LeBlanc."

Now I understood the reason for the gun. Hearing the name LeBlanc sent a tingle down my spine. I wasn't a man that scared easily, but Pierre's brother Jean was a man to be feared. On the outside, he appeared to be the owner of a huge and reputable construction real estate holding company, but the truth was much grittier. Jean LeBlanc was New Orleans's most notorious drug lord and leader of the city's largest street gang, the Crescent Boys. A kingpin, if you will. He was a dangerous man and one anyone should have been careful not to cross. Including us. So, if indeed Pierre LeBlanc was dead in our club, there would be hell to pay.

"Shit!"

Momma was now halfway to the door. "Exactly. I already told Floyd to close that part off to everybody. And hurry the hell up."

Chapter 2
Big Shirley

It was late, almost three a.m., by the time I left my son Marquis and pulled my Jaguar onto the long dirt driveway that led to our family's century-old legacy, the Midnight Blues. The Blues had been in our family since shortly after slavery ended, and despite all the bullshit that had happened earlier tonight with the discovery of a body, I always beamed with pride when I saw the lighted trees that surrounded our plantation-style-house-turned-casino.

I pulled my car into the parking space with a sign that read: BIG SHIRLEY DUNCAN, PROPRIETOR. People had been calling me Big Shirley for as long as I can remember, almost forty-something years. Some people thought it was an embarrassing nickname placed on me because of my stout size, but I wore the name with pride because it meant so much more. I'd always been a voluptuous woman with big titties and a big ass, but I liked to think the name Big Shirley came more for my over-the-top charismatic personality, which had a tendency to take me into places my big titties and ass couldn't. Oh, and of course, when my body or my personality didn't work to open doors, there was always my big-ass .44 Magnum gun I was known to keep handy.

I glanced up at the Blues once more, shaking my head as I thought about the body I was about to encounter once I went inside. Don't get me wrong. We'd had dead bodies at the Blues before, but we'd never had anyone's death that could bring us the problems of Pierre LeBlanc.

I exited the car and entered the building, thankful that there weren't half a dozen police cars and a nosy-ass sheriff asking everyone a million questions. I was greeted by Dice, my six foot four, three hundred pound cousin, who headed our security. Dice wasn't the brightest man you'd ever meet, but he was loyal, and his size was a huge deterrent when it came to patrons getting out of line. Unfortunately, it hadn't deterred Pierre's demise on the premises.

"Where's Moe?" I asked when I was barely through the door.

Dice gestured upstairs. "Your office."

I nodded my thanks, then headed for the

stairs. When I reached my office, Monique Cartwright, my best friend, right-hand woman, and first cousin on my daddy's side, was already sitting in her usual spot beside my desk, looking visibly distressed. She wasn't much of a drinker, but she was in the middle of throwing back a shot of tequila when I stepped in.

"You want one?" She glanced over at me as she poured herself another shot.

"Yeah, but make mine a double." I walked around and sat in my chair as she poured our drinks. "Is Pierre still here?"

"Yeah, he's still here. I told you on the phone the man's dead. You didn't expect him to get up and walk away, did you?" Monique handed me my drink.

"You okay? You sound a little stressed."

"Shit, I am stressed." She downed her second drink and poured another. "You'd be stressed too if you found that fool with his brains splattered all over the room. I mean, that's Jean LeBlanc's brother in there."

"Yeah, I know," I replied, trying to sound comforting. Did Pierre's death ignite a small sense of panic inside of me? Yes. But it had already happened, and there was only one way to go — forward. What would get me through was keeping a clear head and handling only what I could handle at the time. So, my focus would be getting in front of the situation. I'd cross the other roads when I got there.

"We're gonna be all right, Mo. I mean, hell. We didn't kill the man. And at least that part is the truth."

I downed my drink just as Marquis walked in the room. Like us, he had a look of worry on his face, and his first question was, "What the fuck happened?

CHAPTER 3
MARQUIS

I'd dropped Antoinette off a block away from her house and damn near broke every speeding record I could driving over to the Blues, where I found my momma and her cousin Monique in her office. To my surprise, they were doing shots. I might have expected that from my momma, but you couldn't have paid me to think it was something I'd see straightlaced Monique doing. See, Momma had a dark and dirty past. It was one she rarely talked about, but it was what had turned her into the person she was today, a hard-nose, no-nonsense business owner who would do whatever it took to protect her club and her family. Monique, on the other hand, had gone to some fancy college back East, and I'd never seen her drink more than a glass of wine. I guess Pierre's death had everyone stressed.

Don't get me wrong. Despite her small stature — five feet two inches, 100 pounds

— and her by-the-book pit boss mentality, Monique, like the rest of our family, was nobody to fuck with. She could turn from a pussy cat to a damn mountain lion in the blink of an eye. And she was a beast with that eight-inch switchblade she carried at all times.

I let them savor their drinks for a moment, then finally broke the silence in the room. "What the fuck happened?"

Monique shook her head. "I don't know. Pierre was in the high stakes parlor room, playing poker, drinking, and losing, like always."

"You didn't notice anything different or funny about him?" I asked.

"Not at all. Other than he was involved in a pretty bad beat, even for him."

"How bad?" my momma asked.

"I got called in the room when the pot went over fifty thousand. Pierre's full house lost to four of a kind. When it was all said and done, he lost about a hundred grand, and he wasn't happy. He accused the guy of cheating, and things got heated to the point that Dice had to step in. I told Pierre to take a walk. Ten minutes later, the shot rang out. I ran back up and found him dead on the couch."

"So, the guy shot him?" Momma asked.

"No, he was with me cashing in his chips. Dice and I walked him to his car and watched him drive away. That's when we heard the shot."

I was just about to ask Monique which parlor room the body was in when my uncle entered the office. He checked behind him before shutting the door.

Uncle Floyd was Momma's younger brother. He was dressed in pressed slacks and a Versace button-up. Like usual, he was dressed sharp. He was only a few years older than me, and we were practically raised as brothers, although he always reminded me he was my uncle. Floyd was forced to grow up a lot faster than I was. He was out of the house with his own spot, taking care of himself at seventeen. He was one of those streetwise, practical brothers who didn't have any formal education, but you'd be stupid to challenge his intellect, because he could run rings around most college-educated men. Momma may have been the head of our family, but Uncle Floyd was the backbone.

He checked behind himself before shutting the door. Noticing me, he nodded his head in acknowledgement. "Nephew."

"Unc." I returned the gesture.

He turned to face Momma. "All right, I

cleared the other parlor rooms on this floor and gave everyone credits. Folks were asking questions, but only a few people saw the body. The upstairs parlor rooms are completely closed off until further notice."

"Smart. Good job, Floyd," Momma replied. "Now, what are we going to do with his body?

"Hell, I say we call the police. Let them sort it out with Jean," Monique said quickly.

Momma's neck snapped toward her. "Hell no! Are you crazy? We're not talking to anybody until we get our stories straight."

Momma turned back to Uncle Floyd. "Right now, I wanna see the body." She got up from the desk so Floyd and Monique could take us to the scene.

I wasn't sure what to expect. I'd seen my share of bodies before; however, nothing could have prepared me for the gory scene I witnessed when Monique opened that parlor room door. My heart sank, and any hope that we could get out of the situation easily, sank with it. Laying at an awkward angle with the top of his head blown off was none other than Pierre LeBlanc. I didn't have to see his face, which was a bloody mess. His clothes and jewelry told me who he was. Pierre was someone I'd grown accustomed to seeing multiple times a week for as long as I could remember. He was a smooth-talking, impeccably dressed cat with almost as much gold around his neck as Mr. T. Pierre loved to gamble, and the Blues was practically his second home. He was on a first name basis with all of our dealers and most of the cocktail waitresses.

"Fuck." I stepped near the body. His blood and brains had painted a mural on the wall behind him. There was no question about it; he was dead.

"Who else was in here with him?" Momma asked, walking into the room and looking around for clues.

"No one that I know of," Monique answered.

"It looks like he killed himself." Floyd pointed to the gun on the ground by Pierre's hand. "Or somebody got real close and personal."

"Anybody check the cameras?" Momma asked.

"There are no cameras on the second floor," Floyd replied. "You took them out at your friend the mayor's request, remember?"

"Yeah, I remember." Momma groaned. She rented the parlor rooms out to politicians, gangsters, and anyone else who would pay the $5000 a night private room fee, so they could have their secret backroom meetings without being disturbed or observed.

"What the hell would make him do something like that here, of all places?" I wondered out loud, staring at the body.

"As much of his brother's money as he loses, he might have been in some kind of gambling debt," Floyd suggested.

"Nah. Jean wouldn't hurt his little brother over no money," I replied. "This shit just doesn't add up. What would make a man blow his own brains out?"

"I wouldn't put anything past Jean. He's ruthless," Momma said, and I swear I saw a moment of fear flash in her expression. She was not a woman who was rattled easily.

"Ruthless with a capital *R,*" Monique added.

"I know I'm asking a lot, but you're our fixer. I need you to make this go away," Momma said, looking me in the eyes. "We both know we don't need any problems with Jean LeBlanc or the Crescent Boys."

"How the hell do I make something like this go away?" I asked, pointing at the chunk missing from Pierre's head.

"The same way we make everything else go away, nephew. Money." Uncle Floyd placed a hand on my shoulder. "Think about it. You know what to do."

We connected eyes, and I nodded. He was right. I did know what to do, but that didn't mean that I wanted to do it. "All right. I'll make the call, but I need to see everyone who saw this room."

"I thought you might say that. Right this way," Uncle Floyd replied.

He led me out of the room and to another parlor room a few doors down. When we entered, I saw three men sitting uncomfortably around a poker table. The room stank from the nervous sweat seeping through their pores. I knew them by name: Todd, Eric, and Fred. They were all regulars at the Blues, wannabe high rollers who gambled enough to earn access to the parlor rooms.

Fred's eyes were glued to the ground, and he didn't budge, not even when he heard the door open. Eric, on the other hand, was a little jumpy. Todd's brown face was flushed, and his broad shoulders slumped. I didn't think he could seem any more down until he saw me and Floyd and slumped even farther.

"Bruh, I swear none of us had anything to do with that boy being dead. How long have we been friends?" Todd asked Floyd in a shaky voice.

"Too long," Floyd answered. "Long enough for me to know that you didn't lay a finger on Pierre."

"Then why are we still here?"

"Insurance," I said.

I looked at Uncle Floyd, and he gave me a small nod before he left the room. Focusing my attention back on the men, I gave the men a hard stare. I needed them to understand how grave the situation was.

"We all know who the dead body is, right?" I asked, and they nodded. "And we all know what will happen if his brother learns of what happened here tonight, right?"

"But like Todd said, we ain't do it!" Fred inserted.

"We know that. Pierre killed himself," I told them, and they seemed to relax slightly, as if they were exonerated.

"You think that matters?" I asked them. "You know who his brother is just like I do. *And* what he'll do to anyone who he suspects in the slightest. You three saw the body, right? That could be evidence enough for Jean to take off your heads."

The three of them shared a mortified expression. They no doubt were envisioning the horrors that Jean would inflict on them. Good. It was those thoughts that would keep their mouths shut. That, and a nice payoff from us. Uncle Floyd reentered the room, holding a nice stack of cash. He split it equally in three and handed a stack to each of them.

"I'm gonna make this all go away, but let's be clear. Y'all ain't seen *shit* tonight. Understand?"

"Shit, I wasn't even here tonight. I was in Baton Rouge," Todd said, thumbing through the money.

Fred and Eric simply nodded their understanding. They seemed to still be in shock. But who could blame them? I was too.

"Good. Now, all of you get the hell out of here. And remember, don't say shit to nobody," Floyd told them.

The three men stood up and scrambled out of the room, leaving Uncle Floyd and me alone.

How could such a beautiful day end so badly? I wondered. But I didn't have time to be pissed off about it. We had a body to move.

Chapter 4
Floyd

I'd carried a lot of bodies in my past, but there was only one that had fazed me. Years ago, when I found out my son Fabio was murdered, life as I knew it was altered forever. Although I had two children, he'd been my first born and my only boy. I would never forget the call telling me they had to identify him by his dental records because he was unrecognizable. Nor would I forget what it felt like carrying his casket. After that, I was eternally changed inside. A part of me died with him. I always wondered if my days of plundering the streets as a young cat had come to serve me my karma. My son being gunned down at a fresh twenty-five was the worst kind of trauma.

I rarely tried to live in that memory. It was too painful still even years later. I went from being on top of the world to having no world at all. Fabio and my daughter Fanny had been truthfully the only thing holding together the loveless marriage between their mother and me. The divorce papers were signed soon after he died. My ex-wife, Amina, was the most money-hungry witch I've ever known. She tried to take me for everything I had, and she would have succeeded if it weren't for the prenuptial agreement she'd signed decades ago. I let her keep the house and put a nice amount in her bank account, but that was it. Fabio was gone, and Fanny was grown and traveling the world. I knew losing her brother had cut her deeply too. It probably didn't help to see her parents arguing all the time. I didn't blame her for staying gone.

All I had left was Big Shirley, Marquis, and the Blues. At least I knew I was with people who genuinely loved me. And I loved them right on back. I'd do anything for them, including getting rid of the body of Pierre LeBlanc.

One thing I'd learned from being in the game for so long was that one should always keep tarps laying around. I had some in the closet of my office, and Marquis and I used that to wrap the body. There was a part of the Blues that was under renovation and had been closed off to everyone, the staff included. We took that route to get the body to where my pickup truck was parked in the back. It wasn't a short distance carrying literal dead weight, but it was the best way to take. So, we huffed and puffed our way to the door.

"Shit! Did this motherfucka eat a cow before he died?" Marquis asked breathlessly.

We set the body down and stopped to catch our breath. I peered out of the window to make sure nobody was around. The coast was clear.

"All right, let's do this," I told him.

"One, two, three."

On the count of three, we hoisted the body. I opened one of the doors with my back and stepped out backward, walking to the pickup truck. Knowing we were at risk of being seen, we moved as fast as we could and dumped the body in the bed of the truck.

"Damn, Unc, you did that like it was nothing to you," Marquis said, studying me. "You barely even broke a damn sweat!"

"I've been around a lot longer than you, nephew," I told him. "And I was much younger than you when I had to get rid of my first body."

"Really?"

"You know me and your mom have different daddies? Well, my daddy was a short-tempered motherfucka. Trigger-happy, too.

I was just fifteen years old the first time I dug my first makeshift grave, all because my daddy thought he was being cheated in a poker game. I never even knew the poor bastard's name. Just knew my daddy put a bullet right between his eyes."

"Damn. He sounds cold blooded." Marquis let out a low whistle.

"He was. But he always would tell me, 'The body doesn't matter if the soul is gone.' I guess that helped me not be, I don't know, creeped out looking at a dead body. It was just a *thing* at that point. There's only one time one of those *things* affected me." I stopped talking abruptly and found myself staring off into the distance. A quick flash of my son's handsome face and his infectious smile came to my mind before I pushed it away.

"I still think about him too, you know," Marquis said softly.

I looked at him, shocked.

"What?" I asked.

"Fabio," he said, looking sincerely into my eyes. "I think about him all the time. He was the closest thing I had to a brother. It still fucks me up that he's gone."

"Yeah . . . well, it's just one of those things."

"I know why you don't talk about him.

But Fabio was a forgiving man. Don't for a second think he doesn't forgive you for —"

"You call Clay already?" I interrupted him, not interested in rehashing those painful memories.

He gave me a knowing look but didn't push the topic.

"Yeah, I called right before we grabbed the body. She wasn't too happy about it, either, but we don't have a choice. I don't know how she's gonna help us get out of this one, but she's gonna have to."

"You sure you don't want me to go with you?"

He shook his head. "Nah, I got it. You and Clay don't get along too good."

"Nope. I got a problem with snakes, and Clay is as big a snake as they come."

"She's just a mercenary, that's all."

I handed him the keys to my truck and placed my hands on his shoulders. No more words needed to be said between us. He knew what he had to do. I gave him a quick embrace and sent him on his way. I stepped back while he got in the truck and watched him drive away until I couldn't see the red rear lights anymore.

When he was gone, I went back into the Blues. The second stop would be finding my sister, but the first would be to the bar.

I needed something dark and strong to hit my chest. Anything to rid my mind of that last fight I'd had with my son before he died.

Chapter 5
Jean

I waited for the last patrons to walk out of La Nue, a popular gentlemen's club in New Orleans. It was a little after three in the morning, closing time. The business I had with the owner, Red, didn't require any extra eyes or ears. Saint, my right hand and close friend, sat passenger in my Rolls Royce, watching the club. He didn't look too happy, which was understandable. I'd sent Saint to La Nue a week prior with a proposition for Red. Saint didn't like it whenever I had to step in.

Before me, my father, Julien LeBlanc, ran New Orleans with an iron fist. Not only did he control the drug trade, but he made sure to have a piece of almost every profitable business that he wanted. Whether it was buying them out or offering them start-up money, he made sure his name was somewhere in the paperwork. He taught me at an early age that the best money was the money that other people made for you. They built the businesses up, and we sat back and collected our duckets. When it was my turn to take over, I followed the blueprint entirely, spinning it to my favor, of course.

There were some businesses that my father never wanted to be a part of. For instance, he never wanted to own a gentlemen's club. He said they were too sleazy, and he only wanted the most upscale establishments attached to his name. Me, on the other hand? I saw nothing but profit. It was in my interest to have my hand in the highest grossing establishments, regardless of their business. Out with the old, and in with the new. La Nue, that is.

Currently, La Nue was one of the most popping joints in all of NOLA. Although it was smaller than the Midnight Blues, it seemed to never be empty, just like the casino. Seeing that kind of business and being of no benefit to me felt like a waste, especially with it being in Crescent Boy territory. The olive branch I'd extended Red was very much one-sided, but he would have still made out nicely. However, when Saint told me Red had all but spit in his face when he was presented with my offer, I was forced to make a house call. It was something I rarely did, but if the most decorated killer on my roster couldn't persuade Red, then it was time to show my hand. It wasn't unusual that an owner didn't want to bring in other parties when it came to their establishments, but I could be a very persuasive man. Whether it was with my checkbook, finding the skeletons in someone's closet, or completely getting rid of them, I always got what I wanted.

"What you wanna do?" Saint asked while checking the magazine in his gun.

"Talk," I said with a smirk.

We opened our doors and got out. So did a small entourage of Crescent Boys in an SUV parked next to my car. The Crescent Boys were one of the biggest gangs in New Orleans, and their allegiance was with me. See, before my daddy, my grandfather was in charge. And before him, it was my great grandfather, Jaleel LeBlanc. He was the one who started the current LeBlanc legacy — and what a visionary he was. He figured that instead of hiring bodyguards, he would start a gang that served the specific purpose of protecting his family and pushing his weight. In return, they would have all the money and weapons they could ever dream of. Not only that, but they would be able to operate in the shade of one of the wealthiest and most prominent black men in society.

That gang was the Crescent Boys, and their service was for a lifetime.

I smoothed out my Brioni suit, and when I started walking to the club entrance, they all followed me. Two security guards that I knew as Gio and Mario were standing in front of the club. Gio was Red's oldest son and protector. Mario was their cousin. They seemed to be having an amusing conversation, until they saw me approaching them. In unison, they stepped in front of the door. The two men looked like night and day, with Mario being light skinned and Gio being dark. Mario crossed his arms and looked at me like he had a bad taste in his mouth.

"Red in?" I asked.

"Nah, he left," Mario told me.

"You sure about that?"

"I work for the man, don't I?"

I found myself chuckling at his words. "Do I need to remind you who I am?"

"That means step aside, motherfucka. Unless you want us to be the last things you see." Saint touched the gun on his hip.

Mario looked down at the pistol and then at Gio. They communicated wordlessly, but it seemed that they got the message because they stepped out of the way. Gio opened the door for us to walk through the entrance hallway. When we got to the main floor, I noticed a few bartenders cleaning their work stations and a janitor mopping the floors. The music had been turned off, but the lights were still dim.

"I think it's time for y'all to go on home." Saint's voice boomed.

Everyone stopped what they were doing. The bartenders took one look at me and grabbed their purses without a second thought. The janitor looked up at me with low and dopey eyes. He had to have been in his late forties, and it was obvious that he was as high as a kite. He grinned as he pushed his mop and bucket past us, talking to himself.

"Big Red think he's the big man in town. Wait till he see that the real big man in town is here, and he don't look too happy," I heard him say as he exited. When he was gone, I could still hear him laughing down the hall.

Mario passed us and went to fetch Red from his back office. Gio hung back and stood across from us, giving us the evil eye. His gaze lingered on mine for a second before he looked away. As I waited patiently for the man of the hour, I looked around the lavish club. I had to admit, I was impressed with what Red had done with the place. The deep red velvet chairs went well with the chandeliers hanging from the ceiling and the sparkly black marble floor. The VIP booths looked like something out of a Vegas nightclub. On the walls next to them were empty crystal picture frames, I assumed for whoever rented the section to put a blown-up photo of themselves. Nice. He'd taken an old, run-down building and flipped it into a five-star establishment.

"Jean LeBlanc!" I heard the loud, raspy voice of the one and only Red Baskin. "You missed the party. The club is closed."

Red was a tall, very light-skinned man, hence the name. He also often wore the color, like his suit that night. Walking beside him was his shadow, Kendall. Kendall was a trans man who stood at about five feet eight inches, with a slim but muscular build. He might have been easy on the eyes to the women, but he was also a straight killer.

When Red stopped, so did Kendall, but he made sure to stand a few steps back like a good shadow should. Mario and Gio stood on either side of Red, showing that he was protected from all sides. Hanging in one hand at Red's side was a shotgun. In the other, a cigar rested between two of his fingers. He took a long draw of it as he looked at me and my entourage.

"Then it's the perfect time to discuss business, don't you think?" I asked smoothly.

"And what business do you have with me?"

"This club. I sent my man Saint over to work out a business deal for me to buy half of it. It hurt my heart to know you gave him such a tough time."

"He didn't tell me how important this was to you," Red said unconvincingly.

"A part of me is telling me that you knew." I gave Red a hard stare for a few moments before he chuckled and waved his lit cigar in the air.

"If I did know, I might have given him a few more seconds of my time, out of respect. But either way, Mr. LeBlanc, my answer is still the same. No."

"Well, that's fine, because that offer is no longer on the table anyway. Now I want it all."

Red scoffed and studied me as if to see if I was serious. He looked from Saint and then back to me like I was out of my mind. In truth, he was the one out of his mind, because everyone in New Orleans with half a brain knew that it would not be healthy to piss me off.

"Like I said to your man Saint last time, with all due respect, La Nue is not for sale." His voice was firm. "Now, I'd appreciate it if you boys went ahead and left. It's way past closing time, and I need to lock up."

It was almost funny the way Red thought he could tell me what to do. So funny that I laughed. "You almost had me going there with the whole 'with all due respect' thing. Made me feel like my daddy for a minute."

"Your daddy was a good man. A fair man."

"What you tryna say, Red? That I ain't a fair man?"

"I'm sayin' that you ain't your daddy."

Although I smirked, I felt a small twinge inside. That was something I'd been hearing since I was a boy. No matter how high I went in the world, Julien LeBlanc had already been there. Instead of dwelling, I reached into the inside pocket of my suit jacket and pulled out a couple pages of folded paperwork and a pen.

"I'm going to give you the easy way out and two hundred thousand to boot. All you need to do is sign here, and the money will be in your account in the morning."

Anger flashed across Red's face. "I just told your ass that La Nue ain't for sale! And two hundred thousand is chump change. I see that in a month with all the high rollers that come through here. Take that paperwork and shove it up your friend's ass. Get out!"

I sighed and looked up at the ceiling in annoyance. "Stop being so difficult and sign the papers, Red."

"Can't do that." Red dropped the cigar and cocked the shotgun he was holding, aiming it right at me.

"I didn't want it to be this way. I hope you know that," I said calmly.

Two shots rang out. Nobody on my side of the floor moved, but on Red's, I watched as Mario and Gio fell dead to the ground with bullet holes in the backs of their heads. Gio's eyes were still open as his blood began to seep onto the floor, and Red stared, horrified by the sight of his dead son. Confused, he turned around to see Kendall's gun pointed right at his face.

"I'd appreciate it if you stopped pointing that shotgun at my uncle," Kendall told him tersely.

"U-uncle?" Red was in such shock that he didn't fight when Kendall snatched the shotgun from him.

"Your dumb ass didn't even know I had my family working for you." I chuckled. "How else do you think I knew how lucrative La Nue has become?"

Red's eyes went back to Gio. "My son . . .

you killed my son."

"No, you killed your son. All you had to do was sign the fucking papers. And now that you know how serious I am about owning La Nue, it's in your best interest to comply. Unless you want the rest of your family to face the same fate as Gio."

Kendall shoved his gun in the back of Red's head and nudged him, forcing him to walk toward me. I knew that if he could, Red would have tried to rip me to shreds. If he attempted it, he would receive a bullet in his skull, as would his family members, and he surely knew that. So, he acquiesced and signed the papers on every dotted line when I handed him the pen.

Once he was finished, I took the paperwork back and looked it over. "Thank you, Red. That wasn't that hard, was it?" I tucked the papers in my suit jacket. "Have a good night."

I motioned my head toward the door, and my crew turned to walk away. Kendall stepped around Red with the gun still pointed at his head. When he got to me, he let his arm down, and we both turned to walk away.

As we neared the door, I heard what sounded like a war cry behind me. I turned around in time to see Red running at me with a blade raised high in his hand. Blocking the attack just in time, I twisted his wrist so I was able to snatch the blade from him. He was staring me in my eyes as I shoved it through the side of his neck.

"You . . . bastard." Those were his last words before I let him fall to the ground.

"It didn't have to be like this. But it's better this way. I didn't need an annoying pest at my heels." Not caring to watch him take his last breath, I turned to Kendall. "Clean these bodies up."

Chapter 6
Floyd

Hanging around the Blues that night, my thoughts were on Marquis. He was a grown man, but as his uncle, I was finding it hard to take the training wheels off. I often gave Big Shirley a hard time for hovering over the boy, but quiet as it's kept, I did the same thing. It might have been the pain of losing my own boy that made me overprotective of Marquis.

I'd been feverishly checking my phone, waiting for any updates from him about Clay.

Sheriff Clay had taken a liking to him, unlike her feelings about me. That woman couldn't stand me. It could've been because I didn't watch my mouth for anybody, or it could've been because she knew that if she ever tried to cross Big Shirley, it would be me who stuck it to her.

I forced myself to stop looking at my phone and decided to trust my nephew to take care of Pierre LeBlanc's body. For the right amount, I knew the sheriff would help us, and Marquis would do whatever needed to be done to protect the family, just like we'd taught him. If I stuck around the Blues, my anxiety would eat me alive. So instead, I decided to indulge in my favorite stress reliever.

It was late, but the lights of an old, eccentric house deep in the bayou were still on when I parked in front. When I got out of my car, there was an uneasy feeling that overcame me as it always did from all the witchy energy coming from the place. I preferred the bustling energy of the city, and this house was in the middle of nowhere. It was surrounded by wilderness and nightlife sounds that made the hairs on the back of my neck stand up. Still, that didn't stop me from walking up to the front and raising my fist to announce my arrival. Before my hand even hit the door, it swung open, revealing the most beautiful and mystical-looking woman. Her name was Ernestine Wicks, and it was she who was my biggest stress reliever.

My eyes trailed down her shapely body as I admired the matching black lingerie set she was wearing. I couldn't help the smirk that came to my face. "You knew I was coming, didn't you?"

"The spirits might have whispered something in my ear. But then again, I'm sure they knew you were on my mind. Come in."

She pulled me into her home and into her arms. Our lips met, and we shared a deep and sensual kiss right there in the doorway. When she finally decided to come up for air, she pushed the door shut and led me to her bedroom. Ernestine was deep into her Creole heritage, and that included the voodoo stuff. Her home was filled with crystals, jars filled with God knew what, and hanging talismans. I didn't mind and often went along with it all because it seemed to make her happy, but the truth was that I didn't believe in any of it.

When we got to her bedroom, the first thing I noticed was the glass of what looked like red wine on her dresser next to a black leather book and a chicken's foot. Curiosity got the best of me, and I tried to take a step toward the dresser, but Ernestine stopped me, pulling me close to her again.

"What's that?" I asked.

"I've been worried about you, mon cher. You had a troublesome night?" she asked, disregarding my question.

"Yeah, it's written all over my face, isn't it?"

"Yes . . . but I can also feel the dark energy radiating off of you. What is troubling you?"

"My night just wasn't so great, that's all. That's why I came here for some relief." My hands found their way to her backside.

"You'll get your relief," she said with a naughty grin.

"Is that right?" I asked, kissing her gently.

"Yes." She stepped away from me. "But first, I have something for you."

She walked to the dresser and grabbed the chicken foot. It was then that I saw that it was attached to a leather string. She held it delicately and muttered something I couldn't make out. When she was done, she kissed it and brought it to me. She tried to hand it to me, but I pushed it away.

"The fuck I'ma do with that?" I asked, shaking my head.

"Wear it," she told me in a tone that said, *what else would you do with it?* "And don't ever let anyone take it from you. It's not only your protection. It is your power."

"Look, baby, sometimes this voodoo shit turns me on, but I ain't wearing no damn chicken foot around my neck. That's crazy."

Ernestine laughed at the seriously disturbed look on my face. Tenderly cupping one side of my face with her free hand, she looked up into my eyes. I hated when she did that. Her doe-eyed look could get any and everything up out of me. It could even get me to wear a damn chicken foot.

"I don't have time to fight with you, Floyd. There is trouble brewing, and you must be protected from it. So, if for nothing else, wear this for me. It will protect you. It's filled with strong magic, and you will need it. Understand?"

She held it out to me again, and after a final, brief hesitation, I took it from her. She waited until I put it on before giving me an approving nod.

"There. You happy?" I asked.

"Yes. Now, in order to make the magic work, I need you to make love to me three times before the sun comes up. My power is in my womb, and in order to release it, you must be inside of me as the sun rises in the east."

"You shoulda led with that. I woulda put this damn thing on as soon as I walked through the door!" I felt my third leg jump in excitement, and a grin came to my lips. I scooped Ernestine up into my arms and laid her on the bed.

I might not have believed in her voodoo shit, but I had no doubt in the truth that once a man got some witch pussy, there was no going back. Ernestine had me in a chokehold, and I gladly let her. Every time we made love, it felt like magic.

Like right then. I didn't remember even taking my clothes off. One minute, I was fully dressed, and the next, the two of us were rolling around naked in her bed sheets. If I could, I would have spent every waking moment inside of her juicy, warm love tunnel, but with everyday lovemaking came everyday commitment, and I wasn't ready for that. Or that was what I told myself.

I rolled over on my back as she straddled me. My eyes were glued on her while she pleasured herself by pleasuring me. Now, I wasn't a small guy. I was blessed between the legs. But watching her repeatedly pounce and take every inch of me made me want to give her a reward. My eyes clenched shut as I tried to hold my orgasm back until she reached her climax.

She fell on top of me while still working her hips, and I felt her lips come to my ear. "Cum with me, baby," she whispered. "My juices are about to flow."

The words were out of her mouth for maybe a second before her body jerked, and I felt the warm gush of her secretions pouring down onto my groin. I was glad, too. I wasn't going to be able to hold my orgasm for another minute. Our moans became louder as we released together in each other's arms. A chill overcame me — the good kind — and I felt the energy leave my body.

When she was done, she lifted herself slightly to kiss me on the lips and grin tiredly into my face.

I asked, "We get to do this two more times, right?"

Chapter 7
Marquis

"You heavy bastard!" I cursed through gritted teeth as I struggled to carry the tarp-wrapped body through a small clearing.

A part of me was regretting not letting my uncle come along. I hadn't thought at all about how I was going to get the body out of the truck alone. It had taken a good five minutes for me to figure out the best way. At first, I was just going to put him on the ground and drag him, but I figured it would be best to hoist him over my shoulder to evenly distribute his weight. As I brought the body to a big pile of twigs and leaves, I didn't even try to gently lay Pierre down. I dropped the body like a sack of potatoes. A part of the tarp got loose, and a hand flopped out.

"My bad, Pierre. But you probably coulda did without going to the buffet every day," I said as I tried to catch my breath.

I wasn't a small man, and I frequented

the gym, but that had given me quite the workout. I looked down at the tarp, not liking that it was just out in the open like that. It was likely nobody would come that way for some hours, but still, to be on the safe side, I decided to cover him up right away. I kicked leaves and branches over the tarp until it was completely covered.

Walking back over to the truck, I leaned on it and checked my watch. It was a little after four in the morning, and I couldn't believe that I still hadn't been back home yet. A shower would do me a lot of good, especially with all the sweating I'd been doing, but instead, I was standing by a swamp in Gator Lake. Anything for my momma, though.

I looked at the murky waters uneasily, knowing that they didn't call it Gator Lake for no reason. I kept one of my hands on the gun on my hip, just in case one of those overgrown reptiles jumped out on me. With all that had just happened, the last thing I needed was to be a gator's breakfast.

I heard the sound of tires approaching, and then I saw the headlights of a car. Once the car parked and turned off its headlights, I could read the word "Sheriff" on the side of it. The driver's side door swung open, and I stood my ground. An average height woman hopped out, wearing a tan uniform that fit perfectly around her slim figure. Her sandy blond hair was in a ponytail, and she walked over to me with her lips slightly pursed, looking annoyed.

Sheriff Clay worked in conjunction with Mayor Simms, and because Momma had the mayor in her back pocket, she had the sheriff as well. The mayor often counted on Momma during election time because of her influence in the Black community. She also helped fund his campaign and paid a nice monthly stipend to keep any unnecessary static from coming the Blues' way. For those things, the mayor would do mostly anything to keep Momma happy. He had informed Sheriff Clay of this "unholy alliance," and instructed her to be available to us when we called. For the more strenuous tasks, there was a higher fee to pay, but it was always worth it. I was sure this middle-of-the-night call would cost us more than a little bit.

"Sheriff Clay, I'm glad you came," I said.

"This better be important, Marquis," she told me with a thick Southern accent. "I hate being outta bed before the sun rises."

"I wouldn't have called you if it wasn't."

"I'll be the judge of that. What's the big emergency?"

I motioned for Sheriff Clay to follow me and took her over to where the tarp was haphazardly buried. A couple of swipes with her foot were enough to move the leaves and reveal the tarp.

"Holy shit!" She looked back at me. "Marquis, is that a body?"

"It is."

"This is a first. Even for you."

"You might wanna take a closer look. This shit gets worse."

I knelt down and lifted the tarp away from Pierre's head, just enough for her to see his face. I stepped back, and she looked at me warily before she leaned in to get a better look. She turned on the light from her phone and shone it on the ground.

I counted down the seconds in my head until I heard her gasp. It only took three seconds.

"Oh my God, Marquis. Is this —"

"Pierre LeBlanc," I finished for her. "Yes, it is."

I watched her turn her light off and stand back up with the utmost shock frozen on her face. She turned to me, and I saw her mouth moving as she tried to find words. Finally, she calmed herself by taking a big breath.

"Why in God's name is Pierre LeBlanc

lying dead in front of me? Jesus, Marquis, did you kill him?"

"Why the hell would I do that?"

"I don't know. But I see you didn't answer my question."

"No, I didn't kill him. Believe it or not, he shot himself." I shook my head. "The motherfucka shot himself in the Blues."

"Why would he do that?" She gave me a skeptical look.

"Your guess is as good as mine. But I'm sure you don't need me to tell you this ain't good for business."

"It's not. I ain't saying I don't believe you, but this doesn't add up. And I know I'm not the only one around who won't believe that Pierre LeBlanc killed himself. I'm for damn sure his brother ain't gonna believe it. This is a heavy one."

Her eyes fell on the dead body before she closed her eyes and sighed big again. When she opened them, she had an expression that said she wished she'd never answered my call. But she had, and since she was there, I really needed her to make the problem go away.

"What the fuck is he doing in a swamp?" Sheriff Clay finally asked.

"You know we don't need any problems at the Blues, Clay. That's why we pay you and your crooked-ass boss."

"Milton is a good man. You watch your mouth when you speak about him," she snapped. "Now, I don't know how you expect me to make something like this go away."

The way she spoke about the mayor was not surprising. Momma had always said he was more than just her boss. Not that I gave a shit. Those two could do whatever they wanted with each other, as long as Clay took care of this problem for us right now.

I looked around the swamp, and my eyes fell on the murky waters once more. A revelation suddenly came to me. "Well, what if he got lost in the swamp and the gators had their way with him?" I suggested. "Wouldn't be the first time. You can call it in like you just happened to come across the body."

"I don't know. Something like that could be very expensive," Sheriff Clay said with a shrug. "Keeping secrets from Jean LeBlanc ain't cheap." Just as I had expected, we had to talk about a price before she would do the job.

"Ten thousand," I said, and she laughed.

"A situation like this, I wouldn't even be able to wipe my ass with ten thousand dollars."

"Fine. Twenty."

"Fifty."

"Hell no. Thirty thousand dollars."

"I think I might need to get the coroner out here and let them know we have a body on our hands with a gunshot wound to the head. And of course, notify the family."

"All right, all right. Fifty thousand. I'll have it to you sometime later today."

There was a brief silence. Sheriff Clay put her hands in her pockets and walked around Pierre's body. She began to make a "tsking" sound with her tongue as she gazed down at him.

"Damn shame what them gators done did to this boy. We're gonna have to use dental records to identify him since his body was so . . . mangled." She shook her head. "Go on and get outta here. Looks like I have some work to do. Have my money by lunch. I'm supposed to meet with the mayor."

She didn't have to tell me twice. Fifty thousand dollars was a steep price, but if it made all of that go away, it was well worth it. I got in the car and drove away. I trusted Clay to do what she said, but that didn't mean I didn't still have a bad feeling about it all. A man had died in our establishment, and we didn't have the slightest clue why. Nor were we even trying to find out. We were just getting rid of the evidence. I felt a twinge of guilt, but it was still nothing in comparison to the dire need to protect my family.

As I drove in the direction of the family mansion, my phone began to ring. Seeing Momma's contact pop up on the screen, I answered immediately.

"Yeah, Momma?"

"How much did it cost us?" she asked.

"Fifty thousand."

"Goddamn Clay! That sorry son of a bitch wasn't worth ten thousand, let alone fifty."

"Well, that's what it cost. She does have to split it with your good friend the mayor."

"I know, and I'm hoping it doesn't, but in the long run, it might cost us more." Momma sighed. "Listen, baby. I've been thinking. Maybe you should take a vacation for a few weeks — to Europe or maybe to Africa — until this mess blows over."

As she talked, I rolled my eyes. I knew where she was going with it. She was my mom, and her first instinct would always be to protect me from the fire, but who would protect her?

"Leave for what, Momma? My place is with you and Uncle Floyd. I'm not running from Jean LeBlanc or nobody else. Believe that."

"Marquis, you know what the LeBlancs are capable of just like I do. They've been known to wipe out entire bloodlines. The blowback from Pierre's death could end up destroying all of us."

"How, when we've got the sheriff in our pocket? And more importantly, we didn't kill him. Plus, if it comes down to it, we can have Todd, Fred, and Eric vouch."

"Boy, if your Uncle Floyd was killed in one of Jean's massage parlors, would you listen to any witnesses he brought you?"

She made a good point. "No. He'd probably have paid them off."

"Exactly. He wouldn't believe us either. Jean LeBlanc won't care if it was our fault or not. If he finds out his brother died in the Blues, he'll blame us because he won't have anyone else to blame, suicide or not."

"You're right," I conceded.

"You're damn right I'm right. I'm not gonna let anything happen to you, Floyd, or Monique."

I heard the power in her voice. The kind that came with the job of being everyone's armor. I'd been hearing it since I was a boy, and sometimes I wondered if she knew she didn't have to be that for me anymore.

"I can handle myself, Momma," I told her, and I heard her scoff.

"There you go, thinking you're a damn gangster like your uncles."

"Speaking of my uncles, why don't we call Uncle LC? They owe us a favor after what we did for Orlando. I'm sure he could —"

"No!" She cut me off with irritation in her tone. "Hell no. We are not asking LC for a thing. Do you hear me, Marquis Duncan? We are not going to LC! We don't need their kind of help. Understand?"

"Yeah, Momma, I understand."

"Good. Now hurry up and get home."

Chapter 8
Jean

All day, I was a businessman, but no matter what, I was a father first. My wife, Marie, and I had Simone when we were young, so one could say we'd all grown up together. Simone had become a beautiful and fine young woman. She'd graduated top of her class with a scholarship to the finest performing arts school in the state. Words couldn't express how proud of her I was, and I made it a point to attend as many of her recitals as I could.

My wife and I sat side by side, watching the elegant ballet dancers own the stage. The melody of classical music played by the orchestra alone was enough to impress me. But watching Simone perform her solo was a breathtaking experience. She danced with the grace of a professional ballerina. That and her impeccable beauty made her stand out from the other dancers. She easily let it be known why she was the lead. And judging by the round of applause she got when she was done, it was clear I wasn't the only person who felt that way.

At the closing credits of the performance, I reached over and grabbed Marie's hand. It was meant to be an affectionate gesture, but her hand felt stiff in mine, like she didn't want me to hold it. Before leaving the house that evening, we'd had an argument about me being late to pick her up for the performance. Although we still made it on time, she seemed to not have let it go. It was no secret that she had been unhappy lately about me being gone all the time, and she made no attempt to hide it now. I never understood why she would fuss at me for being the same man I'd been ever since she met me.

Marie was a poised woman, but I could tell by how her nose slightly flared that she wanted to roll her eyes. Even with her attitude, she was still the most beautiful woman I'd ever seen. The mint green slip dress she wore draped delicately over her body, accentuating her shape. The color of the dress made her olive skin radiate, and I loved when she wore her long hair in a bun.

I leaned over to kiss her on the cheek, but she turned her head so I couldn't. "Be nice," I said as the orchestra played their last notes.

"I am being nice," she responded and took her hand back.

We stood up with the rest of the audience to give a standing ovation before curtain calls. My phone began to vibrate in my pocket, and when I checked the screen, I saw that it was Saint. I excused myself before stepping out into the aisle and walking out of the auditorium. I answered on what was probably the last ring.

"Everything smooth?" I said into the receiver.

"Yeah," Saint answered. "You know we handled that. I had Kendall and Prince get them bodies up outta there and all that blood up. We should be able to open La Nue tonight."

"Good. Find Pierre, and the two of you meet me at my house now. We're leaving Simone's recital."

"Pierre?"

"Yeah." I sighed, thinking about my knucklehead little brother. "I'm thinking about putting him in charge of La Nue. It might keep him out of trouble. Keep him busy enough to not blow all his money. And mine."

"You sure that's the right choice? I mean, this is Pierre we're talking about. This the same motherfucka who almost burned down the house you bought him frying chicken."

"Yeah, I'm sure, man." I found myself laughing. "I think this will be good for him. I'll see y'all in a bit to discuss things in detail."

"Yeah, a'ight."

I disconnected the call and tucked the phone back in my pocket as people began to spill out of the auditorium. My wife spotted me and came to stand by me as we waited for Simone together.

"Your daughter was looking for you during her curtain call," Marie told me in a bitter tone.

"I had to answer a business call, baby. She'll understand."

"Yeah, until she doesn't. When are you going to start putting your family first?"

"How don't I —" I stopped myself and took a breath, not wanting to cause a scene in front of everyone. "You know I love my family more than anything, and that's why I do what I do. I'm a businessman, Marie. There used to be a time when you understood that."

"I guess back then I thought you'd be more settled down by now."

I didn't get a chance to respond to her

because Simone came bounding toward us, carrying her dance bag. She had changed into a pair of jeans and a pink shirt. Her eyes went to my hands, which were empty, and I felt a twinge of guilt. I usually had a bouquet of roses for her after every recital, but we had been running late and didn't have time to stop and buy flowers.

"I'm sorry, Money. I forgot your roses," I said, calling her by her nickname. I reached in my pocket and pulled out my wallet. "But how about I make up for that with a shopping spree for you and your friends?" I handed her my credit card, and she took it with a smile.

"I wish you forgot the roses more often!"

She and I laughed, but Marie just shook her head. I didn't have it in me to go back and forth with her anymore, so I just ignored her. I walked arm in arm with Simone out of the building, and Marie followed closely behind. Once we were outside of the grand theater, we walked down a flight of stairs to the valet, and I gave the attendant my slip.

While we waited for the car to be brought up, Marie hugged Simone tightly. "Baby, you were spectacular. I knew all of those private lessons would pay off," she said.

"She's right, baby girl. You looked like an

angel floating around up there. How about we celebrate and go to dinner?"

"Thank you guys so much. I don't think I could ask for better parents. But . . ." Her voice trailed off.

"But what?" Marie asked.

"I kind of already made plans to go meet with the girls tonight." She pointed toward a few of her friends waiting for her.

They waved at us, and I waved back. Marie, on the other hand, didn't look too happy about it.

"Well, surely you can reschedule. I don't know the last time the three of us have sat down and had a decent meal together as a family."

"With dance and my school schedule, I barely have seen them either." Simone pouted and turned to me. "Dad?"

I looked at Marie and saw her shake her head slightly. I sighed and smiled at my daughter. "You can make it up to your mother and me, sweetheart."

"Okay! I love y'all. I'll see you when I get home."

Before Marie could protest, Simone ran off to join her friends. My wife cut her eyes at me as my Rolls Royce pulled up. She got in without another word to me.

■ ■ ■ ■

When we got home, I saw Saint's car parked in front of our lavish home. I ignored Marie's eye roll when she spotted his car too. She got out almost as soon as my foot hit the brakes. Her bad vibe was something I wasn't in the mood for. I'd just acquired an amazing club, and money was pouring in from all other angles. I should have been celebrating, and that's what I was going to do.

We went inside the house. Marie bounded up the stairs, but I went to find Saint and Pierre. I knew they would be in the kitchen, and when I got there, I saw that I was partially right. Saint was seated at the table, eating the brunch my chef had whipped up for him, but Pierre was not with him.

"Where's my brother?"

"I don't know." Saint shrugged. "I called his phone like ten times. He didn't answer."

"It's just like him to miss out on a business opportunity," I said, shaking my head. "Look, I'ma go change my clothes and be back down so we can head out."

He nodded, and I left the kitchen. I went upstairs to the master bedroom, and I heard the shower going. Glad I wouldn't have to go another round with the gladiator, I went to the closet and changed out of the suit I'd worn to the recital.

I heard the doorbell ring. Thinking it was my brother, I headed down the stairs, eager to give him the good news about La Nue. However, standing outside the front door of my home, talking to Saint, was Sheriff Joan Clay.

Seeing her put a sour taste in my mouth. Any chance she got, she was trying to round up a Crescent Boy or two to get information about me. Although my operation was iron clad, it didn't stop her from trying to bring it down. I wasn't really surprised, seeing as how she was the mayor's bitch. High society talked, and it was no secret that Mayor Simms was nervous that one day, I'd decide to run for mayor. It would all but make him cry tears of joy to learn that I was in some federal prison doing life.

"Can I help you?" Saint was saying.

"I'm here to see Mr. LeBlanc. I need to speak with him about a police matter," she said.

"Do you have an appointment?" Saint asked.

"No, but I think this here badge speaks for its fucking self. Now, are you going to get Mr. LeBlanc, or do I have to shoot off a few rounds to get his attention? Not sure how the neighbors will like that, but I really don't give a shit either way."

"Let her through," I said from the stairs, and Saint looked back.

Seeing me, he nodded and stepped out of Sheriff Clay's way. As she passed him, Saint gave her a distrusting look. I motioned for the sheriff to follow me into the kitchen, and Saint stayed on her heels.

I gestured toward the food still out, neatly lined on the island. "So, Sheriff, I heard you saying you wanted to discuss a police matter. My chef just made us a late brunch. How about we chat over some good food? These are some of the best homemade beignets you've ever had. I can bet my life on that."

"Thanks." She grabbed a few of the pastries. When she turned back to me, she wore a serious expression. "You might wanna sit down for this. Unfortunately, this house call isn't the nice sort."

There was something about the way she said it that made a gray cloud come over my head, although the sun shone brightly through the kitchen windows. I sat down slowly, and Sheriff Clay remained standing.

"I got some bad news for you, Mr. LeBlanc."

"What kind of bad news?"

"It's your brother," she said, and I groaned.

"What the fuck has Pierre gotten himself into now?"

"A gator's stomach," she said.

Her tone was so detached that I didn't know if I had even heard her correctly. "Come again?"

"I'm sorry. I haven't had my coffee this morning. What I meant was we found a partial body with your brother's identification among the remains, Mr. LeBlanc."

I looked at Saint to make sure he was hearing the same thing I was, and the appalled look on his face told me that he was. I replayed the sheriff's words over and over in my head, but nothing was making sense to me. Did that mean . . .

"Are you telling me that my brother is dead?" I asked in disbelief.

"Yes, sir, he's dead. Deceased. Gone to the other side. A lot of ways to say it, depending on what you believe, but *dead* sums it up the best."

"How?"

"Like I said, most likely gators got him. His body was found in the damn swamp, ate on up."

The way she was so casually talking about

Pierre made me want to get up and strangle her. But then again, my body felt so light, I couldn't move right away. I just wanted more answers.

"The swamp?" I heard my voice raise. "How did my brother get into the swamp? He didn't put himself there."

"We're still looking into it. When I have more information, you'll be the first person I call."

I heard the sound of footsteps entering the kitchen, and when I looked up, I saw Marie. Her eyes curiously darted from the sheriff to me, and I could see the question in her gaze. She wanted to know why the sheriff was in our home.

"Jean, what's going on?" she asked nervously.

The lump in the back of my throat almost prohibited me from answering her question. I felt my jaw clench as I fought back my emotions. Finally, when I was partially gathered, I looked into my wife's eyes. "It's Pierre. The sheriff just told me he's dead."

Her hand went to her chest, and she gasped. She looked at Sheriff Clay for confirmation, and the sheriff nodded her head. It was true. My brother was gone.

"Where is Pierre now?" Saint asked the sheriff.

“Down at the county morgue. I wouldn’t recommend going down there. It’s a pretty gruesome sight. I can have them send the body to whichever funeral home you like.”

“I’ll handle it,” Saint told me.

“I’m gonna head out. I’m sorry for your loss. Please feel free to give me a call or come down to the station. Oh, and thanks for the beignets. These are good.” She took a bite of her beignet and walked out of the kitchen casually, like she hadn’t just delivered devastating news.

Saint followed her to let her out, and Marie rushed to me. Regardless of whether she had been unhappy with me earlier, now she sat on my lap and wrapped her arms around me. I allowed myself to relax into her embrace. My wife was always there for me, no matter how rocky things between us got sometimes.

Chapter 9
Big Shirley

I'd stayed up most of the night. I told myself it was to make sure Marquis got in safe and sound, but even after that, I stayed awake. There was an unsettled feeling in the pit of my stomach, and it didn't seem like it would be going anywhere anytime soon. It wasn't the amount Sheriff Clay had charged us to clean up the mess. My issue was the fact that even if Clay had handled that, I would need to cover every base ten times. I'd been around a long time, and I knew to always expect the unexpected — especially when it came to Jean LeBlanc and those damned Crescent Boys.

Sleep didn't find me until almost six in the morning, and I was awake only a few hours later. Most days, being the boss meant late nights and early mornings, so those few hours of rest were just enough fuel to get me through the day.

When I got out of bed, I opened my

blackout curtains to let the sunshine into my room. Then I went to the shower to cleanse my body and clear my mind. I thought the hot water would be healing, but I was wrong. All I got was a bunch of steam and more intrusive thoughts.

"This is some bullshit," I said to myself as I rushed through the shower that was doing nothing to relax me. Then I got out to get dressed. I opted for a sexy peach pantsuit with an open two-button blazer and my hair pulled back into a neat bun. No matter what, I never looked like what I went through. I was a boss, and I would always look like one.

I gave myself a once-over in the full-length mirror in the corner of my bedroom. Sliding on my heels and grabbing my Chanel from the purse shelf I'd had imported from Italy, I left my bedroom. As I walked down the hallway and descended the staircase, I noticed the silence, even though I knew the help was bustling around somewhere. It wasn't abnormal for my home to be quiet, although I could vividly remember the sounds of Marquis running around with his friends when he was younger. I smiled thinking about how the sword fights turned into shouting over video games. That kind of fun ended when Marquis got older and came to work for me at the Blues. He knew his place, and that would always be at my side.

Nearing the kitchen, I could smell all the deliciousness. Our cook made a wonderful breakfast spread every morning and was always done and gone by the time we woke up. I half expected to see Marquis stuffing his face when I walked in, but it wasn't him sitting at the dining table. It was Mo.

She saw me, and a look of relief came over on her face. "Girl, if you didn't come down them stairs in the next thirty minutes, I was gonna go up and make sure you was alive!" she said then stuffed a piece of crisp bacon in her mouth.

"Please. If the world ain't burned down, always know I'ma get my ass up and go to work," I said. "I did have a late night, though."

"Waiting for Quis to get in?"

"That, and I just can't seem to wrap my head around what that dumbass LeBlanc did. A part of me wants it to be a nightmare or a sick joke."

"Baby, you saw the top of that boy's head blew off just like I did. He's dead. Ain't no question about it." She shook her head. "I don't get it, though. Why kill himself? He comes from one of the wealthiest families in all of New Orleans. Ain't nothing coulda been that bad."

"Everybody has their own crosses to bear. Just because we don't look like we're going through hell don't mean we ain't walking through the fire."

"Not a preacher!"

I couldn't help but to laugh. One thing my cousin knew how to do was lighten up a dark room. I made myself a small plate of shrimp and grits, wishing I didn't have to scarf them down the way I did. My chef, Preston, *knew* he knew his way around a kitchen.

I sat down with Mo briefly and relished the decadent taste of my food before it was time to leave. Outside of the unexpected hand that I'd been dealt, there were things that required my attention. First would be a stop at City Hall.

After Mo and I were done eating, we left in her cherry red Benz to take on the mayor's office. When we got there, we walked right in, although we didn't have an appointment. With the "special arrangement" the mayor and I had, my just needing to talk to him was enough for his schedule to be cleared. He wouldn't dare turn me away. Not just because I kept his pockets nice and fat, either. I happened to know for a fact that Mayor Simms didn't make that beautiful wife of his sign a prenup, which meant it would be earth-shattering to him if she found out about his ongoing affair with Sheriff Clay. He would be left with nothing should she decide to leave him, and if she stayed, his life would be hell. The mayor knew to take my meetings, no questions asked.

Mayor Simms had recently raised the amount of the monthly fee I paid him to keep our detractors at bay. Over the years, there had been many people who wanted to see the Blues shut down. I couldn't count the number of petitions that had been presented at city hall meetings, and even some conversation among legislators about ways to make it happen. I never had to worry about anything taking root, however, as long as I made that payment every month. For the most part, I kept my head down and fed the right pockets to ensure the continued success of the Midnight Blues. As a Black woman and a mother, that legacy meant everything to me.

Now I was here to get some of the influence I was paying him for. A pressing matter had come up for us, and it was starting to become a nuisance. For years, I'd been paying the Barnes family off with an annual convenience check and free gambling because the Blues encroached on their land. Usually that was enough to keep them from complaining about the noise that came with the business. Recently, however, they'd been pressuring me to buy the land or threatening legal action. They were crazy as hell to think I'd ever pay a quarter million dollars for the piece of land the Blues occupied. I didn't like being hustled. But that was only one of the reasons I needed to see Mayor Simms.

As Mo and I marched toward his door, his secretary, Debbie, jumped up to try to stop us. "Can I help you?" she asked, looking over her wide-framed glasses.

"Is he in?" I asked without stopping my stride.

"Yes, but —"

"Good."

She tried to hold her ground in front of me, but I easily sidestepped her, and Mo gave her a look that told her to go play with something safe. I burst into Mayor Simms's office and saw him sitting behind his desk. He was a stout white man who looked good to be in his fifties. He wore a navy blue tie and looked to have been in the middle of doing some paperwork. When Mo and I came through, he first had a surprised look on his face, but a smile quickly followed when he realized it was us.

"Mrs. Duncan, this is a welcome surprise," he said in a cheerful tone.

"I don't know how it's a surprise when I told you last week that I wanted to talk about this donation increase," I said, letting the door close behind me.

"Still, I thought you'd set up a meeting," Mayor Simms said.

I pursed my lips, and he understood not to push the issue.

"No matter. I'm glad you're here now. Ladies, take a seat. How is your morning going?"

Monique and I took seats on the opposite side of his desk, but I didn't return his cheery attitude. "Cut the crap, Ronald. What's this about raising my payments?"

"Well, as you know, your donations are always appreciated, but with inflation being what it is, perhaps an increase from seventy-five thousand a month to one hundred thousand should be arranged."

"Perhaps?"

"I need to work on my phrasing. I should have said, 'I need an increase.' Which I'm sure won't be a problem. I've been by the Blues, and it seems like you're having a stellar year."

"Why do I get the feeling that you're trying to hustle me, Ronald?"

He almost looked offended. "Never! If you prosper, I prosper. We're all a team here."

"Glad to hear you say that, because to get the kind of money you want, I'm gonna need something in return."

"And what exactly would that be, Mrs. Duncan?" Mayor Simms leaned forward and clasped his hands together.

"The first out of two things, I need you to handle Jack Barnes. He has been a pain in my ass all year," I told him. "He's threatening to take me to court. Now, I know the Blues encroaches on his land, but he's already taken his yearly payment, and his sons have a ball in the Blues every other night."

"Okay, I'll talk to Mr. Barnes myself and see if we can meet in the middle somewhere."

"Middle?" Monique said. "Ain't no middle. Didn't you just hear Big Shirley say they've already taken her convenience payment for the year?"

"I understand that." Mayor Simms answered. "Unfortunately, a judge can easily throw a side deal like that out, as the land legally belongs to the Barnes family. But until I can get that all straightened out, what is the second thing, Mrs. Duncan?"

"Our hours at the Blues need to expand three hours past two a.m. So we're gonna need an ordinance," I told him.

Mayor Simms groaned. "That's no easy feat. You do have your detractors."

"And so do you. However, for a hundred grand a month, those detractors are now your problem, not mine. I'll expect my ordinance in the next week. Don't look for your money until then. Have a good day." I smiled at the flabbergasted look on his face as I stood up and made my way to the door with Mo. I wiggled my fingers at the mayor before we left the office.

"Girl, I know you're a boss and all, but ain't a hundred thousand a month kind of steep?" Mo asked as we walked down the hallway.

"Chile, to stay open an extra three hours, I would have paid double that. That's damn near giving me an extra day in the week. And think about it. When the French Quarter and Bourbon Street close down for the night, we become the after party."

I watched a sly smile come to her face.

"Shirley, you always were the smart one."

Chapter 10
Marie

I didn't know what to say as I lay in bed and watched my husband prepare to leave for the day. The day and night before had been hard for him. He'd tossed and turned in his sleep, keeping me up most of the night. But then, he just got up and got ready for the day like he would any other time. I mean, it had been a normal part of our routine for a while. He woke up, showered, got dressed, sometimes ate breakfast, and then left for work. In between none of those things was there time for me. However, that morning was different. Normally, I would find something smart to say about how he never spent time with me anymore. Although it was the truth, I didn't feel right saying it. Not after finding out yesterday that Pierre was dead.

Jean was moving slower than usual that morning. Most times, it was like he couldn't wait to get out of the house and away from me. I hated to think like that, but often I wondered if my husband still loved me. I knew I still loved him just by me being guiltily happy that I was able to spend a few more moments with him. I tossed the covers back and got out of bed to assist him with his tie. I smoothed it down with a hand, which I let rest on his chest for a few moments.

"You okay?" I asked, looking in his eyes. There was sadness in them. It was almost surprising, because he and Pierre were two very different people. And by different, I mean Pierre was always messing up, and Jean was always cleaning up after him. Sometimes, I didn't even think Jean liked Pierre. There had been times when Pierre made Jean so mad that he didn't talk to him for weeks. But they were brothers, and Jean always ultimately forgave him for whatever knuckleheaded mistake his baby brother made.

Now he was dead.

"This ain't right," Jean finally said.

"I know, baby. I can't believe Pierre is dead."

"It's not just him dying that ain't right. It's how they said he died. Pierre couldn't have been in no swamp, no matter how drunk he was. He was deathly scared of gators and had been since we were kids. Plus, he couldn't swim to save his life."

"So what are you saying?"

"I'm saying my brother ain't die in no swamp. And I'm gonna find out the truth."

"How are you gonna do that?" I asked, knowing that once he set his mind on an idea, he would pursue it relentlessly.

"I don't know. But I'm sure a hundred thousand dollars' reward will make somebody who knows something say something. I'ma have Saint and Prince put the word out."

I scoffed at the mention of Saint's little brother Prince. Jean didn't know as much about his daughter as he thought he did, because he didn't know that Prince was Simone's current obsession. He was a handsome young man all right, but I would be happy when her infatuation for him passed. She was going places in life, and Prince, well, he wasn't. He was okay running the streets with the other Crescent Boys, and my daughter was way too good for a drug dealer or gang banger. It sounded like the pot calling the kettle black, but the difference with me and Jean was that my husband had always been the boss, and I was always the queen.

"Just don't do anything stupid, okay?

Simone and I need you here," I told him.

He didn't answer me, and that wasn't a good sign. But I didn't press the fact. I couldn't tell him how to mourn. Instead, he kissed me on the forehead and made his way out the door without another word.

When he was gone and I was once again alone in the silent room, I went and stood in front of the floor-length mirror. I knew I was stunning; I'd heard it all my life. It was just crazy how the man I was so sure I'd spend my life with could make me feel so unseen. I needed something to lift my spirits, and I knew just what would do it — a trip to my best friend's salon.

It wasn't hard to talk Simone into a girl's day, especially when she heard that we were going to Raven's House of Beauty.

I'd met Raven at thirteen when my parents shipped me off to Colorado for an all-girls summer experience. They thought it would be good for me, since I'd been sheltered with such an upper-class upbringing that I rarely mingled with girls my age. I was too busy studying or in piano lessons. My parents wanted the best for me, which was why I was shocked when they signed me up for summer camp with the "regular folks." I remember being so nervous about it, until I met a rough-around-the-edges, slickmouthed girl from New York, who also happened to be my bunkie.

It didn't take long for us to become as thick as thieves. The bond we formed was one that went beyond space, and even though we rarely saw each other over the years as we grew up, we always kept in touch. So, I was ecstatic last year to hear that she was moving to New Orleans and opening a salon and spa. To have my best friend in such close proximity meant the world to me, especially with how distant Jean had grown despite my many efforts to close the gaps.

Simone and I walked into the lavish salon, where there was a good reason for the sign just inside the entrance that read: PATRONS MUST BE AT LEAST EIGHTEEN YEARS OLD. Simone and I were greeted by shirtless, muscular gods — the reason for the age restriction. Okay, they weren't gods, but they were some of the finest men I'd ever seen, wearing tight pants and little else. They were all shades and so perfect that I was almost convinced that Raven had them manufactured, especially since their godlike physiques were paired with magical fingers as well.

As Simone and I were led to the pedicure chairs, I saw many women in pure bliss. I chuckled as I passed a woman, who looked to be well into her sixties, ogling the young man who was massaging her legs with hot stones. I could see on her face all the things she imagined doing to him.

I saw Raven coming my way. She gave me a quick hug. "Girl, why didn't you tell me you were coming in today? I would have had a bottle of champagne chilling already."

"Well, it ain't too late. I could use a drink."

Simone was already in her seat with her headphones on, so Raven reached out and tapped her leg to get her attention. When Simone saw her, she smiled and waved, but didn't bother to take off the headphones.

Raven turned back to me. "So, how are things at home?"

"Jean is taking the death of his brother pretty hard."

"I heard about that. I'm sorry for your family's loss." Her tone was sincere at first, but then she pursed her lips and said, "Now that husband of yours has an excuse to be an asshole."

"Raven!" I loved my girl, and she'd heard me complain plenty of times about my marital issues, but I was still shocked that she would be so insensitive this soon after Pierre's death.

She was unapologetic. "What? If you weren't going to say it, you knew I was."

"I'm just trying to be a good wife and support my husband in his time of need," I told her with a sigh. "So I need you to support me while I'm doing that."

"You know I got you, girl. Sit down, and I'll make sure you and Simone are taken good care of."

She walked away, and I sat down in the chair next to Simone's and took off my shoes. The dreamy worker who was in charge of my pedicure ran the water into the basin, and I lowered my feet in. The heat was perfect, and when he turned on the jets, I leaned back and prepared to be taken to pure bliss.

After a few minutes, I opened my eyes and glanced over at Simone. I was surprised to see her looking back at me.

She took off her headphones and said, "I guess I'll do black nails for the funeral to match my dress. I can't believe Uncle Pierre is really dead, Mom."

"Me either, honey. That was definitely the last thing I expected to hear. And you know your father isn't taking it too well."

"Daddy didn't even like Uncle Pierre like that."

"Like and love are two completely different things, sweetheart. That was still his brother," I told her. "He's gonna get to the bottom of it."

"The bottom of what? The swamp?"

"Your father doesn't think your uncle really died in the swamp. And personally, I don't either."

"Why?"

"What would Pierre be doing at a swamp? He couldn't swim, and it just isn't adding up. That's why your father is offering a hundred thousand dollars to anyone who might have information."

"Dang, a hundred thousand dollars. That's a lot of money."

"Enough to get tight lips talking. Somebody knows something, and we're going to find out who. If someone killed Uncle Pierre, you'll see exactly what your father is capable of." I reached out and squeezed her hand tightly.

She gave me a sad smile, then she put her headphones on again, leaned her head back, and closed her eyes.

As I refocused my attention on the fabulous leg massage, I saw Shirley Duncan, the owner of the Midnight Blues, passing by me. She was with her cousin Monique, and they looked like they were in a rush. Shirley was a busy woman, running that casino, so

I was sure she had a million things to do all the time. In some ways, I was envious. There were days that I found myself bored with life as a stay-at-home wife now that Simone was an adult. I hadn't worked in years, but I thought it might be nice to get out of the house and feel like I had a purpose again.

"Shirley Duncan! Hey, girl," I called out to her.

They both stopped and looked at me. I wanted to tell Big Shirley to try one of Raven's facials. The poor woman had bags under her eyes like she hadn't been to sleep in days, and she was too pretty for all of that. I admired her more than she would ever know. Being a Black woman and the owner of one of New Orleans' finest businesses was a huge accomplishment.

A small smile came to her lips when she recognized me. "Marie LeBlanc. Baby, it's good to see you. Y'all coming to my masquerade ball, aren't you?"

"We wouldn't miss it for the world. We'll need a lot of cheering up after we bury my brother-in-law."

Shirley glanced at her cousin, and then their faces seemed to melt into sad expressions. They almost looked uncomfortable. I didn't pay that any mind, though. Some people just get awkward when they're talking about death. She was just trying to be kind.

"I heard about that. I'm sorry for your loss," Shirley said.

"Thank you. I appreciate that so much. My husband is taking it pretty hard. That was his only brother."

"So sad. I hate to hear it," Big Shirley said, speaking quickly. She looked eager to get back to whatever she was rushing to before. "But you let me know if y'all need anything. Until then, I'll see you at the ball."

She gave me a small wave, and Monique offered me a head nod, then they left. I was glad that they had reminded me about Big Shirley's annual masquerade ball. It was one of the biggest events of the year, and it gave me something to look forward to.

Chapter 11
Marquis

The sound of loud cheering filled the casino floor at the Blues as I stood near the craps table, watching a gentleman roll the dice. He was on fire — and I mean fire. He'd hit six times in a row, and if there weren't cameras everywhere inside our family establishment, I would have sworn he'd swapped out the dice with trick dice. But no, apparently he was just a lucky fella. He was up about twenty thousand. I wasn't the only one noticing his winning streak, either. He had multiple women standing by him with money-hungry eyes, probably hoping he would break them off a couple dollars when he cashed out. I'd witnessed it many times, the women who came to the casino and didn't play a single game. Those were the ones in search of a dummy or a sugar daddy, but I couldn't hate. They had their game, and I had mine.

"You must see something you like over

there." A sweet voice made its way into my ears.

I smiled, because I'd recognize that voice anywhere. I liked it best when it was calling my name. I turned around and saw Antoinette standing behind me, looking sexy as ever in her cocktail waitress get-up.

"Nah, but I do now," I said.

"Mm-hmm," she said skeptically, but the smile on her lips was undeniable. "How did things go with Big Shirley after I left?"

"Man, Momma is gonna be Momma." I shrugged it off, but she gave me a serious look.

"Marquis. I never planned for *anyone* to find out about us. I can't have this blowing back in my face."

"Damn, and here I thought you were gonna say you don't wanna lose me."

"That too. But I can't have you if my husband finds out about us."

"I understand, baby. I'll handle my Momma. In the meantime, you see dude over there in the middle of all those ladies?" I nodded my head toward the craps table.

Antoinette strained her neck to see the man I was talking about. "With the Versace shirt on?" she asked. "He looks like he's winning big."

"That's him. I need you to go over there,

turn on that charm, and hype him up to bet it all."

"Ohhh, you're a cold piece, Marquis Duncan."

"The goal for any good businessman is to keep money in, not give it out," I said with a wink.

"I'll see what I can do."

She bit her lip lustfully at me before sashaying that big butt of hers over to the craps table. I watched as she moseyed her way close to Versace shirt and whispered something in his ear. I had no idea what she said to him, but when he got a good look at her, his eyes said it all. I watched his gaze undress her as she smiled in his face. He wanted her, just like most men in the Blues.

I watched Versace shirt bet all his chips. Just as he was preparing to throw the dice, the feeling of my phone vibrating in the pocket of my silk pants grabbed my attention.

"Hello?" I answered.

A disappointed chorus of "awwwwww" erupted from the craps table. I looked over and saw the sick expression on Versace shirt's face as the crowd dispersed, letting me know he had crapped out. As Antoinette walked away, she shot me a sly look, and I winked at her.

"Marquis? Where are you?" Momma's voice came through the phone.

"Making my rounds on the floor."

"Come up to my office. It's an emergency."

"I'm on my way now."

We disconnected, and I left the casino floor. As I turned down the hallway that would take me up to the offices, I ran into my uncle Floyd. His sharp suit was giving my fit a run for its money. But then again, I'd gotten my clean-cut swagger from him. He always told me, "Dress every day like you're going to be in the presence of greatness."

"What's up, nephew? You headed up to your mom's office?" he asked after dapping me up.

"Yeah. She called me up. Any clue what she wants?" I pried as we continued down the hallway, side by side.

"I don't know. She sent me a 911 text, but it probably has something to do with last night. Speaking of which, how'd things go with Clay?"

"Good as far as I know. She spoke with Jean earlier, and the medical examiner's on board. The official cause of death will be gator attack."

"That's what I like to hear."

We went up the staircase and walked down another hallway, passing our offices to get to Momma's. I had my hand on the doorknob, about to enter, when something caught my eye. I stopped Floyd to get a closer look at it.

"Unc, hold up. What's that around your neck? Is that what I think it is?"

"Nothin'." He tried to tuck it away, but it was too late.

"Is that a chicken's foot?" I couldn't help but laugh as I asked the question.

"Maybe it is," he said, cutting his eyes at me.

There was a smirk frozen on my face as we walked into the office. I'd heard Momma talking about how he messed with some witch out in Voodoo Lake, but I'd doubted the rumor until now. Growing up, those were the kind of women I was always told to stay away from. Swapping liquids of any kind with them could tether me to them for eternity. Of course, back then, that sounded like a bunch of hoopla, but seeing my uncle, the most solid and headstrong man I knew, walking around with a chicken's foot around his neck made me think differently.

"What's up, sis?" Uncle Floyd greeted Momma before taking a seat in one of the comfortable chairs in the room.

I sat down as well and took note of the unhappy and uneasy look on Momma's face. That worried me. I would have thought she'd be happy that the situation had been handled. In fact, I thought I'd be walking into some praise.

"Everything all right, Momma?" I asked.

"I got something I need to tell y'all," she said as her serious eyes went from Uncle Floyd to me.

"Well, spit it out," Uncle Floyd said.

"It's Jean LeBlanc. I overheard his wife talking at the salon today. That crazy bastard done put out a hundred-thousand-dollar reward for information about Pierre's death."

I felt my heart drop to my balls. Any hint of a smirk was long gone. A hundred thousand dollars was a lot of money, especially to someone who didn't have any.

Uncle Floyd seemed to share my sentiments. "You do know that for a hundred grand, those boys are going to sing like canaries. And you know what that means, don't you?"

"We're about to be in the middle of a damn war with him and the Crescent Boys if we don't figure this thing out," Momma said.

"Why don't we just make a call to New

York? Uncle LC and his people would even up the odds." I couldn't mask the pleading in my tone. Next to Uncle Floyd, Uncle LC was the baddest man that I knew. He ran a luxury car dealership, but that was just a front for his real moneymaking business — a crime syndicate that supplied drugs to practically every region of the United States.

Not only that, but he had the manpower to help us if things got too bad. The people he controlled made the Crescent Boys look like a bunch of pussies. They wouldn't be scared to get their hands dirty or do anything they had to do to keep the odds in their favor. That was the kind of energy we needed on our side — a strong front, one anyone would be scared to cross. With Uncle LC and his sons, my cousins Vegas, Orlando, and Junior, we would be untouchable.

As soon as the words were out of my mouth, Momma turned into a whole dragon. As fast as she turned on me, I could almost swear I saw fire coming out of her mouth. "No. Hell no! Boy, how many damn times do I have to tell you that?"

"But, Momma, Jean's got an army. Uncle LC has —"

"Goddammit, didn't you just hear what the fuck I said, Marquis?"

"What is your issue with Uncle LC anyway?"

"I told you. I don't like the drugs and the violence."

"Momma, you keep a pistol in your purse and at your office desk."

"For protection!"

"Something is telling me there's more to the story." I looked deep into her face, trying to find some sort of answer. "What happened between you and Uncle LC?"

"This isn't what we're talking about. Not right now."

"Then what are we gonna do, Momma?" I asked, exasperated.

"*We* ain't gonna do nothing. But *I've* got a plan."

"I'm listening," I said, leaning forward in my seat.

"Good, 'cause the first part of my plan is to send your narrow ass to Houston until things cool down."

"Houston?" I couldn't believe she would even suggest that. "Why would I go way out there to the country when we're in the middle of a damn crisis?"

"As much as I want you by my side, son, I don't know what I'd do if something were to happen to you. I need you out of harm's way."

"So you trust me to get rid of a body, but not to help fight?"

"Yes," she said simply, like it was a good enough answer. But it wasn't.

"Momma! That doesn't make sense. You know, just like I know, you need me here."

"I don't. What I need is to know you're alive while I handle this."

I was dumbfounded. Apparently, she didn't trust me to handle a serious situation like the one we were in, and that hurt. She wanted to send me away like I was still a little boy.

"Momma, I been training to take this place over since I was ten, doing every shit job there was because you two said I needed to know every job to run this place. How the hell am I supposed to take over the business if you expect me to run at the first sign of trouble?"

I could see Uncle Floyd nodding his head in agreement, but Momma shot him a look as if to say, "stay out of it."

"Can't you see I'm trying to keep you alive, boy?" she shouted.

"I'm a man, not a boy!" I yelled back. "I'd rather go down fighting for this family and for the Blues. It's my legacy too."

"Well, that's not going to happen. You're going to Houston, and that's that. You're my only son, and I'd give my life to protect you. I'm driving you to the airport myself." She stood up from her desk.

"There's nothing else to talk about." She turned her back on me, letting me know that she was done with the conversation.

I looked at Uncle Floyd, hoping that he would back me up, but he shrugged helplessly. He knew it was a battle neither one of us could win.

I let out an angry groan before jumping up and leaving the office.

Chapter 12
Floyd

I'd known at an early age that I had a different kind of beast living inside of me. I could do the most terrible things without batting an eye or losing a moment's sleep. I used to think it made me soulless, but when I grew into a man, I knew it was the thing that made me a boss in a different way than my sister. I wasn't scared to do the dirty work or make the tough calls. Any successful organization needs someone like me in a high position. My sister Shirley was the face of it all, but we both knew nothing moved without me by her side. I loved the bond my sister and I had. There was no power struggle. We both respected each other's positions.

I rarely questioned her decisions, but the way she'd sent Marquis off just wasn't sitting right with me. I'd been trying to hold my tongue about it, but there were some things that needed to be said. Although I understood the strong feeling to want to protect him and keep him safe, there was a way she could have done that while still respecting him as a man. I had my own strong feelings about letting the boy spread his wings, but in the end, I knew I had to trust him to be the person we'd raised him up to be. My nephew was the perfect mixture of both of his parents. He had critical and logical thinking, but he also wasn't scared to get in the mud if need be. Knowing that should have been enough to keep him here with us.

I found myself knocking at my sister's office door early in the morning. She called for me to come in, and I entered to find her dressed in all black for Pierre LeBlanc's funeral. I too was in all black, out of respect, but I would be missing most of the funeral.

Big Shirley was standing in her mirror, wrapping a string of pearls around her neck, and I saw a big, festive hat sitting on her desk, ready to be mounted on her head.

"You ready for today?" she asked.

I nodded, knowing she wasn't talking about the funeral. "I am. But first, we need to talk about something," I said as I made myself comfortable in my favorite chair in her office. I crossed my right ankle over my left knee and clasped my hands together, waiting patiently for her to finish doing what she was doing.

Her eyes found mine in the mirror, and she squinted, trying to read me. When her necklace was wrapped the way she liked it, she walked back to her desk. I watched her open the top drawer, grab a shiny chrome pistol, and tuck it away in her black Chanel bag.

"Well, are you gonna speak, or do I gotta pull it out of you?" she said finally.

"I'ma speak. You might not like what I have to say, though."

"Well, I don't like you fucking that voodoo witch and wearing that chicken foot around your neck. Can we talk about that next?" she taunted me in annoying-little-sister fashion.

"No, because my lady is my personal business. But Marquis is fair game because he's family," I said, looking her square in the eyes.

She rolled her eyes. "I was waiting for it. I knew you were gonna have something to say about that. Anything between me and my son is none of your business, Floyd."

"It is when you aren't allowing him to be the man that you raised him to be."

"Well, it's too late. He's in Houston as we speak."

I shook my head at her. "That was the stupidest shit you coulda did."

"Protecting my baby was stupid? I sent him off for his own good."

"You shouldn't have done that. Marquis ain't a baby anymore, Shirley. He's a grown man who's tryna stand on his own two feet and see the world for what it is."

"Don't tell me what I should and shouldn't do with my son."

"He's my damn nephew, and I'm telling you, you're making him weak. And a weak man can't run The Blues."

"I'm making sure he has the opportunity to fight another fight when it's his time to take over. But this one here is on me."

"Sis, I know you don't want to go through what I went through with Fabio. But I'm telling you as your brother, you can't shelter the boy. One minute, you have him front line, and the next, you push him to the back. I want to protect him too, but as a man, I only learned how to swim by being thrown in the water."

"I hear you, Floyd, but that's my only son. I'll throw him in the water one day, but that day ain't today," she said tersely.

I sighed, knowing that nothing I said would change her mind. "Fine. Let's just hope your plan is enough to win this fight,

’cause I’m starting to think Marquis was right about calling your folks from New York.”

Once the words were out of my mouth, I was happy to be out of her arms’ reach because I was sure she would have tried to hit me — even if she knew I was right. She had some of the most lethal in-laws at her fingertips, and she always refused to reach out to them. It was beyond pride at that point, pushing more on the brink of stupidity. But, if she was rocking, I had to roll.

She glared at me for a moment before finally calming herself down. “LC Duncan runs his business one way, and I run mine another. Accepting his help would be like saying I’m okay with his way of things as long as they benefit my purpose. And I just don’t roll like that. Do you get it?”

“Partially. But still —”

“Stop your worrying. You know the plan, and I just hope your gun is loaded and you’re ready to use it.”

“You know my gun stays ready.”

“Good. Meet Mo and me at the funeral when you’re done. You know I’m not one for theatrics, but we have to put on a face for the LeBlanc family.”

I got up and prepared to leave. I felt strongly that Marquis should be there by my side, but I wasn't going to argue with Big Shirley. She was smaller than me, but her anger could come on like a tsunami.

"Floyd?"

I was almost out the door when I heard her call my name. I stopped and turned around. "Yeah?"

"Be thorough. The fate of our family depends on it."

Chapter 13
Marquis

Me and busy airports didn't mix, but there I was, maneuvering through a large crowd of impatient people with just a duffle bag on my shoulder. I was uneasy about being away from home, but I knew Momma had some peace of mind knowing I was somewhere other than back home in New Orleans. Words couldn't express my relief when I approached the exit and saw a man in a black flak jacket, holding a sign with my name on it.

"Marquis Duncan?" the man asked in a New York accent that told me he had grown up in the streets.

"That's me."

"I'm DJ. I'll be your driver today. Is that all you brought?" He pointed at my bag.

"I travel light."

He tried to take it from me, but before he could get a grip around the strap, I moved back. "No need for all that. I can carry my own stuff."

"All right then. Follow me."

He led me out of the airport to a Mercedes SUV and opened the back door for me. I hadn't expected to have a car service waiting for me, but I had absolutely no problem with riding in style. I tossed the bag in first then got inside. DJ shut the door, got in the driver's seat, and pulled off.

DJ had some morning show playing on the radio that was making him chuckle in the front seat. I wasn't paying it any attention because my thoughts kept going back to the words Momma had said to me. I hated how sometimes she treated me like an adult, but others she treated me like a child. Whichever one suited her interests at the moment was the one she went with. Well, no more of that. I would be a man all the time, whether she liked it or not, starting with making my own decisions. When she had dropped me off at the airport that morning, she thought I would be boarding a flight to Houston. Now I was looking out the window at all of New York's scenery whizzing by.

It had been a while since I'd visited my father's side of the family. In between running the Blues and doing Momma's bidding, I barely had time to visit. But when I shot a text to my cousin Vegas, letting him know I was in town, he'd sent a car for me. I wished my trip could have been under more pleasant circumstances, but we needed help, and Momma was being too bullheaded to ask for it. It was ironic, actually, how she always talked about doing what was best for the Blues, but her distaste for Uncle LC was getting in the way of that.

See, although gambling was surely on God's list of *hell no,* it was legal, and it gave us a way to make a so-called honest living. Uncle LC was the biggest drug dealer on the East Coast, and he ran an iron-clad organization. I didn't know all the details, but I just knew Momma and drugs didn't mix. Or at least that's what she always told me. There had to be more to the story. Anytime I brought up Uncle LC, you'd think I was talking about Satan himself.

I had been so lost in my thoughts that I didn't even realize we had reached the gates of the Duncan mansion until we were through them. As we approached the breathtaking home, I saw some big dudes that I didn't recognize. By their stature and the guns on their hips, I could only guess that they were security guards. The Mercedes came to a halt as DJ parked, and the security guards approached the vehicle. I stepped out with my bag, which was taken from me before I could protest.

"I'm C-Note, and you already met DJ," the man who took my bag said, motioning to his partner. "We're the ones who protect the Duncans at all costs."

"And since you're a Duncan, you fall under that umbrella. Follow us."

I nodded and let them lead me to the front door. Before we reached the door, it swung open, and I saw my first cousins Rio and Curtis standing there. Our fathers were brothers, and we used to spend part of our summers together when we were kids. They were a little older than me, but that didn't matter to them. We were family, and they let me tag along no matter what they were doing. Those summers were some of my best memories.

I was a little surprised to see Curtis standing there, because he wasn't native to New York. He'd grown up down in Waycross, Georgia, with my Uncle Larry and Aunt Nee Nee. Since we were kids, Curtis had been proud to call himself a country boy.

"Marquis!" Rio happily pulled me in for a hug.

C-Note took my bag up the stairs, presumably to the room where I'd be staying for the night. DJ stayed planted right there with us while I greeted my family.

"Cuz!" Rio and I slapped hands and embraced before I turned to Curtis and did the same thing. "Man, it's good to see y'all!"

"What's up, dog? It's been a long time!" Curtis stepped back to look at me. "My little cousin is a grown man now."

"Been a grown man," I said, playfully popping the collar to my jacket.

"The same one who was scared of lightning bugs when you were little?" Curtis teased.

I laughed. "Aye. Them things is unnatural! What you doing up this way?" I asked.

"I've just been helping out. Truth is, I've just been waiting on my Momma to say the word and we out."

"That's 'cause you never were big on this city shit."

"Not at all. I'll be a country boy till the day I die. But enough about me. What brings *you* up this way?"

When I sighed big, he and Rio exchanged a look.

"Let's just say I need to see Uncle LC and get back home before the shit hits the fan. My Momma's letting pride get in the way of common sense, and we could use his help."

"Ma and Pop aren't here. They're Upstate," Rio said.

"Will they be back soon?"

"Not sure, but Vegas is in the kitchen. Come on. He's expecting you."

We went into the spacious kitchen, and sure enough, there was Vegas, talking on the phone. His back was to us, but he heard us enter and cut the call short, then set the phone on the counter. A big smile came to his face when he turned around and laid eyes on me. I wasn't prepared to receive the bear hug he gave me. I forgot dude had always been built like a stack of bricks. I wasn't able to breathe again until he finally let me go.

"What's up, cousin? It's good to see you, man."

"You too, seriously. I'm glad to see you out and free," I told him sincerely.

I knew he'd been locked up for quite some time, and prison was no place for any man, especially one who had experienced the luxuries of life being a Duncan. I was happy that he was able to be with his family again.

"I appreciate it. I was shocked when you called and said you'd be in town. I was happy, but I can't be so sure whether this is a family visit or business."

"I can't lie. As much as I'd love to shoot the shit and catch up on old stories, I'm here on business," I told him.

He nodded. "All right, what's the business?"

"I came to see your pops. I . . . we need help, Vegas. The family's help."

I watched the curious expression on Vegas's face turn to one of downright alarm. "Aunt Shirley would bite her foot off before asking Pop for help. What the hell is going on?"

"I'm glad you know, because you're right about that. She isn't the one asking, though. I am. You ever heard of a dude named Jean LeBlanc?"

Vegas shook his head, then glanced over at Curtis and Rio, who made the same gesture.

"Nah, never heard of 'em. What's his deal?" Vegas asked.

"He's like a New Orleans godfather. He runs most of the gambling, drugs, and prostitution in the city."

Curtis stepped forward. "He trying to squeeze y'all out of your casino, cuz?"

"Nah, his brother killed himself in the Blues, and I'm afraid they're going to think we had something to do with it."

"Did you?" Rio asked skeptically.

"No, but we did help get rid of the body, so it won't matter that we didn't do it. Plus, now Jean put up a hundred grand reward for information about his brother's death. It's not looking good."

"All right, little cousin. How can we help?" Vegas asked.

It felt good to know that although it wasn't their problem, they were willing to help. I didn't understand why Momma had kept us away for so long when the love was clearly ever present.

"I was hoping you could lend us some muscle. Maybe you, Junior, and Orlando could come back with me. Let the word get out that y'all in town and have our backs."

Vegas shook his head. "See, the problem with that is we're in the middle of some shit ourselves, and it involves Junior. He's in a bad way. I'm gonna need O here with me."

"Shit, what about me?" Curtis volunteered. "I'll go down there and smack a couple motherfuckas around. Ain't nobody gonna punk my family."

"Yeah," Vegas nodded, and I could see he liked the idea. "Yeah. You and Lauryn can go back down to New Orleans with Marquis and sort this shit out."

"Lauryn? As in little Lauryn?" I asked, scrunching up my face.

Lauryn was Curtis's little sister. He also had a brother, Kenny, but just like Curtis and Lauryn, I hadn't seen him in years. In fact, the last I remembered of Lauryn was when she shaved a patch in the back of my head. We were kids, and it was a childish grudge, but I'd never forget not knowing why everyone was laughing at me when I walked by.

"Just like you ain't so little, neither is she. She's a thoroughbred Duncan and mean as hell with her hands or a pistol. Trust me when I say she's a soldier," Vegas assured me.

"All right, then." I grinned at Curtis. "I guess it's settled. New Orleans will be your new home for a while. But until then, can we enjoy the weekend? I've been pretty damn stressed lately."

Chapter 14
Floyd

A pleasant whistle escaped my lips as I bounded up the walkway to a quaint house in a quiet neighborhood. The grass was freshly mowed, and the sprinkler was going as the sun settled high in the sky. When I got to the front door, I knocked as I looked back at the clean black Honda Civic I'd driven there. I hit the lock button on the key fob in my hand because a person couldn't trust anyone those days. I turned back around when the front door opened, and I saw my old friend, Todd. When he saw me standing there, a smile came to his face.

"Floyd? Man, it's crazy how shit works. I was just about to call you! Come on in."

He stepped back and let me inside the house. I looked around and noticed that it was even quieter inside than it was on his empty street.

"The wife isn't in?"

"Nah. She's on her morning grocery store run. I don't know why we need shit from the store every day, but hey, if it keeps her happy, right?"

"Happy wife, happy life."

"Amen. Let's sit down in the living room and rap like men."

I followed him to the living room and sat on a sofa across from him. I could tell that he had nothing to do with the décor of the place. From the frilly blinds to the upholstered couch, all the way down to the fluffy rug, it had a woman's touch written all over it. I took in the happy expression frozen on Todd's face as he stared at me.

"You want some water or something?" he asked.

"Nah, I'm good. I just wanted to stop by before I went to LeBlanc's funeral."

"Good thing about being rich. You can bury your kin quick without having a fish fry. Speaking of the LeBlancs, I —" He stopped speaking suddenly and leaned forward, staring at my neck. "Floyd, is that a chicken's foot around your neck?"

He was truly bewildered, like most people had been when they saw it around my neck. Not wanting him to lose focus, I tucked the chicken foot inside my shirt.

"That's not important right now. What

were you about to say?" I asked, and he cleared his throat.

"Well, word on the street is Jean LeBlanc is offering a hundred large for information about his brother's death."

"Yeah, I heard about that," I said. "Shit for that kind of money, I might tell him what happened myself."

"Dog, I'm hearing what you're putting down. Me and old Fred was just saying the same thing. I mean, what we keeping quiet for? It's not like we killed him. The man killed himself! Might as well get this money."

"You think Jean gonna go for that?"

"Why not? It's the truth, and if we all saying the same thing, he's got to believe us."

"I don't know . . ." I let my voice trail off and shook my head dramatically.

"Well, I'm supposed to meet Fred down at his house now so we can head over to Pierre's funeral and talk to Jean, but now that you're here, maybe we can split it three ways? Strength in numbers, you know?"

"Nah, that ain't gonna work for me." I sighed and shook my head in disappointment before standing to my feet. "That ain't gonna work for me at all."

"What ain't?" Todd asked, and then his eyes widened. "You telling me you're tryna keep it all for yourself? That's a lot of money."

"To be straight-up honest with you, Todd, now that I've given it some thought, I was thinking maybe we'd just let Jean keep his money."

"Wait, I'm . . . I'm confused. A second ago —"

"A second ago I was testing your temperature to see if you were still as solid as the old days. I guess things change. Where I come from, a man's word is his bond, and you took my sister's money in exchange for your silence."

"Floyd, are you crazy? This is a hundred thousand we're talking about. And she ain't pay us that."

"No . . . no, she didn't."

I watched as fear took over Todd's whole body as he saw me remove the pistol on my hip. Now, sometimes when a man drew a gun, it was for scare tactics; however, when there was a silencer screwed onto it, there was a plan to use it. Todd raised his hands and didn't make any effort to run.

"What the fuck, Floyd? We been friends for damn near forty years! You can't kill me."

"I wish shit could be different, but unfortunately, I have to, and I'm truly sorry about that, buddy. I can't let you or anybody else fuck with my family and our business."

"No. No, I have a —"

I didn't care to hear him say another word. Without remorse, I pulled the trigger three times, the first bullet landing a fatal blow. I watched Todd's lifeless body fall to the floor, knowing that his wife would be in for a surprise when she returned from the store.

Before I left, I gathered my shell casings and wiped off anything I might have touched with my handkerchief. Whistling the same tune, I made my way out the door.

Fred was another person I'd grown up with. He and I had graduated in the same class and remained in communication for years. It was why he and Todd frequented the Blues. On the outside looking in, I could be seen as a monster for so easily following the order to take them out. But then again, who was the real villain? Our history hadn't meant a thing to them when they made the choice to try to sell my family out to Jean, knowing what Jean would do to us. So, the truth to it was that they'd chosen their fates for themselves.

Fred didn't live too far from Todd. When I knocked on the door and he answered it, he had a look of anticipation on his face. It quickly faded to disappointment when he saw that it was me.

"Expecting somebody else?" I asked.

"Yeah, I —"

"Was expecting Todd?"

"Yeah. How'd you know?"

"A gut feeling," I said with a sly smile. "Sorry to be the bearer of bad news, but Todd won't be able to make it."

There was a split-second realization that came to Fred's eyes before he gave a small gasp. "Shit!" He tried to slam the door in my face.

I caught it with my foot at the last minute and pushed it back open, entering the home. I gave an annoyed groan as I watched Fred running down the long hallway, no doubt going for his pistol. Knowing I didn't have time for a long, drawn-out shootout, I quickly raised my weapon and fired a few shots, gunning him down as he ran. He fell face down, and I heard his labored breathing as he struggled to take his last breath before succumbing to death.

"You stupid bastard," I said, shaking my head.

I erased any evidence of my presence there that morning before once again taking my leave. Two down, one more to go.

Chapter 15
Marquis

It was my last morning with my Duncan family, and I was disappointed that I hadn't seen my uncle LC, but there would always be next time. Well, unless Momma mauled me like a bear when I got back to NOLA. I would cross that bridge when I got to it. Right then, I wanted to hit the Duncan gun range and get some shots off before it was time to go.

On my way there, the smell of something delicious being cooked hit my nose, and I couldn't help but to make a pit stop in the kitchen. A smile came to my face when I saw my aunt Nee Nee over the stove, whipping up some shrimp and grits with some sides of toast and bacon. Vegas and Curtis were already seated at the dining table, stuffing their faces, and when Aunt Nee Nee saw me, she returned my smile.

"Don't be shy now. There's more than enough," she said and pointed at the table.

"Go on and sit down. I'll make your plate, baby."

"Thanks, Auntie." I joined my cousins at the table.

"You ready to be leaving us so soon? Pop would have loved to see you," Vegas said in between bites.

"I would have loved to see him too," I said earnestly. "But I really need to get back home. Plus, I want to get the heat from the dragon's den out the way sooner than later."

"Don't you talk about your momma like that," Aunt Nee Nee said as she placed my plate in front of me. "Comparing her to a damn dragon."

"Y'all don't know how she is. Momma don't play, especially when I go against her wishes."

"I know exactly how Big Shirley is. I've faced her wrath a time or two, but trust me when I say she has one of the biggest hearts I've ever come to know." She said it in a matter-of-fact tone and sat down at the table with a cup of tea.

Curtis sat up straight in his seat and wiped his mouth before focusing his attention on his mother. "What ever happened between you and Aunt Shirley anyways, Momma? I mean, I remember always going to visit, or Marquis coming to visit us. But then it just stopped." Curtis looked at me. "Does Aunt Shirley mention it at all?"

"Nah. Momma is real private about her past. And even though I'm a grown man now, she'll tell me quick to stay out of grown folks' business."

Everyone laughed.

"Let's just say your momma and I had a bit of a disagreement a long time ago. It was never meant to get out of hand the way it did, but it did. I'd like to say there's no bad blood between us, but I can't speak for your mother, baby."

"Well, what happened?" Vegas asked. "You know Duncans are always stronger together, but it feels like Aunt Shirley would rather be apart."

"Well, for one, Big Shirley has never been one for drugs or violence. Don't get me wrong. She'll defend herself or her family in a heartbeat, but she's always been an earner versus a taker, if you understand what I mean. Second, years ago, when your mother and father had gotten into it bad and separated, she needed all the help she could get. She was hurting bad, real bad, and your momma don't ask nobody for help, child."

"I know it," I agreed.

"Well, she called on me, and of course I

came. But then Chippy called on me, and I left."

"That's all?" I asked, and Aunt Nee Nee gave me the most serious look she'd ever given me.

"Child . . . that's everything. When a woman experiences a life-altering experience, especially with a young child, the people closest to them are supposed to form a fence of protection. Big Shirley was always one of those people who didn't trust a lot of people, but the ones she did were ones she loved dearly. She was always the person who was there for everyone around her, but she was also the person who had to get through everything alone. Which is probably why she's such a control freak. In hindsight, I wish I would have stayed and been the friend — no, the sister she needed me to be. My decision to leave truly drove a wedge in our relationship. It was never the same again."

I watched my aunt's face grow sad as she stared into her teacup. Curtis reached an arm over and patted her arm in a comforting way. Her words gave me a different perspective of my mother. I had always thought she was such a control freak because she just wanted things her way. I never thought it was because she had to be her own rock and pull herself out of every fire. I felt a strong fondness for her, and it made me ready to get back to her even more.

"Well, hopefully one day, you two can iron those wrinkles out," Vegas suggested.

Aunt Nee Nee just smiled and nodded her head.

When I finished my breakfast, I got up from the table and stretched my arms. "I'm gonna head down to the range and get some practice in," I said and looked to Curtis. "Join me?"

"Nah. I gotta finish packing. But Lauryn is down there already. Maybe she can teach you a thing or two."

"Me?" I laughed. "I think you said that backward, cuz."

He grinned. "No, I said it right."

I shook my head and left the kitchen. My full belly had me feeling energized, and when I got to the range, I sure enough found my cousin there, shooting the hell out of a target. She looked like she was ready to go into battle, wearing a black jumpsuit and black ear coverings. I wouldn't have been impressed if it weren't for the distance of the target. Not only was she hitting it with ease, but she made nothing but head shots.

I didn't announce my presence until her

magazine was empty. “Nice aim,” I complimented her, and she looked over her shoulder and grinned.

“Thanks, cuz. You tryna get some shots in?” Lauryn asked.

“Shit, if you tell me what kind of pistol you’re shooting with to hit a target that far out. What’s that, like, eighty yards?”

“A hundred,” she corrected. “Walther P99. It gets me right every time. Of course, I had to train vigorously to shoot so accurately. With brothers like mine, I have to keep up. You know?”

“Understood. How is Kenny anyway?”

“Somewhere out there being Kenny, I guess.” She shrugged, and I didn’t push. “Anyway, the range is all yours. I’m about to go finish packing. Rio’s dropping us off at the jet in a couple hours. Ammunition is over there, and if you want to shoot with something new or different, guns are there.”

She tucked her gun away and pointed me in the direction of the Duncan armory. My eyes got big when I saw all of the shooting options. I hated that I didn’t have more time to shoot them all. She handed me the earmuffs and walked away. I rubbed my hands together in excitement as I stared at the AR-15 on a table to the side.

“I know what I’m shooting first.”

Chapter 16
Big Shirley

Although it was supposed to be a somber affair, the classic New Orleans homegoing for Pierre turned into almost a party. The band in the middle of the street was playing like their lives depended on it, and the singers were heartily belting out their songs of goodbye. Even I couldn't help but to move my body while holding my black umbrella. I wasn't the only one, either. The French Quarter was filled with people who had come to pay their last respects, and we were all dressed to impress. All I could see for a mile were people dancing in black clothes and umbrellas.

Beside me, Monique was putting on a show as well, but I could tell that she wasn't thrilled about it. She had been born and raised in Cleveland, so some NOLA festivities didn't make sense to her. But I knew she wouldn't break character, not until what had to be done was done.

The hat I wore had a veil that covered my eyes and nose, and I used that to my advantage as I scanned the scene. A little ways away, a horse and carriage was coming our way. It was carrying Pierre's coffin, and I could see the LeBlanc family walking beside it.

"You sure about this?" Monique stopped dancing to ask me, and I nodded.

"Today, I settle all our family's problems."

"All right. He's right there. Do you see him?"

"I do. Slimy son of a bitch." I shook my head just as the horse and carriage reached us.

My eyes fixated on the casket, a symbol of finality, knowing it carried Pierre's body. A coroner might have been able to give the LeBlanc family an open casket with the gunshot wound, but after the gators did what they had to do to make our story sound believable, I knew there wasn't much left of him in there.

As the LeBlanc family passed, I saw Jean's stoic face. The only tell of his emotions was how tightly he was holding his wife's hand. Saint was walking near him and observing the scene. As crazy as he was, I knew nobody was going to be able to get close to Jean without joining Pierre.

Still, I stepped forward to address the family. They paused when they saw me.

"Jean, Marie, I am so, so sorry for your loss," I said, laying on the sympathy as thick as I could.

I offered my hand, and Jean took it, to my surprise. He nodded his head in appreciation of my words. "Thank you. He had a lot of fun at your place. Sometimes I don't think anything made Pierre more excited than being at the Blues."

"It really was his happy place," Marie added, giving me a sad smile.

"He'll be missed," I said.

Jean nodded and let my hand go before continuing on his walk. Saint and I connected eyes, and although I offered him a smile, he didn't return it. He walked after the LeBlancs, and when they were past me, my smile turned into a smirk. That was easier than I thought it would be.

I went to rejoin Monique on the sidelines.

"He doesn't have a clue," she said.

"Good. If my plan is going to work, he can't."

"Well, now that you've given him your condolences, can we stop putting on face? You know I hate these things. Ain't nobody supposed to be dancing at a damn funeral."

"You need to stop," I said with a laugh.

"You know this is how we do it in New Orleans."

"That don't mean it ain't creepy as fuck. Whoever heard of dancing around a dead person? Besides, my ass is from Cleveland."

"Well, your Cleveland ass better get to dancing harder, so we can do what we gotta do and get the hell out of here. You see anything yet?"

With grand theatrics, Monique raised her umbrella and twisted it while dancing in a circle. Only I knew she was really scanning the crowd. I moved my body along with the saxophone notes so I wouldn't look out of place standing beside her. Suddenly, she stopped and lowered her umbrella.

"Over there." She motioned to something near the street that the LeBlancs would be turning down. "If we cross now, we can beat him."

"Let's go."

Although there was a large crowd following behind the LeBlancs and the band, we were able to make our way to the other side of the street without an issue. The problem was getting to where we were going before Jean did. Luck seemed to be on our side, because Jean was stopped once again in the street when someone he knew wanted to pay their personal respects. We maneuvered through the dancing crowd until we reached an overzealous man waving and trying to get Jean's attention. The man? None other than Eric McMan. The same Eric that had been at the Blues the night of Pierre's death.

See, the thing about a place like the Midnight Blues was that folks often went in there and got a little lippy. Even when they thought they were being inconspicuous, the liquor made them obvious. Eric had been bold enough to not only take my money, but to come back to the Blues, bragging at the craps table about a big check he was about to get from Jean LeBlanc himself. When it got back to me that he planned to go talk to Jean at the funeral, I knew I had no choice but to get rid of Eric.

I was happy that he wasn't making it a hard decision. As we neared, I could hear him shouting and trying to be louder than the already loud music and crowd. "Jean! Over here, Jean! I need to talk to you!" He was waving his arms like a madman.

The only reason Jean hadn't heard him was because he was too far out, but as he got closer, it would be impossible to ignore Eric's behavior. I looked at Mo, who nodded back. She detached the handle from her umbrella, revealing that it was really a sharp dagger, and handed it to me just as I reached Eric. I shoved it into his back, aiming for his heart.

I heard the pained choking noise come from his mouth, and I placed my lips by his ear. "Shhh," I said as I twisted the dagger.

He made a gurgling noise, but it blended in with the other sounds around us. I pulled the dagger out of his back and wiped it on his shirt before handing it back to Mo. Eric stumbled forward a bit before he fell to the ground, face first. Nobody seemed to notice the man dying in front of them as Jean had finally arrived at their part of the street. He had their attention and focus, which made Mo and I getting lost into the sea of black an easy feat.

Chapter 17
Marquis

I didn't know just how much I needed the warm love of my family until it was time to go. The weekend had been filled with good food and a lot of laughter and partying, but I knew I had to get back to New Orleans. Still, as I stood there about to board Uncle LC's jet, telling Rio goodbye, it was harder than I thought. He must have seen it in my eyes, because he reached out and gave me an encouraging shoulder pat.

"I've never been good with goodbyes either," he said.

"Am I that transparent?"

"Beyond see-through, cousin." Rio grinned. "As much fun as it is when we're all together, family affairs always come first. You'll be back before you know it."

"Yeah, maybe Momma will come with me."

He and I shared a look before we both burst out laughing. We embraced one last time before Curtis, Lauryn, and I continued up the steps. Vegas had been right about my little cousin Lauryn. She had gone from the nerdy kid with glasses to a beautiful killing machine. I'd had a chance to see firsthand how lethal she was in the Duncan gun range on my visit. Although I wasn't leaving with who I thought I would be, she and Curtis should be enough muscle for now.

Suddenly, I heard screeching of tires on the tarmac, and when I turned to see what it was, I noticed a silver SUV flying toward the jet. Instinct took over, and I reached for the gun on my waist, pointing it toward the speeding vehicle.

"Curtis, Lauryn, Rio. Nine o'clock!" I shouted in warning.

I glanced toward my cousins just as the car came to a dramatic stop about fifteen feet away from the plane. They were standing there calmly, no weapons in sight. Why was I the only one ready for battle?

Curtis placed a hand on top of my gun and gently forced me to lower it. "Duncan plates. It's one of ours. Vegas must have come to see us off. Might be a change of plans?" Curtis said with a perplexed shrug.

We watched as DJ got out of the driver's side and opened the rear door. Expecting to see Vegas get out, I was surprised when

Aunt Nee Nee hopped out, carry-on bag in hand. I looked at Curtis, but he was too busy watching his mother sashay over to the jet.

"Momma?" he and Lauryn said in unison.

"Aunt Nee Nee?" I pointed to the bag in her hands. "You going somewhere?"

"And if so, where?" Lauryn threw in.

"If my children are going to New Orleans, then I guess I am too."

"What?" Curtis exclaimed. "Momma, you can't come with us. I thought you said you and Aunt Shirley didn't get along."

"We don't. But that doesn't mean that we won't," she said cryptically.

"What does that mean?"

"It means that sometimes family has their ways, and they have their days, but it's been a while since I've seen my sister-in-law. I think it's about time for a visit. There was a point that we were the best of friends. That kind of love never fades."

"Momma, this could get dangerous."

"Dangerous?" Aunt Nee Nee let out a loud laugh. "Boy, do you know who I am? I've been a Duncan a lot longer than either of you. Danger is my middle name. It comes with being part of this family. Now, move."

She pushed her way past us, and I could see Curtis eyeing me as if to tell me to try to stop her. However, I was still too startled to say anything. Besides, I wouldn't be opposed to Aunt Nee Nee coming. Growing up, she was the fun auntie, the one who shot water guns with us and who snuck us more snacks way after bedtime. She and Momma really did used to be best friends until they had their falling out. I didn't know what it had been about, and since Momma wasn't forthcoming about it, I didn't press the fact. I just knew I started spending less and less time with my father's side until I rarely saw them at all. By then, I was older and more focused on high school and girls to care anyway. But now, I was back to wondering what had really happened.

"I guess it's settled then," Curtis said, shaking his head.

"That's Aunt Nee Nee for you," Rio said, laughing.

"And you know there is no stopping her when she acts like this," Lauryn added, adjusting her knapsack before continuing up the stairs after her mother.

DJ grabbed a few more bags from the trunk, and he too walked toward the jet. It was Rio's turn to look confused. He pointed at the extra luggage, and then at DJ.

"Vegas thought it would be wise for me to tag along too. He thought they might need an extra body."

"Good thinking," Rio gave an approving nod and let him pass. Curtis and I stepped out of his way.

"Welp, you've got some of the best muscle around. But you know the rest of us are just a phone call away," Rio told me.

Curtis and I bounded up the steps into the jet. It was time to go home. When we got there, I just hoped Momma wouldn't kill me.

Chapter 18
Jean

The outpouring of love for Pierre was almost overwhelming. But then again, it was to be expected. Since we were kids, Pierre had always been a charming bastard. He had an easy-going personality that made him easy to get along with, and the nigga was smart. Back in our younger days, he had so much promise. He could have been anything he wanted, but where my father piled on the discipline with me, he practically let Pierre roam free. I was the one who was made to carry on the family legacy, while Pierre was the baby boy, full of entitlement. He was spoiled rotten and had everything handed to him, while I had to earn it. I never understood why it was so surprising to anyone when his life went to shit.

Instead of going to work in the family business like me, or going to college, all he did was chase hoes and travel on the old man's dime. It was during that time that he started gambling. He was actually pretty good at it. Like I said, Pierre was smart and knew how to calculate the odds like a motherfucker, but what he didn't know how to do was get up when he was ahead. You sit there long enough, and eventually, the odds aren't going to be in your favor. The house always wins. Hell, it didn't matter, because the more he lost, the more the old man gave him. He was the golden child, and it wasn't a secret.

When our father fell ill and I became the controlling power of all of the LeBlanc legal and illegal businesses, Pierre's free ride ended. If he wanted anything, he was going to have to work for it. However, a cushy job at LeBlanc Construction still wasn't enough to keep him out of the casino. Without my father giving him the all the money he requested, Pierre began to resent me. But I didn't care . . . until I did.

"Your job as a big brother is to protect your little brother at all costs."

During the funeral, my father's words played over and over in my head. I couldn't help but think that Pierre's death was on my hands. It had been my responsibility to keep him out of trouble. It had been my responsibility to take care of him. I thought by making Pierre responsible for his own actions I was doing that. I thought my brother had time to iron out his crooked ways. I thought there would be a time that we could be actual brothers. Partners, even. Those were the parts about his death that were eating me up. And that was the reason I had to get to the bottom of it all.

I let out a sigh as my thoughts consumed me, and I felt a pressure on my right hand. I looked down and saw Marie's delicate hand squeezing mine. She was staring at me, wearing a look of concern. She brought my hand up to her lips and kissed my knuckles.

"You all right?" she asked.

"I don't know," I told her honestly.

We reached the end of the procession and continued walking to where my Rolls Royce was parked next to a lifted shiny pickup truck. Beside it stood Prince and his best friend, Jace. Among the most thorough of the Crescent Boys, they were the personification of "don't let a handsome face fool you." Prince had always been what girls called a pretty boy, and it was how he could remain under many radars. Nobody suspected anyone with his charming features to be such a savage, and it worked in my favor every time.

He and Jace were waiting with a look of

anticipation on their faces. Saint went over to them first and talked to his little brother Prince. Watching them exchange words, I felt a sharp pain in my chest. It wasn't jealousy; it was longing. Their tight bond was how siblings, especially brothers, were supposed to operate. Prince looked up to his brother and was loyal to him, and because Saint was my right hand, that meant he was loyal to me too.

I got Marie and Simone in the Rolls Royce. Once they were comfortably seated, I shut their doors and went to the driver's side. I could hear Prince speaking, and his tone sounded urgent. As I opened my door to get in, Saint looked over his shoulder and motioned for me to join them.

"Babe, give me a second," I said into the car to Marie.

She pouted. "You said no work today."

"I know. But this will only take a minute," I promised.

I couldn't miss the annoyed look on her face, but I still shut the door and went over to where Saint and Prince were standing.

"What's this about?" I asked.

"Tell him," Saint urged his brother.

"Me, Kendall, and a couple of the boys was dumping Red and his son like you told us, and we came across something," Prince told me.

"What?"

"Your brother's car. It was out there by the swamp."

"The swamp?" I had been wondering where my brother's car was. The sheriff never found it, and that was a big part of the reason I believed there had been foul play. If he didn't drive himself, how had Pierre gotten out there? Now I was a little confused, because it seems his car was at the swamp after all.

"Yeah, but that's not the craziest thing." Prince exchanged a look with Jace. "There was somebody in that motherfucka."

"Were they dead or alive?" The alarm in me went off like someone had flipped a switch.

"Very much alive. Kendall got him tied up at La Nue right now. Just waiting for you to give the word."

"Who the fuck is it?" I asked.

"No idea," Jace chimed in. "But I know for a fact that he ain't from around here. Motherfucka was dressed like he was ready for LA fashion week."

They definitely had my attention. Who the hell had access to my brother's car, and what did they know about my brother's death? I glanced back at Marie, who was giving me the death stare through the window. I offered a smile, knowing that I was about to piss her off even further, then I turned back to the boys.

"Keep him on ice until I get Marie and Simone situated at the house. I'd like to meet this mystery man. A little stress relief could be fun. It's been a while since I've had a chance to get my hands dirty."

"No doubt," Prince said. He motioned his head for Jace to get in the truck.

"I'ma follow them over there to make sure their trigger-happy asses don't kill the motherfucka before you get a chance to talk to him," Saint said.

We slapped hands and parted ways. As I went back to the Rolls Royce, the thought of cracking my knuckles on a jaw sent a chuckle through my lips.

Chapter 19
Big Shirley

After getting Eric out of my way, I could focus on preparations for the annual Midnight Blues masquerade ball. It would not only help me get my mind off my troubles, but it would add a little excitement back into my life after so much stress. The ball was one of the most anticipated events of the year, so much so that I was able to sell tickets for $250 a pop. And don't get me started on how much money guests spent during the ball on gambling. Nothing opened a purse or a wallet like free liquor and a good time.

Monique and I were walking around the Blues, noting where we wanted the ice sculptures, tables, and decor. Just like every other year, we weren't agreeing on a thing. She wanted one side reserved for a dance floor and one side designated to seating in the grand hall. I wanted the dance floor in the center of the grand hall, with the seating around it so it could be more open. She'd already chosen the color theme, midnight blue and silver. She should've been happy I let her do that.

"If we do it that way, the refreshment tables will look like we just threw them somewhere," I was telling her when Antoinette sashayed her fast behind by us.

I couldn't help the fact that my nose turned up as she made her way to the bar near the slot machines. She had never been my favorite worker, but she *was* my best cocktail waitress and brought in the most tips. However, knowing that she was fooling around with my son even though she had a crazy-ass husband wasn't gonna cut it for me.

"Mmm, mm, mm," Monique said distastefully as Antoinette began serving a few customers. "I can't believe that slut. Have you talked to her since you caught her in Quis's bed?"

"No, I haven't had a chance to with everything else that's on my plate. And now that Marquis is gone, it kept slipping my mind. But trust me, I'ma get that girl together."

"You better. You don't need any of these little bitches walking around here thinking they run shit," Monique said, raising her brows at me.

"I know. I know."

"Good. Anyways, back to planning." Monique looked down at the iPad in her hands. "Let's talk food and drink. We've got plenty of high-end liquor, but we're running low on beer, crawfish, and crab legs."

"Oh, hell no! The free drinks and food is what makes these fools spend two hundred and fifty on their entry tickets. When's our next shipment?" I asked.

She scrolled some more. "Thursday."

"Shit, that's cutting it close. I might have to make some calls."

"Yeah, because we don't need a repeat of last year when we ran out of crab legs." She started laughing. "Remember those two old ladies jumped Skunk's ass for making a plate damn near a foot tall? He was limping for a week!"

I laughed too, thinking about one of our regulars. Skunk was the kind of guy that seemed to always be around even when he shouldn't have been. He was a weaselly fellow with a scruffy beard, and his clothes always looked like he had pulled them out of a dirty pile on the floor. He never had any money to gamble, and he always dined good on the buffet, knowing he didn't pay a dime for anything. Floyd hated that I allowed it, but for some reason, I had a soft spot for him. He brought laughs wherever he went, so he was all right with me.

"He scrounged up enough money to buy another ticket," I said with a chuckle. "I wanted to tell him that I knew he stole it from his momma's purse again."

"Oooh, Shirl, not you done took the man's momma's money," Monique teased.

"I like Skunk. He ain't too bad once you get to know him."

We continued on our journey. Next on our list were the bars. Surprisingly, Monique and I agreed on how we wanted to decorate them, like something out of a fairytale. Each one would have its own signature drink. As we prepared to go to the VIP lounge area, something in the distance caught my eye, and I stopped walking. A squeal came out of my mouth, and not the happy kind.

"You've got to be fucking kidding me," I said. "That better not be who I think it is."

Monique stopped walking and turned to see what had me so upset. Walking in our direction was my son — the same son who wasn't supposed to be in New Orleans — and he wasn't alone. In tow, he had my meddling sister-in-law, Nee Nee Duncan, and her children. I hadn't seen Curtis and Lauryn in years, and had it been under different circumstances, I might have been happier to see my niece and nephew. Nee Nee, on the other hand, was up in the air. I could feel my anger with my son taking over my whole body. He had deliberately disobeyed me. I'd thought he was in Houston, but really, he'd bamboozled me. *Me.* The one pulling all the strings to keep his behind safe. I was livid.

"Oh, shit. Shirl, calm down," Monique said, but there was no calming a raging bull.

"Too. Fucking. Late." I stomped my way to my son and estranged family. I couldn't believe Marquis had defied me like that. The only saving grace was that he'd gone to Waycross to get help, and not New York. Had he gone to New York, I would have wrung his neck right then and there in front of everyone.

The space between us and them closed in quickly, and I could see Monique beside me, shaking her head. I took a breath and tried my best to take the high road. Instead of ripping Marquis's head off, I concentrated on Nee Nee, who I was sure would have my other sister-in-law, Chippy, on the phone first chance she got, telling all my business. We quickly engaged in a tense stare down.

"Well, if it isn't my long-lost sister-in-law,"

Nee Nee finally said. "You looking good, Shirley Duncan." Nee Nee's lips twitched until a full-blown, genuine smile spread across her face. To my surprise, a wide grin spread on mine too.

"Not as good as you, Nee Nee Duncan," I replied playfully. "And I can't be too lost if you know where to find me. Now, bring yo' ass over here, girl."

We laughed and gave each other a warm embrace. Don't get me wrong. I had always liked Nee Nee, but she was entirely too close to LC and Chippy for my taste. I couldn't stand them because although my son Trent had his problems, they were responsible for his death.

When we separated, I turned to my niece Lauryn and marveled over her. "Oh my God! I know this ain't little Lauryn with the braces who used to terrorize Marquis." I had to give it to the girl. She was tall, fine, and with a real pretty shape on her. I know people who'd pay money to have hazel eyes like hers.

"Hi, Aunt Shirley," Lauryn said bashfully then hugged me.

"Girl, you are as easy on the eyes as a Siberian Iris. You must be fighting them off with a stick." I let Lauryn go and admired her for a few more moments before turning to my favorite nephew, Curtis. "And you! Boy, get over here and give your auntie a hug. You just as handsome as you wanna be. Lord, that Duncan blood runs deep, don't it?"

"Don't it?" Nee Nee agreed as Curtis and I shared an embrace.

"Thank you, Auntie," Curtis said, letting me go and then motioning around the Blues. "This place is more amazing than Marquis described. Why we never came here before, Momma?"

I glanced over at Nee Nee. I had thought many times about inviting her to visit so we could reconcile, but I could never be sure she'd leave that crazy-ass husband of hers at home. Not that he wanted to visit, considering he was in and out of mental facilities most of the time. As expected, Nee Nee avoided Curtis's question.

"Yeah, girl, you've really got something here," Nee Nee said proudly.

"Thank you. Outside of Marquis, the Blues is my pride and joy. It's been in the family for a very long time," I said. "Now, not that I'm not happy to see you, but I don't know what to make of it. What are y'all doing in my neck of the woods?"

I'd asked the question to Nee Nee, but my eyes traveled to my intended target,

Marquis. Nee Nee sensed the trouble and slightly sidestepped, blocking him from my piercing gaze.

"We were visiting up there in New York, and well, you know, one week became a month." She chuckled.

"Is that right?" I glared at Marquis. "And here I am thinking my son went down to Waycross, when he really went to New York."

I could see Marquis trying to make his body small enough to hide behind Curtis. He could try it, but his ass was mine once we were alone. I needed to change the subject before I smacked the shit outta my son.

"So, how's Larry?" I asked.

"I don't know if you heard, but Larry's no longer at the mental health facility up there in Pennsylvania."

"Oh, I might be out of the loop, but I keep my ear to the wind. Is it true that he escaped?" I asked rather bluntly.

"Yeah." Nee Nee shook her head. "But that place was no good for him anyway. He had too much free rein, and he wasn't taking his medication like they promised they'd monitor him to do. It was just a mess. But since I don't have a clue where he is right now, I figured why not come visit New

Orleans and see some more family? So, here we are."

"Mm-hmm, that you are." I shot Marquis another death stare.

"While I'm here, I'm hoping we can iron out that last disagreement that we had?" Nee Nee asked hopefully, and I gave a little chuckle. I had much bigger problems to deal with at the moment, so there was no sense in revisiting the past.

"Honey, that's been ironed out. You made your decision. You chose Chippy like I knew you would."

"Big Shirley, it wasn't like that. I —"

I put my hand up to cut her off. "Nee, it's water under the bridge," I said, but I didn't mean it. I was sure Nee Nee knew that, too, but she didn't press the subject. "Well, y'all here now, and I know y'all have to be starvin' after all that traveling. Let us show y'all to the buffet."

"Buffet?" Nee Nee scrunched up her face as if I had insulted her. "What I'ma do with a buffet? My kids don't eat at buffets. We can go to the house, and I can whip us up something real quick."

"Nee Nee, everybody know you the best cook this side of the Rio Grande, but you ain't the only cook. Now, you want a job in the kitchen, or you here to eat?" I snapped with a hand on my hip.

"Don't mind her, Aunt Shirley. A buffet is just fine." Knowing his mother, Curtis stepped in and moved Aunt Nee Nee to the side.

"Good. Now, y'all remember Monique. She's my first cousin on my daddy's side. She'll show y'all to where the food is at, and I'll be right behind you. I need to talk to my son."

"Come on. Follow me," Monique said with a wave. I watched them walk away, smiling like I'd just gotten paid — until they were out of sight. Then I snapped my head toward Marquis to rip him to shreds.

Chapter 20
Marquis

Before they walked away, Monique and Aunt Nee Nee both gave me sympathetic looks. They obviously knew there was nothing they could do to save me. It was time to own up to my choice, and I stood there with my head held high. Momma's eyes rested on me, and I swore I didn't see her blink once. She held her tongue until the rest of our family was out of earshot.

"You think I'm stupid? You went to New York behind my back?" Her voice was eerily calm.

"The honest truth is, yeah, I did. But —"

"Get your black ass to my office now," she interrupted through gritted teeth.

I watched her storm off, and I waited for her to get a good distance away before I hesitantly followed. I moved so slowly that eventually I lost sight of her. I had half a mind to leave the Blues all together and go home. That would only postpone my problems, however, because of course, she lived there too.

The moment I stepped inside Momma's office, I received a forceful smack in the face. It took a few seconds of feeling the sting for me to register that Momma had just slapped the hell out of me. I held the burning spot on my face and looked at her with wide eyes.

"That's for going behind my back!" she told me. "What in the name of heaven and hell were you thinking about? Have you just lost your damn mind?"

"I was doing what you were too proud to do. We needed help."

"You damn right. I'm too proud to crawl to LC."

I let my hand fall to my side, and I looked defiantly at her. "I didn't crawl. I flew."

She got in my face with a balled fist. "Boy, do you want something more than a smack? Don't be disrespectful. I'll knock that big-ass head off your shoulders and shoot hoops with it! You betrayed me, Marquis."

"Ma, I didn't betray you. I love you! But you wanted me to run like a scared baby. That's not me. I'm a Duncan, and I'm a fighter. Just like them, just like you. You may not want to admit it, but being a Duncan means something."

Frustrated, she stepped away from me and went to her desk. She rubbed her temples with her fingertips, and I could tell she was trying to find the right words to say. I could understand her anger because I had disobeyed a direct order; however, she couldn't deny that I was her son through and through. If the shoe was on the other foot, she would have made the same call, and I knew it. Finally, she looked back at me with an unwavering gaze.

"Boy, you don't know what that family is about. What being a Duncan stands for in New York. It's not just private jets and fancy cars. It's a lifestyle built on drugs, high stakes business, and violence."

"Momma, I get it. I get it. You don't want me to be involved with drugs. Fine, I won't. But there are going to be times when I'm going to have to fight and use every weapon in my arsenal. And if that means calling my drug-dealing cousins in New York or my bounty-hunting cousin from Waycross for help, then so be it. I'll do anything to protect my family and our club. Just like you."

It took a few moments, but I saw her eyes soften. I stepped forward and took her hand — the same one she'd smacked me with — in mine.

"Marquis, I'm just trying to protect you."

"Then learn to protect me *and* respect my position by your side."

"Okay," She nodded and pulled her hand back. "Okay. And now that this situation with Jean has died down for the moment, I won't be as on edge."

"Died down?" I asked. "How?"

Momma walked around her desk, sat down, and clasped her hands, looking very much like a boss. No, like *the* boss. She smirked. "Like you said, sometimes you have to do what you have to do to protect our family and our club."

CHAPTER 21
JEAN

"I know you're not leaving. You promised."

Marie's terse voice caught me off guard as I was opening the front door to our home. I sighed and closed my eyes. All I wanted to do was get the fuck outta there, and she was smothering me.

Emotions were high that day, and a normal man would have spent the night after his brother's funeral with his family, but that was not Jean LeBlanc. My affairs required my attention at all times of the day. I couldn't change that. There was no way I wouldn't address the buster who was in my brother's car just to lay up with my wife, someone I'd been with for two decades. Not to downplay our relationship, but Marie knew what it was with me. She also knew that even if I came home late, I always came home.

I turned around and saw her standing on the stairs in her robe with her hand on her hip. I caught my breath for a moment when I saw her skimpy lingerie set and the bottle of wine in her free hand. Both her puppies were popping almost to the point I could see nipples, and the way she was positioned gave me a glimpse of her perfect ass from the side. No lie, my wife had an immaculate body, even if her face looked like she was ready to kill me. I searched for an excuse, because it was true, I'd told her earlier that morning that I would take the day off to focus on family. I just didn't know that the current business would also involve family.

"Hello?" she pressed. "Marie to Jean. Come in, Jean?"

"I got some shit I need to take care of over at the clubhouse," I finally said, giving up on excuses that I knew would never be satisfy her anyway. "I'll be back."

"I knew you were gonna pull this shit," she scoffed. "Today wasn't about family. It was about you, just like every other day. You got me fucked up, Jean, standing here looking like a fool."

"How do I have you looking like a fool?"

"Because you don't love me anymore," she whined.

"Oh God, Marie, not this again. You know I love you, honey."

"Oh, really? Do you know how long it's

been since you *touched* me?"

"I touch you all the time."

"Don't play games with me, Jean Paul LeBlanc. We haven't made love in over a month."

"Baby, please. I really have to run. Let's not do this tonight. I'll make it up to you. I —"

"Promise?" She finished for me. "Do you know how many promises you haven't cashed in on? You know what? Let's cut to the chase, 'cause it ain't that much business in the world. Who is she?"

"What?"

"You heard me. Who is the bitch you're clearly fucking? Because we both know that if you go out that door, I won't be seeing you until three in the morning."

I couldn't believe what she was insinuating. I mean, sure, when we were younger, I was a ladies' man, but when I'd made the decision to be a husband and to make her my wife, I'd left that part of me in the streets. I wasn't perfect, but I wasn't a cheater, not with a woman like her at home.

There was a fierceness in her eyes that I bypassed, focusing instead on the hurt. "Marie, you are and have always been the woman for me. There is nobody else."

"Then why have you been rejecting me

for months? Just because I'm a woman doesn't mean I don't have needs." She pouted.

"Will you stop it? I'm not rejecting you. I'm just preoccupied. It will always and forever be you and only you, Marie. You're the love of my life. I have no other. Now, I'll see you when I get home."

Not wanting to continue the back and forth, I left and shut the door behind me. As a man, did I understand that there were worse things I could do than cheat? Yes. But at the moment, I couldn't focus on that. Marie's problem wasn't just me being gone all the time. It was the fact that she hadn't sought out a purpose for herself since Simone became an adult. If she found some way to preoccupy her time, she wouldn't be so bored when I was out of the home.

The drive to La Nue was filled with Teddy Pendergrass in my ears. I hummed along to "Love T.K.O." as I navigated. For the most part, I was calm, but listening to my favorite oldies was how I prepared for a night of potential murder. Yes, I was an amazing businessman, great father, and okay husband, but I was also a killer. It was what my father had raised me to be. I was his oldest son, his heir, and many times, I was his bodyguard. Ever since I could remember, I had been prepped for exactly who I turned out to be. There was a lot of blood on my hands — although I still slept very well at night. I would always do whatever needed to be done without feeling the slightest twinge of a guilty conscience.

When I arrived at the strip club, I pulled to the back and parked. Kendall, my nephew who used to be my niece, was already there waiting for me. He was dressed in Crescent Boys colors, a loose purple pants set with a lavender bolo hat on his head.

Since he was little, he'd been tough. Back then, we knew him as Kendallise. His mother, my late sister, never accepted that Kendallise didn't feel like herself in her own body. The saddest thing was that they never made amends before cancer took her life. I made sure that Kendall knew that I accepted him gay, straight, trans, or other. He was and would forever be family.

I noticed that the brass knuckles on his wrist were covered in blood. If he had killed the man I came to see, there would be hell to pay.

"He alive?" I asked, pointing to his hand.

Kendall looked down at the droplets of blood falling from the brass knuckles and grinned. "Yeah, he's alive, although it was hard not to kill him. He's a cocky bastard, that one. Won't stop talking shit to save his life."

"Well, I appreciate your restraint. Take me to him."

Kendall led me through the back entrance of La Nue into a room that looked like an old, forgotten locker room. Standing around a man bound to a chair were Prince, Jace, and Saint. Saint gave me a quick head nod as I approached the man in the chair. He had a bag over his head, and he was making loud, angry hums that told me his mouth was taped shut.

Snatching the bag off, I stared at the man for a few moments. Judging by the dried blood under his nose and the shiner forming under his eye, I could tell he'd had quite the tussle with Kendall's brass knuckles. I studied him and realized I hadn't the slightest clue who he was. He was fair-skinned, with wavy hair and very expensive taste. I could tell by the colorful Armani suit he was wearing. I had the same one in gray.

I watched as the man's eyes adjusted to the lights and focused on me. I couldn't get answers with his mouth taped, so not knowing if I would regret it, I snatched the tape off his lips.

He yelped loudly. "You motherfuckas

don't know who you're fucking with!" He looked me up and down like I was a turd on the street. "And who the hell are you supposed to be?"

"I ask the questions," I told him.

"I don't give a fuck what questions you ask. I thought they were bringing the boss, not another flunky. Where the hell is Pierre?"

"Hmm, well, now we can skip to the second question. What business do you have with Pierre LeBlanc?" I asked.

"The business I have with him ain't got shit to do with you."

He glared at me for another moment before shifting his hateful gaze to Saint, who laughed and shook his head. Clearly the man thought Pierre was the boss. Actually, it wasn't too hard to imagine Pierre telling him that. He had always wanted to be in charge, without putting in any of the manual labor, of course.

I sighed and turned back to the man. "Unfortunately for you, whatever business you have with him has everything to do with me. See, I'm Jean LeBlanc, Pierre's brother. And it don't strike me well to find out some high yellow bastard who clearly ain't from around here was driving his car."

"Brother?" The man's interest was piqued.

"Well, if you're his brother, you can tell him that Sebastian is here, and this isn't how I do business. And he's liable to slap the shit out of you for how you've done me, brother or not."

"Slap the shit out of me?" I laughed. "Let me ask you a question. Who the hell told you that Pierre runs shit around here?"

"Well . . ." An unsure look came across his face. "He did."

"And you believed him why?"

"Because he looked the part . . . I guess."

"Well, that was your first mistake. *I* run shit around these parts. I don't know what all he told you, but when he was alive, my brother was known to tell some far-fetched stories."

"Wait." Sebastian's forehead crinkled. "Pierre's dead?"

"Buried him today," I confirmed and then pulled the shiny chrome pistol from my hip. "So once again, who are you? And I ain't talking about just a name. And why were you driving his car?"

"Well, like I said, my name's Sebastian. And it ain't just a name. It holds weight. You had to have heard of me."

"Nah, never." As I cocked my gun, I felt a tap on my shoulder.

"Hold on, boss. I've heard of him," Saint

said, stepping forward, and I saw Sebastian smirk in satisfaction. “Sebastian from South Florida. He’s supposed to have some of the best shit.”

I looked from Saint to Sebastian. Sebastian nodded his head feverishly.

“Is that right? Hmm. Then what business did you have with my brother? His ass was more liable to party with the product than sell it.”

“Pocket change, really. I had his car loaded up with five keys of that pure, uncut shit. Only thing was, he didn’t show up. Your goons did.”

“Five keys?” I asked. “They still in the car?”

Sebastian glared at me without answering, and that was all the answer I needed. I looked at Prince and Jace. Before I could give them the order, they were already making their way to the door. Sebastian made a pissed off noise and lowered his head, no doubt thinking he was about to be robbed. A few moments later, Prince and Jace returned, and Prince was holding a leather bag. He brought it to me, and they resumed their posts.

Taking the bag to a nearby table, I unzipped it, and sure enough, there were five uncut bricks of that all-white stuff. Kendall handed me a switch blade, which I used to make a small incision in one of the keys.

"Let me," he said and tested a small amount of the powder. I watched the bored expression on his face turn into a highly impressed one. He put the knife away and nodded his approval. "That's some of the best shit I've ever had."

"You stand on that?" I asked just to be sure.

"Hell yeah."

Satisfied with his feedback, I closed the bag and turned back to Sebastian. What the hell was my fool of a brother doing with a miniature kingpin? I said miniature, because if I didn't know him, he couldn't have been making too much noise. But according to Kendall, he was working with some good product.

"How did you meet Pierre?" I asked.

"Back when I came to visit my sister for Mardi Gras, the motherfucker was balling out of control. I mean, thousands upon thousands of dollars. He had the money, the women, and the respect of everyone around him. He told me he was the boss, and I believed him."

"Well, you were wrong about that." I shook my head. "He was just the boss's annoying kid brother. What was his ticket?"

"Fifteen a key," Sebastian told me. "But I'm sure y'all are about to just take my shit for free."

"No. I'm a fair man. Now, my brother isn't around, but luckily, I am. What if I take these and give you thirteen five a key? Plus put in an order for thirty-five more?"

I could almost see Sebastian's mind going as he contemplated my offer. I didn't know how long he thought he had to decide, but the real number was only thirty seconds. Finally, he looked down at his torn clothing.

"What about my Armani suit? That thug of yours really did a number on it."

"I'll replace your fuckin' suit. Now, what do you say?"

"If my hands weren't tied behind my back, I'd say give me my damn money," he said with a grin.

Chapter 22
Larry Duncan

I used to think growing older would be a hindrance. That I wouldn't be as cunning or precise as I was when I was younger. Oh, how wrong I'd been. See, when you look like a harmless old man, people will let you fly under their radar. The unchallenged egos of young men make them think they don't have to worry. They assume they can take you out with ease. The short attention span of women barely makes them look twice at you or the people you're with. So, being myself had proven to be the perfect disguise. The night I walked into the pharmacy with my crew of nuthouse rejects by my side, nobody gave us a second look. Well, maybe they glanced twice at Holly with her all-black attire and her gothic makeup.

My crew consisted of my youngest son, Kenny, who had become one of the best marksmen I'd ever seen, thanks to the help of Sergeant Dennis Cook, my old friend and war buddy. Dennis and I had seen a lot of crazy action together in Vietnam. Probably too much action, which was why we were both diagnosed with PTSD. Dennis eventually ended up locked up at Fresh Meadows psychiatric hospital after he killed his wife and all her relatives. I'd lost track of him for almost a decade, until my family worked out a deal to have me sent to Fresh Meadows instead of jail. Locked up in that nuthouse, Dennis and I rekindled our friendship like a day — let alone a decade — had never passed. The things that made sense to us went over everyone else's heads. Dennis once again became one of my closest confidants, and he would do anything I asked of him.

Then there was Holly. She looked a little eccentric with all her piercings and tattoos, but she was still a beautiful young woman. Holly was as good with a knife as anyone I'd ever seen. She was also a serial killer who'd used her knife skills on more than twenty people, hence her stint at Fresh Meadows. She took a fatherly liking to me when I stopped a couple of sex-crazed patients from raping her. Since then, she had proven her loyalty to me time and time again.

When Dennis, Holly, and I escaped Fresh

Meadows, Kenny was there as our getaway driver. Together, the four of us were unstoppable. But before we could continue our travels, I needed to make a very important stop at a pharmacy.

Kenny stayed by the pharmacy entrance as Dennis, Holly, and I made our way toward the back. There were a handful of people in the store. As I said, nobody gave us a second look, so they didn't notice us or the pillowcases Dennis and I were carrying. As we made our way toward the pharmacy counter, we had to pass the security guard on duty. I gave Dennis a look, and my good friend nodded his understanding. The officer was in hearty conversation with a worker — until Dennis walked up on him. Sensing someone nearby, the officer turned around with a smile on his face. When he saw Dennis's big, menacing frame, his smile faded.

"Can I help you?"

"Awake? No. Unconscious? Yes," Dennis answered with an eerie smile.

Before the officer could make a move, Dennis pulled out a shiny .32 and whacked him in the temple. He hit the officer so hard the first time that one hit was all it took to knock him out. When he hit the ground, Dennis turned the gun to the ceiling and shot twice, creating a chaotic environment. Everyone in the store beelined it to the exit.

I looked toward Kenny, who had removed the sawed-off shotgun from inside his jacket. Anyone who thought they could just run out was sadly mistaken. I cleared my throat and put on a big smile for the scared eyes that were now focused on us.

"Yes, ladies and gentlemen, it's a robbery, but you are all in charge of your own fate this evening. No funny business, and you'll all make it home in time for the five o'clock news."

Kenny made sure no one could get out as the three of us continued toward the back. When we got to the pharmacy, Holly jetted from my side with lightning speed. She hopped the counter and hemmed up the gutsy female pharmacist, pinning her against the wall. I was surprised that she hadn't hit the floor after hearing the gunshots, but when I saw a phone fall from her hand, I understood why. She stared into Holly's threatening eyes and started trembling. The whimpering started when Holly pulled out a sharp knife and put it to the woman's neck.

"Please don't hurt me."

"Didn't he just say no funny shit?" Holly hissed. "I've been wanting to kill somebody all day. One more move and you'll make my wish come true."

She held her there as Dennis and I went around the counter. As fast as we could, we began dumping every pill bottle we saw into the pillowcases. We were almost done when Holly grunted, and I heard a shriek followed by a thud. I turned around and saw the pharmacist on the ground, holding her hand over a large gash in her cheek.

Holly was holding the phone she'd dropped. "We need to hurry up. She was able to get a call off to the boys before I got to her. They could be here any second."

"We're done. Let's go!" I shouted.

The three of us hightailed it back to the door, where Kenny was still manning his station. Seeing us running toward him, he opened the door, and we all ran to our car. Kenny and Holly got in the front, while Dennis and I clambered into the back. My son didn't waste any time to peel out of that parking lot.

As he drove, I started sifting through my bag of goodies. "No, no, no!" I tossed bottles of pills to the side.

Beside me, Dennis picked up the codeine and oxycodone I'd thrown. When he realized what they were, he looked at me like I was crazy. "Boss, ain't these opioids the reason we hit this pharmacy in the first place?"

"No, I'm looking for something else. That shit ain't no good to me."

"You good, Dad?" Kenny glanced in the back seat.

I ignored him as I continued searching the bag, fearing that maybe the robbery had been in vain. Finally, I found three bottles with the correct dosage of Asenapine. It was the medicine I had stopped taking at Fresh Meadows because I believed it was poisoning my mind. Now I understood it had been the only thing helping me control my urges. I needed it. There was nothing wrong with having a monster inside of you; we all do. But I needed a little extra something to keep mine from running wild.

Feeling a sense of relief wash over me, I looked up and smiled at my son. "I'm fine now, son. Just fine. I found my medicine." I held up one of the bottles.

"Is that what we broke in there for? I thought we were gonna get some shit that we could sell," Dennis said.

"No, we broke in there so I could find my medicine. I want to be with my family again, and in order for that to happen, I need to be in my right mind."

Kenny was usually one who didn't show

his emotions. He was tough. But I saw all kinds of relief wash over his face, and I reached out to pat his shoulder lovingly. I knew all my kids loved me and I them, but Kenny was the only one who had chosen to be by my side no matter if I was on my medicine or off it. I knew the things I'd done to my brother LC had split my family apart, but Kenny chose to love me through it, rather than keeping me at a distance like the others. I owed it to him to make us a unit again. Not only that, but I missed being with my wife. Everything about that Nee Nee Duncan made me want to sing, and I didn't want to go another day without her. So, the next thing on my to-do list was to find her.

"Now, let's go home," I said with a smile.

I was surprised when Kenny shook his head. "You don't want to go home?"

"I do," Kenny said, "but Mom isn't at home."

"How do you know?" I asked.

He showed me the screen on his phone. "I have her location on my phone. She shared it with me a long time ago. I guess it's her way of letting me know she's here for me wherever she's at."

I took the phone from him and looked at the dot that read Mom. I wondered if my eyes were playing tricks on me. If her location was correct, she was in New Orleans.

The only family we had in New Orleans was Big Shirley. She was married to my brother Levi, and one thing about her was that she rarely reached out for visitors. I couldn't imagine why my wife would be there with her, but the way Big Shirley was with us Duncans, I knew it wasn't for no family reunion. I got a nasty inkling that something was up, and it was something I wouldn't know unless I went there and found out.

"I guess we better strap in for a long drive," I said, getting comfortable in my seat. "Looks like we're going to New Orleans."

Chapter 23
Floyd

The sun shining on my face reminded me that it was time to get up and head to the Blues. That morning, it proved to be a hard feat, and the reason why was lying next to me. Once again, Ernestine had shown me why there was no need for any other woman in my life. She did freaky shit to me that I didn't even know I enjoyed. But with her, there was no door I wouldn't open and nothing I wouldn't try. As scary as that sounds, it was the God's honest truth.

I sat up and removed the leather belt that was still loosely wrapped around my neck from our lovemaking less than an hour ago. Ernestine looked up at me with lustful eyes, and I grinned down at her. I'd given just as good as I got, which was evident from my handprint left on her neck after she begged me to choke her as she climaxed. I was starting to love the benefits of wearing a chicken's foot. She could recharge it whenever she wanted to.

"Are you about to leave, mon cher?"

"Yeah. I gotta get to work. Shit gets crazy this time of year around the masquerade ball, and my sister wants all hands on deck. She can be a real pain in the ass with this shit."

"Leave her be. As a woman, I admire your sister. She's a boss, and that's what happens when you work on something you love and want it to be perfect."

"Yeah, yeah. See how you like it if she calls you a bunch of worthless motherfuckas," I teased. I leaned down and gave her a wet kiss before getting out of bed to get dressed.

Ernestine and I weren't an official couple because we'd never spoken it out loud, but as long as I kept extra clothes and a toothbrush at her spot, I'd shoot any man dead for being up in there. Before leaving, I tucked the chicken foot in my shirt. Just because I was getting used to wearing it didn't mean I would ever get used to being ridiculed for it. I waved a quick goodbye to Ernestine, and she blew me a seductive kiss. It almost made me dive back under the covers, but I was already running late.

A week had passed since Pierre's funeral, and the streets had been quiet. I was taking that as good news. With Eric, Fred, and

Todd out of the picture, nothing else could bite us in the ass. I didn't even bat an eye when Todd's wife, Jenna, called me and said she found him shot dead when she came home. She said the neighbors saw a black Toyota outside of the home and had given the plate information to the police. They'd be lucky if they found even a piece of it, the way I'd burnt it to a crisp. There was nothing left but scrap metal.

Jenna also asked me to be a pall bearer at her husband's funeral, and I, of course, accepted. To some, it might have been a foul move, knowing I was responsible for sending him to the other side. But to me, it gave me a last chance to pay my respects to an old friend. I truly did hate that it had to be the way that it was, but family always came first.

I drove to the Blues in my blue '67 Impala with my windows down, letting the wind hit my face and wake me up. It was my favorite car, and Big Shirley would blow a gasket if she knew where I'd gotten it. Two years ago, she thought I'd taken a trip to Miami for my birthday. The truth was, I'd taken my own little trip to New York, and LC hooked me up the right way. It was a secret I'd never divulge, especially after how my sister had lashed out at Marquis. I found myself laughing as I drove, thinking about how he'd run to tell me, in hopes I'd be on his side.

I'd told him, "The cost of making big-boy decisions is sometimes taking the punches — or in your case, slaps."

I pulled into the Midnight Blues and saw that we already had a packed house. I parked and got out, walking to the entrance with a little umph in my steps. Before heading up to my office, I made a stop at the restaurant. It was still early enough for me to get breakfast, and some hotcakes and bacon sounded mighty good right then. My sister was already in there, placing flyers about the masquerade ball on the tables. I was about to go up to her when I heard the most annoying, high-pitched voice. It could only belong to one person.

"Aye, Shirleyyy!" Skunk yelled.

I cut my eyes at him as he beat me to the punch and approached Big Shirley. He had a cunning grin on his face, the kind a person wore when they wanted something. Although my sister seemed to be in a hurry, she paused for a moment.

"Hey, Skunk. What can I do for you?" she asked, then put her hands up. "And before you ask, I don't have any free vouchers for the buffet."

"Hmm, that would have been nice, but I have some important business I need to run by you. Some life-or-death shit. You got a minute?"

If it were anyone else, the use of "life-or-death" might have gotten her attention, but Skunk was so insignificant that I'm sure she assumed it was bullshit that would just waste her time. "Sorry, I don't. I was headed up to my office to take care of payroll."

She tried to move around him, but he sidestepped to remain in front of her. "It'll really only take a minute," he pressed urgently.

I shook my head and walked up to them, standing next to my sister.

Shirley looked at me as if I were there to rescue her. "Whatever you need to say, tell Floyd. Like I said, I'm busy."

Skunk turned toward me. He sized me up and had the audacity to look unimpressed. Him. Mr. Two-dollar-Goodwill-suit himself.

"Nah. I need to talk to you about this. This is some serious business."

"And that's why Floyd is your guy. Right, Floyd? He's our manager, and he handles all our business affairs. He'll take care of you."

Big Shirley walked away before Skunk

could protest again. When it was just the two of us, I saw his eyes go from my face to my chest. I almost had forgotten what was hanging around it until he pointed at it.

"Aw, man. You been talking to one of them voodoo witches, huh? Man, one of those crazy-ass broads gave my brother one of them things, and he ain't have as much as a mosquito bite the whole time he wore it."

"Really?"

"Yeah. Only problem is his dick won't get hard unless she say so. But that's the price you pay when you mess with voodoo."

I hadn't thought about those ramifications, but then again, I didn't have to. I planned to keep Ernestine in my life for as long as she would have me. I checked my watch and saw that I didn't have much longer if I wanted to get my breakfast.

"What was it that you wanted Skunk?"

"You heard Shirley. She said I should talk to you about some business I have."

"Well, I'm askin', ain't I?"

"Fifty thousand," he said with a straight face.

I didn't understand the statement. "Look, I don't have time to be sitting around here listening to your bullshit get-rich-quick schemes, Skunk."

"Bullshit? This is life or death," he said

seriously.

"You're right. You're lucky I don't kill you right here on the spot. Look, I don't know what Big Shirley sees in you, but you're nothing but a two-bit con man as far as I'm concerned. Now, get the fuck out my club."

I could see that my words had hit a nerve with him. I saw his mouth open and close a few times as he tried to find his words. Finally, he shoved a finger toward me.

"You know what, Floyd? Fuck you. It might be a good thing you got that around your neck for protection, 'cause I'm about to bring shit crashing down around your head."

"That a threat?" I asked, getting in his face.

"Nah," Skunk answered boldly, not backing down. "It's a fuckin' promise!"

I grabbed him by his collar and hoisted him up on his tiptoes. Although there was still defiance in his eyes, I saw him take a huge gulp. He knew, like most people around did, that I was not one to be trifled with. It would be nothing to get rid of Skunk and hide his body. He wasn't like Pierre. He didn't have a rich family that would come sniffing around for answers.

"Get the fuck out of here before I throw you out." I shoved him back.

When I let go, he stumbled back, glaring at me. He didn't try any funny business, though. Instead, he heeded my warning and took his leave, muttering curses under his breath.

Chapter 24
Jean

The ghastly screams that filled the air in the warehouse were like music to my ears. I was enjoying them much more than I was the smell of seafood invading my nose. As a businessman, oftentimes you were in business with certain people for a long time. Decades, even. And sometimes, in those instances, you'd get a cat who got too comfortable and didn't do the things expected of him. Take the Shark family, for example. My father had given them the startup money for their seafood business and had continued doing business with them for years after. By business, I mean we continued taking our cut of their monthly revenue.

"Agh! No . . . no more. Please, no more."

The screams and begging came from Martin Shark, son of the original business owner, Michael Shark. Martin had taken over as the head of his family, and for a while, he had been doing a good job. Recently, though, his actions, or lack of them, had led him to be bound to a chair in his own warehouse in front of me. Bloodied and beaten, he wasn't looking at all like the confident man he liked to portray himself to be.

I watched Saint and Kendall pummel him some more before I motioned for them to stop. Then I went to stand in front of Martin with a lit cigar, which I put out on the bloody gash on his forehead. He screeched loudly in pain, bringing a satisfied smile to my face.

I tucked the cigar in my suit jacket pocket. "After all my family has done for you, Martin, this is how you show your gratitude?"

"Jean . . ." Martin panted. "I'll pay you your money. I'm the only one here right now, but my crew will be in soon. I'll —"

"Unfortunately, this has gone way past money. This is about more than that now. It's about loyalty, honor, and most of all, respect. When your family first started out, you had nothing. How many warehouses did you have, Martin?"

"N–none."

"And now how many do you have?"

"Eight."

"And how many restaurants and grocery

stores do you provide your fresh seafood to?"

"Hundreds."

"Hundreds!" My voice boomed in the warehouse. "All because my daddy gave you an opportunity that has shaped your current reality in the best way possible. Julien LeBlanc not only put up the money, but he also insured that local restaurants and stores would only buy from you. The Sharks are forever indebted to us. Your grandbabies' grandbabies owe us."

"My father was a coward! He was your daddy's bitch. And you know what? I won't be yours." Martin glared at me from where he sat. "We've paid our debt to you tenfold."

I paused for a moment at his outburst, then clapped slowly, applauding his last burst of courage. The fear had left his face, replaced with hatred. The nerve of that ungrateful little shit. Teach a man to fish so he can feed his family, and he eventually acts as if he taught himself.

"Then I guess it's lucky for me that you have cousins who have no problem falling in line," I said.

I motioned to my man Saint, who was standing next to me. He pulled out his pistol.

"Kill him, Saint," I ordered.

Fear overtook Martin's features. "Okay, okay! I'll get you the fucking money!" he yelled. "Just don't kill me. I got a family."

"Oh, now you wanna pay?" I laughed as I took out a handkerchief to wipe a spot of blood from my hand.

"Yes, please. The money's in the safe. Just tell him not to shoot."

"What's the combination?" Saint asked.

Martin blurted it out.

"Cool. But I do have one more question," I said.

Martin gave me a pleading, anything-you-want look.

"Whose bitch are you now?"

Martin exhaled and looked across at me, and with tears in his eyes, he muttered, "Yours."

I smiled, nodding my head at Saint. He put a bullet in Martin's right temple. The closeness of the shot snapped Martin's neck to the side, and I could tell by the way his bone was protruding that his neck was broken. What a terrible way to die when all he had to do was pay me.

"Clean this up and open up that safe," I instructed Kendall. "Saint, walk with me."

He followed me out of the warehouse to our vehicles. I got in mine and rolled down my window to talk to him. "Make sure any security footage and evidence of what just happened is destroyed. And let Martin's cousin Dino know he's in charge now."

"Already done," Saint said. "Where you going?"

"Home to shower. I smell like fucking fish. You know the ball is tonight."

"I'll meet you there. I gotta go to La Nue. Prince got some motherfucka he wants us to meet."

"Oh, yeah. I forgot about Chino."

"You wanna come?" he asked.

I tried to decide if I would have enough time. Prince was in charge of all the new recruits for the Crescent Boys, and he'd brought forth some promising prospects. I trusted him.

Finally, I shook my head. "I'm gonna pass. You handle that. I promised Marie I'd pick up her dress for the ball and wouldn't be late. But call me if you run into any problems."

"Bet." Saint stepped away from the car. "I'll get up with you later."

I gave him a nod and drove away from the murder scene, like I'd done probably a hundred times before.

Chapter 25
Curtis

One thing about me was that I loved seeing my Momma smile. But that night, her smile came with a cost, and that made me uncomfortable as hell. She, Lauryn, and I were occupying one of the parlor rooms as we put the finishing touches on our costumes and had a few private drinks. Marquis would have joined us, but duty called, and Aunt Shirley had him manning the entrance of the Blues.

While Momma was dancing happily near me in her masquerade gown, I was standing in front of the mirror, tugging at the tie to my tuxedo. Now, I'd worn a tux, and I looked damn good in one, I might add. But this wasn't just a regular tuxedo. I never in a million years thought I'd wear one that was black with shimmery sparkles all over it. Apparently, it was festive, but it made me look like a whole —

"Curtis! Stop standing over there looking

all sad. It's a happy night," Momma said as she stepped over to me.

My facial expression didn't change as she fixed the tie I was fidgeting with. I just shook my head at my reflection. When she was done, she handed me my masquerade mask and turned around to look at me in the mirror.

"I look like a fool," I said.

"No, you look like a fine gentleman. Now, put a smile on your face. We're gonna enjoy our night. Lauryn, you come over here next."

Momma gently pushed me out of the way. Lauryn gave me a smug look as she took my place in the mirror. She'd just touched up her makeup and fixed her hair. She'd opted for a more flowy pink gown than a form-fitting one, and as a big brother, I approved. I much preferred when my sister was going through her nerdy stage and had acne all over her face. It had been hard to let her bloom and go off on her own, but there she was, looking like something right out of a fairytale.

Momma admired her in the mirror. "Perfect. Just . . . perfect." She placed Lauryn's mask over her face and kissed her on the cheek.

"Thanks, Momma," she said.

I took one more look at my reflection and let out a breath. Might as well make the best of it. Usually, I wore my clothes; they didn't wear me. And I did have to admit, I looked kind of sharp. I just wasn't happy about being in costume.

"I never thought I'd say it, but I wish I was back in New York with Uncle LC," I said.

"Why? We're the ones who get to have all the fun," Momma said as she ran her hands down the sides of her red dress. Instead of a mask, she wore an elaborate headpiece that hung over her eyes. I loved when she got dressed, because she was the most beautiful woman in the world to me.

She went back to dancing, and I went to the window of the parlor room. We were on the second floor of the Blues, and we had the perfect view of all the excitement outside. I didn't believe Marquis when he'd told us how big the event would be, but the cars lined up farther than my eyes could see told me that he didn't hype it up enough. There were elegant costumes everywhere I looked.

"Look at them. They really love this shit."

"Oh, boy, hush and meet me downstairs when you're done up here. I'm about to go find that sister of mine."

When Momma left the room, Lauryn stood next to me by the window and looked down. A look of utter excitement came over her face, and she did a little twirl in her pink gown. "I've always wanted to come to something like this. It's gonna be fun. Lighten up, Curtis. Aunt Shirley put this whole thing together. And I made a special request for them to serve gumbo tonight." She winked at me, knowing the way to my heart.

I reached out and tucked a piece of hair behind her ear. "Thanks, sis. You look beautiful, by the way. I wish Pop was here to see you."

"Yeah, well, you know him. Gone in the wind." There was a hint of salt in her tone, and she looked away.

Lauryn and I were close, and I could tell that our dad's absence was affecting her differently this time. Before, when he was in Fresh Meadows, we knew where he was, and we thought he was getting the help he needed. We eventually found out he'd been up to other things, like completely taking over the facility and holding Uncle LC hostage, not to mention almost murdering him. Thank God he didn't, but because of the attempt, my dad escaping the mental facility still had everyone's antennas up.

When he was in the facility, it gave us an excuse for why he wasn't with us. But now, it was like he was choosing everything else over being with his family. Just lost in the wind. Even though she didn't show it, I knew that seeing Uncle LC be a father to all of his children, even while recovering from the torment our dad had caused him, affected Lauryn. Whenever she was ready to talk about it, I would be there. And hopefully one day, so would our dad.

Chapter 26
Saint

When I pulled into the parking lot at La Nue, I was pleasantly surprised by the crowd we'd brought in that night. It was a strip club, but there were just as many women standing in line as men. All of them were dressed in their weekend's best and sexiest, ready to see something and be seen. Our hostile takeover had proven quite lucrative for Jean, and what was lucrative for him was lucrative for all of us Crescent Boys.

I pulled my phone out and called him.

"Hello?"

"Yo, I just got here. Finna go see what they're talking about," I told him.

"Cool. You know I trust your brother's judgment, but if a motherfucka is gonna be down with my shit, I gotta know that he's thorough. And fa sho that he ain't no cop."

"I hear you." I laughed. "Also, I gotta give you credit, my brother. I knew muscling in on Red's business would be good, but I never in a million years thought it would be this damn good. You should see the crowd tonight."

"Yeah, it's good, but it's chump change compared to what they gonna rake in over at Midnight Blues. The real money is gonna be over there with the ball tonight."

"Tell me about it," I agreed. "My lady says that they gonna rake in half a million on that ball alone. That place is like a fucking goldmine."

He grew quiet for a few moments. "Yeah, but more importantly, think about all the money that could be washed through that motherfucker," he said finally.

It was a thought that I knew he'd had often. So did I. The Blues was the perfect front for a much larger-scale operation. It was a wonder Big Shirley didn't dabble in the drug trade. Her profits would triple, if not more. But then again, some people didn't think as big as we did.

"Why don't we do it, then? We could take Big Shirley out like that." I snapped my fingers. "She ain't never had no real muscle. The only one who's a real threat is Floyd. And Kendall, Prince, and I could take care of him. Shit, I probably wouldn't even need them for his ass."

Jean chuckled. "Floyd ain't no joke. You

forgetting what he did to those Texas boys who came through a couple years ago?"

"Oh, shit. I forgot about that."

"Uh-huh. And don't sleep on Marquis. He ain't no punk. I know that because his mother is a huge threat. I'm sure she raised her son to be just like her."

"Big Shirley, a threat?" I was glad he wasn't there to see me roll my eyes.

"Hell, yeah. Big Shirley has the new mayor, the sheriff, and half a dozen aldermen of Gator Lake in her back pocket. Right now, the politicians and the law are leaving us alone, but if we pluck their golden goose, things would be different: We'd become public enemy number one."

"I never thought about it like that."

"That's why I do the thinking," he said. "The only way we're gunning for Big Shirley and the Blues is if they make things personal. Understand?"

"I hear ya, boss. Anyway, I'm finna head in here."

"A'ight, I'll see y'all in a couple of hours at the ball."

"For sure." I hung up as I got out of the car and went to the entrance of the club.

I skipped the line, and when I got inside, the smell of smoke and perfume hit me. I saw many eyes following me like I was some sort of celebrity. In a way, I was in New Orleans. Most knew I ran with Jean, and others knew the weight my reputation carried.

It was a packed house, and if they weren't in a VIP section, people were shoulder to shoulder. However, they parted like the Red Sea as I came through and headed for the stairs to the VIP.

Prince was up there popping bottles with a few other Crescent Boys and some dancers. I was starting to make my way to them when I felt a hand grab my arm. Turning my head, I saw Cheyenne, a chick I used to get down with back in the day. She didn't look like she'd aged a day — still beautiful, thick, and kept herself together. I couldn't help admiring the one-piece red outfit she was wearing.

"Long time no see, stranger." She seductively flicked her tongue across her front teeth.

"I be around. But something tells me you know that."

"I do, but whenever I try to get up with you, I see you're dealing with business."

"That's 'cause I'm a businessman," I replied.

She moved closer to me with a pout on her lips. Her hands explored the muscles on my arms as she looked up into my face, trying to break my resolve. Back in the day, I had a thing for a pretty and slim thing with a big behind. Cheyenne hit all the markers, and although I remembered just how much I liked how she would roll her tongue around the tip of my dick, I had to push her up off me, mainly because I loved my wife.

"I'm also a married man, but then again, you know that. Have a good night." I stepped past her, not caring about the dejected look on her face.

In the VIP section, about a dozen of the Crescent Boys cheered my arrival. I grinned at Prince and embraced him after we slapped hands. I gave everyone else a head nod, then focused on the face I didn't recognize mixed in with them. He was a Latino man who looked to be a little older than my brother, with a muscular build and a mouth full of gold teeth.

"It's lit tonight! Bruh, this spot is everything," Prince said, taking a swig out of the bottle in his hands. He put it down when he saw me eyeing the new guy. "Shit, my bad. Yo, Saint, this is my man Chino. The one I wanted you to meet. He really looked out for me when I was upstate. Chino, this my older brother Saint I was telling you about."

"Prince, man, you ain't gotta introduce

me to Saint. He was just getting outta Angola when I went up. Your brother's a living fucking legend. He used to run the place."

Chino stood up and offered me his hand. I still didn't recognize him, but off the strength of my brother, I grasped his hand. Like me, Prince had a mean streak, but he was really a good kid at heart. He wanted to see everybody come up, and to be honest, I needed that kind of attitude around me and the boys. Otherwise, I'd leave a trail of blood wherever I went.

"Everything's good, Chino. Glad to see you back home in one piece. Angola ain't no joke."

"You ain't never lied. You looking good. I heard y'all run with Jean LeBlanc, and I can see that he's taking care of you." His eyes went to the diamonds around my neck and the encrusted watch on my wrist.

I laughed. The young ones were all the same. It was always about the bling. "Yeah, man. You know. Family ties. So, what's up? You tryna be down or something?" I asked just as a very sexy dancer passed us.

"Your brother promised me a whole bunch of bread and all the fine women I can fuck, so hell yeah, I'm in." Chino's eyes left my diamonds and went straight for her ass. It was like he'd just jumped off the porch.

He turned back to me with a grin on his face. "I remember they used to say you fucked with a real bad stripper from the Fifth Ward. They said she was a cold piece, and I heard a lot of freak stories 'bout that bitch. Said she had a mean mouthpiece and some good-ass pussy. What happened to her? She round here?"

"I married her." My cold stare wiped the smile right off Chino's face.

He looked at Prince for confirmation, and my brother gave him a warning look because he knew how I was about my lady. I didn't care what her past was. There would never be a man who could disrespect her in front of me.

Chino must have missed the signal, because he turned back to me with wide eyes and dug his grave a little deeper. "You married that girl?" he asked in disbelief. "Bro, that bitch is a —"

Before the word was out of his mouth, my fist slammed into his face. His top grill flew out of his mouth, and blood spilled down his chin. The monster inside of me was wide awake, and he wanted to be heard. I could see that Chino realized he'd made a huge mistake, but he was bold enough to step into the beast's den, so he had to see it through.

Before Chino could regain his bearings, my hands were wrapped around his throat. "A ho?" I asked. The entire club faded to black around me as I focused my rage on Chino. "Was that what your stupid ass was about to call my wife?"

Chino was struggling for air.

"Oh, shit! Saint! Saint! Chill, man!" Prince pleaded. "He ain't know y'all was married. Did you, Chino?"

Chino shook his head in a desperate attempt to keep me from putting his lights out permanently. I let him go, and he fell to the ground, gasping for air.

"Disrespecting my wife was the worst thing you could ever do."

"My bad. It won't happen again," Chino said in a raspy voice.

I locked my eyes on his. "So, we good?" I asked.

"Yeah, we good."

He was down but not out, and a man like him would never truly be able to let go of something like this. It just wasn't in his DNA. "You sure?"

"You good, Saint." My brother answered for Chino.

"Nah, we ain't." I shook my head. The monster inside of me was refusing to let him go. I already wasn't a very forgiving man, and he'd trotted into the land of no return. In a quick motion, I pulled my pistol from my hip and aimed it at his head. I doubted that he had even formed a final thought before I pulled the trigger and snapped his head back, killing him in front of everybody in the VIP section. I knew that even with the loud music blaring from the speakers, the gunshot was audible, but I didn't care.

I saw some people who were near the section scrambling to get away, but others continued to party like nothing had happened. Calmly, I turned to my brother, whose jaw dropped open.

"You — you killed him," Prince mumbled. "What'd you kill him for?"

"If I left him alive, I'd have to look over my shoulder the rest of my life," I explained to my shocked brother. "Come on. Let's head out. Time to get ready for the ball."

Chapter 27
Marquis

The Midnight Blues masquerade ball was an event that all of New Orleans looked forward to every year. Everyone loved being able to dress up in their costumes and wear their masks. It was almost like becoming another person for a night, and it made people feel like they could act out on all the things they'd thought about but wouldn't dare to do when they were their everyday selves. There were so many colors and so many different masks in the crowd. The ladies all looked edible in their ballroom gowns, and the men were dressed to impress. They were ready to party the night away.

Usually I enjoyed myself too, but tensions were still high. I told myself I was going to try to have a good time, or at least look like I was. On my face I wore a golden half-cracked mask that matched my fitted black-and-gold print blazer. Looking good and smelling good was my specialty, even on a bad day.

Cars lined the entire road trying to get to the Blues. The excited sound of laughter and knee-slapping music filled my ears as I watched people valet park their cars and others posing on the red carpet. It was looking like one of the best turnouts so far.

I stood at the entrance, looking out at what seemed like a star-studded event. Anyone who was anyone in New Orleans would be there that night. From where I stood, I could see Mayor Simms doing an interview on the side and Sheriff Clay standing not too far away from him. I knew that it would only be a matter of time before Jean showed up, but the truth was that I wanted to avoid him at all costs.

I continued assisting with security at the entrance doors, ensuring that everybody who came in had a legitimate ticket. Every pocket was being checked and every purse was being rummaged through, and that meant there was a nice crowd in line, waiting to get through to the grand hall. Security was only getting a few more moments of my time, because the party was in the grand hall, and so was the food. I wanted to go mingle, and more so, spend time with my family.

A smirk found its way to my face, knowing that Curtis was probably throwing a fit about having to dress up. When we'd gone for our fitting, he complained loudly, "It ain't Halloween. Why the hell I gotta wear this shit?" Aunt Nee Nee had talked him into purchasing his getup, and at that moment, I was sure she was talking him into actually wearing it. I'd see him soon, with or without it on. Momma was somewhere crossing T's and dotting I's, and I could only guess that Mo was with her, a goblet of tequila in her hand.

I felt myself growing more relaxed, but that feeling went away when I saw Jean and his wife enter through the far doors. My jaw clenched as I watched him guide his wife through the crowd. When our eyes connected, it was like time around us stopped. Two alpha males trying to assert their dominance. We held each other's stare for a moment before he finally nodded his head. I returned the gesture.

I didn't know why I was holding my breath. As far as he knew, Pierre had died at the swamp. However, I knew differently, and life as I knew it had shifted forever. I wasn't especially comfortable with him moving so freely around the Blues, but appearances had to be carried on.

A sudden commotion caught my attention. Looking around, I groaned when I saw Skunk standing in front of DJ and Tea Tree, a Blues security guard. *His ass is always in some shit,* I thought, heading over to see what the problem was.

Skunk seemed to be having an issue with security checking him, and I could only imagine why. Skunk was what some would call a wild card. He played all sides, and with him, you never knew what you were going to get.

Dice had him by the hem of his suit, and he was trying to snatch away, with no luck. "We caught him trying to sneak in one of the side doors."

"Marquis, tell this big dinosaur-lookin' motherfucka to unhand me!" Skunk said loudly.

"Let him go," I said.

Dice begrudgingly let go. When he was free, Skunk flinched at the guard like someone was supposed to be scared of him. Sometimes I think he forgot that he was only five foot eight.

He angrily fixed his collar. "This suit is rented! If somethin' is wrong with it, one of y'all owes me three hundred dollars."

"Oh, really? Because that Goodwill sticker says it was five dollars." I was pointing at

Skunk's jacket sleeve.

I couldn't help but laugh at Skunk's "caught" face. But even without the sticker as proof, we all knew Skunk wasn't buying anything expensive. He barely had money for a shot of our cheapest liquor, let alone a three-hundred-dollar suit.

"Skunk, what the fuck are you doing, trying to sneak in? I thought you had a ticket."

"Well, Marquis, it was too many people coming through the front, and I don't like waiting. And what's up with all these metal detectors?"

"A precaution."

"A precaution? For what?"

"A precaution for that," I said and calmly moved his suit jacket to the side. Poking out, clear as day on his hip, was the handle of a revolver. "I'm thinking that's the real reason you were trying to sneak in. Either that or you don't have your ticket."

There was a sheepish look that came across his face that told it all. "Man, go ask your momma. Ask Big Shirley. I bought my ticket directly from her," Skunk said, speaking quickly. "And I had it on my way in here, but some Cyrano de Bergerac–looking dude bumped into me and took it. He had to have!"

I shook my head at how crazy he sounded.

And I couldn't stand a liar. I looked at DJ and Dice before making a shooing motion with my hand. They grabbed Skunk by his arms and hoisted him into the air. It was like something out of a movie, the way he began shouting his protests and kicking his swinging feet. I was still chuckling when I walked away.

I left the security checkpoint and made my way into the grand hall. The good vibes were the first thing that hit me. The bars were packed with people, and I knew the casino was making a killing. We had both a deejay and a live band, and there were people already on the dance floor, having a great time. I was rubbing my hands together, thinking about the new suits I was going to buy, when I felt someone brush against me. From the sensual feel of the touch, it could only be one person.

I turned around to see her by my side. Now, she was already sexy, but the very short, feather-sequined romper she was wearing with the very low V-cut had her looking delectable. Instead of a mask, she wore glitter face paint the color of the bar she was working that night.

"Mr. Duncan, why, you look mighty fine in that getup if I do say so myself."

"Me?" I leaned back to get a better view

of her ass. "Mm, mm, mm!"

"You better stop!" She looked around nervously. "There's too many people here."

"They're too busy filling up on seafood and free liquor. They aren't concerned with us."

"Then you won't mind meeting me upstairs in your office in say, ten minutes?"

"Ten minutes feels like forever. Why don't we head up now?"

I tried to tempt her, but she wagged her finger. "I can't. I have to help Dice. A table just placed a huge order, and he'll kill me if he knows I ran off with you again."

"Again? He knows?" I asked, suddenly alert.

"Don't worry. He won't tell a soul. I know his secrets too." She winked at me as she walked away. "Ten minutes, Mr. Duncan."

She made sure to switch hard as hell. The way that booty shook, that ten-minute wait would feel like an eternity to me. I looked at my watch, knowing Momma would be making her speech soon. My meeting with Antoinette would have to be a quickie, but even just a little taste was the right way to get my night started.

I didn't notice Lauryn had come up to me until I looked up from my watch.

"Wow, you clean up nice. What should I

call you? Princess?" I teased her about her slightly over-the-top gown.

"As fabulous as I look, you can," she shot back, and we laughed. "Anyways, you don't look too bad yourself. In fact, you could pull any woman in here. Why focus your sights on one who's married?"

"Married?"

"Cut the shit, Quis. The diamond on her finger is big enough for me to see across the room." She gave me a knowing look then glanced over to the bar where Antoinette was busy making drinks.

I looked around to see if anybody else might have been paying attention to the exchange between Antoinette and me. Sometimes, I was so captivated by that woman that I could forget where we were.

Lauryn laughed at me. "Relax. Nobody was paying attention. The only reason I saw was because my momma told me to come fetch you for Curtis."

"He good?"

"He refuses to get up from his seat because of the tux you talked him into getting. Maybe if he sees you in your costume, he'll feel more comfortable."

"A'ight, I'll go find him in a second. I have something to take care of first."

"You mean fall into?" She didn't even try

to hide the smirk on her face.

"You know what? Forget you. I'm a grown man."

"I know you are. Just be careful playing with that kind of fire, okay?" There was sincerity in her voice.

"I know." I sighed. "But it's gonna take a *whole lotta* whole lotta to get me to leave that alone. She does this thing where she —"

"Too much information!" She interrupted me with a disgusted look. "I'm gonna go somewhere that I don't have to hear about your nasty-ass sexual exploits."

She walked away, still wearing a look of distaste.

Chapter 28
Jean

Marie was in a trance as she looked around the Midnight Blues. "Oh my God! It looks fantastic in here," she marveled as we made it through the security check.

I wasn't viewing the place through the same lens, though. Sure, it had been dressed up for the ball, but it still had that old school feel to it — old fixtures, the walls needed a more welcoming color, and even the floors could do with a facelift. It all would be changed if I were in charge. Out with the old and in with the new.

Most of the folks that hung around the Blues were middle aged or elders. Once in a while, I'd see some younger people when I stopped in, but not a lot. That was a shame, given today's climate and how rich some of these youngsters were getting. If this place were mine, I would capitalize off their need to stunt and spend everything in their pockets. I'd have it looking and feeling so popping in the Blues that the young cats would be in there every day, and not just for their Instagram shots.

I stopped paying attention to the building and focused on my wife's sexy frame through my *Phantom of the Opera* mask. She had opted to wear a rhinestone-encrusted gown that clung to her shape and made her look ten times curvier. She'd wanted real diamonds, but knowing she would only wear the dress once, I told her no. If I had known she would look so ravishing in the gown, I might have changed my answer.

We walked hand in hand to the grand hall, where the main events would be taking place. She glanced up at me, and even though her white tasseled mask covered most of her face, I saw the dreamy look in her eyes.

"You are really wearing that suit, Mr. LeBlanc," she told me.

"Not nearly as well as you're wearing that dress, Mrs. LeBlanc."

Saint and Prince had met us in the parking lot and were walking a few steps behind us. Both had been unusually quiet, and I wondered how everything had gone with the new recruit at La Nue. I'd ask later. Right now, I didn't even want to say the word "work" in front of my wife when she was in such a good mood.

We found an empty table for the four of us. It was the perfect distance from both the dance floor and the refreshment table. I pulled my wife's chair out, then sat beside her. A waiter in costume approached us with a tray filled with champagne glasses.

"For you and the lady," he said.

He placed the glasses in front of us. As he was walking away, the music stopped, and a center light focused on the top of the grand staircase in the hall. Big Shirley's cousin Monique was bathed in the spotlight, wearing a feathered mask. The red sequins on her dress sparkled in the light.

She spoke into a microphone in her hand. "Ladies and gentlemen, if you don't know, now you know. The Midnight Blues is the place to be!"

The crowd cheered, and even I had to join in. The energy was contagious.

"Now, for the lady of the hour. I'm sure she needs no introduction."

In a wide motion, she waved her arms, and Big Shirley materialized beside her from the shadows. She was looking good in an asymmetrical black gown with a thigh-high slit up one side. There were sparkly crystals along the opening that matched a crystal tassel hanging from her facemask. Her hair was pinned up, and when she turned her head, the diamonds in her hair clip sparkled. That night, she wasn't just the boss. The way the crowd was whooping and hollering for her, she was queen of the night, and I couldn't be mad at it.

"Good evening, everyone, and welcome to our yearly Midnight Masquerade event. We wouldn't be the Blues without you, so I want you all to have a great time. And tonight? The drinks are on us." She waited for the cheering to die down before she added, "Notice I said the drinks, 'cause that gambling is on you! Enjoy now!"

The music cut back on, and the crowd went back to partying. Saint and Prince were across the table, talking among themselves. Whatever it was, it seemed serious. Marie grabbed my attention again before I could focus my ears on their conversation.

"Big Shirley sure knows how to throw a party," she said.

"She does. And you know what I'm thinking about?"

"What?"

"Hitting the dance floor with my wife. So, may I have this dance, Mrs. LeBlanc? And then after, we can get you something to eat. I know you starved yourself all day to wear that dress, and you didn't need to."

"Jean!" She hit me playfully before taking my hand.

"I'm 'bout to work my magic on the floor," Prince said, getting up and walking away.

I watched him curiously for a moment then looked at Saint. "What's his problem?" I asked.

"I'll tell you later. For now, enjoy your evening with your wife. I'm sure mine is around here somewhere." He too got up from the table and went his own way, while Marie tugged me toward the dance floor.

As I followed behind her, I had the hint of a smile on my face. It felt pretty good to be just a face in the crowd for a night. Nobody coming up to me asking me about work or wanting to talk about —

"Mr. LeBlanc?"

We were just about to get our groove on when I heard my name. I almost kept going as if I hadn't heard it, but because I was a gentleman, I stopped and turned around. Mayor Simms and Sheriff Clay were standing behind me. Neither was in costume. The mayor had on a plain old suit, and the sheriff wore her uniform.

"Evening, Mayor. Sheriff," I said, nodding at the two of them.

"I want to offer my sincerest condolences

about the unfortunate events involving your brother," Mayor Simms said earnestly. "As a man in your line of work knows, those gators can be ravenous."

His word choice threw me for a loop because on paper, I was a construction magnate and business owner. Nothing more, nothing less. Sure, I had a reputation that would follow me, but no matter how true most of the rumors rang, none of them were on paper. Especially for Mayor Simms to speak of so casually.

It was good to have the law in one's back pocket, especially living the life I lived, but it was also important to be choosy about it. Mayor Simms had too much power, which could have been a good thing; however, blackmailing a man like that would be close to impossible. I would never trust someone like him with too much of my business. One wrong move and he could have me put away at the snap of a finger. I didn't like those odds. The lowly deputies working closely to Sheriff Clay, on the other hand, weren't hard to put on payroll.

"And what kind of work would that be, Mayor?" I asked, smirking at his attempted jab.

"Ahh . . ." The mayor suddenly seemed so tongue tied that Sheriff Clay cleared her throat to step in.

"What the mayor means is with your construction businesses being so close to the swamps, your men are bound to run into gators."

I held my smirk and purposely didn't speak right away. I knew my momentary silence would make the air around us awkward. Good. They were fools to think they could play around with me.

After I felt like I'd enjoyed their uncomfortable expressions long enough, I said, "Thank you for your condolences. Of course, I'm not so convinced that my brother died in a swamp. And I for sure don't think gators killed him."

"I didn't peg you for a conspiracy theorist, Mr. LeBlanc," Sheriff Clay said.

"No conspiracy. I just knew my brother."

The sheriff and I held each other's gazes for some seconds.

"Well, unless you have other evidence, that's where the investigation led. I hope you're not planning on taking the law into your own hands, Mr. LeBlanc," she finally said.

"Now, Sheriff, do I look like the type?" I motioned toward the food table. "Now, if you'll excuse me, my wife and I were in the middle of something."

I turned back to Marie and pulled her into my arms as Usher's voice blasted through the speakers. Being the boss meant sometimes playing nice with the local powers. One of the ugliest truths I'd learned in the game was that everything had a price tag, people included. Sheriff Clay didn't know it, but I would have my eyes on her.

I enjoyed moving and grooving with my wife for a while. It was like when we were younger all over again. In fact, I think that was the last time I saw Marie smile so hard that there were wrinkles under her eyes. I was glad when the music slowed and I was able to just hold her in my arms and slow dance.

"We haven't had fun like this since Simone was little," she told me.

"Yeah, and I bet you didn't know I still had my moves, did you?"

"I mean, you still got it. Even though for a minute there, I thought you'd stepped on a tack!" she teased.

"Oh, you got jokes. That's cold, even for you," I said with a laugh.

"You deserved that one," she said, looking deeply into my eyes. "But what I'm not joking about is spending some alone time with you tonight. I miss you."

"I miss you too," I said. "And I'd like that

very much. I know work has gotten in the way of our relationship, and I'm sorry. I'm really trying to build something here, and I believe this is my time."

"I'm all for that, Jean. Are you forgetting who hid the gun and the coke from the cops the night we met? I'm ride or die, but you have to let me in the damn car before you pull off."

"I just don't want anything to happen to you when we pull off. That's all," I said earnestly, and she chortled.

"A little late for that, now, isn't it? My name's on half the shit you own. You go down, I go down."

Maybe I really was a cocky son of a bitch, because until then, I'd never thought about it like that. Of course there were ventures Marie's name was nowhere in writing, but on the main ones like the construction company, it was. If the feds ever found out how much drug money I washed through there alone, Marie would go down right along with me. She knew it too and had chosen to stand by me. Years ago, before we got married, my father had tried to talk me out of it. He'd told me she wasn't the type to be in it for the long haul and she just saw dollar signs. He'd been wrong.

As I stood there holding her, I felt a sudden wave of affection. I opened my mouth to speak on it, but a tap on my shoulder interrupted my thoughts.

It was Saint. “Don’t mean to interrupt you and the missus, Jean, but something has come up that requires your attention.”

I looked from him to my wife. Marie was giving him the evil eye, but that look was nothing compared to the one she gave me right after. She was daring me to leave.

“Right now?” I asked Saint. “Can’t this wait until the morning?”

Saint shook his head and leaned in, whispering something in my ear that made my breath shallow.

I looked to my wife and gave her an apologetic look. “I have to go,” I told her.

“What do you mean, you have to go? You’ve known about this ball for weeks! You said tonight was all mine.”

“I know. That’s why I want you to stay and enjoy yourself. Have a good time for the both of us. I love you, and I’ll see you at home.”

I left her and Saint standing there and made a beeline for the exit.

Chapter 29
Lauryn

It didn't matter that I didn't know anybody at the Blues that night because what I did know was good music. I also knew a few of the line dances, so I fit right in with all the masked people around me on the dance floor. New York had been a time, but New Orleans was a *vibe.* The only thing that got me off the dance floor was looking across the grand hall and seeing my brother, looking upset. He was staring at something on the dance floor, and when I followed his gaze, I saw my mom getting her groove on — and she wasn't alone. She was dancing with someone who had her cheesing from ear to ear. I wouldn't be able to place the man if I wanted to. He was in costume from head to toe.

I forced myself to leave the fun I was having. "What's wrong with you?" I asked when I approached my brother.

"You don't see that shit?" He pointed at

our mother.

"Yeah, so?"

"So?" He gave me an incredulous look.

"Yeah. We're having a good time. Why can't Momma?"

"Speak for yourself," he said, tugging at the collar of his costume.

I rolled my eyes. "The only person in the way of you having fun is you." I hip-bumped him, and he gave me a death stare, but I just laughed. "Seriously, bro, loosen up. We're probably going home soon since Aunt Shirley took care of everything."

He thought about it for a minute, then said, "You're right." He finally took his eyes off Momma. "I think I'ma head over to the craps table for a little while. You seen Marquis? I wanted to have a drink with my cuz before our ride together ends."

"He's uhh . . ."

"Right here." My cousin's voice came from behind.

He walked up to us wearing a Cheshire cat grin, and I knew there could only be one reason why. I glanced across to the bar, and sure enough, I saw the cocktail waitress I'd seen earlier moseying her way back behind the bar. The male bartender was yelling at her, no doubt about going missing when they had a full house to tend to. I turned back to Marquis and shook my head. He gave me a sheepish shrug.

"A mess," I said, unimpressed. "You two go and get your drink. I'm about to go outside and take the edge of the night off."

I left them and made my way to where I'd seen people exiting to a patio. I noticed a guy in a shimmery mask eyeing me as I passed by. That kind of male attention wasn't abnormal for me, in costume or not. He had a nice build, and from the part of his face that I could see, I figured he was probably handsome. But I really wasn't in the mood to be hit on.

"Leaving so soon?" he asked, flashing his perfect pearly whites. "Something as beautiful as you should be on my arm, dancing the night away."

I kept right on walking to the patio, which was set up like a midnight wonderland. There was a separate bar out there. The bartenders were dressed like fairies, and the drinks they were serving had colored sugar on the rim. If I'd come out there to drink, I would have indulged, but I was looking for a different kind of buzz.

I found an area that wasn't overcrowded with guests and sat down at a table by myself. From my purse, I pulled out a perfectly rolled joint and a lighter. The first drag instantly relaxed my body, and I blew out a small cloud of smoke. It was a habit my mother couldn't stand, so I didn't do it anywhere she could see.

"Your lips are gonna turn black as night smoking that shit!"

I chuckled as her words played in my head. It was a parent's job to try to keep their children on the straight and narrow, but I didn't know how straight she expected my path to be when I was a practiced killer. So, the things she chastised me about would always tickle me.

"I thought I smelled somebody blowing that good shit."

The voice caught me off guard, and I instantly put the hand holding the joint under the table. Turning my head, I saw the same guy with the shimmery black Zorro mask approaching me. His cape fluttered a little in the slight breeze. I looked him up and down, not knowing where or how to place him.

"You ain't gotta hide shit from me, Cinderella, but you better be careful. I seen Sheriff Clay lurking around, and she don't play."

"Thanks, I guess," I said, bringing my hand back up. I hesitated for a moment, but then I held my hand out. "You smoke?"

"Every day," he said, sitting down and taking the joint. As it hit his lungs, he nodded his head, impressed. "Damn, this is some good shit." He hit it a few more times before passing it back to me.

"I brought it from New York. My cousin owns a dispensary there."

"Dope."

Out of nowhere, he started laughing. I put the joint out and gave him a wary look. I hoped he wasn't one of those guys that smoked and got weird.

"What's funny?" I asked.

"I never thought I'd see Cinderella getting high, that's all."

I couldn't help but join him in his laughter. "You're funny."

"Nah, I'm Prince. And you? Should I address you as Cinderella, or Your Highness?"

"Your Highness will do. So, are you dressed up as a prince? As in Prince Charming?" I made a face, letting him know that I wasn't buying it.

"Nah, for real. Prince is my government. My mom always said when I was born, I was perfect, her little prince, so that's the name she gave me."

He sounded earnest, and when I searched his face for a lie, I couldn't find one. "Well, it's nice to meet you, Prince. My name's

Lauryn."

He held his hand out, and I took it. I thought he was just going to shake it, but instead, he brought it to his soft lips and kissed it. I hated the electrifying fireworks that went off in the pit of my stomach. Where had they come from? I quickly took my hand away and looked down so he wouldn't see me blushing.

He chuckled. "You're not from 'round here, are you, Lauryn? Are you from New York?"

"No. Georgia. You?" I asked, looking back up at him.

"Right here. Born and raised."

"And what do you do besides smoke weed with strangers?"

"A little this, a little that. Nothing that makes for good party conversation."

"In other words, nothing legal."

"Do I look like a criminal?" Prince pretended to be shocked by my statement, but the smirk on his face was a dead giveaway.

"No, but most men don't just walk around with Patek watches on their wrists and diamonds in their mouth."

"Good eye. I could be a lawyer or something. You never know."

"You expect me to believe you're a lawyer?" I pursed my lips in a disbelieving manner, and he laughed a deep belly laugh.

"Nah. I'm just sayin' —"

Suddenly, there was a loud uproar coming from inside. We whipped our heads just in time to see people running inside, like kids used to do when there was a fight in high school. The music had cut off, and I heard lots of shouting.

"No, Saint! Saint!" Someone was yelling repeatedly.

It sounded like someone was having an awakening in there. I knew they were differently religious and spiritual in New Orleans, but I wanted no parts in it. Prince, on the other hand, jumped up and started running toward the commotion.

He paused for a quick moment and looked back at me. "You still owe me a dance!" And with that, he was gone.

Chapter 30
Antoinette

"Oh, shit! Oh, shit! I'm cummin' again!" I moaned again and again as I felt the delightful sensation of Marquis's hardness sliding inside me. He had me bent over his office desk with my skirt hiked up, my panties on the floor, and his trousers around his ankles, hitting it from the back. We'd been at it for the last twenty minutes. It was so damn good that I didn't want it to ever stop, but I was sure people were starting to notice that one, if not both of us, were gone. Like I had a crystal ball, someone knocked on the office door at that moment. We both froze, with him still deep inside of me.

Marquis whispered in my ear, "Shhhh. Maybe they'll go away."

They knocked again, this time even harder. "Boss, you in there?"

I let out a sigh of relief when I heard Dice's voice. He was the head of Midnight Blues security. He was a friend, and because he always seemed to be around, I was sure he knew about Marquis and me, although he kept it to himself.

"Yeah," Marquis replied.

"You seen Antoinette?"

"No." He pushed himself a little deeper inside me, and I had to stifle my moans. He was trying to be cute, but he had no idea what it was doing to me physically and emotionally. We'd only been screwing for a few weeks, but Marquis was starting to take over my soul. "You might wanna check the powder room," he told Dice.

There was a slight hesitance before Dice responded. "Sure, boss. But if you see her, tell Antoinette that her husband is on the warpath. She might wanna make an appearance."

A shiver of fear rushed through my body. Why the fuck was my husband looking for me? He was supposed to be working.

"Yeah, I'll let her know if I see her."

"Cool. See you downstairs."

The moment it appeared that Dice had walked away, Marquis slid out of me, stepped back, and pulled up his pants. No words were necessary. We both understood that it would be dangerous for us to continue now. I retrieved my panties, kissed Marquis, and headed toward the door.

I hadn't made it five feet out the door before I heard a man clearing his throat. I stopped dead in my tracks. *Please, Lord, don't let my husband have seen me slip out that door.* I slowly turned around, and a scream almost escaped when I saw a tall figure standing in an alcove.

"Dice, you scared the shit out of me!"

"It's not me you should be scared of. It's your husband," he said, walking up to me. "Dude's walked into two ladies' rooms looking for you."

"Oh Lord." The two of us began to walk toward the stairs. "That man needs to calm down and relax."

"Yeah, and you need to be more discreet. Fucking in the boss's office during an event like this is just plain stupid."

I shot him an annoyed glance, but he wasn't wrong. It was stupid. However, every time I looked at Marquis, I wanted him.

"Y'all keep it up and somebody's gonna end up getting hurt."

"Antoinette!" My husband's voice came from the other side of the room.

I glanced at Dice, and he rolled his eyes as if to say, "I told you so."

"Antoinette!"

I turned, my body tense and full of anxiety as I watched my husband push his way through the crowd. The closer he got, the higher my blood pressure rose.

"Antoinette!"

"What, Saint?"

His hands were balled up into fists, which was never a good sign. I braced myself for what might come, whether it was a punch, a smack, or just plain roughhousing and a cussing out.

Saint raised his hands to throw a punch. I braced myself for the impact, but to my surprise and Dice's, his fist landed on the big security guard's jaw. Caught off guard, Dice fell back, and then Saint was on him like white on rice, repeatedly punching him with lefts and rights until Dice was a bloody mess despite his size.

"Saint! Saint! Stop, baby, please! You're gonna kill him!" I screamed, but the beating continued. "Somebody help him!"

Saint clearly had a demon on his back. His eyes seemed blank. DJ and Floyd suddenly appeared beside me.

"Saint, you crazy bastard, get off him! Get the fuck off him before I put one in your fucking skull." Floyd pointed a gun at Saint's head.

A crowd had formed around us, as everybody wanted to know what the commotion was about. More security came running over to pull Saint off Dice, but it was too late. The poor man was unconscious.

Floyd shoved Saint back and jammed a finger in his face. "You better get the fuck out of here before I do something you'll regret," Floyd said.

Saint was glaring at Floyd like he was contemplating whether Floyd would be his next target, until his brother Prince ran up to him.

"Saint, bro, calm down. It's all right. Just calm down, bro," Prince told him.

Those were the only words Saint seemed to hear. He blinked and looked at Prince, snapping out of his daze.

He turned to me. "Get your shit. It's time to go."

"I still have to work," I told him.

"Not anymore you don't! You just quit."

He grabbed my arm and snatched me away. Prince and a bunch of Crescent Boys followed closely behind us, boxing me in so that even if I wanted to run, I couldn't. I looked at the security guards trying to get poor Dice up off the floor, and I shook my head. What a damn shame. That man did nothing wrong. Then I shot a quick glance up at the top of the stairs, where Marquis was watching. I was sure he was thinking the same thing I was: *that could have been him.*

Chapter 31
Marie

There I was, walking aimlessly around a party, thankful for the mask on my face. While everyone else was having a good time, I was trying to hold off my tears. Not only had Jean left me, but his flunky Saint had caused such an embarrassing scene in the ballroom. I wanted to shrink into the nearest corner. No, I wanted to get a hold of my husband and chew his head off. I was tired of being number two. But then again, I couldn't even remember the last time that I was number one.

In my heart, I just knew he wouldn't leave me at such a grand event to handle his so-called business, but when he gave me that fake apologetic look with his eyes, I knew it had been a stupid fantasy. He was gone, and I was on my own for the night. I replayed the memory of him walking away from me as I snagged my third drink.

As I walked around the grand hall, I

sipped my drink, trying to banish thoughts of Jean. I didn't want to have a bad night when everyone else was happy. Even after the fiasco in the ballroom, everyone had gone back to enjoying themselves. That was New Orleans for you. A fight wasn't nothing but a little added razzle dazzle. Even still, I was glad that the mayor and the sheriff had left shortly after arriving as well. I didn't need anyone connected to my husband to be arrested.

Before I made my way over to the casino where all the fun seemed to be happening, I slid my wedding ring off my finger and put it into my purse. I was going to be just Marie that night. My plan was to find a slot machine and blow a couple thousand dollars of my husband's money, but an uproar coming from the craps table changed my course.

"I can't lose tonight, baby! I'm on fire!" a man was shouting to a large group of onlookers.

It must have been the liquor, because the first thing I noticed was how easy on the eyes he was in his tuxedo. He had fair skin and beautiful curls in his hair. His eyes were a tantalizing green, and I went to stand close by as he threw the dice. The crowd cheered when he hit.

"Somebody better tell my aunt to get ready to cash me out because this fire doesn't seem to be going out!" He rubbed his hands together excitedly.

It was at that moment that he took notice of the crowd around him, particularly me. Our eyes met, and the big grin on his face retracted into a sly smile. The butterflies I felt in my stomach were a sensation that had been foreign to my body for quite a while. I felt my cheeks grow warm when he held his hand out to me. I hesitated to take his hand since I was a married woman and most people knew who I wa— wait a second. I was wearing a mask with fringes. No one knew it was me. Plus, I wasn't wearing my wedding ring. With liquid courage coursing through my veins, I took his hand and allowed him to pull me close.

When the dealer handed him the dice once more, he held them out to me. "I think this throw, I might need some luck," he said.

"Is that right? It looks like you were doing just fine before I got over here."

"I think it might've run out by now. Do me the honors?"

I kept my eyes locked on his as I leaned forward and blew a slow, cool breeze onto the dice. Someone standing around the table whistled, and he threw the dice without looking.

"Seven!" the boxman shouted.

"I knew you were a lucky one," the green-eyed man said and kissed my hand before turning to collect his chips.

"You're done playing? I thought you were on fire," I teased.

"A wise man knows to quit while he's ahead. Plus, I saw you sitting alone in the ballroom earlier. Someone as beautiful as you should have a companion on a night like this. Let me buy you a drink."

"Hmm. Assumptions usually don't belong to a wise man."

"So, you aren't alone?" he asked with a disappointed look on his face.

I should have told him the truth, but I didn't want to.

"I am tonight," I finally answered.

"Then tonight, let me change that. How about that drink?"

"You didn't hear? The drinks are free," I said with a giggle.

"Let me buy you a free drink then."

He gathered his chips and put them in his pockets, then led me away from the table. I thought we were going to the bar that I'd passed earlier, but to my pleasant surprise, he took me outside to the back. The Blues sat on the water, and it was beautiful back there. The moon reflected off the water, and the music from inside still played softly out there. There was a manmade path near the water that led to a willow tree in the distance. It had small lights wrapped around every branch. When a breeze blew, the branches waved, and the lights looked like twinkling stars. There was a bar out there and a handful of people dancing under the night sky. The ambiance was more of a chill vibe, and not as crowded.

He ordered a Jack and Coke, and I ordered a sex on the beach. I thought we were going to sit at the bar and drink them, but instead, we went on a walk. It was all a whirlwind to me. There I was, walking and drinking with a strange man who I knew nothing about. The thought made me laugh out loud.

"What's funny?" he asked.

"I just realized I'm outside with a stranger by a big body of water. Anything could happen."

"Well, kindred spirits can't be strangers, but if it will make you feel better, here." He gently grabbed me by my waist and swapped sides with me so that way he was the one walking by the water. "Now if I say anything you don't like, just push me in. Hell, you'd be doing me a favor. I hate this damn tux.

And this stupid mask."

He took his mask off, and I finally saw just how fine he was. I audibly gasped and felt my cheeks grow warm again. I looked away, not wanting to stare too long, and focused my eyes on the path in front of me.

I found my voice. "So, are you in town visiting? I can tell by your accent that you aren't from here."

"Yeah. My aunt needed help with a few things, so we came on down. Don't know just how long we're staying yet."

By then, we had reached the willow tree, and my drink was almost gone. I was already feeling a buzz before that, but by now, I was well on my way to drunk. It felt good to have him near me. It felt so . . . natural.

He towered over me under the moonlight, forcing me to look up into his pretty eyes. "Hmm . . . does he protect you?" he asked as he lifted my left hand.

I quickly pulled it out of his grasp and tried to turn away, but he stopped me and lifted my chin with his finger.

"I noticed the ring indent back at the craps table."

"And you pursued me anyway?" I asked.

"I just figured a happily married woman wouldn't have looked at me the way you did. And she surely wouldn't have said yes when I asked her to have a drink with me."

I sighed. "It's . . . complicated. But I'm happy?" Even I heard the question in my tone.

"Are you telling me, or asking me?"

I groaned. "I try, you know, to be a good wife. The loving wife. The supporting wife. But somewhere along the line, I lost touch with who I am. I used to love getting out and going on adventures. I used to love going horseback riding and hiking. But being ignored has made me channel all my energy to just being seen in the moments when I can. And that's not saying much."

"Well, what happened?"

"I don't know. Most days I just feel like a prop. Like something that can be traded in at any time. You know?"

"Nah, I don't. But it sounds horrible, like you're in a loveless marriage. Why not just leave?"

Flashes of Jean came to my mind. I hated the fact that this moment I was having with a stranger was sending more tingles down my spine than my husband had in the past I-don't-know-how-many years. I wasn't a hard woman to please. Simply prioritizing me at night would have had Jean in the clear with me. But no. Even that was made to seem like I was asking for too much. I was tired of the empty-ass promises. Like that night. I was a fool to think that Jean would really commit to the no-work clause.

"It's not that simple," I finally said.

"Do you still love him?" he asked, pulling me closer.

"I–I don't know," I breathed as his lips got closer to mine.

"There's only one way to find out." He kissed me deeply.

Chapter 32
Saint

There was pure rage coursing through my body as I tugged my wife out of the Blues. I didn't care what kind of spectacle I'd become, but it was time to go before I caught my second body that night. I had an iron-clad grip on Antoinette's wrist, and it didn't matter how much she tried to yank away. She wasn't going anywhere.

"Saint, let go of me!" she yelled as I pulled her through the parking lot.

I acted like I didn't hear her, stopping only when we were at my car. I looked down at her flushed face. There were tears in the corners of her eyes, but they didn't move me.

"I can't believe you did Dice like that!" She hit my chest. "What's wrong with you?"

"Maybe if you weren't fucking him, it wouldn't have happened!"

"I'm not!" She finally freed her arm from my grasp. "He's not interested in me."

"Please, try that with another sucker. The way you be prancing around in there with your ass hanging out."

"He's gay, you fucking idiot!"

"Gay?" I was thrown for a loop. "That big ass motherfucker?"

"Gay, as in he likes dick. And he's the bottom. You better hope nobody recorded it because your ass will be going down for a hate crime."

"Shut up and get in the car." I opened the door, not completely buying what she was selling.

"No."

"Get in the car, woman, before I put you in it!" I bellowed. With an attitude, she obliged.

"I hate this shit!" She slammed her own door shut.

"Yeah, well, I hate when you whore around," I murmured to myself as I opened the driver's side door.

"Bro!"

I heard Prince's voice, and when I turned, I saw him jogging toward me with a disappointed look on his face. I knew what he had to say, and I didn't want to hear it.

"You need to get back in there and look after Mrs. LeBlanc while I take my wife home," I told him.

"So we ain't gonna talk about what just happened back there?" he asked. "Because I think we need to."

"I don't think we need to talk about shit. Like I said, I'm out."

Prince looked up at the sky in frustration. He ran his hands down his face as if he were contemplating his next move. It had never come to blows between my brother and me, but if it did, he knew he couldn't beat me. Still, Prince was the only person besides Jean who wasn't scared to step to me.

"Saint, I love you, but you're dumb as fuck." He jabbed his finger into my chest. "Two times in one night you did some crazy shit in front of countless eyes. Are you good? Because your anger is getting the best of you. You gotta get that shit under control or you gon' send us crashing down with you. You ain't untouchable. None of us are."

He was shaking his head as he turned around and walked away, leaving me speechless. He wasn't necessarily wrong, but I did not appreciate being reprimanded by my little brother.

"Excuse me, Mr. Saint? Is this a bad time?"

"What now?" I asked in pure annoyance before turning to see who was speaking. It was the annoying little dude who seemed to always be around.

"What the fuck you want, Weasel?" I asked.

"Actually, it's Skunk. But I'ma let that slide because I can clearly see you're not in a good mood right now. But I know somethin' you might wanna hear."

"There ain't nothing you got to say that I could possibly want to hear. Get the fuck on," I said, turning to finally get into the car.

"Even if it has to do with the truth about Pierre LeBlanc?"

I dropped my hand from the door handle and turned back to him. "What did you just say?"

"I got something to say about Pierre. Is that hundred thousand still on the table?"

The last person I thought I'd ever be standing with in Jean's foyer was right beside me. I was watching Skunk like a hawk to make sure he didn't go scurrying off. He was the kinda guy who would make a dumb-ass decision like that, trying to snoop around the LeBlanc household. Prince and Kendall seemed to be watching him also as we waited for Jean to make his way downstairs.

There were a few things I did at the ball that I probably shouldn't have. What could

I say? My temper and liquor don't mix, and I wasn't going to apologize for it. But I knew Jean would eventually hear about the shit that went down, and that wouldn't be good for me. He hated anything public that brought negative attention his way. I hoped that bringing Skunk's news to him would make all that other stuff insignificant.

Of course, that depended on whether Skunk recounted everything he'd said last night exactly how he told me, and it had better be the truth. He wasn't exactly the trustworthy type, and he wouldn't be the first motherfucka trying to lie to get a reward.

"Bruh, how do you know this squealy motherfucka knows anything?" Prince asked me, mean-mugging Skunk.

"I don't. That's what we're gonna find out," I told him just as Jean came bounding down the steps.

After Jean left the ball the night before, I couldn't imagine things had gone well between him and the missus. Jean was wearing a frown on his face that only got deeper when he saw Skunk sullying up his foyer.

He looked at me. "There better be a good fucking reason for him to be here."

"I wouldn't have brought him here if it wasn't," I said and nudged Skunk forward.

"Tell him, Skunk."

"Damn, I don't get no breakfast in this nice-ass house?" he asked seriously. "I know there's a cook in here somewhere."

My reflexes were faster than my thought process. I backhanded him, busting his lip and sending droplets of blood to the floor.

"You think this is a game? I said tell him!"

"Fine, fine! I see y'all ain't morning people around this motherfucka." Skunk angrily wiped the blood from his lip. He looked at Jean. "I know for a fact your brother wasn't killed by no gator."

"Explain," Jean said, his interest piqued.

"He wasn't ate up by no gator. He was shot."

"And who shot him?"

"I don't know who exactly killed him . . ." Skunk said.

Jean flexed his fists, making Skunk talk faster.

"But I do know where he died and who carried the body out."

I shoved him again.

"This ain't no cliffhanger to no movie, motherfucka. Tell him who."

"What about my money?" Skunk asked.

"You'll get your money," Jean promised right before his eyes got dark. "But if you don't tell me what I want to know, there will be hell to pay for wasting my time."

Skunk swallowed and looked around at all the menacing eyes on him. Finally, he leaned in toward Jean. "Get this," he said. "The night Pierre died, I was smoking a cigarette after my usual dumpster dive — and don't y'all knock it till you try it. You'd be surprised what kind of stuff rich folks throw away! Anyways, as I was hitting the square, I saw something crazy. It was that chicken foot–wearing bastard Floyd, carrying a body wrapped in tarp out of the Blues. Him and Marquis! I couldn't believe my eyes."

Jean looked intrigued, if not entirely convinced yet. "You sure about that?"

"Positive. I saw the hand sticking out of the tarp, so I know it was a body with lots of gold jewelry, just like your brother used to wear."

I watched as slow anger came to Jean's face. Skunk's story was confirming his suspicion that his brother had died before his body went into the swamp.

He looked at me. "Round up the boys and have them at my house first thing tomorrow. Looks like we'll be making a stop at the Blues."

Chapter 33
Nee Nee

There weren't enough words in any language to describe the tingling sensation coursing through my body as a pair of strong hands stroked my back. I had no idea that the events from the night before would lead to an intense morning of lovemaking, but I was glad I'd worn my lace thong. It had been so long since I'd been touched in the places that made me sing, and feeling guilty was the last thing on my mind. Actually, the only thing on my mind was the orgasm rising between my legs.

"Oh my God!" I cried out to my lover. I didn't care that other guests staying at the W New Orleans might be able to hear me. Nobody and nothing was going to ruin my good mood this morning.

I felt him buck, letting me know that he too had reached his climax. He shivered with the aftershocks, and I gently kissed up his neck to his chin, coaxing him through it.

"That was so good, baby," I whispered as he rolled from in between my legs. "Oh, I needed that."

"Me too."

I propped myself up on my arm and stared into the handsome face of my husband, Larry Duncan, the only man who could ever make me feel this good. The smile on my face had been there since last night. I was so happy to be reunited with my love. The initial shock of seeing him pop up in a Cyrano de Bergerac mask at the ball had damn near made me jump out of my shoes. I was so pleased to see him, but I didn't want to draw too much attention to us. I had no idea what he was doing there or how he had gotten there, and until I found out, I didn't want Curtis or Lauryn to know.

"Baby?"

"Hmm?" he responded sleepily with his eyes closed.

I knew I only had a few moments before he was in a full-blown sex coma. He told me he always got the best sleep after we made love. Unfortunately, he'd have to pause on that rest.

I gently shook his arm. "Wake up. I need to ask you something." I shook his arm again.

"Look, I'm not as young as I used to be,

so if you want another round, you're gonna have to give me a minute," he said with a yawn, finally opening his eyes.

"Larry!" I laughed and swatted him. "While I'm not opposed to that at all, I have something else on my mind. Why are you here?"

He turned to face me and took in the searching look I gave him. I surely thought he was going to tell me something that would make my heart drop, which was why I'd waited so long to ask.

Instead, he leaned up and kissed me softly on the lips. "It's simple, really. I missed you. It's been lonely without you, baby."

Instead of making my heart drop, the sincerity in his voice did melt it a bit. If anyone could understand his loneliness, I could. It's rare to find a true soul mate, and Larry was mine. Although having my kids around had softened the blow, it was so hard to be without him after he disappeared from Fresh Meadows.

"I missed you too." I cupped his face. "Now, tell me. Where's my son? Where's Kenny?"

"He's here in New Orleans too. And before you say anything, don't worry. You know I'ma make sure you see him soon."

"You better."

I thought he would go to sleep now, but instead, his expression became serious.

"What?" I asked.

"Why are you here in New Orleans? Last I knew, you were in New York."

When Larry was holding LC captive at Fresh Meadows, he was getting help from my son Kenny. I had left Georgia and gone to New York to try to find Kenny before an all-out war broke out between him and the New York Duncans. After Larry and Kenny disappeared, I stayed in New York so that the bonds between our families might begin to heal. I still held out hope that someday we could bring Larry and Kenny back into the fold.

I was almost hesitant to answer because I still wasn't sure about his mental state. When he was at his sickest, his paranoia made him believe his family, especially LC, was out to get him. I didn't want to say anything that might set him off now.

"Well," I began cautiously, "Marquis came up north to get some help from LC, but they have their own stuff going on right now, so Vegas asked Curtis and Lauryn to come down here and give her a hand."

Larry raised his eyebrows in surprise. "Must be pretty serious if Shirley was willing to ask LC for help. She's not exactly a fan of him or Chippy."

He assessed the situation with clarity I hadn't heard from him in a long time. It gave me hope that he was getting better.

"She didn't ask. It was Marquis. And it's not that she doesn't like LC and Chippy," I said, trying to put a positive spin on things. "She loves them in her own special way. At the end of the day, we're all family. But you know as well as I do that Big Shirley doesn't like the drugs or the violence that comes with them. She never wanted her kids around it, especially after Trent died."

Larry chuckled. "Shirley's got a problem with violence? If I remember correctly, it took a little bloodshed for her to get the Blues, even after her daddy left it to her."

"There are always exceptions when there is no other option," I told him as I got out of bed and started getting dressed.

"I'm not going to argue with you on that. But what's she got going on that she needs Curtis and Lauryn's help?"

"I'm not too sure. Some crime boss here was giving them a hard time, but when we got here, it looked like she had already solved the problem." I walked over to the bed and planted a big kiss on his forehead.

"Where you going?" he asked.

"Back to Big Shirley's. I'm sure they'll be

wondering where I am if they're up. You coming?"

"Nah," he said, then got lost in his thoughts for a few seconds. "Maybe . . . maybe it's best that nobody knows I'm here for now."

"Larry," I said with a warning tone. "Don't go doing no digging. I told you Big Shirley handled the situation."

"I won't. It's just that you know Shirley feels the same way about me as she does LC and them. It's best I keep my distance. The most important thing is that you know where to find me."

I wasn't quite sold, but then again, I hadn't given him enough information for him to dig up anything anyway. I sighed and nodded, letting him know his secret was safe with me.

I blew him one more kiss before exiting the hotel room. It had been so long since I'd gotten it that good, I hoped I wasn't walking funny.

CHAPTER 34
BIG SHIRLEY

Despite my head of security getting the shit kicked out of him by that crazy-ass Crescent Boy, the Midnight Blues masquerade ball had been a huge success, socially and financially. Marquis and I had made a slew of new contacts, and the casino had taken in a record amount. All in all, it was a very successful night. People left feeling good, and that meant many of them would be back soon.

"So, that sister-in-law of yours is a lot more adventurous than I gave her credit for. Did you see the way her wig was leaning to the side when she staggered in this morning?" Monique asked in the casual way she did when she was feeling me out. "Looked like old girl mighta got it in last night."

"Girl, ain't no *mighta* in it," I replied, pulling into my parking space at the Blues. "Nee Nee did a lot more than get it in. She got her back blown the fuck out!"

We burst out laughing.

"I know that's right!" Mo replied. "But who did it? I didn't think she knew anybody other than you here in NOLA."

"Neither did I, but you know what they say. Every rabbit got a hole."

"And if they don't, they'll find one," Mo finished.

We were both cracking the hell up as we headed toward the casino entrance.

Mo stepped inside the casino. I was about to follow until I heard quick footsteps coming toward us. Instinctively, I placed my hand in my Chanel bag and wrapped it around my gun. I turned around and felt a little less threatened when I saw a slightly nerdy-looking Black man wearing a suit and holding a briefcase. He was tall, with a low cut and a neatly trimmed mustache. He was more Monique's type than mine, which was obvious from the way she was cheesing as she looked at him.

"We don't open until noon," I explained, hoping he'd go away.

"I'm not here to gamble," he said. Then he just stood there, staring at me as if we owed him money.

Mo and I glanced at each other, then both spoke the same word out loud. "Salesman."

He looked disappointed by our assessment. "No, I'm not a salesman. You don't remember me, do you, Shirley? Or, as you were known back in the day, Big Shirley?"

I gave him the once over again. I was usually good with faces, but this man I could not recall. Obviously, he didn't know me too well, because he didn't seem to know that they still called me Big Shirley.

"No, sir, unfortunately, you have me at a disadvantage. We have a lot of people strolling through these doors. Now, if you'll be so kind as to state your business, I have some things to attend to."

"Sure, sure. I just need a minute of your time." He handed me a card that read: GABRIEL WILLIAMS, DEVELOPER.

"How can I help you, Mr. Williams? Did that damn Jack Barnes send you over here to barter with me?"

"Is there somewhere we can talk? I have a proposal I'd like to present to you."

Monique stepped in before I could say anything. "You want me to deal with him, Shirl?"

Gabriel snapped, "No! I need to talk to you and you only! What I have to say is very important." He stood firm, like he was a man accustomed to being taken seriously.

I scrutinized him more carefully now. His suit wasn't cheap; neither was the leather briefcase he was carrying. Normally I didn't take impromptu meetings like that, especially from people I didn't know, but there was something about his eyes that felt somehow familiar, and that made me curious. I checked my watch. It was still early enough in the day that I could spare a few minutes. I motioned for him to follow me.

When Gabriel and I were in my office, I sat comfortably behind my desk and he took a seat on the opposite side. I placed my elbows on my desk and clasped my hands. Gabriel just stared and stared at me to the point that it started to creep me out. I hoped I hadn't made a mistake letting him come up to my office without security outside my door.

I cleared my throat. "So . . ."

"Oh, yes!" he said, snapping out of his daze. "I'm sorry. You're just still so beautiful."

"Thank you," I told him, brushing off the odd compliment. "But let's make this short and sweet. You're not the first developer to sit in that chair, though you are the first Black one. So, before you start trying to sell me a dream about what you can do with the place, I need you to know that the Blues and its surrounding properties aren't for sale."

"Big Shirley, I think you have the wrong impression," Gabriel said with a smile, sitting back in his chair. "I'm not interested in Midnight Blues or the property around it."

I felt the hair on the back of my neck stand up. I didn't know why, but it was something about the way his eyes refused to leave mine. It was like he was . . . calling to me.

"Then what are you interested in, Mr. Williams? Because I don't have a lot of time."

"I'm interested in you," he said flatly.

"Me? Why me? I'm confused." I was now wishing I had asked Monique to stay.

"You *still* don't remember me, do you?" He let out a disappointed chuckle.

"No, not at all," I told him, preparing to tell him to get the hell out of my office with his crazy talk.

"Maybe this will jog your memory."

I stared at him.

"Waycross, Georgia," he said.

The word *Waycross* wasn't unfamiliar to me, that's for sure, but it had been a long time and a lot I'd purposely forgotten. "What about Waycross?

"A long time ago, when I was on spring break from college in Jacksonville, some friends of mine took me on a ride to Waycross for my birthday," he said.

I felt my eyes widen because I was starting to understand where this was going, although I still didn't recognize him.

"They took me to a place I'll never forget. A brothel called Big Sam's."

"I should have known," I said with a groan.

It had been a while since anyone brought up Big Sam's. In fact, if I could have forgotten the place entirely, I would. I'd made every possible change to ensure I'd never have to walk that path again. I couldn't remember the last time I'd run into any of my old customers, and never had any sought me out. It explained the lustful look in Gabriel's eyes as he stared at me.

"Ahh, so you do remember."

"Big Sam's is a place I could never forget. It was probably the lowest point of my life. Still don't remember you," I replied. By this time, my hospitality had faded, and I pulled the pistol out of my purse. "If this is some sort of shakedown —"

"There's no need for the gun." He was eerily calm considering the situation. "This isn't a shakedown."

"Then what the fuck do you want?"

I didn't know what he thought would happen. That I'd be flattered about him coming to my place of business, bringing up a past

I'd deaded years ago? He had some nerve. It was taking everything in me not to shoot him right between his too-close-together eyes.

"I said what the fuck do you want?" I repeated louder, pulling the hammer back. That got his attention.

"You. I–I want you," he stammered. "That night was my first time, and you made it special. I've never forgotten it. I've had my share of women over the years, but none have left quite the mark that you did."

I had to stifle a chuckle. Back then, there was a reason why I was such a hot commodity. I knew how to paint a sexual masterpiece and send them over the moon. It was why I was Big Sam's best girl for so many years. I had plenty of men fiending for me, running back every chance they got. However, this was thirty years later, and Gabriel was a cuckoo in the nest.

"Well, thanks for the compliment," I said dryly, "but I don't do that sort of thing anymore."

He stared at me briefly. "Not even for fifty thousand dollars?"

My mouth opened in shock.

Seeing my reaction, he grinned. "I hired a private investigator to find you, and I didn't hire him for nothing. I'm not the kind of man who gives up easily."

"You hired a private investigator to find me? Just so that you could relive a fantasy?" I asked, knowing then that I for sure wasn't going to lower my gun. "Are you serious?

"Very much so."

What kind of freak was he? Well, he couldn't have been much of one if I didn't even remember him. In all fairness, I had blocked out a lot from my time at Big Sam's, even if I wasn't ashamed of my past. I was a boss now, and I saw no reason to hang on to memories of a time when I wasn't the one in charge.

"It's flattering, but no thank you. I don't do that anymore."

"I understand you're more successful now. What about seventy-five thousand?"

"All right, it's time for you to leave. This is getting weird. I just told your crazy ass that I don't do that anymore."

"A hundred thousand."

"No!"

"Two hundred?"

"No!"

"Then give me your 'yes' number. Three hundred thousand?" I hesitated for a brief second, was he serious?

"How about I give you six reasons to get the fuck out of my office?" I was seriously about to pull the trigger at this point.

"What the hell is going on here?" The voice belonged to my dear sister-in-law. I couldn't have been more happy to see Nee Nee. She'd cleaned herself up and come down to the Blues. Her eyes were on the pistol in my hand, and she had a nervous look on her face.

She *looked* at Gabriel and pointed at the door. "I don't know what you did to piss her off, but trust me when I say you need to leave now. She will kill you."

Gabriel looked from her to the gun, then back at me. He reluctantly got up from his seat and walked slowly to the door.

He left some parting words before he closed the door behind him. "This isn't over. Shirley. I always get what I want, *and I want you!*"

Chapter 35
Jean

I remember when I was a kid, the urge to pee grew stronger the closer I got to the bathroom. I couldn't count how many times I'd almost had an accident just because I couldn't unzip my pants fast enough. Now as an adult, I still got that feeling, just not with my bladder. The itch in my trigger finger got stronger the nearer we got to the Blues.

Every fiber in my being wanted the news I'd gotten about my brother's death to be . . . I didn't know what I wanted it to be. But if Big Shirley wanted to live another day, it had better be a lie, especially since she and the rest of her lot had smiled in my face and sent me their sincerest condolences. For the life of me, I couldn't think of a reason why anybody at the Blues would want to hurt my brother. He could be a piece of shit sometimes, sure, but as much money as he'd lost in that place, he should have been like family.

"We're here." Saint's voice snapped me out of my thoughts.

He'd gotten us to the Blues in record time. Kendall, Prince, and some other Crescent Boys parked their car beside us. When I stepped out, Prince approached me.

"You don't look like a man who just found out his brother died from foul play," he said, eyeing me.

"Having a calm mind has always served me well. It's rare that I make emotional decisions," I explained. "Today is business. If that business so happens to get ugly and turn personal, then so be it."

"Word."

"I need you and Kendall to post up outside the entrance and look out. Just in case those flashy lights show up. You know Big Shirley has the sheriff in the palm of her hands."

As we all began walking toward the building, I adjusted my suit jacket to conceal my gun in its holster. Prince and Kendall took their positions near the entrance and casually leaned against the wall. When the rest of us got inside, we had the instant attention of security.

They started to approach us, but Saint put his hand up to stop them. "Not today.

Not if you know what's good for you." He gave them a menacing stare as we continued through.

Of course, the metal detectors beeped. However, the security guards seemed to be heeding Saint's warning. I was sure they'd radio to Big Shirley that she had guests, which was fine with me.

As soon as we stepped foot in the lobby, Monique came rushing toward us. "Uh, Jean, can I help you?" She sounded flustered, which was what I wanted.

"I'm here to see Big Shirley, so if you'd show me to her office, that would do me good. Otherwise, I'll find it myself."

"I don't think you were on her schedule today," she said, still not moving.

"So?" I gave her a deadly stare and watched her shrink under my gaze. I led my crew as I stepped around and left her standing there, looking shook.

I knew the way to Big Shirley's office, and I didn't bother knocking when we got there. Saint followed me in, while the others stood watch outside. Big Shirley was in there, seated at her desk, with a woman I didn't recognize. I assumed she was family or a close friend the way she protectively stepped closer to Big Shirley. Saint slid in front of the door, ensuring that nobody could get out.

I had no smile to offer, nor was I looking for any pleasantries as I calmly took a seat on the other side of the desk. Big Shirley held my gaze.

"I hope I'm not interrupting anything — and if I am, I don't really give a shit. You and I need to speak," I told her.

"Well, this is more than a little unexpected, but it's always nice to see you, Jean. What's on your mind? Does it have anything to do with your man Saint beating up one of my employees last night?"

That was news to me. I turned around and looked at Saint, but he didn't have half an answer for me at the moment. In fact, if he had done it, he looked completely unapologetic. Understanding that I could deal with that later, I turned back to Big Shirley.

"No, it's not about that. I'm here looking for some answers about my brother." I paused briefly, studying her face. Not even a flinch. "A little birdie told me Pierre was here the night he died. That true?"

"I wasn't here that night," she said without missing a beat. "But Floyd did mention seeing him that night, which wasn't uncommon. Pierre was here most nights. You know that boy loved him some poker, even though he wasn't very good at it."

I leaned forward. "That's interesting you bring up Floyd, because that same little birdie told me that your son and Floyd were seen hauling Pierre's body out back and driving off with it."

She slammed her hand on the desk. "That's a goddamn lie! Pierre left here alive that night. And I've got video proof."

I watched her body language, but mostly her eyes. They didn't waver one bit. In fact, they were laser locked onto mine. Our stare-off ended with me nodding when I wasn't able to find any hint of discomfort on her part.

"I want to see the video. It would clear up a lot of this misunderstanding — if it *is* just a misunderstanding."

"As long as you don't mind bringing me that lying piece of shit that told you this crap. I don't do no mess, and we both know folks would do just about anything for the kind of reward money you're offering up."

She had me by the balls because I wasn't ready to give up my source without doing a little more digging. For all I knew, she'd have him killed before I could find anything. At least that's what I would do.

"Let me chat with my little birdie and see what I can arrange. Until then, this thing between us is not over. I'll be in touch."

As Saint and I left the office, I couldn't shake the feeling that there was more to this story. I knew Big Shirley was a tough cookie, but an accusation like the one I'd made should have made her more forthcoming, especially if she truly had a video of Pierre leaving the Blues the night he died.

"Everything good?" Kendall asked once we were back outside and the door was closed.

"Nah." I shook my head. "She's hiding something, but we're gonna find out. Me, Skunk, and my brass knuckles are gonna have a little talk."

"What's there to talk about? I think that motherfucka is playing us like a fiddle. Especially if she's able to show us some footage," Saint said.

"I need every piece of the puzzle. I don't trust either one of them, but one thing I know for sure is that a mother will lie for her son." I looked to Saint. "Have Prince find Marquis. Let's see if their stories line up."

"What about you?" Saint asked.

"Me, Kendall, and Skunk are gonna go pay Floyd a visit."

"And me?"

In truth, dealing with somebody as hard

as Floyd, I would have liked to have Saint by my side. Not saying that Kendall couldn't get the job done, but Floyd wasn't someone to underestimate. Kendall would have to do, however, because Saint had another job. My brother's double-cross with that guy Sebastian had pissed me off, sure, but I'd gotten a new connect out of that betrayal.

I told Saint, "You need to go home and pack. Our new friend from Florida is expecting you."

Chapter 36
Prince

I inhaled deeply, relishing the feeling as the Blue Dream kush hit my chest and sent me into a pleasant daze. I hit the blunt a few more times before passing it to my best friend Jace in the passenger seat of my truck.

"Man, where the fuck is Marquis at?" he asked before taking a hit.

I focused my attention out the window and shrugged. This was looking like an all-day job. There were endless places Marquis could be in and around NOLA, so I figured I might as well be lit and comfortable while searching.

"Chill out. We gon' find his ass."

"Jean is always sending us on some bogus-ass mission," Jace said. I could hear the frustration in his voice. "I'd rather be on the block making some paper. This shit is pointless."

I looked over at him and had to chuckle.

My boy looked like a kid having a temper tantrum. The two of us had been thick as thieves since we were knee high. More than best friends, he was my brother from another. I would bleed an entire city for him, and it was vice versa.

Although we were similar in many ways, Jace was more like a little kid with ADD when it came to being serious or concentrating on shit that didn't interest him. It was showing at that moment. If he didn't get some action soon, he might explode.

"Like I said, chill out. We gon' catch this man, and then we gon' get in better with Jean. Remember the plan."

"Yeah, a'ight."

He went back to smoking, and I turned my attention to driving and looking for Marquis's treasured Lamborghini. A car like that was fun to drive but terrible for keeping a low profile. As I maneuvered through traffic, my mind went to the plan Jace and I had to move up in the ranks. We were tired of being runners and errand boys. Although there were many that surpassed us in age, there weren't many who did so in work. With me being Saint's baby brother, Jean trusted me with more missions than the average cats. They were big ones, too, like taking out anyone who thought they were going to move in on our turf. The one we were on now felt small. I would have rather been getting in on the new thing Jean had going on with that dude Sebastian from Florida.

Saint told me that Jean had him picking up a package and we would have more work to handle soon. Saint would be more preoccupied with being the distro, so he wouldn't have time to manage the Crescent Boys and all the spots we had around the city. Jean had a pretty clean setup when it came to his money and his drugs. Neither stayed in the same spot for more than eight hours. Moving that kind of weight around so consistently with nothing coming up missing had to be managed by someone Jean trusted with his life. For a while, that person had been Saint. However, from the looks of things that person would soon be me.

That was where Jace and I came in at. No more hand-to-hand pass-offs. Selling the product for Jean came with a nice income, but I was trying to move up in the world. So was Jace. We were ready for management.

"You think Jean will really give us that job over Kendall or Bobby?" Jace asked, mentioning Jean's nephew and another Crescent

Boy who was about ten years our senior.

"You know I'ma have Saint put in a good word for us, man. Plus, Kendall might be Jean's nephew, but he's more of a hitter and a mover, feel me? I can't see him wanting to be tied down to any one position. Jean likes him at his side at all times. And Bobby?" I smacked my lips, thinking about his old ass. "He knows the game. I'll give him that. But he just don't got it like he used to. Especially after he got shot a few years back. All it would take is one good thump on the head to knock buddy out."

"You wrong for that, bro," Jace said, laughing. "But yeah, make sure Saint put that good word in. This sunup-to-sunup shit ain't working for me no more."

I nodded, agreeing with him. The job of a Crescent Boy came with many perks but not enough sleep.

"Aye! Slow up. There goes Marquis's Lambo right there!" Jace sat up in his seat.

Sure enough, the sleek blue vehicle was whipping by in oncoming traffic. "That's gotta be him. He's the only one I know with those wheels."

"Follow his ass," Jace instructed like I was new to the game.

"What the fuck you think I'm about to do?" I hit a U-turn, practically sideswiping a minivan full of old ladies. I sped up to try to catch the Lambo, but I didn't want to admit that I'd lost sight of him. *Where the fuck did he just go?* I wondered as I wove in and out of lanes.

Finally, I spotted the Lambo again, but it wasn't in traffic anymore. It had pulled into the parking lot of a rinky-dink motel. There was only one reason a man like Marquis would be at a place like that, and I was a little surprised. I'd never pegged him to be the type to entertain prostitutes. But then again, every man has his vices.

"Who is he fucking in a place like that?" Jace asked, reading my thoughts.

"Gotta be some dirty slut. No respectable woman would ever be seen in a place like this. Feel me?"

"Well, we might be finding out who. Shit, after we apply pressure to that motherfucka, I might get her number next. I could use a new eater on my team."

"Dawg, you crazy," I said with a laugh, making the necessary turn to hit the road where the motel was. "Get your strap ready."

"This thing stays ready."

Chapter 37
Marquis

I knew that when I finally got to the Blues, Momma would have a field day with curse words about me not answering my phone. But the way Antoinette had been putting it on me, I was not about to be interrupted by a phone call, no matter who it was from.

I got dressed and grabbed Antoinette in her sexy lingerie. "You going into work after this?" I asked, cupping her bottom and giving her a kiss.

"Yeah. I wish I could lay up with you all day, though."

"That makes two of us," I said. "I would give you a ride, but it wouldn't be good for business."

"I know."

"The two of us showing up at the Blues together would cause a ruckus that neither of us needs right now."

"I *know.*" She rolled her eyes at me.

"Is an Uber cool? Or you more of a Lyft girl?"

"Uber is fine." She pulled away from me to start getting dressed as I hailed her a ride on my phone.

"All right. It says it should be here in about five minutes. You need anything before I leave?" I asked.

"Yeah, for you to hurry up and get to the Blues before your momma sends a hunting squad out for you. I know she must be fuming the way you were ignoring her calls."

"You're right."

She was laughing, but that was because she didn't know Momma the way I did. If I didn't show up soon, she *would* send somebody to find me. I gave Antoinette one last kiss before I left the room and bounded down the stairs. By then, Curtis had probably returned from his joy ride in my Lambo and would be waiting in the parking lot.

As I went down the stairs, I was checking notifications on my phone, but when my feet hit the sidewalk, I looked up to step off the curb. I expected to see my cousin, but instead, I was met with an unwelcome surprise. Sitting on my freshly washed Lamborghini were two Crescent Boys. I recognized them as Saint's little brother and his best friend, two dudes who could be just as violent as Saint. It was crazy to think that at one point, we'd been cool. Prince and Jace frequented the Blues almost as much as Pierre did back in the day. I had to put a stop to that when they got caught selling drugs out of the casino. To this day, Momma never knew about it, but the relationship between Prince and me had never been the same.

"The fuck is going on here?" I asked as I got nearer.

"What you think, boy?" Prince sneered. "This is what pressure looks like. Now, you gon' tell us what ya mammy didn't."

I felt my stomach do a flip. What did they mean, what Momma didn't tell them? I had a bad feeling, and I knew I needed to get to the Blues quick.

I kept a poker face as I addressed them. "Bruh, I don't know what you're talking about. All I know is y'all better get your ugly purple asses off my whip before I show *you* some pressure."

They started laughing. Prince hit Jace in the shoulder, and it made them laugh harder.

"He got the nerve to talk about ugly when he's leaving a place like this, man," Jace said hysterically, then turned his attention to me.

"What you had up in there, dawg? A five-dollar whore? What you need to do is go get your dick checked out before it falls off. After we talk, of course."

I looked behind me at the motel and prayed that Antoinette had the good sense not to walk out now. It would just make everything worse.

"Ain't shit to talk about. For real, though. Move. I'm a businessman, and my time is worth a lot of money," I said.

"We do got shit to talk about, businessman." Prince got off the car and stepped toward me. "Like I said, we just left the Blues from talking to Big Shirley. Thought we'd ask you the same thing we asked her."

"And what was that?" I tried to hide my alarm. That must have been why Momma was calling me, and I didn't answer because I was knee deep in Antoinette's pussy. If they'd done anything to her, I'd kill them dead.

"We're gonna give you one chance to tell us what really happened the night Pierre died," he said, studying me like he was searching for clues.

The hardest thing to do was keep my face straight. I had felt a pang of alarm shoot through my chest when they mentioned Pierre's name. Why were they asking about him when we'd already buried that? Or so we thought.

"I don't know. I wasn't at the swamp," I answered with a shrug.

"See, I was told that Pierre was at the Blues the night he died. That's more believable than Pierre being found in a fuckin' swamp. Don't you think?"

I could no longer hold my poker face. How could they possibly have known that Pierre was at the Blues that night? Someone was talking, but who?

I spoked through clenched teeth. "I don't know what you were expecting to hear, but all I got for Jean is condolences."

Jace hopped off the hood of the car and got in my face. "You cappin'!"

"What you gon' do?" I asked.

He shoved me hard, but I'd already planted my feet in preparation, so I barely moved. I shoved him back with more power, and he stumbled. As he regained his balance, he went to his waist, but Prince stopped him.

"Bruh, chill out. We ain't here for all that," he told his friend.

Suddenly, I heard my cousin's voice. "I'm glad somebody got some fucking sense."

I breathed a sigh of relief. Curtis was approaching us from the direction of the gas station next door. In one hand he held a soda, and in the other was a pistol pointed directly at Jace's dome. Jace mean-mugged him, but he was smart enough not to move, seeing that Curtis's finger rested on the trigger.

"The fuck y'all here giving my cousin a hard time about?"

"His beef your beef?" Prince asked.

"Always."

"Then you might want to put the gun away. You fucking with mighty powers, my boy. Especially if you ain't gon' make it go boom."

"Where I come from, you can't be scared to pull a trigger," Curtis said icily. "And trust me, killing you and your partnah ain't even enough to make me blink. So tell me, you living or dying today?"

There was a dramatic pause, and for a moment, I couldn't even hear any birds chirping or leaves rustling. Time seemed to stand still. Finally, Prince and Jace got the picture and did what was best for them. Prince hit Jace on the arm and motioned his head to where his truck was parked.

"Like I said, we ain't here for all that," Prince said, then pointed at me. "I'll be seeing you." With that, they hopped in the truck and sped off.

Curtis waited for them to be gone before he put his gun away. "Looks like me and my fam ain't leaving so soon after all," he said.

CHAPTER 38
JEAN

It wasn't hard to find Skunk, since he was sitting front and center at the buffet in the Blues. He had his back to me as he talked his mess to a table of three women next to him. The ladies looked to be in their fifties, and they were dressed in matching sweat-suits. Skunk was happily stuffing his face from a big plate of food in front of him.

Kendall and I slowly approached so he wouldn't see us and bolt.

"You need to stay away from the poker table, Miss Dobby," Skunk was saying. "They're robbing you over there because they know you don't know how to play. All that money you throwing away you could be putting in my pocket."

Miss Dobby, a heftier woman with a head of gray hair, rolled her eyes. "It looks like you have other thangs to be worried about. Not where my money is going." She looked in my direction.

Skunk turned his head around and saw me. He tried to get up and make a break for it, but Kendall's firm hand on his shoulder stopped that from happening. He forced him back down in his chair.

"Ah, ah! Damn, you strong!" Skunk tried to snatch away from him but got nowhere.

"Where you tryna go, Skunk?" Kendall asked.

"Nowhere," he lied. "Actually, I'm glad y'all are here. Mr. LeBlanc, I'll take my reward money now."

He held his hand out to me, and I looked at it like it was the filthiest thing I'd ever seen.

"I'm still waiting for your words to ring true. I need proof," I told him. "You won't be getting a dime until I have it."

"I told you the truth about what I saw. Of course they gon' deny it! What more do you want from me?"

"Take a ride to see good ole Floyd with me," I told him.

He started sweating. "Floyd? Crazy-ass Floyd. Ah, nah. I can't —"

"You will." Kendall yanked Skunk up by the arm. "Let's go."

"Can y'all at least pack my food to go?" Skunk asked as he was being dragged away.

I walked behind them through the restaurant and lobby. He better have enjoyed that plate, because if it turned out that he'd been lying about everything, it would be his last meal. The only reason I still felt his story had some truth to it was the detail. The body rolled in tarp being snuck out the back and hoisted into Floyd's truck? Not even Skunk would be sick enough to come up with such an elaborate story like that unless he had actually seen something.

Kendall shoved him into the back of my Rolls Royce and shut the door. I got in, and we drove off without looking back.

Floyd was rough around the edges, but he still liked to indulge in the finer things. Truman's Country Club was one of the most elite country clubs in New Orleans. Not just anybody could have a membership, and unless some major blackmailing was being done, it wasn't a place you could buy your way into, especially being a Black man. Getting into Truman's was like getting into a secret society, and luckily, I had a membership. I knew firsthand that Floyd golfed every Sunday morning until noon.

"Now, when we get there, you better say everything you told me," I said. My eyes were on the road, but Skunk knew I was talking to him.

"As long as you have your gun drawn and ready to protect me at all costs. I've seen Floyd strangle a man bigger than him with his bare hand. No plural! One hand! That motherfucka is a monster. You might have the Crescent Boys behind you, Jean, but one on one, I'm putting my money on Floyd."

"There are only a few people that I'd protect at all costs, and you ain't one of them," I said. "But if you really want this money, you should be ready to shout the truth from the mountaintops."

"I thought you would do the legwork and I was just supposed to provide the information!"

"You won't need to worry too much about Floyd. If what you say is true, he'll be dead before nightfall." I came up on a stop sign and slowed to a stop. I glanced in the rearview at Skunk, who was acting jittery.

He looked out the window and then up at me. "I don't know. I don't know if I can take that risk!" Skunk shouted just before he opened his car door and his crazy ass jumped out.

"Shit! You ain't lock the doors?" Kendall asked in a frenzy.

"Shut up and get him!"

Instinct and a little anger took over as we hopped out of the car with our guns drawn.

I was so mad and zeroed in on Skunk's running body that I didn't care about the people around. We raised our guns and let off a few shots, but he was a crafty son of a bitch. He weaved in and out of the crowd. I finally realized how many people were out in the French Quarter and stopped firing. Kendall saw me and did the same.

"Let's go before someone calls the sheriff," I said, and we jumped back into the car.

I sped off from the scene, looking in my rearview to make sure there were no flashing lights behind us.

"Where to now?" Kendall asked.

"Same destination. I don't need Skunk to question Floyd, and right now, I'm prepared to do something more than just a little questioning."

"Snatch and grab?" Kendall asked with a slight smirk on his face.

I nodded. "Snatch and grab. You know the best way to get answers out of a motherfucka is through a little torture. Call a few more of the boys and have them meet us there. I have a feeling that Floyd might not come quietly."

Chapter 39
Big Shirley

Just as concerning as Marquis not answering my calls was Floyd also going MIA. I sat on the edge of my desk, calling him back-to-back like a madwoman. He hadn't picked up or shot me a text.

When I heard the answering machine for the fifth time, I shouted into the phone. "Dammit, Floyd! Call me back!"

I tossed the phone onto my desk, then went to pour myself a glass of brandy.

"Got one of those for me?" Nee Nee asked. I had almost forgotten she was in the room with me. I poured another one and handed it to her. While she sipped hers, I downed mine in one gulp.

"I take it those two gentlemen that were here a little while ago are the reason Marquis came to New York."

"Yup," I said with a nod, pouring myself another drink. "The one who did all the talking is Jean LeBlanc. He's the local kingpin and the leader of the Crescent Boys."

"The Crescent Boys?"

"The most dangerous street gang in New Orleans. Jean's brother committed suicide in the Blues last week."

"And you don't think Jean will believe that it was a suicide?"

"To be honest with you, Nee Nee, at this point, it doesn't matter what he believes." I took another gulp of my drink. "I'm too far into my lie to change my story now."

"The more you lie, the worse it gets."

She was right, but that didn't mean those were the words I wanted to hear. I rolled my eyes at her and went for my phone. Marquis had one more time to not answer my phone call before all hell would certainly break loose.

Just before his voicemail picked up, my office door swung open. I was relieved and annoyed at the same time when I saw that it was Marquis rushing in with Curtis.

"Boy! Where the hell have you been? I have been blowing your goddamn phone up for an hour. Jean paid us a visit, and it wasn't a social call."

He looked at Curtis then back to me. "You're not the only person who had unexpected visitors today. Prince and Jace just rolled up on me and Curtis, asking questions about Pierre."

"Are y'all all right?" Nee Nee asked with worry in her eyes.

"We're fine, but it's a good thing Curtis was there, or things could have gotten ugly."

Nee Nee and I exchanged a concerned motherly look. I forced mine away so my son couldn't see that I was nervous. I finished my drink and set down my glass.

"Shit," I cursed.

"You think Jean knows, Momma?" Marquis asked.

"It doesn't matter if he knows. He suspects, and that's just as bad. He has somebody singing in his ear."

"How? The only people alive who know what happened are you, me, Uncle Floyd, and Monique."

"And now us," Curtis inserted.

"Yeah, but I trust all of y'all."

"So do I. But somebody saw you and Floyd put that body in his truck. Jean ain't pull that shit out of his ass." I paced back and forth as I tried to wrap my buzzing head around the day's events. Suddenly, I stopped and looked at my son. "Wait. If Prince and Jace pressed you, where the hell were Jean and Saint?"

"I don't know, but they weren't with them."

I looked around the room, and suddenly a cold sensation grasped me. There were only two people involved in the coverup who were missing from the room now. I knew Monique was downstairs in the casino.

"Oh Lord. Floyd!" I exclaimed. "Marquis?"

Marquis was halfway out the door with Curtis when he yelled, "Already on it, Momma!"

Chapter 40
Sheriff Clay

A high-pitched cry slipped through my lips, and my back arched. My orgasm was completely taking my body over, and I shivered as I felt a set of strong hands etching down my spine to my waist. I waited for the blissful feeling to pass, but it didn't. I was straddling the thickest horse ever, and just because I had climaxed didn't mean the ride was over.

"Oh my God!" I grabbed my partner's shoulders, needing to hold onto something as he continued to stroke my insides.

I tried to match his strokes, but as an alpha male, he preferred to be in control. He tossed me on the bed and got on top. Before diving back into my ocean, he stared down into my face, devouring me with his eyes right before our lips met for a sloppy kiss. Screwing a married man had never been on my to-do list, until I met Mayor Simms. There was something about his power that had intrigued me all the way to the bedroom, and now I was hooked.

As he prepared to enter me again, I raised my legs and opened them as wide as they would go, giving him full access.

"Sheriff Clay, you don't know what you do to me," he mumbled as he slid back in.

I felt the tip thumping against my G-spot with every thrust and knew he was about to take me to my favorite place again. I tried to hold onto him to brace myself, but he pinned my arms down above my head. Holding my wrists, he watched me intently. He might have been admiring me, or he might have been admiring what he was doing to me.

"Let it out," he coaxed. "Let it out. It's mine. I deserve it."

His breathy tone and the sweat beads glistening on his forehead turned me on immensely. But it wasn't until he placed his lips at my ear and I felt the warmth from his quickened breaths that I unleashed a waterpark.

"Oh my God. Oh my *God*!" I quivered helplessly underneath him.

"That's right. The mayor said cum on his dick, and you did like a good girl," he said into my ear. "Now it's my turn."

His pace quickened as he pumped in and

out of me. It didn't take long for his body to begin twitching, letting me know his climax was near. He hurried to pull out of me and jacked himself off the rest of the ride. His warm semen shot out of his manhood and found a home on my stomach. He jerked a few more times before he fell onto the bed beside me, completely worn out.

"Shit!" he said as he caught his breath. "That was good."

"It was, wasn't it?" I reached for the warm wash rag I'd placed on the nightstand beside the bed. It wasn't warm anymore, but I still used it to wipe the mess off my stomach.

When I was done, I rolled back over to the mayor, hoping to get some cuddles, but he was already getting out of bed. I tried to hide the look of disappointment on my face as I watched him getting dressed. It didn't work. Mayor Simms took one look at me and sighed.

"Not this again," he groaned.

"You don't have to just fuck me and leave all the time," I said.

He gave a small laugh. "Well, then what exactly do you expect me to do? Cuddle?" he asked, and the question cut me. "I mean, look at where we are." He waved his hand around the nice hotel room he'd gotten for us that afternoon.

I looked at the disheveled sheets and my work uniform on the ground beside the bed. I'd momentarily gotten lost in the fantasy, but reality was setting in. He was the mayor; I was the sheriff. We were having an affair, and there was nothing romantic about that.

"I need to get back to the office," he said, buttoning up his shirt. "Did you take care of that body found after Pierre LeBlanc's funeral like I asked?"

"Yes. You know he was murdered, right? The man had a stab wound to the back."

"Well, we don't need any kind of bad press right now, so you make sure you do what you have to do so that bit of information doesn't get out. Say he passed out due to all the excitement. Heart attack maybe."

"I know how to do my job, Ronald," I snapped.

He whipped his head in my direction. Just a moment before, he'd been looking at me with care in his eyes. Now when he stared at me, they were cold. He approached the bed, and I sat up and scooted back into the headboard.

"What have I told you about using my first name?"

"I–I'm sorry, Mayor Simms." I stuttered

as I corrected myself, feeling slightly embarrassed.

No matter how good he made me feel momentarily, it was always that. Just for the moment. He never had an issue putting me back in my place. He stared at me for another brief moment, and I didn't know what he was going to do; however, the intense way he was leering down at me made my body naturally brace itself. He'd never hit me before, but he was a powerful man, and I didn't want to be on his bad side. Suddenly, his lips broke into a smile. He reached out and gently rubbed my chin.

"Good girl. I left a gift for you in the nightstand." He stepped away from the bed and put on his suit jacket. With one final wave to me, he was gone, just like that.

A part of me felt almost regretful about being the new mayor's secret side piece. Sometimes I just wanted to end that part of our arrangement. But then again, the other part of me still longed for his presence. I pulled out the drawer on the nightstand and saw a single rose inside. A smile came to my face as any regret I felt faded away.

I got out of bed and took a quick shower before I got dressed in my uniform, put my tactical belt on in front of the full-length mirror, and pulled my hair into a ponytail.

On the way out, I made sure to pick up my rose. Then I grabbed some coffee from the dining area and made my way out to my police cruiser. I drove off blasting Nicki Minaj's new song loudly through my speakers. I was feeling good and refreshed, and the freshly rolled joint I pulled out of my pocket would make me feel even better.

I wasn't a conventional sheriff, and that might have had something to do with the fact that I never really wanted to be a sheriff. As a child, I wanted to be a veterinarian, but my father had different goals for me. He had all girls, and with me being the oldest, he projected his wishes for a boy onto me. I had to do everything he would have done with a son, including pursuing a career in law enforcement. I wondered just how proud he would be now if he knew what kind of sheriff I'd turned into. I laughed at the thought of the look on my old man's face if he ever saw me smoking a joint.

What was the point in having power if I didn't use it? I had told myself that I earned whatever perks came my way for giving up my own dreams for my father. The moment I got my star, I was going to run the game however I wanted to play it. Legal or not, if there was a benefit for me, I was in. I also aligned myself with those who had more power than me. The mayor landing in between my legs hadn't been part of the plan. Neither was falling for him, but for the time being, it was all working in my favor. I had more money than I could have ever dreamed of having, and the entire Gator Lake Parrish knew to stay on my good side.

I took another hit before I placed the joint in my ashtray and picked up my coffee. I had just put it to my lips when a flash of something ran right in front of my cruiser. I hurried to turn my wheel and barely avoided hitting it.

"What the fuck was that?" I shouted as I came to a screeching halt.

I looked over my shoulder and saw that the "something" was a man. Not just any man, either. It was Skunk, a fool I'd arrested more times than I'd like to count for being drunk in public or disorderly conduct. Now I was going to arrest him for making me spill my coffee all over my freshly dry-cleaned uniform.

I got out and prepared for a foot chase, but to my surprise, he ran *to* me, not away.

"Skunk, what the fuck is wrong with you?" I asked, taking in the terrified look on his face.

"Sheriff! You gotta help me! He's tryna kill me!"

"Kill you? Who?"

"Jean LeBlanc. He just shot at me. You gotta help me, Sheriff! Fuck that hundred grand."

"Hundred grand?" I was more than confused at that point. "Hold up. You telling me that Jean LeBlanc just shot at you in broad daylight?"

"I look like I was running for my health?" he asked as if I were slow to catch on. "Yes! That crazy motherfucka shot at me in a crowd of people."

"Skunk, you better not be lying to me," I warned, pointing my finger in his face. "Because that's the stupidest thing anybody could do."

"Why does everybody think I'm always lying? I just got shot at!"

"Get in the damn car," I said.

Before Skunk could take a step, Deputy Douglas's voice came through my walky talky. "Sheriff, come in. Over."

"This is Sheriff Clay," I said into the device.

"Sheriff, we've got multiple reports of gunshots fired in the vicinity of River Road. Callers say the shooter was driving a Rolls Royce."

“A Rolls Royce?” My eyes went to Skunk, who was standing there with a look that said *I told you so!*

“Yup,” Deputy Douglas said.

“Roger that. I want all available cars to converge to River Road. Find me that Rolls Royce.”

I turned to Skunk. “Do you know where he is?”

“If he ain’t looking for me, he’s at Truman’s looking for Big Shirley’s brother Floyd.”

“All right. Once again, get in the damn car!”

I didn’t know what on earth would possess Jean LeBlanc to do something so stupid, but it looked like it was time to catch me a big fish.

Chapter 41
Floyd

Golfing was my stress reliever, so I tried to play at least nine holes two days a week and eighteen on Sunday. The Sunday after the masquerade ball was no different. I set my phone on silent and went out to enjoy a morning on the course by myself. I needed some peace and quiet after everything we'd been dealing with lately.

The course was surprisingly quiet for a Sunday, but maybe people were still recovering from last night's festivities. I could see other golfers in the distance, but they were far enough away that it almost felt like I had the whole course to myself — until I got to the tenth hole. As I bent down to place my ball on the tee, I heard a rustling sound coming from the bushes and cattails nearby. The club swore they'd never had a gator pop out, but I always kept my pistol on my hip just in case. When the bushes started moving like something was coming at me, I whipped out my pistol and faced whatever was coming. Then I dropped my arm just as fast when I saw that it was no gator.

"Ernestine?"

I couldn't believe my eyes when she walked out and brushed a few twigs off her long, flowing dress. She had the most disappointed look on her face, although it was me who should have been wearing it. She was spying on me like a woman who didn't trust me.

"What are you doing here?" I asked.

"I woke up with the most uneasy feeling. I felt . . . I felt like I couldn't breathe. It was a feeling of death. And you were gone, but this was on my nightstand." She held up the chicken foot necklace. "Without it, you're not protected, Floyd."

"Damn. Baby, I'm sorry. I forgot I wasn't wearing it," I lied. I'd left it behind on purpose to get a break from all the shit people were giving me whenever they saw it. I couldn't tell her that, though. She would just start speaking about omens and whatnot.

"Floyd, how many times do I have to tell you that you're not protected without this? You have no idea what kind of danger surrounds you, but I can sense it."

"I hear what you're saying, baby, but I'm just out here playing some golf. Ain't nothing gonna happen to me."

She pointed at my gun. "So why are you carrying that?"

"Oh, this?" I asked sheepishly. "This is just a precaution in case a gator hops out on me."

Not wanting a long, drawn-out argument over the damn chicken foot, I took the necklace from her and put it on. Then I grabbed her and pulled her in close, planting a kiss on her lips.

"Better?" I asked.

"Yes. All I could smell before was your death. Now, that smell is gone."

I knew Ernestine called herself a seer, but truthfully, I'd never believed none of that mumbo jumbo. I'd grown up in New Orleans, and I knew plenty of people who were just as eccentric as she was. But me? I believed in what I could touch and see. Mostly, anyway. Ernestine had slowly but surely been getting to me.

"It will come back to you," she said like she really believed it. "It's of your energy. It will always belong with you. Now, I must go to work. Will I see you tonight?"

"As long as you promise to ride me like you did last night," I said with a wink.

"Come on. I'll drive you to the front."

I started toward the cart but noticed that she hadn't come with me. I turned around. She was giving me what looked to me like a sneaky smile.

"I can't go out a way I didn't enter through and risk your membership."

"Baby, stop playing and get in the cart."

I turned around again, expecting her to follow, but instead, I heard the bushes rustling. I looked over my shoulder, and Ernestine was gone. The only thing left in her wake were a couple of moving branches. I couldn't help but smile and shake my head, envisioning her hopping a fence or two with her kooky self.

Chapter 42
Jean

"Pierre, that's not how you shoot the ball. Here. Let me show you," I said to my little brother.

We were waiting after school for our father to pick us up and had decided to shoot some hoops. Although he was still in elementary school and I was in middle school, our schools were adjacent. We often played ball after school, and Pierre always tried his best to beat me at one-on-one. It hadn't happened yet. I was just too good. If my dad didn't remind me every day that one day I'd take over the family business, I might have set my sights on being a pro ball player. But I knew he wasn't going for that.

"I don't need your help," Pierre said, rushing to get the rebound of his missed shot. "You'll probably try to sabotage me."

"I don't need to sabotage you to win. I'm good regardless. But you? You have room for improvement. What kind of brother would I be if I let you be weak at ball? Now, come here."

I pointed at the spot on the outside court beside me. Reluctantly, he dragged his feet and stood next to me. I snatched the ball from his hands and pointed at the hoop.

"You keep shooting and hoping it's going to go in. That's not how you play."

"Oh, yeah? Then how I'm s'posed to shoot, big man?"

I laughed because I really was a whole head taller than him.

"Bro, you're stupid. Look, aim your shot. *Be* your shot. When you trust your shot, there ain't no hope. You know it's gonna go in. And flicking your wrist helps guide the ball. Like this." I demonstrated with my signature jumper, and as I knew it would, the ball went straight in, all net. "Now you try."

He went and got the ball, dribbling a few times before choosing where he wanted to shoot from. He bent his knees a few times as he aimed his shot. When he glanced at me, I gave him an encouraging nod, and he mimicked my shot exactly. I grinned when I heard the "swoosh" of the ball hitting all net. He gave me an excited grin.

"Now practice that a hundred more times and you might get one win to my one hundred."

"Showoff," he said as he went to grab the ball.

I heard a voice that I recognized all too well.

"Well, what do we have here?"

It was deep, almost too deep to belong to a kid, but it did. Turning around, I saw a group of about five boys making their way toward us. Most were my age, but the one who had spoken was a grade above me. His name was Jimmy "Two Times" Bennet, and he earned his nickname because all it took was for him to hit an opponent two times for a fight to be over. I never really had any problems with him or his crew, but the way he was walking over to us let me know that we might have an issue.

Pierre appeared by my side, and I held an arm out to keep him slightly behind me. I didn't know what the boys wanted, but I knew their rep. They were usually up to no good. I recognized the other boys in his crew as Taylor, Bruno, Justin, and Saint. Saint and I had a few classes together, but we weren't friends. He was the quiet type, but I got the vibe that was just what he wanted people to think.

"What's up?" I asked.

"Why two rich boys like y'all out here after school? Don't you have a butler to pick you up?" Jimmy asked, and his boys laughed.

"Why they even at our school in the first

place? Shouldn't you be in private school with the rest of the rich pussies?" Taylor chimed in.

"Nah. My dad thought it would build more character to go to school with regular pussies," I said, getting a laugh from Pierre.

It was funny, yet true. My father, Julien LeBlanc, had transferred us out of private school to public school for the new school year. He thought private school was making us soft, and he didn't want any soft sons. He chose one of the nicer public schools in our area, but it was still like a lion's den. He said it would make us strong.

"What are you laughing at, runt?" Jimmy took a step toward Pierre.

"Yo, watch out," I warned, pushing my brother farther behind me. I stepped forward fearlessly. "We ain't got no problem with you."

"Yeah, well, I got a problem with him. He missed his weekly payment. Pierre, where the fuck is my money?"

"What's he talking about?" I asked, looking at my brother's guilty face.

"Yeah, Pierre. Tell big brother what you pay me for," Jimmy said.

I focused my attention on my brother, but he didn't want to look at me.

"I–I pay for protection," he said quietly.

"Protection? What do you need protection for? I'm right next door."

"It's not for me." He finally looked up at me.

I was even more confused. If he wasn't paying for protection for himself, who was it for?

"You never wondered why your pockets ain't never been ran by my crew, or why your face ain't never hit the concrete?" Jimmy asked. "Little brother here pays me every week to stay away from you. The moment y'all came to this school, I was on his scary ass. I told him I was going to beat you up every chance I got unless he paid me fifty dollars a week. Easy money."

His group of flunkies started laughing — except for Saint, who seemed to be just quietly observing everything.

"Is that true, Pierre?" I asked without taking my eyes off of Jimmy.

"Yes," Pierre answered meekly. "I just didn't want him to hurt you."

The rollercoaster of emotions I felt at that moment made me unsure of what I wanted to do next. I was touched by Pierre's love for me. It had always been my job to look after him, but now to know that he'd do the same for me even without my knowledge made me love him even more. He had to do chores to get an allowance, so knowing that someone was extorting him for his hard-earned money sent anger through my body. It was the rage inside of me that made my decision.

"I guess I just have to show you I don't need protection. Huh, little brother?"

"Motherfucka, you saying you wanna fight me?" Jimmy growled.

"Let's make a deal. If you win, I'll double my brother's payment to you every week. If I win, you give him back all his money and leave us alone. Indefinitely."

"Jean, no!"

"Hush, Pierre," I told him and then looked back to Jimmy. "Deal?"

"Shit, that's easy money. And y'all rich, so I know you got that good insurance for when I break your jaw."

I motioned for Pierre to move so he wouldn't get in the way of the fight. I could see the fear on his face, but he stepped aside. As Jimmy and I squared up, I truly took in how much bigger he was — and I wasn't small for my age. There was no way he was supposed to be in the eight grade. Still, for my brother, I wouldn't back down.

As cocky as Jimmy was, I knew he would go for the first blow. So, when he swung, I was ready. My father had taught me that it took more energy to swing and miss than swing and hit your target. I moved out of the way of Jimmy's fist and used his lunge to my advantage to launch a powerful fist at his jaw.

Anybody else would have stumbled and

fallen, but Jimmy ate it up like a champ. We went blow for blow, and one of his hits landed in my ribs. I felt the pain, but I couldn't fall back. I countered with a three-piece combo, only landing two punches. Jimmy must have noticed that he'd hit me more than two times, because on my missed punch, he wrapped his arms around my waist and hoisted me in the air.

I heard Pierre's shouts as Jimmy threw me to the ground. The back of my head hit the concrete, and my eyesight went blurry for a moment. I knew the fight was over, and as my eyes cleared, I could see Jimmy rushing toward me, ready to stomp me. Just as I was about to cover my face with my arms, I heard a quick and sharp "snick" and saw a sharp blade at Jimmy's throat.

"Enough," Saint said from behind Jimmy, holding the knife steadily.

"Man, what are you doing?" Jimmy put his hands up nervously.

"About to slice your throat if you or anybody else makes a wrong move," Saint shot the others a warning look. "I'm tired of you, man. You're like fifteen in the eighth grade, picking on little kids. Your brain just don't work right."

"I told y'all we shouldn't let him be down with us," Bruno said, but he didn't make a move.

Saint looked at him like he was stupid. "I

only became part of your crew 'cause I been planning to rob this oversized giant." With his free hand, Saint went into Jimmy's pocket and pulled out a big stack of money. "Now, get the fuck out of here before I turn your neck into sushi. And if you try some shit tomorrow, I'ma get my uncle to shoot your house up."

Jimmy's hands were still up as he backed away slowly from the knife. When he was far enough away, he and his other friends made a break for it. When they were gone, Saint put the knife away and helped me to my feet.

"You good?" he asked.

"I think so."

"Nah, you gon' have one hell of a black eye tomorrow at school," he said with a laugh. "But I ain't never seen nobody get with Jimmy like that. Respect."

"If it weren't for you, I might be dead."

"It's a good thing I was here then. The real look after the real." He held his hand out, and I dapped him up.

He turned to Pierre and broke off a nice portion of the money. "Here, little man."

"Thanks!" Pierre excitedly took the money.

Saint broke off another portion and tried to give it to me, but I shook my head. I'd taken notice of the scraggily jeans he was wearing and the slightly too-tight shirt. "You keep it."

"I ain't no charity case. You earned it. Here."

He tried to offer me the money again, and I refused.

"The real look after the real, remember?" I said.

My father pulled up then and leaned on his horn.

"You need a ride home?" I asked Saint.

"In a Rolls Royce? Hell yeah!"

He followed Pierre and me to the car. My dad was standing outside of it, watching us with his arms crossed. I opened my mouth to ask if he would take Saint home, but the way he was looking at him made me nervous.

"Your parents know you walk around carrying a knife like that, boy?" he asked, shocking us all.

"I —" Words seemed to fail Saint as he looked up at my father.

I couldn't blame him. My dad was an intimidating man. His eyes bore down on Saint as he waited for an answer. Had he seen it all? Wanting him to know that Saint wasn't a threat, I stepped up in his defense.

"Dad, he —"

He interrupted me by placing his hand on my shoulder. To my surprise, his eyes softened.

"You boys did good. Let's get pizza."

Replaying one of my fondest moments with Pierre heightened my thirst for blood as Kendall and I made our way through Truman's golf course, looking for Floyd. I needed answers, and I needed them now.

"Over there!" Kendall said.

Sure enough, there was Floyd parking his cart at the fifteenth hole. It wasn't hard to tell it was him, because besides us, he was the only other splash of color at the golf course. I pulled my pistol out as we made our way across the greens. Floyd was going to come with us even if I had to put a bullet in his foot and drag him through the woods.

"Come on, let's get his ass," I said.

We were still a nice distance away when I heard a golf cart speeding toward us. It came to a halt in front of us, and to my unpleasant surprise, out jumped Sheriff Clay and a couple of her deputies. Seeing my gun, she drew hers.

"Have you lost your damn mind?" she shouted. "Where do you think you're going? That ain't a golf club in your hand, and it sure as hell ain't duck season."

"Louisiana is an open carry state, if I do recall. It's not illegal to possess or carry a firearm, Sheriff."

"You're absolutely right. But if you're using said firearm to do all that shooting over on River Road, we got a problem. Now, hand over the fucking gun. Don't make this any worse for yourself than it is."

"Shooting? I don't know anything about a shooting."

"Tell that to every eyewitness that saw you and your nephew here acting like it's the wild, wild West and then driving off in your custom Rolls Royce."

I clenched my jaw and glanced at Floyd, who seemed oblivious to what was happening as he stood on the putting green. I wanted him badly, but not bad enough to get a bullet in me.

"Fine." I handed the gun over to the sheriff.

"Great. Now cuff these two trigger-happy motherfuckers," Sheriff Clay said right before a deputy forcefully turned me around and locked the bracelets on my wrists.

Chapter 43
Big Shirley

Whew. The throbbing headache sneaking up on me was no joke. Too much was coming at me at once from all sides, and I was worried about everything and everybody. I'd been around the block a time or two and something about Jean's little visit to my office earlier was even more trouble than I wanted to admit. Especially since I hadn't heard a word from Marquis about Floyd, and my head and heart were thumping. I knew he wasn't going to back off anytime soon. Not unless I did what I told him I could — AKA, the impossible.

"You okay?" Nee Nee asked.

I looked over at her, sitting next to Monique on the couch, both watching me with concerned eyes. I understood why. Ever since Marquis and Curtis had left, I'd been pacing back and forth like the world was about to end.

"I could say I'm fine, but we'd all know

I'd be lying. So, I'ma just skip to the 'I'm worried as shit.' Jean ain't playing about Pierre, and if we don't figure something out soon, there's going to be more dead bodies." I rubbed my temples. "Dammit! I'm supposed to be running a business, not knee deep into some bullshit with a fucking gangster."

"We gon' find a way out of it, Shirl. We always do," Monique said, and as sincere as she sounded, that shit was easier said than done.

To my great relief, Marquis and Curtis burst through my office door with Floyd in tow. I was happy as hell to see him, but he had still earned a good cussing out.

"What the fuck, Floyd?"

"What?" Floyd looked kind of lost.

"Where the fuck were you? And why the hell didn't you answer your phone?"

"I forgot to charge it last night, And you know I play golf every Sunday. How you think they found me?" He gestured to the boys.

"Well, you scared the shit outta me. Jean came by here asking a lot of questions about his brother. *Detailed* questions. Shit I didn't really wanna talk about." I picked up my half empty glass and drained it of its contents.

"Shirl, I'm sorry," he said humbly. "I was just playing golf. I ain't mean to have you worried."

"I know, but somebody's talking," I said, looking around the room.

"We got rid of everybody who was there, except for Dice, and he ain't saying shit."

"Or so we think," I interjected. "Somebody knows something, and we have to find out who, pronto, before Jean drags their ass in here."

"Well, we might have some time to make that happen," Marquis said. We all turned toward him. He was looking down at his phone.

"Looks like Jean was arrested today," he announced, holding up the screen to show us.

"Arrested? For what?"

Marquis came closer and held the device in front of my face. On the screen was a news article that had just been published. The headline read: New Orleans Construction Tycoon Jean LeBlanc Arrested.

"Remind me to put a little something extra in the church offering plate next Sunday, 'cause this here is God sent," I declared.

"Yeah, but we can't assume they'll be able to hold him for long," Floyd added, lifting his head from his own phone. "If I know Jean, he already has a team of the best lawyers working to get him out."

"True, but at least this might keep him and those Crescent Boys distracted while we figure out a way to make Jean believe his brother left the Blues alive that night. I told him we have surveillance footage. The only thing is, we —"

"Don't have the footage." Marquis finished my sentence.

"Exactly."

I skimmed the article, which stated that Jean was arrested for discharge of a deadly weapon and the attempted murder of Sean Perkins. Attempted murder? I almost wouldn't have believed Jean could be so sloppy if his picture weren't attached to the article. He must have really been on a rampage, but why?

"Who the fuck is Sean Perkins?" I asked.

Floyd chuckled. "Seriously, you don't know?"

I shook my head. "Not a clue. Who is he?"

"Skunk, Momma," Marquis said. "Sean Perkins is Skunk's government name."

"Get the fuck outta here. Why would Jean be shooting at a nobody like Skunk?" Monique asked, and just like that, all the pieces of the puzzle came together for me.

"Because Skunk's the snitch," I replied. There was no need to explain my theory, because looking at the expressions on everyone else's faces, I knew we had all reached the same conclusion.

"Yep, that motherfucker is always lurking around somewhere," Floyd growled angrily. "And with the reward money, I could see him ratting us out big time."

He glanced over at me, and his eyes told me all I needed to hear. Floyd hated Skunk and had been trying to get me to ban him for years, but I just wouldn't. I honestly felt sorry for the man. I should have just listened to my brother.

"Well, I know one thing, Momma," Marquis began, looking me square in the eye. "We need to find Skunk before Jean gets bail."

I snapped, "Then what the hell are y'all standing around here for? Find his ass!"

On that note, Floyd, Curtis, and Marquis quickly marched out of the room to locate Skunk's snitch ass.

Chapter 44
Marie

Whenever I was down, shopping was one of those things that made me feel better, so after our weekly lunch date, Raven and I decided to hit some of our favorite stores. This time, retail therapy wasn't working. There I was, walking through the French Quarter, my hands full of high-end shopping bags. Raven was chattering on and on about something I didn't care about because I'd long since tuned her out. All I could do was think of the man I had met at the masquerade ball. He was so easy to talk to, and that kiss he planted on me still had the hairs on the back of my neck standing at attention. No one — not even my husband — had ever kissed me so passionately.

I didn't even know the man's name. Before things could get too heated, I heard Kendall calling my name in the distance, and suddenly, I remembered I was somebody's wife. I'd left him standing by the river alone. Now he occupied my mind, and just the memory of a kiss had me hot. That morning, I'd given myself more than one orgasm, imagining what could have happened if I hadn't been called away. I knew I should have felt guilty, and part of me did. I was a married woman who'd made vows. But I also felt intrigue and . . . longing. I tried to rationalize my thoughts. Maybe I was just projecting. Maybe I didn't want the mystery man, and what I truly wanted was for Jean to sweep me off my feet like he had in the beginning. Yes, that had to be it, I hoped.

"Uh, hello? Earth to Marie." Raven waved her hand in front of my face. "Have you heard a thing I said?"

"Oh, ummm. Yeah," I lied. "You were talking about um . . ." I smiled sheepishly.

Raven stopped walking. She took off her oversized sunglasses and gave me a long stare. I hated when she looked at me like that. It was her "search and find" look that she gave me when she knew something was off. It meant she wouldn't leave me alone until I fessed up.

"What?" I asked.

"Girl, what is going on in that head of yours today? After a day of shopping on Jean's dime, I would think you'd be floating. I know I am."

"I just have a lot on my mind, that's all."

"Spill the tea then! Did something happen at the ball?" She stopped and stared. "Dammit, I knew I should have gone."

"Nothing happened at the ball," I said defensively as we started walking again. She was my sister, but I wasn't ready to share what had happened. Not everything, anyway. "Jean just left without me."

"He left you?"

"Girl, left." My voice was full of attitude. "Like an old pair of shoes."

"Damn, where the hell did he go?"

"I don't know, but when I got home, he was there already. Taking a shower like he was washing some bitch off or something," I said. I couldn't help but think there was another woman. There had to be. Something was off; I could feel it. How long had he been seeing her? How would he feel if I strayed?

Her eyebrows shot up. "There's a lot of reasons he could have been taking a shower, girl. You can't think —"

"That he's cheating on me?" I sighed. "Why go home and shower instead of coming to pick up your wife? He's hiding something, Raven. I can feel it. Plus, we haven't had sex in weeks."

"I haven't had sex in years," Raven said, laughing. "Isn't that why you bought the Rose Toy?"

"Raven, this is serious," I said with a pout. "Men don't go weeks without sex. Plus, you know he owns that fucking strip club now."

"This might not be what you want to hear, but you know I keep it real. Jean *is* a rich man, and we all know rich men do some cheating. But then again, you've said it yourself. His businesses will always be his mistresses."

"No, this is something else. He's being way too sneaky and secretive. I can usually read him like a book, but not lately."

"Well, I know the perfect place to find out some answers." Raven stopped walking in front of a store with a flashing neon sign in the window that advertised psychic readings.

"Hell no! You know I don't dabble in that crazy shit," I told her.

"Well, I do, *and* they're having a full moon sale on crystals? I need some rose quartz because I need a man. Come on! Let's go in."

She dragged me and my bags inside. Although it was well lit, there was a dark ambiance to the store. No, not dark. Heavy, like there was some kind of energy coursing through the place. There were crystals for sale on the shelves, and tapestries with different mystical symbols decorating the walls. The soft New Age music playing in the background was actually kind of pleasant. We passed a doorway with beads hanging down, and I almost didn't notice the beautiful woman standing there. I jumped when she greeted us.

"Welcome. I am Ernestine. Welcome to my shop." Her hair was in long braids with beads, and she wore a flowy red dress with abstract designs all over it.

"Hi. I'm Raven, and this is my sister Marie." Raven stepped forward.

"Pleasantries. Can I help you ladies find anything in particular?" Her eyes rested on me, and there was a knowing twinkle in them. "Or perhaps I can interest you in a reading?"

"N—"

Raven didn't even let me get the whole word out before she interrupted. "We would love that."

Ernestine smiled. "Follow me."

She walked away from us, and I shot Raven daggers with my eyes. "Girl, what are you doing?"

"Baby, live a little!" She shrugged her shoulders then followed behind Ernestine.

I hesitated to go after them. The woman could be an axe murderer for all we knew, and we were walking right into her dungeon. But when I didn't hear Raven scream for help after a few moments, I went through the beaded entry.

Ernestine's tarot room looked exactly how I might have imagined. It was dimly lit by candles, and the flames flickered off the walls. In the center of the room sat a very low table with soft-looking meditation pillows on either side. Ernestine had already taken her seat on one side and motioned for us to sit on the other.

She held out her hand. "Readings are fifty dollars apiece," she told us.

"Fifty dollars? Just to make up some stuff? This is a scam." The words slipped out of my mouth.

Ernestine cut her eyes at me. "Knowledge and understanding isn't cheap, my child. Neither is truth."

The way her eyes bore into me made me feel like I was shrinking. I had clearly offended her with my words, and I regretted saying anything at all. Beside me, Raven reached into her purse and pulled out some bills.

"I'll pay for it. Here." She handed Ernestine the money.

She counted the money and put it in a small billfold beside her before grabbing her tarot deck. As she shuffled the cards, she closed her eyes and mumbled some words I couldn't make out. After a moment, she opened them and looked at Raven.

"I will do your reading first," she said.

Ernestine shuffled some more before she laid out three cards. "I read them in the order they came. The Tower, The Chariot, and The Wheel of Fortune."

"What do they mean?" Raven asked anxiously.

"You've had a dark past. A very dark past. One that you want to leave behind you," Ernestine said as she pointed at The Tower card. "Things haven't always been easy for you. You've had to work hard to prove yourself, and sometimes even that hasn't been enough. The roads you've been down . . . most have been terrible."

Raven shook her head. "You have no idea."

Ernestine pointed at The Chariot. "But one was the right road. You've recently made a move for yourself that is going to shift your entire life." She pointed at the Wheel of Fortune card. "If you continue down this path, it will be filled with abundance. But you must free yourself of the anchor holding you down. If you don't, you'll lose everything. And this time, you won't be able to get it back."

She stopped talking, and the two of them connected eyes. Finally, Raven nodded.

"You know who the anchor is, don't you?"

"Yes," my sister said, sounding a little sad. "My daughter's father."

Raven reached into her purse, and I was surprised when she pulled out a twenty-dollar bill to tip her, as if the hundred dollars she'd just given her wasn't enough. Ernestine graciously took the money and put it with the other bills.

"You believe that shit?" I asked Raven, and Ernestine's chuckle vibrated off the walls.

"There's always a skeptic in every group. Let's see what the cards say about you, shall we?" she picked up the three cards and put them back into the deck.

I watched her hands skillfully shuffle the cards as she mumbled some more words. She might have been putting a spell on us for all we knew. Every fiber of my being was telling me to get up and leave, but morbid curiosity made me stay planted on the pillow. Ernestine finally stopped shuffling and laid three cards out: Ten of Pentacles, Death, and Ace of Cups.

"Interesting," she said.

"What?" Raven asked, her eyes glued to the Death card.

"I see love."

"I'm sure you do. You saw my wedding ring as soon as we stepped foot through the door."

"A wedding ring doesn't always symbolize love," Ernestine told me with a smirk. "You've been with your partner for a long time, but that love has been fading. And then there's this."

She pointed to the Death card, and I got chills, although Raven's loud gasp might have had something to do with it.

"Death?" she asked. "Don't tell me my girl's gonna die."

"Death does not always mean the end of life. It can signify the end of patterns, or . . . the end of a relationship," Ernestine said.

"Mmm. Girl, you said he was cheating," Raven said.

"You are at a crossroads," Ernestine continued. "If not, you will be coming to it soon."

"A crossroads?" I asked.

She nodded, pointing at the Ace of Cups. "There is another man who will love you like no other. I can't see his face. He's . . . masked. You know this masked man, yes?"

I couldn't help but intake a sharp breath. She couldn't be talking about the man from the ball, could she? I hadn't even told Raven about that.

"No." I shook my head.

"You can choose to play the game for a time, but sooner or later, it all will be exposed. And *you* will be exposed. Then, you'll have to make a choice. But no matter what, the Death card will come into play."

Her voice seemed to echo in my head as the meaning of her words settled. My chills were so bad I felt like I had a fever. I jumped up from the pillow and grabbed all my bags. "No! This is stupid!" I said forcefully. "Raven, I told you I didn't want to do this. I'm leaving." I stormed out of the tarot room, ignoring my sister shouting for me to come back.

CHAPTER 45
GABRIEL

The room smelled heavily of cigarettes, the drinks were flowing, and the R&B piped into the room through several speakers made me want to grab a lady nearby and take her to the dance floor. However, in a brothel, you had to pay for that too. I couldn't believe I'd let my friends talk me into going to a place like that. I'd always been kind of a late bloomer. In fact, some might call me a nerd. As an 18-year-old college kid in the South, I'd been to my share of bars and even a couple of strip clubs, but Big Sam's was unlike anyplace I'd ever been. The atmosphere was somehow both relaxed and jumping, with dozens of super-friendly, fine-ass women walking around half naked, flirting with the clientele.

I was sitting off to the side with my best friend, Earl, watching our other friends try to mack with a few of the girls. I sat back, enjoying the show but not planning to indulge.

"Man, why you over there looking all blue in the face? It's your birthday!" Earl said.

"Me? Blue in the face?" I asked.

"Yeah, you. All these fine women walking around us, you should be jumping for joy. Especially after midterms. That shit was rough!"

"So, this is what you do when you had a hard week of class? Come up here and buy some pussy?" I joked.

He laughed. "Motherfucka, fuck you! Ain't nothing like getting straight to the point without any strings attached. The best thing about these women is that they know the deal. They don't even expect you to call them. We ain't nothing but a wallet to them."

"And that doesn't make you feel a way?"

"Yeah, happy! I got enough on my plate as it is. I don't need a woman chasing me down on top of it."

"I don't know, man. Sex is supposed to be something that's cherished."

"You're talking like a virgin right now, Gabe." Earl shook his head. "Time to pop that cherry."

At that moment, a sexy woman with the lightest skin I'd ever seen on a Black woman approached the table. She had some meat on her bones, but I preferred my women thick. A homegrown woman, but still, she was beautiful. She walked in a seductive way and rubbed her hands down her bustier. Each step she took lined up with the music, and she had our attention. She went right to Earl and sat on his lap. Placing her lips by his ear, she whispered something that I couldn't hear, but from the way his face lit up, I knew it must have been something good.

"Hell yeah, let's go!" he said excitedly and threw back the rest of his drink. He stood up and looked at me. "I'll be back. Do me a favor and do something other than keep that seat warm."

And just like that, he let the woman take him away to one of the private rooms. He hadn't even gotten her name or anything. All I could hope was that he was smart enough to use protection.

Now completely alone, I swished the last of my bourbon around the bottom of my glass. I figured after that, I could just go out and wait in the car until my friends were done getting their rocks off. Who was I kidding? That was no kind of place for a small-city boy like me. I drank the last of the liquor and let out a hiss once it hit my chest.

"Why is someone as handsome as you sitting over here by yourself?" someone with a soft voice asked from behind. Then I felt a hand on my shoulder.

"Listen, my friends over there are who you're

looking for. This isn't really my thing. I —" When I turned around and saw the finest woman I'd ever seen in my life, I lost the ability to speak.

She was voluptuous, just how I liked, and had the face of a goddess. The sexy corset she wore showed off her assets, which were spilling over the top of the bustline. Her hair flowed freely around her face as she batted her long eyelashes at me.

"If this ain't your thing, baby, why are you here?" she asked.

"I . . . I don't know."

"Then I'll tell you why. You came here to see me. Come on and dance with me, baby. Let Big Shirley show you a good time."

She held her hand out to me. I didn't know if the liquor had me in a trance or if it was her rotund backside, but either way, I placed my hand in hers and got up from the table. She led me to the floor for a slow dance. I tried to be respectful, but she pulled me in close, placing my hands on that extra-large ass and pushing my head down on those DDD titties. We danced for a good half hour, and I thought I'd died and gone to heaven.

When we finally stopped dancing, she took my hand and led me through the crowd to a back hallway.

"Where are we going?" I asked.

"To my room." She looked back at me with a wink. "Something tells me you need some special loving. This way."

We reached a room toward the end of the hallway, and she opened the door. When I peered inside, I saw a red canopy bed with the most comfortable-looking oversized pillows. Next to the bed was a dresser with all sorts of whips, handcuffs, and condoms on top of it. She shut the door behind us as soon as we stepped inside.

"So, what now?" I asked.

"Take those off." She pointed at my pants.

I hesitated at first. I hadn't been naked in front of a woman since I was a toddler getting a diaper change.

"Don't worry, baby. I'll be gentle," she coaxed.

Slowly, I undid my belt buckle and unfastened my pants. I let them drop to the floor, then I stepped out of them and sat on the bed in my underwear. She sat next to me and began gently caressing my leg.

"Now, tell me. What occasion done brought you here to see Big Shirley?" she asked.

"It's my birthday. My twentieth birthday."

"Your birthday, huh?" She gave me a seductive grin. "Well, we're gonna have to do something special for you. What's your fantasy?"

"I . . . I don't know."

"You don't know your fantasy?"

"No. I've never done this before."

"We get a lot of first timers in here, but trust me when I say I'll be worth every penny, baby."

"No." I shook my head. "That's not what I meant. I'm a virgin."

"A what?" Her shocked expression embarrassed me a little.

"A virgin."

"Well, I'll be damned." An excited smile spread across her face. "Well, baby, you might have walked into this room that way, but when you walk out, you're gonna be a man. I promise you're gonna remember this for the rest of your life. Lay back."

I did as I was told, and it felt like paradise when she straddled me. Her softness on top of my body instantly gave me a hard-on. She didn't even have to do anything. I didn't think I could get any harder until she kissed me, and then I was damn near bursting out of my boxers. Sensing that I was ready, she reached down and pulled my manhood out, gently stroking it.

"Shit. That feels good," I whispered.

"Just a second," she said, getting up momentarily to grab a condom from the dresser. "You ready for me, baby?"

I nodded enthusiastically. She ripped open the condom and slid it down my throbbing third leg, then climbed on top and straddled me again. Pulling out her succulent breasts, she put them in my face and let me suckle them like a newborn baby while my hands caressed her incredible backside. After a while, I let my hands explore some more, moving her underwear to the side. Her not being completely naked added a filthier feel to what we were about to do, and it turned me on. Once I slid into her for the first time, I swear there were fireworks. There is no other feeling that can compare to the sensation of friction of wetness combined with her weight on top of me.

The way she rode me wasn't the way a woman getting paid for it would, in my opinion. She kissed all over me and gently massaged my head, all the while whispering sweet nothings to me, coaching me through the experience. My only regret *was* that it was my first time, and I wasn't able to last but five minutes. Still, it was the most magnificent five minutes of my life. I couldn't stop looking at her through the whole encounter, not even when I felt myself about to explode.

"Big Shirley," I moaned as I shot my load inside of her, filling up the condom.

"That's my name, honey," she said breathlessly and kissed me one more time.

She stayed on top of me for a moment, looking me deep in my eyes with her own beautiful brown ones. Mustering up the energy I had left, I reached my hand up and caressed her cheek.

"I . . . I think I love you," I blurted.

"Honey, if I had a hundred dollars for every time someone said that to me, I'd finally have enough to leave this place."

She'd said it matter-of-factly, but I heard the sadness in her undertone. She got off me and went to her closet for a robe. After she put it on, she slid off her old lace panties and went into her dresser for another pair. I lay there motionless, partly because I was still regaining my wits, and partly because I was truly mesmerized.

"If you want to leave, why don't you just leave?" I asked.

"It ain't that simple," she said. "I need the money. Who else is gonna take care of little ole me? You?"

"I would," I answered without hesitation. My feelings were doing all the talking. I'd never had such a warm sensation come over me, and I attributed that to her. I felt an overwhelming urge to help her in any way I could. "I really think I love you."

"Then that just means I'll see you again

soon," she said, opening the door. "I need to get cleaned up. You can leave my money on the dresser. That'll be fifty dollars, and please don't try to run off without paying. I'd hate to have to get Sam to cut you."

I snapped out of my fantasy, staring out the window of my limo at the Midnight Blues casino that was now lit up. I'd been there about two hours, and my wait was finally over when I saw Big Shirely exit the building and sashay over to her car. Even after all these years, with me being a wealthy businessman instead of a nerdy teenager, she still did something to me. I snatched my briefcase and opened the limo door.

"Big Shirley!" I shouted as I ran across the parking lot.

"Do I need to call security? What do you want?"

I could see immediately that she wasn't happy to see me, but I was about to change all that. I'd learned a long time ago that sincerity was the best way to melt the coldest of hearts.

"First, I wanted to apologize for my actions earlier. I realized offering you two hundred thousand dollars was insulting. I should have known better."

I could see her face soften. "Well, thank you, Gabriel. I appreciate that."

"No problem. I embarrassed myself and you. I'm truly sorry." I offered her my hand, and she took it.

"Water under the bridge," she replied, letting go of my hand.

"I'd like to make it up to you if I can."

"That won't be necessary." She turned toward her car like she was done with this conversation.

"I should have offered you half a million," I said, and her neck snapped back my way.

"Are you trying to say you would have paid me half a million dollars?" She stared at me with skepticism.

"Yes, and that offer still stands. If you're interested?" I lifted my briefcase and showed Shirley the half million dollars in cash I was carrying.

She glanced at me, then the money, shaking her head in utter disbelief. "A half a million dollars for some ass?"

"Yup."

"Who does that?" Her eyes were still on the money.

"A man who really wants that ass," I replied, closing the briefcase and extending it to her with a smile. Everyone had their price, and it looked like half a million was hers. I say looked like, because instead of taking the money like I'd hoped, she gave me a hard, heavy-handed slap in the face before she entered her car and screeched away.

Chapter 46
Prince

Let me start off by saying that I ain't never been a thirsty dude, but Cinderella — I mean Lauryn — had been on my mind since I left the ball. It took everything in me to hold out the day and a half I did from calling her and asking her out on a date. Now, there I was, standing outside of Dinero, a nightclub that everyone who was anyone attended, waiting for her to arrive.

I didn't know why I was so nervous, except that she was already fifteen minutes late. I hoped she wasn't going to flake on me, though she didn't give me that kind of vibe. She seemed like the type that would let it be known if she didn't want to do something. Right before I started doubting my assumptions, I saw her weaving through the growing crowd.

"Damn," I said under my breath. She was definitely dressed for the club, and her curves were on full display in a cropped tee and a jean skirt that hugged her hips and bottom. She had more than a few admirers as she passed by, but them suckers were sad to see that I was the one she was floating to.

"Wow, you look great," I told her.

She smiled and brushed a hair out of her face. "You don't look too bad yourself, Prince Charming. Sorry I'm late. My Uber took forever."

"You shoulda just let me pick you up. You wouldn't have had to worry about that."

"My auntie ain't going for nobody she don't know pulling up to her house," she said, sucking air through her teeth. "That lady don't play."

I laughed. "She sounds like how my momma used to be. Come on." I extended my hand to lead her to the front door.

"The line is so long. You sure we're gonna be able to get in?" she asked.

I flashed my pearly whites. "We don't do lines 'round these parts."

"Well, all right then." She took my hand.

We walked to the front of the line, and the bouncer nodded at me. His name was Montclair, and he was also a member of the Crescent Boys. It paid to have friends in all sorts of places. I nodded back and walked through with my date.

Dinero had a full house that night. It was

dimly lit inside, with strobe lights bouncing off the dance floor. There was not one open seat at the wraparound bar, and people stood three deep trying to get the bartenders' attention. The dance floor was jammed, too, with people grinding up on each other to the bumping music.

I'd pulled out all the stops for Lauryn. Not to impress her — well not *just* to impress her — but to ensure we had a comfortable night. I led her to the section I'd booked just for us near the dance floor and sat down beside her. Everything was already set up for us to have a great night. I grabbed a bottle of 1942 off the table and poured us a couple of shots.

"Good taste," she said, then took her shot.

"Only the best for the best," I replied.

We cheered and threw the shots back.

"This might sound like a line, but I been thinking about you since I met you. I ain't worried about nobody else. And I hope this date goes smoothly so I don't gotta be."

I could tell by the blush on Lauryn's face that my words weren't lost in translation. We looked deeply into each other's eyes for a moment before she set down her shot glass. She took mine from my hand and placed it next to hers.

"Dance with me." She grabbed my hand

and pulled me to my feet. I didn't protest when she took me to the dance floor. It was crowded, but we made a spot just for us.

The moment Lauryn began moving her body, I was in a trance. She knew what she was doing, and fortunately, I did too. Anything she threw, I caught. We were in sync completely. Our bodies intertwined together as one, and our hands explored each other's bodies through our clothing.

I didn't know how many songs had passed. I just knew she had me breathless and hot.

When her back was turned to me, I wrapped my arms around her waist and pulled her close. She looked up at me over her shoulder and grinned. It was a new feeling, but it felt . . . normal. Like she was meant to be in my arms.

"I think I need to sit down," she said to me.

We went back to the section, and this time, we sat much closer to each other. I poured us another shot, and we threw them back. I was about to dive into her mind to get to know her better when I felt a presence hovering over me.

I looked up and saw Dante, a dude from a rival gang called Riverside Clique. He wasn't alone. On either side of him were his cousins Jaheim and Jasir, standing way too close to me. If I didn't already know they were up to no good, the looks on their faces were a dead giveaway.

"The fuck you doing in here?" Dante asked.

When I glanced at Lauryn, I saw worry written all over her face. That alone was enough to set me off. It was our first date, and I didn't want her to think she wouldn't be safe with me.

I stood to my feet and squared up with Dante. "I'm just here to have a good time. You got a problem with that?"

"Yeah. You being in the same space as me is a problem." Dante looked me up and down like I was trash. "You real bold to step out by yourself with Jean locked up."

"I don't need Jean or nobody else to handle motherfuckas like you."

Dante laughed. "Oh, this bitch s'posed to protect you?"

"Who you calling a bitch?" Lauryn snapped. She looked like she was about to step to him.

"You, bitch. Now, you and your punk-ass pretty boy need to get the fuck outta here before I bend your ass over a chair and fuck you in the ass."

She made a move to get at him, but I put my arm out and told her to chill. I looked back at her over my shoulder and winked. "I got this."

I wasn't a hothead like my brother Saint, but we did come from the same woman, and neither one of us would tolerate disrespect of our women. Three-on-one seemed like impossible odds, but I liked a challenge. I just wished Lauryn wasn't there.

Before Dante could come out his mouth with any more stupid shit, I headbutted him so hard he stumbled back. It was so unexpected that Jaheim and Jasir had delayed reactions, which was perfect for my fists. I landed earth-shattering punches to both of their jaws, knocking Jaheim out on impact. Jasir tried to stay on me, but he was no match. I dodged his uncalculated punches and crashed into his body with mine. The last two-piece I gave him sent him falling to the ground beside his brother and debilitated him.

Dante finally regained his wits and pulled his gun, but it was too bad mine was already pointed at his head. He froze, but I didn't.

"You callin' my girl a bitch? Who's the bitch now?" I stepped forward and shoved the end of my pistol in his mouth, breaking a couple teeth in process. I was two seconds away from blowing his brains out and ending any future threat when I heard Lauryn calling my name.

"Prince." She came up beside me, aiming a gun at the two brothers. "It's not worth it."

I hadn't noticed before now that the music had stopped, and everyone was watching the scene unfold. Ending Dante then and there would have been a foolish thing to do. Way too many witnesses.

"Let's get out of here," Lauryn said.

"Today's your lucky day, but this ain't over," I warned Dante then snatched my gun out of his mouth. To ensure our safe exit, Lauryn whacked the brothers across their heads with the butt of her pistol, knocking them back to the floor. Damn, the girl was a straight-up G!

We rushed out of the club and didn't slow down until we were down the street where I'd parked. The air hitting my face and Lauryn's tight grip on my arm brought me all the way back to reality. I was ashamed. That wasn't how I wanted our first date to go, and I didn't want her to look at me as some sort of thug.

I hit the unlock button on my truck and opened the passenger door for her to get in.

"My bad," I said when I was behind the wheel. "I ain't want you to see all that. I can drop you off anywhere you wanna go."

"The date's over already?" She put away her gun, looking disappointed.

"You . . . you still wanna kick it with me? Even after all that?"

"You're not the only person who was disrespected, Prince. Where I come from, kicking ass and guns are just another day in the life. I just try not to make a habit out of it."

Damn, I think I found the perfect woman.

"Me either."

"Good, then what's next?"

I glanced over at her, and she was smiling. I knew right then what I wanted to happen next.

"How about . . . an after party at my house?"

I wanted to kick myself when I saw her body language change. *Prince, you idiot, you're moving too fast. She ain't from NOLA. You just met this girl.*

"My bad, Cinderella. With everything that happened and all this adrenaline pumping through me, I'm sure I'm moving too fast."

"A little, but even if you weren't, there's something you should know about me. Something that might change your mind about spending time with me."

"What's that?"

"I'm a . . ." She paused as if she didn't

know if she should continue.

"You're what?"

"I'm a virgin, Prince."

The car got quiet. I didn't even know how to take it. I searched her face for a lie, but I could tell by her body language that she was telling the truth. Surprising even me, a laugh welled up in my stomach, and I let it out.

She looked up from her hands and gave me the dirtiest look.

What you trying to do? Blow it? You like this girl!

"Don't go," I said, stopping her when she moved to get out of the truck. "I'm sorry."

"You think it's funny that I'm a virgin?" She glared at me.

"Nah, not at all, I was just surprised, that's all. Not many virgins running around New Orleans is all."

"I'm too old to be lying about something like that."

"I can imagine, especially with all the pressures in the world for women to have sex. To not give it up is admirable," I said with sincerity, and her face softened a little. "Truth is, that's dope."

"You playing with me?"

"Not at all. So, you waiting on marriage or something? This a religious thing?"

She looked away from me. “No, I just always kind of figured that when the right person came along, I’d know.”

Her sudden shyness added to her allure. I felt an unwavering desire to protect her. I couldn’t explain it, but I felt like there was a reason we had met. Divine intervention.

“So . . . is this the last time I’ll see you?” She looked back down at her hands.

I leaned over the armrest and lifted her chin gently with my finger, forcing her to look me in my eyes. “Nah, for the time being, you’re stuck with me, Cinderella.”

Our lips meeting in that moment felt inevitable. The kiss we shared was more than passionate; it was a promise. Of what? I didn’t know. What I did know was that I loved the feeling of our tongues dancing the same way our bodies had on the dance floor.

Chapter 47
Marie

I came home to an empty house and a husband who wouldn't answer my calls. My conscience was shut away somewhere deep inside of my head as I tried to sort out the many thoughts plaguing me. Him. I couldn't stop thinking about him. Not Jean, but the man from the ball. It had only gotten worse after my reading. I couldn't shake the longing to know more about him. I wanted to be with him again so badly that it was almost a physical ache.

Sitting down on the bed, I opened my nightstand and retrieved the mystery man's mask that I had held onto when I rushed away. Flashes of the kiss we shared ran through my mind, sending a tingling between my legs. I would have been happy to stay in the memory, but that psychic kook and her tarot cards warning of a crossroads invaded my fantasy.

"I don't even know that man. There's no

damn crossroads. There's only one road, and that's Jean," I told myself with a sigh.

However, even as I said it, I didn't believe myself. I set the mask to the side and got up. It was a split-second decision, but I wasn't going to be cooped up in the house, playing with my lady parts all night while Jean was out doing God only knows what with God only knows who. I went to my closet and picked out a pretty dress and a more comfortable pair of sandals, then left the house.

When I got in the car, I didn't have a particular destination in mind, but before I knew it, I was pulling up in front of the Blues as if I had driven solely by muscle memory. Bypassing the valet, I parked in the far back of the lot.

I looked at myself in the rearview mirror and adjusted the strap on my floral dress, then took a deep breath to try to shake my nervous jitters. "Marie, what the hell are you doing?" I asked out loud.

In the perfect story, walking the same path as I had that night would lead me to where my mystery man and I had our first encounter. And he would be there. But that was just too perfect. That was too —

I headed past the casino toward the riverbank where that unforgettable kiss had taken place. I had half a mind to abort the mission altogether and go home to my Rose Toy and my fantasies. Then memories from the night of the ball came to me in the most wonderful way. The way he looked at me and that kiss — that damn kiss. The passion and longing in it had been just what I needed.

I stopped walking suddenly when I noticed something in the near distance. A man was standing there, looking out into the water.

"Impossible," I said, so stunned that I almost couldn't catch my breath. It was him.

When I realized I had spoken out loud, my hand flew to my mouth, but it was too late. He had heard me, and he turned around. Our eyes connected, and the recognition between us was instant.

"Even without the mask, I'd know you anywhere," he said as he approached my frozen body. "You're even more beautiful without it."

He was so close that I could feel the heat coming off his body. He stared down at me, and I wanted to get lost in his dreamy green eyes forever. Nothing about him was disappointing — his tall, muscular frame, his chiseled jaw, his scent. It was even better than I had allowed myself to remember. A small part of me almost hoped he would let me down a little bit so I could snap out of it. However, being in his presence again, I felt myself just going deeper.

As we stared at each other, silent words were spoken that only we could understand. I was happy to see him; so happy that I could feel the energy vibrating up and down my body. I caught myself as the faint smile on my lips threatened to spread like wildfire.

"What's your name?" I asked. "I don't think I ever got it."

"Because you ran away from me," he reminded me with a chuckle. "My name's Curtis. You?"

I hesitated, wondering for a second if I should give him my real name. "I'm . . . Marie." My heart won out. "So, Curtis, why were you just standing there like that?"

"You might not believe me, but I was thinking about you." He shrugged. "A lot."

"I've been thinking about you too," I admitted. "Last night was —"

"Over too soon," he said. "This time's gonna be different." He grabbed my hands, and I didn't pull away.

"In what way?" I asked, letting a little flirtation enter my tone.

"This time, I'm not gonna let you go."

He pulled me into him, and I let myself

melt into his body. Our lips merged. This time, it was more than just a kiss of longing. It was one of inevitability, and I was now officially at a crossroads.

Chapter 48
Saint

I arrived in Miami around two in the afternoon and went straight to bed after checking into a motel in South Beach. I woke up to the sound of my phone's obnoxious alarm going off around 11 o'clock that night. Staring at the ceiling, I allowed my eyes to focus before I reached over and turned it off. My first instinct was to call Antoinette, but she was probably still pissed about the ass-whupping I'd put on the security guard at the Blues.

I took a deep breath and blew it out. I'd have to call her later. Right now, it was showtime. I got out of bed and took my time getting dressed. As usual, I opted for Crescent Boys colors — purple pants and a gold paisley silk shirt that I left half unbuttoned, thinking it would give my look a Miami vibe.

I heard my phone sound with a notification. It was a text from Sebastian with an address. Our meetup spot would be a nightclub about thirty minutes away from the hotel.

On my way, I responded.

I got my car from the valet and headed out.

At the club, I took notice of two ogres in suits standing outside the building. It was obvious to me they were security, and they watched me closely as I parked. I grabbed my knapsack and sauntered toward the building. One of the goons opened the door for me.

"He's expecting you. The stairs are down the hall. Top floor."

It was early for South Beach, so there weren't many people in the lavish club. Just a few people dancing and a couple others at the bar. I went in the direction security had pointed me in and climbed the stairs to the top floor. When the doors opened, I was greeted by an even uglier security guard.

"Right this way," he said when I stepped up.

He turned and began to walk away, and I followed behind him. At a door down the corridor, he stepped out of the way and took his post on the side. I raised my fist and knocked.

"Enter," Sebastian yelled through the door.

I turned the knob and stepped through into the extravagant office. It was a large space filled with grand furniture pieces and bright paintings on the walls that looked expensive. Sebastian was seated behind his desk with his feet kicked up. He took a toke from his vape and blew a stream of smoke into the air. On either side of his desk were two of the sexiest chocolate women I'd ever seen in my life, but they left no doubt that they were also some of the deadliest. Their heads were shaven bald, and they wore matching tactical outfits with guns resting on their hips. Dark sunglasses shielded their eyes so I couldn't see them, but I was sure they were trained on me.

"I was expecting your *boss.*" Sebastian looked at me mockingly.

"I don't know why," I said, stepping closer to the desk. "Only thing we promised you was the money." I held up the knapsack to show him.

Sebastian glanced at it briefly before giving a satisfied nod. Removing his feet from the desk, he reached down and picked up a black duffle bag, placing it with a thud on top of his desk.

He motioned for me to come closer. "This

is for you."

I peeked in the bag. When I saw the pure bricks, I dug my hand and counted them to make sure they were all there.

I handed over the knapsack full of cash. "And this is for you."

He grinned when he opened it and saw all the blue faces staring up at him. "Between sex, drugs, and money, money will always be my favorite," he said excitedly. "It can always buy the others and so much more."

"We done here?" I grabbed the work and was just about to turn around to leave.

Sebastian's voice stopped me. "You know, when I came to New Orleans, I thought I was gonna be among friends."

"Sometimes things don't work out the way we want them to," I answered. "If they did, Pierre would still be alive."

Sebastian scoffed. "You know I shoulda outted you to Jean that night, right? Being as it's you who was Pierre's business partner."

And there it was. The truth and biggest elephant in the room. Secretly and unbeknownst to Jean, Pierre and I had decided to go into business together. Nothing major to where Jean would notice the difference in his cash flow, but enough to put more than just a little bit of extra money in our pockets.

Well, until we decided to expand.

In the beginning, Jean operated by the motto "teamwork makes the dreamwork." I didn't have an issue with him being in charge, until I *felt* that he was in charge. The more money he made, the more Jean reminded me that I was nothing more than a hired hand — a well-paid one, but a hired hand nevertheless. Of course, he didn't come flat out and say it, but he didn't have to. We'd started off as friends . . . family, or so I thought. But the last few years, everything was strictly business. I realized I was a loyal hired hand. Nothing more, nothing less.

Everybody knows hired hands are expendable, especially once they prove not to be useful anymore. That was why I decided it was time to branch out into business on my own. With the help of Pierre, of course. As Jean's little brother, he had the name to lure the connects. I still couldn't believe he'd done something as stupid as kill himself. Now I was stuck under Jean's iron fist, and with his new connect knowing my secret.

I froze as I gave Sebastian my full attention. He looked amused, eyeing me like a lion toying with its prey before devouring it.

"Funny thing is, I've been wondering. Why didn't you?" I finally asked.

"Easy answer there, bucko." Sebastian leaned forward at his desk. "Finding out Jean is your best mate made this all a bit more interesting. Especially since he doesn't know you and his dear brother were in cahoots."

"I guess it worked out better for you this way. You get to move five times more weight than me and Pierre would have been able to push for you. More money, less problems. So, I expect our previous dealings to stay in this room," I said and cut my eyes at him in warning. "If not, you're gonna need thirty bald-headed bitches to protect you."

"No need to get all hostile!" Sebastian threw his hands up theatrically. "You should know, I'm a sucker for a good underdog story. I like people who go enterprising on their own. Who knows? Jean might not always be the boss." He winked at me.

"I wasn't trying to change shit. Sometimes a brother just needs to make a little extra."

"Saint, you aren't fooling anybody." Sebastian gave me a knowing look. "Nobody likes to be second best."

We locked eyes. I hated that he was reading me correctly. I was tired of being number two. I was tired of Jean not acknowledging my very important part in the makings of his empire. It was *my* little brother who kept the Crescent Boys in check, and he did that at my command. The reason they listened to him was because they feared *me.* Not Jean. But Jean was still my best and oldest friend. In the end, I'd rather find a peaceful resolution. Hopefully, all the power hadn't truly gone to his head because, if after all I'd done for him, he couldn't cut me a larger piece of a pie I helped bake? I might *really* have to take matters into my own hands.

"I'll be taking my leave now," I said and chucked the deuces to Sebastian.

"Nice doing business with you." He held up the knapsack and patted it happily. "Whether it's for yourself or as Jean's lapdog again, I'm sure I'll be seeing you soon."

Chapter 49
Prince

After our first date, I dropped Lauryn off at Midnight Blues around two in the morning then headed over to our clubhouse. It was an old building Jean owned and had fixed up for us Crescent Boys to hang out in. As much as I had enjoyed our date, I was also fiending to hear the latest news on Jean's arrest and to put the fellas on alert about the Riverside Clique and that clown Dante. With my brother Saint out of town and Jean locked up, I was the impromptu leader of our gang, a job I took very seriously.

There was no news about Jean, so after chopping it up with the fellas for about an hour, my man Jace and I headed out to make the rounds. It wasn't uncommon for us to be out all night, making sure Jean's businesses, legal and illegal, were safe and sound. However, no one could do that on an empty stomach, so we stopped to grab some grub at Willie's Chicken on the strip.

They stayed open late, and they had some of the best chicken wings in the city.

Jace and I were so hungry that we didn't even make it out of the parking lot with our food. We sat in my truck and dug in.

"Yo, so what we gonna do about those Riverside dudes?" Jace asked me before stuffing his face with another piece of chicken. "I say we blast 'em."

"Yeah, me too. But we gotta be smart. I was thinking about going to see Jean in jail."

"Good, 'cause, I fuck with your brother and all, but I can't even imagine how shit would be if he ran the show. That shit he did at the strip club and at the masquerade ball is crazy. I'm afraid the motherfucka would kill us all for just breathing wrong."

"Aye, as long as you don't talk about his girl, you good," I said with a laugh. "But you're right, though. I'ma go see Jean tomorrow."

"Cool. So, tell me about this new shorty who got you so open."

"Bruh." I shook my head and smiled. "I ain't never met anyone like her before. She smokes weed, carries a gun, is hella funny, and more importantly, she gets me. She might be the one."

"Whatever. You say that shit about every chick you meet."

"For real, Jace. She ain't nothing like anyone I ever met."

"What about Simone?" he asked, giving me a knowing look that annoyed the shit out of me. "She asked about you when I dropped off Jean's car at the house."

"That girl gets on my nerves. Clingy as hell and never cared to know me for real. It's all about the lifestyle for her. Good girl/bad boy type shit. If she wasn't Jean's daughter, I would have dumped her a long time ago."

"But she is Jean's daughter," he replied, giving me a pointed look. "That's the problem."

"True, but he don't know I smashed it. As long as I keep my distance, I should be good." I sighed. "Seriously, Jace, Lauryn is wifey material."

Jace's attention suddenly shot to something out the window. He leaned in to get a better look, and I saw the alarm on his face. Instinctively, my hand went to the gun on my hip, thinking something was about to pop off.

"Yo. Speaking of wifey, ain't that your brother's right there?" He pointed.

When I saw what he was looking at, a fire ignited in my belly. Sure enough, walking out of Bandos was my sister-in-law, Antoinette. At first, I thought she was alone, until I saw the man who came out the door behind her. It was Marquis Duncan, and that bitch was all over him. He had his hand on her ass as he led her back to his car with their to-go boxes. The way they were carrying on, they definitely did not know that we were watching them.

"I can't stand that ho!" I said. "She'll let anybody hit it. What the fuck is she thinking?"

"I mean, we don't know if they're fucking. They do work together, and he's her boss. He might just be giving her a ride home," Jace suggested.

"Hell nah. You see his hand on her ass just like I do. My brother got her off the pole, and old habits die hard. Let's go."

Jace waited for Marquis to pull off before following behind them at a safe distance. We drove for some minutes before they pulled into a hotel parking lot. We parked to the side, but I still had a good view of Antoinette and Marquis as they went up a flight of stairs. Their hands were all over each other's bodies, and they were devouring each other's faces before they went into a room and slammed the door behind them.

I was fuming inside. "That dog-ass bitch. Saint's gonna kill her *and* him."

"You want to call him right now?"

I thought about it. My brother was out of town handling business for Jean. It was important that he knew what was going on, but I wanted him to keep his head in the game, so he didn't mess up the money.

"Nah. He's doing stuff for Jean down in Florida. Plus, if we tell him, she's gonna lie her way out of it."

Jace looked doubtful. "If you say so. But if it was my girl, I'd wanna know."

"I have a better plan. Come on."

I got out of the truck with Jace on my tail. We went up the hotel steps and crept to the room I'd seen them enter. Listening at the door, it didn't take me long to confirm what I already knew was going down in there. She wasn't even trying to be quiet. I knew my brother would be sick to his stomach if he heard another man making his woman moan like that.

I gestured at Jace, and he knocked on the door, then stepped out of the way so they couldn't see him through the peephole.

Marquis's voice came from behind the door. "What do you want?"

"Maintenance," I said, disguising my voice.

"Come back later."

"I'm afraid I can't, sir. Uh . . . there's a

plumbing emergency coming from your room. It's flooding the first floor. I need to take a look at your pipes."

The lock clicked, and the door swung open. Marquis stood in the doorway wearing only a towel wrapped around his waist. I stepped in front of him quickly, my hand reaching for my pocket.

His arms immediately went to a defensive position. No doubt he thought I was pulling out a weapon. As much as I wanted to waste him, it wasn't a gun in my hand. It was a phone. I snapped a few pictures of him. Jace, who caught on quick, kicked the door open wide just as Antoinette was coming out of the bathroom, butt-ass naked, so I got plenty of pics of her too. There was no way Antoinette would be able to explain that shit.

Once Marquis realized what I was doing, he tried to grab for the phone, but it was too late. I had all the evidence I needed, and we were already running back to the stairs.

"Shit!" I heard him belt out behind me, but he didn't chase us.

We were laughing our asses off when we got back to my still running truck and pulled off. Soon, both Marquis and Antoinette would know the repercussions of crossing a demon.

Chapter 50
Marie

I hummed all the way home, until I got there and spotted my husband's Rolls Royce sitting in the front. Then my nerves got the best of me. There was no way I'd be able to sneak in or act like I had been home all night.

Thinking fast, I pulled out my cell phone and called my girl.

"Hello?" Raven answered the phone sleepily.

"Girl, this is an emergency. If anybody asks, I was with you last night."

"Huh?"

"Please, I'll explain later. I was out all night last night."

"Doing what?"

"I said I'll explain later. You got me?"

"Mm-hmm. We had such a good time at karaoke last night. Yo' ass got so drunk you passed out on my couch."

"You're a lifesaver."

"You can thank me by taking me to that new seafood restaurant that just opened up. *And* I want all the details about last night. You got some dick, didn't you?"

"Raven!"

"What? Why else would you be out all night?"

"Girl, go back to sleep. I'll call you later."

"You don't have to threaten me with a good time. Let me know if Jean kills you or not."

"How would I do that if I'm dead?" With a small laugh, I hung up the phone.

Before getting out of the car, I wiped the sand from my arms and prayed I'd gotten it all from my shoes. After fixing my hair, I grabbed my purse and got out, practicing my speech in my head as I walked to the front doors.

When I stepped inside, my husband was nowhere in sight.

"Jean?" I called out timidly as I walked around the first floor. I would rather seek him out than have him ambush me. I was grown, and I could own up to my bad behavior — although I'd be owning up to it with a lie. I looked everywhere, and as each room turned up empty, I felt myself growing frustrated.

"Jean!" I called out a little more aggressively as I stepped into the sitting room.

"He's not here."

The voice belonged to Simone, and I almost walked smack dab into her where she stood. She was looking at me with a distraught expression on her tear-stained face.

"What do you mean he's not here? His car is out front."

"One of the Crescent Boys dropped it off a while ago."

"Hold on. Why was a Crescent Boy driving your father's car?" I asked, trying to make sense of it. "And why are you crying?"

She ignored my questions. "Where were you? You were gone all night."

"I was out with Raven." I struggled to keep a straight face. I'd been prepared to lie to Jean, but not my daughter. "I fell asleep on her couch. I've been calling your father since last night, and he hasn't picked up one time."

"Probably because he's in jail," she said with a flat voice. "He was arrested yesterday."

"Yeah, right. He would never be so foolish."

"I just got off the phone with his lawyer. He's facing attempted murder, and his bond hearing isn't until tomorrow."

Worry, fear, and even anger battled inside me. Why wouldn't Jean call me and let me know something? And attempted murder of who? I knew the man I married and what he was capable of. If he had to go that route with anybody, the word "attempted" held no weight. He got the job done. Just that quick, my thoughts of Curtis faded, and I was back to being Mrs. LeBlanc.

"Come here, baby." I pulled Simone into my arms. "It's gonna be all right. I'll call the lawyer and we'll figure this out."

"Okay, Mom. I just don't want him in there." She broke down crying on my shoulder.

"I know, baby. I know. But don't ever forget who your daddy is," I said, rubbing her head. "He's Jean LeBlanc. He'll be home soon."

Chapter 51
Marquis

Usually when Curtis cooked, the aroma made me want to run to get a plate, but that morning, it was making me sick to my stomach. I moped into the kitchen and couldn't return my cousin's bright smile if I wanted to. It wasn't just Curtis's food, though. My world had come crashing down, and everything was making me sick to my stomach.

"Mornin', cuz. These grits are almost done," he said from where he stood over the stove.

"No, thanks." I sat down at the island, dropped my head into my hands, and rubbed my forehead. How had I gotten myself into such a messed-up situation? Why hadn't I left Antoinette alone when I had the chance? Now I'd be looking over my shoulder for the rest of my life. There was no way Saint would let something like that slide.

"I fucked up, Curt. Fucked up real bad," I began to explain.

"What the fuck happened now?" Curtis asked. "You still trippin' about that Skunk dude? I thought we had that under control."

"We do. This is something worse. Much worse."

He wiped his hands off before turning off the stove, then faced me, looking like he was braced for a catastrophe.

"A couple of Saint's boys spotted me and Antoinette at the motel."

"Damn," he muttered.

"Man, I can't believe I got caught slipping like that. I can't lie. I'm worried."

"Yeah, you fucked up all right, but is it really that bad? Ain't there some kinda innocent excuse she can come up with?"

"I wish, cuz, but they came right to our room. Told us they were maintenance, and my stupid ass was damn near naked when I answered the door. And then one of them whipped out his fuckin' phone and took pictures."

Curtis shook his head. "Shit. Ain't no innocent excuse for that. What you think is gonna happen?"

"You saw what Saint did to Dice, and that was with his hands. I heard he just killed somebody at a strip club the other day, and that dude was only *talking about* his wife. I'm screwing her. Cuz, I don't know what I'ma do."

Curtis tried to quell my fear. "He's just one man."

"Yeah, a psycho who has an army of psychos behind him. This shit is so fucked up." I put my face back in my hands, and my mind went to Antoinette. I was worried about her safety too.

She hadn't answered my calls the next morning, and she didn't show up to work, so after waiting all night for her to call me, I finally went over to her place to check on her. All the lights at her condo were out, and there was no sign of life. It was practically five o'clock in the morning, though, so she could have been asleep. *Or she could be bleeding on the floor after Saint beat the shit out of her,* I thought. I had to know for sure.

I was about to get out of my car, but then the front door of the duplex opened, and Saint hurried out.

"Shit!" I leaned back in my seat.

He looked around before rushing to his car. When he ran under the lights outside the building, I could see how mad he was. He got inside the car, and I watched him go crazy. I couldn't hear him, but I could see him shouting as he pounded on his steering wheel so hard that the car rocked. That lasted for about fifteen seconds before he finally started the car and pulled off. I slid down in my seat and held my breath as he whizzed past, hoping he couldn't see me. I could only breathe again when I heard his car engine roar away into the distance.

Grabbing my gun, I hopped out of the car and went to the condo. I placed my ear on the door and listened. Nothing. I started banging hard.

"Antoinette?" I called out. "It's Marquis. Please open up if you're in there. Please open the door."

I kept knocking, until I heard a dog barking behind me. I turned around and saw an old man in his pajamas, walking by with his dog on a leash. He was looking at me curiously, probably wondering about all the racket I was making, and then his eyes went down to my hand. That's when he started speed-walking away from there, practically dragging the dog with him.

Looking down at my hand, I realized what had spooked him. Shit. I had forgotten the gun I was holding. The old man was probably rushing home to call the cops. I had no choice but to retreat. I bolted back to my car and got the hell out of there.

I still hadn't heard from Antoinette, and I

was really concerned. If Prince and Jace had brought him the pictures, there was no telling what Saint would do to her. I'd witnessed his blind rage, and the thought of him directing that toward her was making me feel sick.

"I'm worried about her too, man. If they showed him the pictures, who knows what that psycho is doing to her. She might be dead."

"Maybe it's time you told Aunt Shirley," Curtis said. "This shit is serious."

"I can't tell Momma, and you can't either. She would be livid if she found out I was still sneaking around with that girl. I gotta figure this out on my own."

"I got you, cuz."

"You got what, Curtis?" Momma asked when she entered the kitchen with Aunt Nee Nee.

"Uh, Curtis is just in here giving me dating advice," I jumped in.

"Mmm, Curtis needs to mind his business. That's what he needs to do," Aunt Nee Nee said, pursing her lips at her son.

He looked like he wanted to say something, but that one eyebrow she raised stopped any statement from forming. He sheepishly went back to fixing breakfast.

Momma disagreed. "Girl, somebody

needs to give his ass some advice the way he's been carrying on with a certain married cocktail waitress we will leave unnamed. That girl ain't no damn good. We all knowing how crazy that husband of hers is."

"Momma, we have bigger things to think about. Have you talked to Monique?" I asked, trying to change the subject.

"Yes. She's on her way to Jean's bail hearing right now. If all goes bad, he'll be released, and we'll be having a meeting tomorrow. If all goes well, he'll be locked up for a little while longer."

"We both know that won't happen."

"Mm-hmm. And don't think you're slick changing the subject like that. We were talking about that skank Antoinette. You better not be seeing her anymore, Marquis Duncan."

I stiffened up at the second mention of Antoinette. Curtis glanced at me, but we both kept our mouths shut.

Chapter 52
Jean

"To freedom!" I belted out and raised my champagne glass.

My family and friends cheered enthusiastically. After spending the weekend in the Gator Lake jail, the judge had set bail at five grand, and I was released. That weasel Skunk would get his soon enough, but now, it was time to celebrate.

My daughter Simone had booked us a private room in one of my favorite restaurants, Mardi Gras Tuesday. I threw back my champagne, grinning at everyone who'd come to celebrate my safe release. The only person missing was my man Saint, who had an excuse because he was handling some very important business.

My wife stood next to me wearing a sexy black number. She was playing her devoted wife role well — so well that nobody even noticed that she'd barely said a word to me. I felt like I understood it a little better now, though. As I sat in that jail cell, I'd had a lot of time to reflect about life, my marriage, and what I wanted going forward. Top on my list was a better marriage. I was happy to be back home, and I wanted to make Marie happy too. The only question was how? I hadn't figured out yet how I would give her all the time she wanted from me and still run my business, especially since our new connect meant we'd probably be even busier.

Kendall walked up and we slapped hands. "Good to see you on the other side, Unc."

"I could say the same thing to you. Any problems in there?"

"Hell no! I was up in that bitch in heaven," he said, laughing. "Females and pussy everywhere. I almost didn't wanna go home."

Marie made a disgusted noise and walked away from us.

"Nah I'm just playing," Kendall continued. "Ain't nothing like freedom. Shit, I got so many women out here in the world, what I need a jail bitch for?"

Prince came over to us looking a little antsy. He gave Kendall a head nod. "Glad y'all home," he said, giving us some dap.

"Glad to be home, Crescent," I said, clasping his hand with a smile. "I 'ppreciate that money you put on the books."

"Me too," Kendall added.

"No doubt. I was trying to come visit, but Sheriff Clay was on some old bullshit about only two visitors a day."

"Yeah, my wife and Simone were up there most of the day." I glanced over at Marie, who seemed to be in her own world, nursing her champagne. I was going to have to figure something out because I could feel that something about her had changed.

"Hey, Jean, I wanted to let you get your celebration on first, but I got something I need to tell you in private," Prince said.

"Yeah, I got a minute." I turned to Kendall. "Go check on your aunt Marie and Simone, while I chop it up with Prince."

"For sure," Kendall said, then walked away.

"What's up, young buck? This about that nigga Skunk?" I asked. " 'Cause you know I told y'all I'm paying a hundred grand to the first Crescent who brings his ass to me."

"Nah, I'm gonna find him, but this is about my brother."

"What about him?" I cared about Saint, but I was more concerned about the dope he was picking up in Florida. I'd put out a lot of money, and a loss like that would set me back plenty.

"I ain't spoke to him, but I know he's back. The package got in last night, and they're at the clubhouse chopping it up as we speak. That shit should be on the streets by tonight."

A smile crept up on my face, knowing my dope was safe. "Good. So, what's this about? You haven't heard from him since he got back?"

"Nah. Only time we spoke was to tell him you was locked up, but right now, he's probably sleeping that drive off," Prince said. "Honestly, I'm glad I ain't heard from him, Jean."

As long as I'd known the brothers, they were close. It wasn't normal for Prince to say he didn't want to hear from Saint, or vice versa.

"Something happen?" I asked.

"Yeah, and it's gonna be a real problem if we don't handle it quick." Prince looked around to make sure we were still alone. "Look at this."

He pulled out his phone, and I nearly dropped it when he handed it to me and I saw what was on the screen. It was a photo of Big Shirley's son, Marquis Duncan, wearing only a towel and looking furious. His arm was outstretched like he was trying to grab for the phone. Antoinette was in the background, wearing absolutely nothing.

I looked up at Prince. "What the fuck? Saint seen this?"

"Nah. I knew he was handling business, and I wasn't tryna fuck up the money. I wanted to bring it to you first to see how you wanted to handle it. You know how Saint can get about Antoinette."

"Good thinking." I nodded. "Never fuck up the money. We need Saint to keep his head on straight and in the game. Maybe you don't need to show this to him."

"I don't feel right about that, boss. I don't keep secrets from my brother. Especially shit about his wife."

I looked across the room, and my eyes fell on my wife. She was speaking to one of my cousins. There was something about the way she tucked her hair behind her ear as she laughed that made me smile. I'd do anything to get us back on track. Suddenly, an idea came to me. There might be a way to use these photos and make my wife happy at the same time.

"How about you pass the entire load over to me and let me deal with this?" I said as I sent a copy of the photos to my phone. I erased them completely from his device, and also trashed the message thread that had sent them to me. "This new business endeavor with Sebastian is big. I need your brother focused. Understand? If he finds this out, he'll kill Marquis Duncan, and we can't have that right now. If Marquis drops dead, it better be by someone else's hand."

"Got it." Prince looked relieved to have that burden off him. "Enjoy your party. I'ma head out. I need to holla at Jace about looking for Skunk. Once again, boss, I'm happy you're home."

I reached in my pockets and pulled out a thick wad of cash, mostly hundreds. I handed it to Prince.

"What's this for?" he asked.

"That's for being a soldier. My soldier, Crescent."

"To the day I die," he replied.

We slapped hands and pulled each other into a quick brotherly embrace. I had no doubt in my mind that he was going to be a huge contributing factor in flipping the new bricks. Prince's eye was always on the prize. I knew him and his boy Jace were looking to be promoted, and it just might happen sooner than he thought.

Chapter 53
Big Shirley

"You sure you don't want me to do it? Or at least go with you?" Floyd asked as he held out the keys to his truck. The two of us were alone in my office, and I was preparing to leave. I looked down in my bag, and my eyes lingered on the .44 Magnum inside. After a second, I closed the bag and took the keys from my brother's hand.

"We wouldn't have this problem if it wasn't for me. I'll be fine," I reassured him.

"Sis . . ."

"Floyd, like I said, I'll be fine. This is my mess to clean up. What I need you and Marquis to do is doctor that video the way I told you. Now, I'll see you later."

Floyd gave me an unsure look. "You can't blame yourself. But I do understand why you want to go it alone. I'll be waiting for your call."

"Thank you." I gave him a quick hug. "Now let me get outta here. I'm supposed to meet her in a half hour."

Outside the Blues, I found his truck in the parking lot. I paused with my hand on the door handle and took a few breaths to steady my heartbeat. The truth was, I wasn't fine. Violence was one of those things that seemed to be ever-present in my life. First we had to take care of the witnesses from that night, and now Skunk if we ever found him. But just because I had to indulge in it here and there didn't mean it didn't wear me down. I didn't like it, not one bit. That was half the reason LC and I didn't get along. He and his family practically made drugs and violence their trademark.

With that said, I'd do just about anything to keep my family safe, so I got in the truck and drove away from the Blues. Sheriff Clay had sent me her location, and I followed the coordinates exactly. They led to a dirt road along the swamp. There were ROAD CLOSED signs posted, but I maneuvered right around them in Floyd's truck. I didn't stop until I saw the police cruiser parked on the side of the road. I pulled the truck in front of the car, cracked the window open slightly, and watched the cruiser in my rearview mirror.

Sheriff Clay got out of her vehicle with

her revolver drawn and went to the other side.

Through my open window, I heard Skunk's voice. "Something ain't right about this. What we doing here?" he asked nervously.

"Goddammit, Skunk. Go!" Sheriff Clay shoved him forward.

When Sheriff Clay had called Marquis to tell him she finally located the slippery snake, I volunteered for the opportunity to deal with him. After all the kindness I'd shown him over the years, he was now my enemy. Plus, despite my aversion to violence, I was no fool. A man with Jean's social standing, influence, and money would not be held for long. He had one of the best damn lawyers in all of New Orleans. Time was short, so I couldn't afford to think twice about taking care of Skunk before he could do any more talking.

"Oh, shit. That–that's Floyd's truck." Skunk stammered.

"Get in the fucking truck," Sheriff Clay demanded.

Skunk looked at the revolver in her hand before slowly and reluctantly walking to the passenger side of the truck. My windows were tinted dark, so Skunk couldn't see inside until he opened the door.

"Sh–Shirley?" he stammered.

"You were expecting the fucking tooth fairy? Get in!"

"Where are we going?"

"Somewhere you can get some rest from all that running you been doing."

"I don't think I need any rest. I–I'm fine."

I chuckled as I reached under my seat for my purse, then withdrew it with my fingers wrapped around a gun, which I pointed directly at Skunk's head. I gave him the sweetest smile.

"Get in," I repeated.

His eyes jumped, and he looked from my gun back to Sheriff Clay's gun, which was still pointed at him. He had a choice to make. Swallowing hard, he looked around for an escape, but there was nothing but open field. If he ran, he'd be an easy target, and he knew it. Finally, he got in the truck and shut the door, staring straight ahead as if everything would just disappear if he didn't look in my direction.

I hit the locks and lowered my gun, but I kept a firm grip on it. Sheriff Clay got back into her cruiser, and I watched as she drove off, leaving Skunk with what would be his worst nightmare.

"You and I have some things we need to discuss," I told him.

"Like what?" He chose to play dumb, though his nervous demeanor told me he already knew that we'd pegged him as a snitch.

"Pierre LeBlanc."

As casually as he could, he shrugged his shoulders. "W–what makes you think I know anything about him?"

"The hundred thousand dollars I'm sure you were hoping to cash in on," I said.

"I don't know —"

"Cut the shit, Skunk! I saw the surveillance footage. You were standing by the dumpster, watching Marquis and Floyd, so let's not play games with each other."

"Big Shirley, I can explain. I —"

"You tried to shit on me. After how good I've been to you." I shook my head. "I never understood why it was so hard for you out in the world, but that don't mean it's not. And that's why I let you eat for free every day. I let you, a motherfucka who don't spend no money, come into my place of business to escape *your* fucked-up life, and *this* is what you do to me?"

"Big Shirley. Please," he begged. "I made a mistake."

"You damn, right you made a mistake."

I could see the tears welling up and threatening to tread down the bags under his eyes. His sorrow didn't mean much to me. I held my gun up to his temple and applied pressure to the trigger.

"You knew what Jean would do to Marquis and Floyd if he found out what they'd done, and you told him. You just . . . know too much, Skunk. You gotta go."

Chapter 54
Saint

I drove from my condo in the French Quarter to Jean's place doing about a hundred miles an hour. I'd missed the celebration at the restaurant earlier, but I still wanted to stop by to welcome him home. It was a miracle I didn't kill myself on one of those winding roads. Not that I gave a shit, because a huge part of me wanted to be dead.

I did a crappy job of parking. Half my car was on Jean's lawn, and the other half was in the driveway. I stared at my car for a moment, then decided fuck it. I was just too drunk and depressed to care. If Jean wanted me to move, I would. Otherwise, it would stay like that until I left.

I made my way to the front door and rang the bell. Jean opened it.

"Just the man I been looking for." He studied me, then asked, "You drunk?"

"A little?" I forced a smile to my face, and

we slapped hands. It didn't even seem like he had been in jail. He was free when I left, and he was free by the time I got back.

"What the fuck been going on around here? You got locked up?"

"Skunk tried to pull a fast one on me, that's all. I got people out there looking for him right now. Me and him still have some unfinished business."

"Why didn't you call me?"

"What you was handling with Sebastian was way more important than me getting locked up for the weekend. Plus, if I had to be in there longer, who you think would've had to hold this shit down? We needed that product. Speaking of which, how'd it go?"

"Everything is good. I dropped it off last night."

"Good shit." Jean gestured for me to come inside. "Now tell me why you're at my front door, drunk and looking like you lost your best friend."

He had no idea how correct he was.

"It's Nette," I said with a sigh. It was hard to mask my heartbreak. "She left me, Jean. Nette left me, man."

"It's not like it's the first time. She'll be back begging when she's broke, just like any other time," he told me with a hint of distaste in his voice. His reaction was a punch in the gut. I'd expected some type of sympathy, but Jean gave me none.

"This ain't like the other times. She took everything. The refrigerator, the stove, washer/dryer, all the furniture. Even the damn rugs."

He finally managed the smallest expression of sympathy. "Damn, bro. I'm sorry."

"Not as sorry as I was when I saw my safe wide open and everything in it gone."

Jean raised his eyebrows. "Damn, she took your loot too?"

"Five hundred thousand."

"Got damn! We gonna have every one of the Crescents looking for her."

"Nah, fuck that. Y'all leave her alone. I just want her back."

Jean stared at me with skepticism and confusion. "Please tell me this is the alcohol talking, 'cause you are sounding real crazy right now."

"Crazy in love."

"No, just crazy! Antoinette has you out here looking stupid as fuck. And that makes *me* look stupid as fuck. I had to call in some major favors to keep that shit you pulled with Chino under wraps. Now, I'm sure she has some good pussy, but she ain't got the only pussy."

"You don't understand. I love her. I ain't

never loved no one the way I love her. I just want her to come home. I don't give a fuck about that money," I replied my eyes welling up with tears.

Jean paused for a minute, thinking. Then he said, "Listen, the best way to shift your thought process is to get back to work. Maybe some tunnel vision will help you realize what's more important in your life. I have the perfect endeavor."

"Yeah? What's that?" I asked just as Marie stepped up to us.

"Excuse me. I'm sorry," she interrupted. "I'm going to Raven's for a while."

"You are? I thought we could spend a little time together now that the party is over."

"I bet you were." She left before he could say anything else.

There was an edge to her voice that I wasn't used to hearing when she spoke to Jean, and I saw longing in his eyes as he watched her walk away. It looked like I wasn't the only one having trouble in paradise. At least Marie hadn't left him.

"What's the endeavor you're talking about?" I asked.

"I'm thinking about trying my hand in the casino business."

"How the fuck you gonna do that?" I asked. "Too many sanctions, permits, and other shit come along with that. It would take years before we could open, *if* we could. Plus, you'd have competition from the Blues."

"I'm talking *about* the Blues."

"Huh?"

"I'm gonna obtain a percentage in the Midnight Blues. Become partners with Big Shirley."

"Again, how the fuck you gonna do that? You can't force your way in like we did with Red. Shit's gotta be legal."

"I know, but I got my ways. I'ma go see her tomorrow and give her my proposal."

"Oh, I can't wait to see this shit," I said.

Jean shook his head. "Nah. What I need you to do is find that nigga Skunk. And make sure that the shipment gets packed up and ready for the streets. That's what I need you to do. I'll take Kendall and a few others for back up. Not that I'll need it."

"Do you really think she'll let you buy in?" I asked.

"Oh, I know she will. It's in her best interest."

Chapter 55
Marie

Want a massage?

That was the text message Curtis had sent me while I was sitting in the living room listening to Jean and Saint talk. It made me smile from ear to ear, so much so that I made up a lie to get out of my house. However, now that I was in the hotel where Curtis had told me to meet him, standing centimeters away from the door, I was having second thoughts. I felt like an easy woman. All it took was a simple text message to make me come running.

I didn't know exactly what I went there to do. No, that's a lie. His text had set off a daydream about the way Curtis's lips felt on mine and how he made me feel when he stared at me with those sexy eyes. I went there for more of that, but on the drive over, my conscience had woken up and told me it couldn't happen. If I wanted Jean to be better, shouldn't the same go for me?

There was clearly too much chemistry between me and Curtis, and it was dangerous. Sex with him was amazing, but I needed to put an end to it, for my sake and his. I didn't want to imagine what Jean would do to Curtis if he found out. Although I was sure Curtis could handle himself, he was no match for Jean or the forces he had at his beck and call. It would just be better for everybody if we ended things.

I made my decision. That was what I would do. I would end things.

I cleared my throat and knocked on the hotel room door. When the door swung open, the butterflies in my stomach went straight to my clit, making it throb. Not only was he looking scrumptious as hell in his all-black attire, but he smelled good too.

"Oh my." The words slipped through my lips before I could compose myself.

"Come in." He took my hand and pulled me inside.

The room he'd chosen was elegant, but not too much. It was a mini suite, complete with a kitchen. There was a plate of chocolate-covered fruit and a bottle of wine chilling in a bucket on the counter. My eyes traveled to the bed, and I saw rose petals scattered across the comforter. Luther Vandross was crooning a love song through the surround-sound speakers.

"Oh, Curtis."

"I didn't have time to do much, but I wanted you to feel special when you walked in. I hope that's all right. Here, let me." He tried to take my car keys and purse, but I gripped them tightly. He looked at me with confusion in his eyes.

I felt so bad because I knew I'd wasted his time. "Curtis, I'm so sorry."

"Sorry about what? Is something wrong?"

"We can't see each other anymore," I told him.

"Yeah, meeting in a hotel room is pretty cheesy. I wish I had my own spot here."

"No, not the hotel. *This.* Us. We have to stop before it goes any further. It isn't right. I'm a married woman, and I love my husband. I can't do this. It's over."

I watched as my words settled in and his face dropped. I felt horrible, but then again, he knew he was taking a risk with me. I wasn't an available woman.

"I see," he said. "Well, that wasn't exactly what I was expecting to hear, but I can't force you to be with me. And it's not like I didn't know you were married."

"I wasn't trying to lead you on, and if you feel like that, I completely understand and apologize. I was just in a bad space because my marriage was in a bad space. I should have never let things get this far with you."

"Is your marriage better now?" he asked.

"I want it to be."

He nodded his understanding. "I want you to be happy, so if that means you're with him instead of me, then so be it."

"Thank you. You deserve somebody that can be all in. You really do. I can't give that to you."

"A'ight, I won't hit your line anymore. I'll just leave you be."

"I'll do the same," I said with a sigh.

We stood there for a few moments, staring at each other longingly. Finally, I blinked and turned away. Why was the lump in my throat so thick? And why did I have tears in my eyes? Something about that man just made me feel so good. I didn't want to let it go, but I had to. Right? I grabbed the doorknob, knowing I had to get to my car quickly before I changed my mind again.

"Hey, Marie?" Curtis said before I pulled open the door.

"Yes?" I turned around.

"One more thing before you go." He took my hand and pulled me close.

I let my body melt into his, and our lips met. I should have left when I had the chance. Now, I didn't stop him because I didn't want him to stop. I wanted more.

Chapter 56
Gabriel

As a young boy, I'd hated the word no, probably because I heard it so much. My parents were strict, and most of my teachers in Catholic school were hard-asses. It felt like everyone else was running the show and I had no control over my own life. That changed when I crossed over from boyhood to become a man. Now, the word *no* was meaningless to me. I got whatever I wanted, no matter how I had to get it.

My mind had been fixed on Big Shirley ever since I met her at Big Sam's all those years ago. Our paths crossing was the best and worst thing that had ever happened to me. She rocked my world when we slept together, but afterward no other woman could satisfy me. I mean pulling-my-soul-up-out-my-body satisfaction. Knee-jerking, toes-curling, and shivers-going-through-my-whole-body satisfaction. No other woman ever made me feel the way she had, and every time I slept with someone else, I was chasing that first high.

It was late morning when I stepped through the doors of the Midnight Blues. It was still pretty empty in there because I guess the lunch crowd hadn't arrived yet, but it was a mighty fine establishment, nonetheless. Not only was Big Shirley fine as wine and could knock a brother's socks off, but she was clearly also an intelligent businesswoman. I liked that a lot.

I spotted Shirley by one of the bars and hurried over before she could walk away.

"Excuse me. Can I talk to you for a second?" I asked.

"Yes. How can I he—" She turned around with the smile still on her face, but when she saw me, it faded quickly. "*You* again. You have a hard time taking a hint."

"I wouldn't have the success I do if I weren't persistent. Can we please talk?"

"About how I'd like you to stop just popping up? Sure. The door is that way."

"I just can't stop thinking about how you made me feel that night."

Her eyes opened wide for a second. She looked alarmed by my choice of words in public.

"Keep your damn voice down," she hissed. "I told you those days were long over and way behind us. Now, are you going to leave, or am I gonna get security to toss you up out of here?"

"No need for that. Look, I took care of these for you." I held up a folder and tried to hand it to her.

"What is this?"

"It's a receipt. I had my people do a little research, and I found out you were quite a bit in arrears with the state gaming commission. I paid it off for you."

"Are you serious?" She took the folder and glanced down at the receipt.

"I understand you're running a successful business, but even the best businesses have cash flow problems sometimes. Now, yours doesn't."

"I can pay my own bills." She looked down at the receipt again like it was the vilest thing she'd ever seen.

I was undeterred. Maybe I was misunderstanding her. If the financial incentives weren't enough, then maybe she needed me to romance her first, I thought.

"Shirley, listen. I went about this the wrong way at first. Let me make this right. Let's do dinner, and we can get to know each other better. You know my birthday is tomorr—"

"This him, sis? The sicko who propositioned you?" A man with a deep voice stepped up to us. She nodded her head at him. He sized me up from where he stood next to Big Shirley. I didn't know who he was, but I wanted him to leave so that she and I could continue our conversation.

"If you don't mind, we were in the middle of some —"

I didn't get to finish my sentence because I was interrupted by a fist in my face. The power of the blow made me stumble back, and I could feel blood trickling out of my nose. He came at me again. I defended myself the best I could, but I was a businessman, not a thug.

"Stay the fuck away from my sister, you perverted motherfucka!" he yelled as he pummeled me. "Stalking her at her place of business and shit. I got a proposition for you too, you freak. I propose you take this ass-whoopin'!"

My body was screaming in pain as he let his fists fly. I was afraid he might not stop until I was dead.

"Floyd. Floyd! Calm down," Big Shirley said.

He kept pounding on me. I covered my head the best I could and peeked through my arms just as security came running our way.

"Help! Help me!"

"DJ! Get Floyd. He's gonna kill him," Big Shirley yelled to one of the security guards.

I didn't know how many men it took to get that lunatic off me, but they finally did. Once I felt a rush of air come over me, I caught my breath. It was quite a spectacle, and people around had stopped to watch.

I gave the man who had attacked me the most hateful glare I could muster through my swollen eyes. I was hurt, but I was also pissed off. I would make them all regret what had just happened to me.

I lay back on the floor, holding my head. "Will somebody please call an ambulance and the police? Please call the police!"

"No, no! There's no need for all that." Big Shirley rushed forward. "No need for no kind of law to be called to my place of business. DJ, get Floyd outta here."

I smirked at Floyd as he was forcefully removed by the security guard.

As I was using my handkerchief to dab the blood at my nose, I pulled out my phone.

"The police are gonna love this one," I said. "And so is your insurance company."

"Wait, don't call." Shirley put her hand on mine. "You said . . . you said you wanted me to go to dinner with you, right? For your birthday. I'll go."

"Really?" I could feel my sore face brightening up. A small smile even came to my lips. That was all I had wanted.

"Yes," she said.

"Okay, great. This is great. Tomorrow, your house, eight o'clock. I'll pick you up."

"I'll . . . be there."

I let a security guard help me up from the floor. If I was in pain, I barely noticed anymore. Mentally, I was already planning our night together. I was so happy that I didn't even care that I had let slip that I knew where she lived.

Chapter 57
Floyd

Shirley was pissed, but I really didn't give a fuck. That dude, whoever he was, was not going to disrespect my sister. Not in front of me. Plus, beating the piss out of him gave me an outlet to let off some steam.

I couldn't remember the last time I'd had a moment of peace, and even as I sat alone at my desk in my office, my mind was still in overdrive. We all had a busy morning ahead of us with Jean coming for the meeting. There was a different kind of ambiance in the air, a crackling electricity that came from uncertainty. I had no idea how things would go when Jean saw the footage we had managed to piece together. We had some video of Pierre walking outside, so we spliced it to make it look like he was leaving for the night. If Jean figured out it was a fake, I would need to take him out right then and there. I opened the top drawer of my desk and pulled out a gun wrapped in a handkerchief. I set it on top of the desk and opened the handkerchief, staring at the custom-made chrome Glock as the diamond-encrusted muzzle sparkled under the light. What a beautiful weapon, but it wasn't mine. It was the gun Pierre had used to kill himself.

I couldn't understand how a person with so much life ahead of him could do something so hasty. I guess that's why most places prohibit weapons in places where alcohol is served. It might have been a split-second drunk decision that Pierre made.

I picked up the gun and aimed it. Too bad we'd have to get rid of it. I would love to carry something like that around. I'd only bring it out for special occasions, though. Pierre was much flashier than me.

Muscle memory led me to drop the magazine and check to see how many bullets were in it. *No, that can't be,* I thought, checking again.

"Well, I'll be damned!" I ran out of my office, still holding the gun.

I didn't stop running until I reached Marquis's office. He was sitting behind his desk, looking at something on his computer, wearing the same sad puppy-dog expression he'd had for a few days. I didn't know what that was about, but I would have to wait to find out because there were more pressing matters at hand.

"Neph! Get to the surveillance room. Now!" I yelled.

"I'm kind of in the middle of inventory." He pointed at the computer screen.

"Fuck inventory! Come on. Now!" I didn't give him a chance to respond before I dashed back out. I almost ran smack dab into Curtis, who had been on his way to Marquis's office. "You too!"

"Where's the fire?" Curtis asked as Marquis emerged from the office.

"He wants us to follow him. Come on."

Together we made our way to the surveillance room, and I kicked the security guard out so we could have privacy. Laying the gun on the desk, I sat down behind the computer screens and instantly started sifting through the backup files.

Marquis looked at me like I was crazy. He pointed at Pierre's Glock. "I know that ain't what I think it is, Unc."

"What is it besides a sexy-ass gun?" Curtis asked, eyeing the piece like he wanted to touch it.

"That's Pierre LeBlanc's gun," Marquis told him, and he backed off quick.

"What the hell you doing with that, Floyd?"

"I couldn't bring myself to get rid of it, and I'm glad I didn't," I said. "One of y'all pick it up and tell me what you notice."

Marquis shook his head. "Hell no. I ain't putting my prints on that thing."

"Quis, pick up the damn gun!"

Reluctantly, he picked up the weapon and studied it. I stayed quiet as I watched him, wanting to see how sharp he was. He dropped the mag just like I had. His brow furrowed, and I saw the moment the realization came to him.

"Oh!" He handed the gun parts to Curtis. "You see what I see, cuz?"

"All these diamonds? Hell yeah. This piece is fly as fuck. I'm not too big on flashy builds with guns, but this one — wait." Curtis looked from the mag to the gun. "Full clip, with one in the chamber."

"And what does that mean?" I asked.

"It was never fired. If it was, there wouldn't be a bullet in the chamber." Marquis began pacing in circles with small steps as it came together for him. "And *that* means —"

"Pierre didn't kill himself. There was somebody else there that night," Curtis finished for him.

"Exactly," I confirmed.

"What you looking for, Unc?" Marquis

leaned over my shoulder to look at the screen.

"If they came in, they had to go out," I said as I sifted through the footage.

Unfortunately, the room Pierre was found in was out of view of the camera in that hallway. I couldn't see anyone going in or out. The next best way to hopefully view our culprit would be to pull up surveillance of each exit door after the gunshot went off. That wouldn't be hard, since only two of the exit doors were unlocked at night. Unless a person had a key, they didn't have a choice but to use one of those.

I started playing the footage from the first door. At the moment that the gunshot blasted, hordes of people went rushing for the exit. This might be harder than I thought to identify one person in that crowd, especially if the killer was someone we didn't know. I slowed down the video speed and started searching the faces for anyone who looked too calm among all those panicked gamblers.

The first recording didn't reveal anything that looked suspicious, so I started scrolling through footage from the other door. It's a good thing there were three sets of eyes in the room because I might have missed what Marquis spotted.

"Wait, Unc. Stop. Go back," he said.

I rewound a little, and he said "Yeah, right there. Freeze that frame. Check out the person in all black with the hoodie over their head. What's in their hand?"

I zoomed in on the black object, and when I saw what it was, I fell back in my chair, stunned. "A gun," I said. "Y'all see that? I bet this is Pierre's killer."

"Who is it?" Marquis asked.

Between the hoodie and the grainy quality of the video, I couldn't make out the person's facial features. "The video's not good enough to tell."

"Send it to me. I know just the person who can clean it up," Curtis said.

I wasted no time copying the video onto a jump drive and then handed it to him.

"You gonna tell Momma?" Marquis asked.

I looked at him and shook my head. "Not until we know more. We still have to meet with Jean this afternoon, so she don't need no distractions."

Chapter 58
Big Shirley

There was a heavy silence in my office as Jean LeBlanc and I sat across from each other, neither one saying a word. Floyd and Marquis stood on either side of my desk, while Jean sat there alone. I was more than surprised when I didn't see Saint behind him. Jean was usually never without his right hand; however, even alone he looked more confident and in control than ever.

After everything that had happened earlier with Gabriel, I was flustered, but I had to set that aside in my mind. Considering I was the one who had called the meeting, there was no way Jean could know that I was nervous as hell. Things could either go real good or take a turn for the worse in the blink of an eye.

I could tell that everyone was waiting on someone to speak first, so I finally cleared my throat and began to talk. "Jean, I appreciate you stopping by with everything you've got going on. How are you?"

"I'm a free man, so I can't complain. The real question is, why am I here?" he asked.

"For one, I want to know who you're getting your false information from," I said, playing my part like a pro. Jean didn't know that we'd already pegged Skunk as the snitch.

"Who said it was false?" he asked calmly.

"I do," I replied firmly. "Now, are you gonna give him up? Because that kind of bad blood ain't good for either of our businesses."

"You're right. If you really have a tape and are going to show me, I'll do you a solid as well," he said. "It was Skunk that told me he saw Marquis and Floyd getting rid of Pierre's body."

I forced myself to laugh like it was the most absurd thing I'd heard all day. "Skunk? Are you kidding me? You can't believe anything that comes out of his mouth. Everyone knows he's a liar."

"Even a liar has eyes, Big Shirley. I just need to see the proof with my own eyes that he's lying."

"All right. I have something that will quiet your mind about our involvement in your brother's death — a terrible crime to accuse us of, by the way."

"You can never be too sure. But, if you have proof like you say you do, then we can put this whole thing behind us."

I turned to Marquis, and he handed me an iPad. The video was already pulled up on the screen. All Jean had to do was press play. I slid it to him, and he started the video, watching the screen intently. I could feel myself holding my breath. His face revealed nothing about whether was buying it. I wanted to glance at Floyd, but I feared any sudden movement would give us away.

After what felt like forever, Jean finally nodded his head. "Okay, mystery solved. I can see that my brother didn't die here."

He slid the iPad back toward me, and I welcomed the relief that came over me. I wanted him out of the Blues faster than the Road Runner cartoon.

"Thanks for coming." I stood up and extended my hand out to him. "I'm so sorry for your loss, but I'm glad to conclude our business."

Jean did not reach for my hand. He stayed planted in his seat and studied my face, looking at me, then Floyd, and then Marquis before directing his attention to me again. Sensing that he had no intention of leaving, I sank back into my seat.

"On the contrary," he said smoothly. "Our

business is just getting started. We have something else to attend to." He flashed his pearly whites, and then looked over at Marquis. "You see, you have a problem that's become my problem."

I looked behind me at my son, and he avoided my eye contact. He was standing stiff as a board, and I got a bad, bad feeling in the pit of my stomach. Body language doesn't lie. Something was up.

"What's the problem?" I asked, facing Jean again.

"I guess the best way to put it is this: it's the kind of problem where your son ends up dead."

"Anyone that wants to kill my son will have to go through me."

"And me," Floyd chimed in.

"Trust me, that can be arranged." Jean laughed confidently, telling me there was way more to the story than I thought. "Because this individual will have no issue using you two as a warmup. See for yourselves."

He reached into his suit jacket and pulled out his phone, opened something on it, and slid it over to me. My eyes almost popped out of their sockets when I looked down at a picture of Marquis and Antoinette in a hotel room. This time, I couldn't summon a poker face. The air conditioner was blasting throughout the building, but I was burning hot.

I turned around, and Marquis had the nerve to have a stupid look of shame on his face, like he didn't know it was risky the whole time he was doing it. It took everything in me not to get up and smack the black off of him and put it back on, just to slap it off again.

"You stupid. Ass. Motherfucka. How dumb can you be, Marquis?" I said raising, up outta my seat.

"Momma, I —"

"Shut up!" I shouted. "Shut the fuck up!"

"What is it?" Floyd asked, and when I showed him the photo, he exploded. Even I was shocked, because however hotheaded my brother was, he always kept an even temper with his nephew, even when he did something really stupid. He jabbed his finger in Marquis's chest. "What the hell is wrong with you?"

"I fucked up," Marquis said.

"Damn right you fucked up." Floyd was flexing his fists in a way that made me think he wanted to give Marquis the same beating he'd given Gabriel.

"Dammit, Marquis. How many times did I tell you about that girl?" I snapped. Of course I got no answer.

"I think we all can agree that my man Saint isn't wrapped too tight when it comes to his wife." Jean looked around at us calmly, like he was talking to a bunch of children. And for that moment, he was the only adult in the room. "And that this is a big problem for us all, right?"

"A big fucking problem," Floyd growled, glaring at Marquis.

"So, I need to know what we are going to do about it." Jean's eye roamed from face to face, finally settling on mine. I could see just a hint of a smirk. " 'Cause when — not if, but *when* — Saint finds out, he's gonna kill your son, Big Shirley, and anyone who gets in his way. And if he can't get to him, or if you retaliate, he's gonna send his brother and every Crescent Boy he can to get the job done."

Jean turned his head in Marquis's direction. "It's about to be open season on you, boy."

I took a long, exaggerated breath that turned Jean back in my direction. The moment I saw that picture, I knew there would be a price to pay. I was almost scared to ask what it could be, but his eyes were goading me to. "How can we make this go away, Jean?"

"Well, now you're asking the right question," he said, making himself more comfortable in his chair. "See, Saint doesn't know yet, and I'm the only one with hard proof that your son is fucking Antoinette. I'm willing to keep it that way and help you fix the problem. But keeping a secret like this from my oldest and dearest friend is going to cost you."

"Cost me how?" I braced myself for a price I knew I wouldn't like, and when Jean answered, I learned it was even higher than I'd imagined.

"I'm thinking a piece of the Blues would be nice," he said with a wide smile.

I cut my eyes at him. "The Blues ain't for sale," I said slowly. "You know that. This is my family's legacy."

"Come on, Big Shirley. You've had silent partners before. I'm just looking for a taste."

He was so smug and confident it was sickening. He knew he had us over a barrel. I turned to my brother, who looked like he was going to lose control. I needed counsel, but he was in no shape to give it. When Floyd didn't say anything, I knew my back was against the wall. I had no choice in the matter if I wanted my son to live.

"How much of a taste we talking?" I asked.

"How much is your son's life worth to you?"

I glanced over at Marquis, whose head was hanging low. Pitiful. "Not as much as you would think."

Jean smirked. "That's funny. How about twenty percent?"

"Hell no!" Floyd belted out.

I scowled and shook my head. "Shit, for twenty percent, I'd let his ass get shot. No deal."

"No you wouldn't." He chuckled. "But I get your point. How about fifteen percent?"

"Still too high. You've gotta do better than that, Jean. Work with me here, this is an established business, we are talking about."

"All right, make it ten percent. *And* you let my wife be the floor manger. Get her out of the house." He looked around my office. "She does have an eye for interior design. She could really make this place pop."

"Um, this place already has enough *pop,* and we already have a floor manager. My cousin Monique," I stated.

"Well, I'm sure you can find something else for Monique to do. She's a pretty resourceful woman. But the price of peace doesn't get any cheaper than this."

I squeezed my fists underneath the desk

and clenched my eyes closed. I had to steady my breathing and calm myself down. I was so peeved that I swore I could spit fire if I tried to. I opened my eyes and looked over at Floyd, who reluctantly nodded his head.

"Fine," I groaned. "But the only way this deal becomes reality is if you can ensure my son's safety from Saint and the Crescent Boys."

"The Crescents do what I tell them for the most part, so you don't have to worry about them. And I can personally guarantee Saint won't be in the picture."

Was this man implying he was going to put a bullet in his best friend's head?

"How?" I asked.

"By doing the one thing he'll never expect." Jean grinned. "Not in a million years."

Chapter 59
Marie

I got home much later than I expected, but the way Curtis had flipped me, dipped me, and took me to town for the third night in a row, I was surprised that I was able to make it home in the first place. I was happy to see that neither Simone's nor Jean's cars were in the driveway, despite the late hour. I stepped inside, carrying my shoes in my hand and holding my purse loosely. Although the driveway was empty, I wanted to be sure nobody was there.

"Simone, honey?" I called out. "Jean? Is anybody home?"

I waited a few moments to see if I would hear any feet coming to greet me. Ten seconds passed and nobody came, so I summoned the little energy I had left to go up the stairs to the master bedroom. Jean could be home at any time, and I needed to wash the remnants of sex from my body. We'd used a condom, which Jean and I never did, and in my mind, I was certain my husband would be able to smell the rubber on me.

I scrubbed every inch of my body multiple times and used the shower head to spray my lady parts. I didn't know what to think of myself. No matter what Jean did, I'd never slept with another man since he and I had been together. The only way to describe what I was feeling was to say I was confused. Yes, I was unhappy, but that didn't give me the right to forget about my vows. The deed was done, though, and I couldn't take it back. I had arrived at the crossroads. I could only go forward, wherever that would take me.

I got out of the shower, dried off, and wrapped myself in a robe. Standing in front of the mirror, I swiped my hand across it so I could see myself in the steamy bathroom. That night, I recognized myself. I was just a woman who wanted to be loved and desired, and it wasn't too much to ask.

"I can't do that again," I said to myself. "I can't."

Who was I kidding? I'd said that every day for the past three days, yet whenever he texted, I found a way to get to him. He was quickly becoming my personal obsession, and I had to stop it. Moving fast before my resolve crumbled, I grabbed my phone off the bathroom counter. I went straight to our message thread and, without hesitating, I blocked his number and deleted everything. When it was all gone, I exhaled, feeling a huge weight lift.

I put the phone down and stepped out of the bathroom. I almost jumped out of my skin when I saw Jean sitting on the bed, facing me. His head was bowed. I froze, not knowing what to do. Finally, he looked up and stared into my eyes. My heart was pounding. I thought I was caught, but then he started laughing.

"What's funny?" I asked.

"Me. I'm funny," he said. "I was just sitting here thinking about our future."

"And that's funny to you?"

"No, I just . . . I just know I've been a fucking idiot."

"Can you say that again?" I genuinely wanted to hear him repeat it.

"I've been an idiot. And I know it." He stood up, revealing a small pink gift bag from behind his back, and stepped toward me. "I've been fucking up."

"That's an understatement," I said, rolling my eyes. "Why the epiphany?"

"A couple of nights in jail with nothing to do but think about what's important to me."

He was saying all the things I wanted to

hear him say, but when they fell on my ears, they didn't move me. It wasn't enough. Not anymore anyway.

"I might not be able to make up for past mistakes, but I want to step forward with you and be the man I shoulda been all along. I don't want to lose you."

"You know, there was a time I hoped — no, I prayed you'd do exactly what you're doing right now. But instead, I got lonely days and lonely nights. No communication, no loving, no sex, no emotional support. Just me and this big-ass house you convinced me that you bought for us, but somehow, it's always only me in it. I just accepted it because I got so used to it."

He nodded, taking my words to the chest. He didn't try to argue me down. He was accepting the sting like a man, and that was shocking. Normally, he would tell me he didn't have time and leave the room.

"I shoulda never put you in a position to get used to anything less than what you deserve, baby. And you know what? That's what makes you so deserving. Because you put up with my shit and love me through it." He groaned loudly at the ceiling. "It's just this . . . this fucking business! The game. It takes hold of you, and once it does, it has you. But I finally figured a way out."

He held the bag out to me, and I took it reluctantly. I didn't want to be bought, but only a fool would turn down gifts when she knew her husband had the money to buy the nice ones. I pulled out a small ring box, and even I was floored when I opened it and saw the pink teardrop-shaped diamond. It had to have been at least five carats. A gasp escaped my mouth.

"Jean, oh my God! Oh my God! It's so beautiful." My hand flew to my cheek, and I was having a hard time closing my mouth.

He took the ring out of the box and put it on my right ring finger. I held it up in the air and admired the sparkle.

"I'm sorry for everything. I hope you can forgive me."

"Oh, Jean, it's . . . Wait." I shook my head to snap myself out of the daze. "How is a ring going to get you out of the game?"

"It isn't. That was a gift to my wife to signify my promise to be the best husband to you. The one that you want. And that's just one of your gifts." He paused to give me a devilish grin. "Remember at the ball you were talking about how much you would do differently at the Blues?"

"Yeah . . ." I said tentatively. Where was he going with this?

"How would you like to be an owner and

the new floor manger?"

"Are you saying what I think you're saying?" I asked as hope blossomed within me. "Because I would love that. It would be a dream come true."

"I'm saying I'm about to make your dreams come true, baby." He pulled me to him. "Can I do that?"

"Yes. Yes, you can." I batted my eyes up at him. "But Jean, don't sell me a rose garden you can't deliver."

"Never that, baby. Never that," he said, kissing me with passion.

I felt his manhood grow against my body. For the second time that night, I felt my love button begin to thump, but this time, it was thumping for the man it was supposed to. I should have turned him down, but then again, I was a wife who had her duties. I let my robe fall to the ground as our lips met again.

Chapter 60
Gabriel

Jubilant was the only way to describe how I felt. The time was nearing 7:30, and I was growing giddy like a schoolboy. I was dressed in a dark blue suit, cockily puffing on a cigar as I watched the decorators bustle around. The luxurious yacht was being transformed into a dreamy and romantic setting for a birthday dinner for two. I didn't care that I was in the way of them setting up flower arrangements or the balloon towers and arches I had requested. I wanted to make sure they were doing everything right. It was going to be a night to remember.

Holding a nice-sized box, the baker approached me wearing a black chef coat. His name was Gustavo, and he was the best cake decorator in all of New Orleans. Believe me, I'd checked. I only wanted the best of the best for my lady.

He flipped the top of the box open and showcased his work. "Sir, the cake," Gustavo said, waving his hand over his masterpiece. "Whipped topping like you requested."

"Amazing. I want y'all to set this whole thing up. When I walk in with her, I want her to be more than just a little impressed."

"Of course," he said and went to set the cake down.

As they put the finishing touches on everything, I couldn't help but to look on in awe. My favorite part was the unlit candles surrounded by rose petals that led to the whole setup. My staff was always good, but they had gone above and beyond for this night.

"This turned out lovely," my assistant said.

Sarah had been with me since almost the beginning, so she was practically family at this point. She was responsible for keeping my head on straight, and she was a diligent worker. She also listened and did as she was told, which was the most important thing. Sarah was the one who had found the PI who finally located Big Shirley. I would be forever grateful.

"How's your nose?" she asked, sounding concerned.

"Fine, just fine. That ice pack and ibuprofen you gave me took the swelling right on down. Thank God I don't have a shiner."

"For all of that, I hope she's worth it."

"Yes, she is," I said with a big sigh.

She came and stood next to me with a clipboard and a large bouquet of flowers in her hands. "Your chef will prepare dinner for you and your guest in front of you."

"No need. Just have him lay everything out. This night is for my lady and me. I don't need any extras around. No interruptions."

"Understood. I'll let him know. Your limo should be pulling up at any moment. I will make sure the yacht is cleared out before you get back." She lifted the bag in her hand. "I bought you something."

"For me? You shouldn't have."

"It isn't much, but I think considering the occasion, you'll find it useful."

I took the bag from her and gave her a hug. She walked away, leaving me alone on the deck once more. When she was gone, I peered into the bag and started laughing when I saw a box of condoms. She couldn't have gotten me a better gift.

I took one more look around before I made my way off the yacht. Everything looked perfect for what I hoped would be the best night of my life.

As soon as I stepped onto the dock, my

limousine was pulling up. The driver got out to hold the door open, and I walked toward the limo with a purpose, nodding my head at him before I got in the back. There was already a bottle of champagne chilling and two glasses waiting to be used.

We headed off in the direction of Big Shirley's mansion. I leaned into my seat and let out a blissful sigh. The nervous butterflies in my stomach were in full effect now. I couldn't help imagining all the ways I was going to please her that night. Back then, I'd been just a boy. Now I was a man, one who'd learned some new tricks and a little something about stamina. I was going to knock her socks off. After she spent the night with me, there was no way she wouldn't come back for more. I was counting on it.

We finally reached a long road that led up to a tall gate, behind which sat her very grand and flamboyant home. When my limousine came to a stop, I took a deep breath, picked up the flowers, opened my door, and blessed the pavement with my expensive loafers. My plan had been to buzz the gate and hopefully be invited in to be introduced to her family. Maybe I would even smooth over things from the day before with her brother. Let bygones be bygones.

That dream was shattered the moment I was out of the vehicle and heard a loud *Woot-woot!* Suddenly, there were red-and-blue lights flashing on the limo and my suit.

"What the fuck?"

Whipping my head to the side, I saw a sheriff's cruiser coming to a stop next to my limo. I watched as two officers stepped out of the cruiser, and I thought about Big Shirley. Had she gotten herself into some trouble? Well, no worries. There was nothing money couldn't fix.

To my surprise, they bypassed the gate and walked up to me.

"Gabriel Williams?" the female sheriff asked in a country accent.

"Yes. Who's asking?"

"My name's Sheriff Clay, and this right here is for you." She handed me an open envelope.

I snatched it from her, and my stomach started rolling as I read the enclosed paper. "What the hell . . . What's this?"

"That there is a protection order sworn out against you by Ms. Shirley Duncan. You are not allowed to come within a hundred feet of her, her home, or place of business. If you violate this order, you will be arrested on felony charges."

"You gotta be kidding me. Is this a joke?"

I asked. My eyes were burning like I might be about to cry.

"No, sir, I can assure you this is quite serious."

I turned to the mansion. Big Shirley was standing on her steps, watching this scene unfold and doing absolutely nothing to stop it. I was genuinely hurt, but the rage that followed filled up my entire body.

"Why are you doing this?" I cried out to her, taking a step toward the house. "I just want to spend my birthday with you. We had a deal!"

The deputy grabbed me.

"Mr. Williams, I'm gonna have to ask you to leave, or else I'ma be forced to arrest you," Sheriff Clay warned.

"Fuck that. She's gonna talk to me, dammit! You're not ruining my birthday."

The deputy had a firm grip on my arm, so we tussled a bit before I finally got away from him. I heard a set of quick feet behind me, and before I could get to the gate, I was tackled to the ground. My face scraped against the pavement as I struggled to get free again, but this time, it was no use.

"Don't fucking move!" Sheriff Clay must have seen the determined look in my eyes because she drew her weapon and pointed it in my face. "Don't you move one fucking muscle. Cuff his ass, Brown!"

Deputy Brown roughly slapped a pair of handcuffs on me. I looked across the lawn at Big Shirley one last time as I felt the cold metal on my wrists for the first time. She'd planned this. Big Shirley had set me up.

I drowned out the sound of the deputy reading me my rights. All I could think about was my ruined day and how I was going to make Big Shirley pay for her betrayal.

Chapter 61
Larry

Kenny, Holly, and Dennis were sitting with me in a booth at a restaurant called Mardis Gras Tuesday. I was avidly trying to convince Kenny to go see his mother. She was growing impatient with me because she hadn't laid eyes on him like I told her she would. But she knew just like I knew that the boy was stubborn.

"She really wants to see you, son," I was saying to him as he ate his Cajun pasta. "And I know you want to see her too."

He just shrugged his shoulders. I knew Kenny loved his mother and his siblings, but he had mixed emotions. Although he and Lauryn got along, he and Curtis had never been the best of friends. While Curtis was more of a Momma's boy, Kenny had been attached to me at the hip since he got off his Momma's breast. He still hadn't forgiven Curtis for siding with my brother LC, even though, in the end, it was the right thing to do. To Kenny, right or wrong, Curtis was supposed to be loyal to me like he was. That reunion was the one he was really avoiding, not the one with his mother. I wouldn't give up, though. Being at odds with your big brother was hard, but it would be better to make amends than to let the relationship fizzle away.

"Kenny, listen. I know —"

"Y'all bring Marquis Duncan to me and there's ten stacks in it for you." A rough and angry voice behind me made me stop midsentence.

There was a small group of thuggish-looking men seated in that booth. I'd seen two of them when the hostess seated them, and the third joined them a little later. Hearing my nephew's name coming from their mouths put me on high alert. I knew Kenny had heard it too because although he didn't look up, he stopped chewing and stayed perfectly still. Dennis and Holly were still talking amongst themselves, but my son and I were tuned into the conversation behind us.

"Let me get this right. We ain't gotta kill him, Saint?"

"I want that motherfucker alive so I can kill him myself," the man called Saint replied.

"A'ight, can we bring in a couple of the Crescents?"

"I don't give a shit who you bring in. I just want the job done. And I'll throw in an extra three if you can get that pretty-eyed motherfucka he's been rolling with. Him, you can kill."

Kenny and I exchanged a look. I only knew of one pretty-eyed motherfucka Marquis would roll with, and it was my son Curtis.

The moment the men had stepped in the restaurant, I knew they were no good. The flashy purple designer clothes and gold chains told it all. Gangbangers. How the hell had Marquis gotten entangled with them to the point where they wanted him dead?

I listened to their plans a little longer, until one of the men got up and walked away, and I got a good look at his face. I had a feeling he was the one they called Saint. He wouldn't be hard to find because like the rest, he was wearing purple. I stayed tuned into their conversation.

"Aye, yo, what the fuck was that all about?" one of the others asked.

"I don't know, Tiny, but for ten grand, I'll kill your momma."

"Shit, for ten grand, I'll kill her ass too."

They both laughed.

"Aye, let's head to the clubhouse and get some of the boys so we can handle this shit. We might be able to get it done tonight if we plan it right."

Kenny and I exchanged another look. We both knew what we had to do. As the men behind us got up from the booth, I waved the waitress over to ours. She was a pretty, dark caramel thing, and minus the accent, she reminded me a lot of Nee Nee when she was younger.

"Check please," I said when she got to the table.

"Of course, Bay-be. Can I get y'all some boxes?"

"No, thank you."

Dennis looked at me with wide eyes. "Boss, I barely finished my crawfish étouffée!"

"You can't take it where we're headed. We got work to do," I told him and gave him a look that only he could read.

Dennis looked back and forth from me to Kenny, seemingly confused. He accepted it, however, and pushed his bowl forward. I handed the waitress some cash, and she walked away from the table.

Holly, who was sitting beside Dennis, clapped her hands. "Oh, goody! What kinda work we gonna do?" she asked at the very moment the young men made their way to the door.

"Them," I told her.

"Oh! Do I get to cut somebody?"

"Probably a lot of somebodies. Let's go before they disappear," I said when the men were out of the restaurant.

We got up from the booth. As I walked to our vehicle, I watched the young men get into a gray Dodge Durango. The four of us piled in, and I waited for them to drive off before we fell in behind them.

Just when I thought New Orleans wasn't exciting, some fun just fell into my lap.

Chapter 62
Saint

It took everything in me to go back to the condo Antoinette and I shared after I met with the boys at the restaurant. It would take a whole crew to clean up the mess I'd made in my rage earlier. I sat there, parked in my car, staring up at the home and knowing I could never call it that again. It felt like the wind was shaking my car, but then I realized there was no wind outside on that still night. It was my body shaking in anger as I thought back to the events of the day.

The place was trashed. Anything that could get thrown and broken did, and I wasn't excited to truly see the extent of the damage. It probably looked like a tornado had run through it. Not only that, but it was a reminder that my wife was gone.

Instead of going inside, I called Prince. I hadn't seen or talked to him since I'd been back. Up until I saw Jace earlier at the clubhouse, it was purely coincidence, but for the last few hours, I'd been purposely avoiding my brother.

"What's up, bro?" He answered the phone after letting it ring four times.

"I don't know. You tell me," I replied sarcastically. I wanted his backstabbing ass to know I was irritated.

"Tell you what?"

"So, that's how we're gonna play it? You gonna act stupid?"

"Saint, what the hell you talkin' about, man?"

I wasn't trying to beat around no bushes. I wanted to know why my brother, my flesh and blood, would withhold that kind of information. "Why didn't you tell me about Marquis Duncan and Antoinette as soon as you found out?"

The phone went silent for a good thirty seconds before he finally said, "I didn't wanna hurt you, man."

"Yeah, well, you did worse than that, Prince. You broke my fucking heart. Me and you supposed to be better than that. You're my little brother, man."

"We *are* better than that, but I didn't know what to do. You know how you are."

"And how am I? Tell me."

"You know how you overreact to shit, man. I love you, but I am not about to let you mess up my money over no dog-ass bitch that you *know* is a dog-ass bitch! A good wife is supposed to bring out the best in your life, not provoke the worst in you. But you never want to listen to nobody when it comes to her. So, I went to Jean for advice, and —"

I cut his ass off. "Jean knows about this too?"

"Yeah," he said. "He ain't tell you? He was supposed to talk to you about it for me."

"He ain't say shit. Jace told me."

"Jace! Jace sold me out like that?" he groaned.

My breathing grew shallow as I thought about my oldest friend and our conversation the night before. I'd never felt more betrayed in my life by the people I loved the most. And now I didn't feel bad for trying to branch out on my own. Business was business, but they'd turned it personal.

"Fuck Jace. I can't believe you and Jean knew and didn't tell me. And that son of a bitch is trying to partner with him and his family?" I said out loud to myself.

First I was going to kill Marquis; then I was gonna have some up close and personal words with my good friend Jean LeBlanc.

"Saint, don't go doing nothing stupid,

bro," Prince begged.

"Fuck you, Prince." I hung up on him and turned the car on. There was nothing he could say to calm me down. Forget going into the house. I was going on a manhunt.

Woot-woot! I hadn't even put the car in reverse before I was surrounded by three cruisers. The flashing lights startled me, and I was even more startled when five deputies and Sheriff Clay jumped out with their guns drawn. They pointed them at my car and eased up on it slowly.

"Saint, come out with your hands up!"

"For what? What the fuck I do?" I shouted back.

I seriously contemplated having a shoot-out with them, but then I'd never get to exact my revenge on Marquis if I did. So, I did what I was told and stepped out of the car with my hands up. Two deputies rushed me. While one put my hands behind my back, the other snatched the gun from my waist.

"Hey, hey! What's going on?" I asked them.

"You better stop resisting, or we're gonna have to tase you," Sheriff Clay warned, standing over me. "You're under arrest for murder."

"Murder? I ain't kill nobody."

"I got a half dozen witnesses from the strip club and the body of Chino Santana that we pulled out of Gator Lake that says differently. If the bullet in him matches up with that gun you're carrying, you're up shit's creek."

Chapter 63
Jace

I was starting to feel a little uneasy when Montclair and Tiny, two of the youngest and most trigger-happy Crescent Boys, walked in the clubhouse and started whispering in the other youngins' ears. Usually, something like that wouldn't bother me, but both of them had left with Saint after I'd slipped and told him about his wife's affair. Slipped may not be the correct word, because my dumb ass was really trying to be important and curry favor with one of the bosses, and it blew up in my face. After seeing Saint's reaction, I wish I had kept my mouth shut like Prince had told me. I probably should've called Prince and told him what was going on, but I didn't want to hear his mouth. Not yet at least.

I studied Tiny and Montclair's little clique cackling like a bunch of old hens and checking their guns, and I knew that something was about to go down.

"Aye, Tiny. Come here, man."

Tiny glanced at Montclair, then headed over to where I was counting and wrapping money.

"What's up, man? Why you interrupting the workflow?" I asked. "We got a lot of shit to pack up tonight."

"Ain't nobody trying to stop work. We trying to *put in* some work. How's that trigger finger, OG?"

"Depends on the work. What you got in mind?"

"Saint put ten bands on that nigga Marquis Duncan and another three on his pretty boy cousin. We going down to the Blues after we finish this. Gonna take him down when he leaves."

"Is that right?" I asked just as my phone rang. I looked down and groaned when I saw Prince's number. I gestured to Tiny that I had to take the call, and he wandered back to his friends.

"What's up, partner? I thought you was on a date," I said into the phone.

"I am on a date. A date that was interrupted by my brother cussing my ass out! Did you tell Saint about Marquis and Antoinette?" He was shouting so loud that I had to pull the phone away from my ear.

"Yeah, yeah, but —"

He cut me off. “I fuckin’ told you not to say shit, Jace! I told you I’d handle it, and because of you, my brother’s on the fucking warpath!” I don’t think I’d ever heard Prince that upset.

“Yeah, but —”

“But what, you stupid ass? Now we gotta deal with Jean.” His words rang through my ears like a drum beat over my head.

“What’s Jean got to do with this?”

“I told you he said he was going to handle it,” he snapped at me.

Fuck, I did not want deal with Jean.

“You think he’s gonna be ma— What the fuck?” All of a sudden, all the lights in the clubhouse went out. “Y’all stop playing with the lights!”

“It ain’t us,” Tiny shouted. “You motherfuckers need to pay the bill.”

“Somebody go check the power breaker!” I yelled.

“We don’t know where that shit is,” Montclair yelled back.

“It’s in the cellar.”

“I ain’t going in nobody’s cellar. There might be rats down there,” someone cracked back.

“Y’all some childish motherfuckers,” I said.

I could hear Prince, who was still on the

line. "Jace, what fuck are you doing?"

I moved the phone back to my ear. "Hold on, Prince. These niggas in here playing with the lights and shit."

"Ain't nobody playing," Montclair said.

"Crescent Boys, come out and playeeee!" A creepy, almost witchlike voice squawked from somewhere in the room. It was a sound that sent chills down my spine and put me on high alert.

"What the fuck was that?" Tiny asked in the dark.

"I don't know, but it didn't sound friendly." I pulled my gun out. "Hopefully it was someone's phone. Yo, is that back door locked?"

"Yeah, it should — oh, shit! What the hell was that?" a dude named Nate said before I heard him yell, "Heeeelp!" in a gurgling voice.

"Nate, you all right, Crescent? Nate!" I'm not gonna lie. That shit didn't sound good at all, and when he didn't answer, I was scared. "What the fuck is going on?"

Tiny pulled out his cell phone and turned on the flashlight so that he could find his way through the dark. He left the living room and went to the small kitchen where Nate's voice had come from. I followed his example, shining my phone's light toward the kitchen entrance. After taking one step inside, Tiny shouted in a way I had never heard a grown man shout in my life. It was a mixture of shock, terror, *and* him trying to catch his breath.

"T–they're . . . they're —" Tiny's voice faded, only to be replaced by him making gurgling sounds.

"What?" Zay said, rushing to the kitchen. He stopped abruptly at the entrance and raised his gun, firing off a few shots as he backed into the living room. Almost as soon as he started shooting, I heard a shotgun go off from the kitchen, and I watched the flash, then the spray, catch Zay in the chest and send him flying. I knew he was dead before he hit the ground.

Rapid gunfire came from one of the back rooms, and then the pained shouts of my friends.

"Jace! Jace!" I heard Prince shout through my phone, and I put him on speaker so I could keep using the flashlight.

"Someone's in the clubhouse shooting at us."

"Someone like who?" Prince shouted in a panic.

"I don't know, but we got dead Crescents."

A flash of a woman in all black running

out of the kitchen startled me into dropping my phone. In both of her hands were bloody knives, and she had the eeriest smile on her face. It was like something straight out of a horror film.

"You wanna play?" she asked in a girly voice.

"Hell nah!" Montclair shouted, and we both started firing wild shots in the direction she came from.

"What the fuck is going on? We need to get the fuck up outta here!" Montclair shouted.

"He's right. Everybody out!" Prince screamed through the phone.

It was too late. We weren't going anywhere, as a wave of machine gun fire splashed through the room. I pulled my trigger until it clicked, and so did all twelve of the rest of us. My heart was pounding, and I tried to slow my breathing so that I could listen in the dark. The only thing I could hear was Montclair panting beside me.

"Did we get her?" he asked.

"She ain't the one you should be worried about," a ghastly voice announced.

"Jace! Jace!" Prince shouted as the gunshots continued, but I was out of ammo and too preoccupied to answer.

There was a loud gunshot, followed by

pain in my body. I let out a cry of agony. There was another shot, and I felt a burning pain in my stomach before I fell to the ground. As I lay there feeling the blood seep from my body and my life fading, I focused on where Montclair had dropped his phone. The flashlight was still on, and I caught a glimpse of the scary-looking woman standing behind Montclair. I wanted to warn him when I saw her lift her blade, but I couldn't speak.

"You didn't think I came here alone, did you?" the woman said into his ear.

He tried to turn around, but her knife was already at his throat. I watched the sharp blade cut mercilessly into his neck, slicing his throat open. It was a sight I'd never wish on my worst enemy. Montclair began gasping for air, making the same gurgling sound Tiny had. Finally, he dropped to the ground, holding his neck as he died.

More gunfire erupted. I could still hear Prince screaming through my phone, shouting my name, before everything went black.

Chapter 64
Lauryn

I didn't know how it happened, but talking to Prince had slowly become the highlight of my day. I liked him, and I could tell he liked me. I'd never tell him how my stomach tingled when he called me Cinderella. Well, maybe one day. Just not that night as we sat on a bench on the Riverwalk. He had other things on his mind.

"Jace! Jace! Jace!" He shouted, pacing around like a wild man in front of me.

He'd been fussing for the last forty minutes with people on the phone, and this latest conversation, he was straight up yelling. From what I could put together from his side of the call, he was dealing with some major shit. He finally hung up the phone looking pale as a ghost.

"You okay?"

"No. Something bad just happened." His voice was trembling.

"Bad like . . . what?"

"I think my friends are dead." He plopped down next to me. I wasn't a doctor, but he looked like he was in shock. I reached over and took his hand, watching him slowly come back to life.

"Look, I'ma need you to take an Uber or Lyft," he said. "I need to check this out."

"If it's bad, I'm not going to let you go alone," I said.

"You don't understand. It could get dangerous."

"Then I guess it's a good thing I brought this." I opened my purse.

He stared down into my bag at the gun casually resting there. His eyebrows shot up, and he looked back up at me, impressed.

"Trust me when I say I can handle myself."

He nodded at me and gave me a soft kiss on the lips. I didn't think he really wanted to go alone. His eyes had real worry in them.

"A'ight, let's go," he said, standing up and leading me to his truck.

Prince drove like a bat out of hell. Wherever we were going, he wanted to get there fast. While he drove, he reached into his armrest and pulled out a black gun and a loaded magazine.

"Nice choice," I said, taking it from him

so he could focus on the road. "I prefer the Sig P365 for everyday use. Lighter, not too much recoil, and *very* accurate."

I'm not even sure he heard a word I said. I loaded the gun and cocked it back to put one in the chamber for him. The shocked expression on his face was priceless when I handed the weapon back to him. His eyes kept fluttering from the road back to me.

"Who *are* you?" he asked.

"Just a girl who likes guns." I smiled at him.

He forced a small one back before he focused on the road. He pulled onto a block with only a few houses and drove to one at the end. When he sped to a stop in front of it, I watched him look around at all the parked cars. There were at least seven of them outside the house. I was no fool. I knew the cars weren't there for a party. The way Prince scanned the area, it had to be their trap house.

He gripped his gun tightly and got out of the car. "Stay in here," he said and shut the door.

"Not a chance." I grabbed my gun from my purse and swung my door open. I hopped down from the tall truck and followed behind him.

He stopped abruptly and turned to face

me. "Lauryn, please get back in the truck."

"I know you call me Cinderella, but I'm not a helpless damsel. Now, come on. I got your back."

He could see that he wasn't going to change my mind, so he didn't even try. He continued creeping to the house, and I covered his six. When we got to the door, we noticed that it wasn't shut all the way. We paused to listen but were met with nothing but quiet. Too much quiet.

"This door is never unlocked," he said and slowly pushed it open.

I aimed my weapon, just in case something jumped out at us. The only thing that did was a swarm of flies. As I swatted them away, Prince took a step inside. He stopped, and the hand that held his gun flopped to his side. He was as motionless as a statue.

I stepped inside to see what had him in such a state and gasped when I saw the grim scene. There were three dead bodies in the living room and blood splatter everywhere.

"Montclair," Prince whispered, staring at a man on the ground with his neck slit.

Montclair's eyes were still open and were beginning to turn a milky white. Prince regained his motion and made his way to another body on the ground. I heard him take a brisk breath as he stared at it tearfully. His free hand formed into a fist so tight that he began shaking.

"Who's that?" I asked.

"The guy I been telling you about. My best friend, Jace."

Prince stepped away from him, and I saw water in his eyes as he passed me. He began defensively moving throughout the rest of the house, and I understood why. The killer could still be there. I decided to stay put to examine the grizzly living room murder scene. I looked at the doorknob and saw no signs of forced entry.

I stepped around to each victim. One had a shotgun wound to the chest. There was no way he'd have been able to survive a hit like that. The slit in Montclair's neck was so deep that his killer had to have used a lot of unnecessary force. It was sickening.

I knelt next to Jace just as Prince came back to the living room. "They're dead. They're all dead," he said, putting his hand to his head and frantically pacing.

"Breathe, Prince. It's going to be okay," I said, but even I didn't know how to fix a massacre. "Were any of the other doors broken? Any sign of forced entry?" I asked, and he shook his head. "Not up here either. You're either dealing with a professional, or it was someone they knew and let in."

"I don't know anyone who would do something like this. I don't —" He suddenly stopped talking, and his eyes grew big as saucers.

"What about those dudes at the club?" I asked, but the feeling of something touching my ankle made me forget my question. I gasped when I realized that it was Jace, weakly reaching for me. "Prince! Prince, he's alive. We need to get him to a hospital!"

"Prince?" Jace croaked weakly.

"Save your strength, bro. Don't talk. Help is on the way."

Chapter 65
Saint

Was it my first time being behind bars? Not at all. I'd seen the back of more police cars than I'd like to count. Still, I couldn't help but feel like Jean and I had switched places. The only difference was I couldn't afford my bail. I wasn't flat broke, but I definitely wasn't in the position to put up bail for a capital murder charge. Shit, after Nette took my money, I wasn't even sure I had enough for a halfway decent lawyer. If that wasn't bad enough, both my resources to get the fuck outta there, Jean and Prince, had recently stabbed me in the back.

I went to the cell bars and peered out just as Sheriff Clay was walking by. She had the biggest smile on her face.

"Well, ain't you a sight for sore eyes. Looks like this is the end of the road for you, Saint," she said when she saw me. Apparently, there really *were* people willing to talk for the reward money Chino's family had offered. None of what they said had mattered before because there wasn't a body. Now that it had somehow turned up, they had a case against me — one I didn't know if I could beat alone.

"We'll see," I said as confidently as I could.

"Once we match your gun with the bullet we found in Chino, you're toast." She shook her head dramatically and laughed. "Don't you watch *Law and Order*? You always get rid of the gun."

"When can I get my one phone call? I need to call Jean so he can get me out of here."

"Jean?" she asked, laughing. "I hate to break it to you, but you're the last thing on his mind right now. Actually, I'm getting the notion that he wants you as far away from his ass as possible when he finishes his deal with Big Shirley."

"I want my damn phone call!"

"You'll get it when I say you get it. And right now, I say you ain't getting shit."

I hated law enforcement. Everyone had to obey the law *but* them. My eyes bore a hole through the sheriff's face. If I could, I'd reach through the bars and choke the life out of her. Technically I could, but then I knew for a fact I'd never be a free man again.

"Hey! You're violating his rights. The man's entitled to his phone call." The voice came from the cell next to mine. It sounded close, like he was right up against the bars.

Sheriff Clay shifted her attention to whoever he was, the scowl evident on her face. "Mind your fuckin' business, rich boy. That uppity shit might work where you're from in Atlanta, but this is Gator Lake. I run the show here."

"Once my lawyers are finished with you and the rest of these hillbillies, I'm gonna own this town," the rich boy yelled back.

"Keep dreamin," she said with a smirk.

She made good on her statement and walked away without giving me my phone call. I let out all the air from my lungs to try to calm myself down. Closing my eyes, I rested my forehead on the cold cell bars as thoughts ran through my mind like a track relay.

Antoinette had taken all my money, and I couldn't call her if I wanted to. I also had no clue where she was. She could have been halfway across the world by then. A flash of her naked with Marquis came to mind, and I envisioned him touching her, kissing her, and fucking her. I knew the faces she made when I hit certain spots. Had she made the same ones for him, and did he know her spots? Did she love him? Did he love her?

I'd never felt a pain cut so deep until another cut came right after it. I never in a million years thought I'd be looking at Jean from across the river. I figured we'd always be at each other's sides. But things had changed. I didn't want to think that he was responsible for my predicament, but every mental route I took led me straight to him. It was just hard to believe. I didn't know what to do with my pain, I didn't know where to put it. Naturally, it just bottled up in my throat until I opened my mouth and let it all out. My curses filled the jail, and when I was done, I felt no better.

"That bad, huh?" the man in the cell next to me asked in a low tone.

"What's it to you?" I growled back.

"I heard them talking before they brought you in. Saint Charles, right?"

"That's me."

"I'm Gabriel. I've never seen officers more excited and terrified to arrest one man. You must be something special."

"You could say that. I guess just not right now. What you in for?" I asked, and he gave a resentful chuckle.

"Loving the wrong woman. Got locked

up on my birthday."

"Damn, that's fucked up."

"Tell me about it. What about you? Why are you here?"

"Murder," I said coldly, and he got quiet for a few moments.

"Did you do it?" Gabriel finally asked.

"Let's just say them cops weren't scared for no reason."

CHAPTER 66
MARIE

He'd done it. He'd really done it. Jean had found a way to purchase a share of the Midnight Blues nightclub and casino. I was ecstatic, full of myself, and feeling good with a thousand dollars in my purse that Jean had given me to buy a dress for our big meeting with Shirley Duncan. We were going to sign papers, then I would be officially installed as the casino's floor manager, and he wanted me to look good. I'd happily spent most of the morning in Irene's, a high-end boutique. Oh, and honey, when I walked out of Irene's, you couldn't tell me shit, 'cause I looked like a million dollars in my designer suit and red bottom shoes.

Coincidentally, Irene's was just a few doors down from the spiritual shop that Raven had dragged me into — the one that I had called utter nonsense. However, when I walked past it this time, I slowed my steps and stared at the flashing OPEN sign in the window as I remembered what Ernestine had read in my tarot cards. I had to admit that she'd been more right than wrong with her predictions. I had indeed come to a crossroads with Curtis and Jean, no matter how much I had wanted to avoid it. Maybe there really was something to the psychic stuff I had previously dismissed. Now that I was about to embark on a new career and, hopefully, a renewed marriage, it might be nice to get an idea of what the future held.

One reading couldn't hurt, could it? I stood outside the door and seriously contemplated going in. Then, I lost my nerve.

I shook my head. "What am I doing here?" I asked myself, then started to walk back to where I'd parked.

I'd only taken a couple of steps before I heard the melodic sound of a door chime behind me.

"I've been waiting for you."

I turned around and saw Ernestine standing in the doorway, wearing a long, loose-fitted black dress. Her hair was pulled up, showcasing her marvelous light brown eyes. She had a mystical smile on her lips as she stared back at me.

"You've been . . . waiting on me?"

"Yes. We have much to discuss. Please, come in."

She stepped out of the way and waved me inside. It was like an invisible magnet pulled me, because I didn't hesitate to go in. She shut the door behind me and led me back to her reading room. Once there, she ushered me to sit down on a pillow across the table from her.

The two of us just stared at each other. I was waiting on her to say something, but then I remembered that *I* was the customer.

"How did you know I was coming?" I finally asked.

"Just a feeling." She studied my face with an interested expression. "You seek answers. Perhaps another reading?"

"O . . . okay." I nodded.

"This reading requires me to pull an extra card. The cost of this reading is one hundred and fifty dollars. If you'd rather not, that is okay, but then you may never know what lies ahead."

She had me hook, line, and sinker. No matter how many times I thought about just getting up and leaving, I knew I wasn't going anywhere until I got my reading. I gave her a wary look before I grabbed the money from my purse and put it in her hand.

"There. Now, let's just do the reading or whatever. I have to be somewhere soon."

"Of course."

She began shuffling a deck of tarot cards, pulling out four. One was face up, and the other three were down.

Ernestine pointed at the one that was face up. "Ahh, the Lovers card. I see that the masked man has returned. No . . . you sought him out! He is an exceptional lover, yes?" She looked up at me and smiled.

I lowered my head. "I put an end to it. I'm back with my husband."

That seemed to amuse her. "Sure you are."

As she turned over the next card, a look of worry came across her face. "The Three of Swords. There is trouble brewing, and it appears you will be in the middle of it."

"What does that mean?" I asked as my husband and my lover both came to my mind.

"I think you already know," she said with a raised eyebrow.

She turned over the third card. "The Fool inspires courage, and with that comes a mixture of anticipation, wonder, awe, curiosity, and danger."

"Danger? What kind of danger?"

"Let us see." Ernestine turned over the final card. It was the Moon.

"You have a secret." She sat back and stared at me. "A deep, dark secret."

"Duh. You already know that," I said plainly.

"This secret is separate from the masked man. It's . . . one that scares you. One you don't want anyone to know. But I do."

"What is that supposed to mean?" I snapped angrily, although I had my suspicions.

"The truth and only the truth will set you free, because he will find out."

Her eyes held mine, and it felt like she was reading into my soul. I felt as cold as a block of ice as fear slowly trickled through my veins. I hoisted myself to my feet and ran out of the store, gasping for air. I didn't know whether to hold in Ernestine's words or let them go.

After shaking off the ghostly feeling of the store and catching my breath, I looked down at the gold watch on my wrist, remembering Jean and my meeting at the Blues.

Chapter 67
Gabriel

I was still in the previous day's clothes, brooding at the head of the dining room table on my yacht. The untouched meal the private chef had prepared the night before, along with the huge birthday cake with fifty burned-out candles, was in front of me. I'd been sitting in that spot ever since my bail hearing three hours ago, which turned out to be a farce. It had only cost me five hundred dollars, along with a promise to stay away from Shirley Duncan and appear in court in three months. That smug-ass sheriff was there, snickering behind my back, but that was all right. She'd get hers in the end.

"Gabriel?" Sarah called from the entrance to the dining room. She stepped into the room, studying me and the expensive, ruined meal on the table. I'm sure she thought I was starting to lose it. Truth was,

I was kind of worried about that myself lately.

"How did it go?" I asked.

She shrugged. "It was more expensive than we expected, but he's here."

I nodded, and she disappeared, returning a moment or so later with the man who, only a few hours ago, had been in a jail cell across from me.

"Welcome, Mr. Charles. Please, have a seat." I gestured to a chair beside me.

Saint's eyes roamed around the room. "Y'all having some kind of party or something?"

"We were supposed to have a little birthday celebration last night, but as you know, I ran into some trouble with the law." I gestured again to the chair. "Please, please, have a seat, Mr. Charles."

"That's Saint. My daddy was Mr. Charles." He sat down.

"Okay, Saint it is. Please, call me Gabriel."

"So, what's up? You some kind of kingpin or something? I don't know many people who got five hundred grand just to throw around at somebody they don't even know. And what exactly is it that you want? For all I know, you might be a cop they planted inside."

"Oh, no." I laughed. "I'm not a kingpin,

and I would never waste my time to do the job of a cop. It doesn't pay enough. I'm just a man who knows how to make money make more money. You can google me if you like."

"That sounds cool and all, but why am I here? You didn't bail me out because you heard my story and was feeling charitable," he said.

I was starting to like him more and more. Straight to the point and all about business.

"No, I'm not that charitable at all. In fact, I'm rather cheap unless I want something real bad."

"And what exactly is it that you want from me?"

"Well, after what you had to say last night, I'm hoping you'll be able to give me a belated birthday present," I explained. "You see, I missed out on the present I was hoping to receive last night, and I would love another shot at it. This time, on my terms."

A slow grin spread across his face. "This have anything to do with the Duncans?"

"Oh, my dear Saint, this has everything to do with the Duncans."

Saint picked up the thousand-dollar bottle of champagne sitting in a bucket of melted ice and popped the cork. He placed it to his lips, took a long swallow straight from the bottle, then looked at me. "Well, shit. Then I'm in."

He began to laugh, and I joined in. The two of us were going to be quite a team.

Chapter 68
Marie

I pulled up to the Blues parking lot right on time. Jean was waiting there for me, looking fine as shit in a gray suit with a purple tie.

"You look nervous," he said as I stepped out of my car. Doyle, his attorney, was there also, just a few steps behind him. I was still shaken up after my encounter with Ernestine, but I snapped out of it because this shit was really about to happen.

"I am a little nervous," I replied.

Jean gave me that million-dollar smile. "Don't be. This is our time. When I get finished, we won't own ten percent of this place. We'll own the whole damn thing. I just need you by my side. Now, come on. All eyes on us."

God, his confidence could be so damn sexy. I took his arm, and we made our way up the walkway with Doyle behind us. When we walked into the Blues, sure enough, heads turned. Big Shirley's brother greeted us in the lobby with a smile faker than Donald Trump's hair and his bronzer makeup.

"Jean," he said dryly as he held out his hand.

"Floyd!" Jean said with enough energy for both of them. "You know my wife, Marie, and this is my attorney, Patrick Doyle."

"Pleasure to see you again, Mrs. LeBlanc," Floyd said, dipping his head in my direction and completely ignoring Doyle. "If you all will please follow me. My sister's expecting you."

Jean and I smiled at each other as we followed him. There was nothing that could stop us now. Nothing at all, except hearing Curtis's voice as we went up the stairwell. I swear I was so petrified I let out a little pee.

"I'm about to look at it right now, Li'l Vegas," he said.

I wished I was just hearing things, but that would be too good to be true. Curtis came bounding down the steps with his phone to his ear and almost ran right into us. I squeezed my husband's hand a little more tightly as we came around the turn on the winding stairs.

"Whoa! Slow down, Curt. You almost took us out," Floyd said.

"My bad. My little cousin Nevada just sent me that updated video. I'm about to go look at it now," Curtis said.

"Bet."

Curtis almost stumbled and broke his neck when he saw me. He caught himself, but when his eyes met mine, a blind man could see there was something between us. Thank God only Floyd seemed to notice. Before Jean caught on, I faced forward and continued up the steps like Curtis was any other stranger.

I was sure Curtis was wondering why his messages weren't getting through to me, or how I could just sleep with him and discard him like junk. I liked him, I really did, but he was a risk I couldn't take anymore. It looked like he was connected somehow to Big Shirley, so him being around the casino could be awkward, but like Jean said, this was our time.

Floyd took us all the way to Big Shirley's office, where she was waiting for us. She wasn't alone. Monique sat to the side on a comfortable-looking sofa with an uncomfortable look on her face. Her grim expression matched Floyd's, and her eyes remained blank even when she smiled. Floyd ushered us in and closed the door behind us. Doyle, Jean, and I took seats opposite Big Shirley at her desk, and Floyd took his place beside her. He remained standing.

"I'm starting to know this office like the back of my hand," Jean said to Big Shirley.

"Don't get any ideas. Ten percent doesn't come with an office. Especially *this* office," Monique told him briskly.

"But shouldn't it?" Doyle interjected. "I mean, it's only ten percent, but it's ten percent *ownership.* The LeBlancs should have their own offices. And don't worry. I've already added that in the paperwork."

"Have you now?"

He pulled a small stack of papers from his briefcase and slid them over to Big Shirley. She picked them up and began reading. It was obvious that they weren't happy to be giving up ten percent, and my husband had most likely forced Big Shirley's hand. I didn't care. I just wanted her to sign on the dotted line and make it official.

"Oh, Big Shirley, I can't wait to get started. This place just has so much potential," I gushed.

"I think it's just fine the way it is. Your job's going to be floor manager, not interior decorator."

She made it apparent that she wasn't okay with me changing anything, but I would fix that. I believed some people were just stuck in their ways until they were shown a new one. If she had any eye at all, she would see that the Blues could use a coat of paint and some renovation.

"I mean, yes, it is nice, but you have to admit, other than the main gambling area, it's a little outdated," I said, standing my ground.

"Outdated?" She looked up from the paperwork to glare at me.

"I'm sure we can discuss building updates sometime in the near future." Jean jumped in, sensing tension forming on top of the tension that was already in the room. He took a pen from his pocket and slid it over to Shirley.

"If everything is to your liking, please sign on the dotted line, Mrs. Duncan. I'll register the paperwork and have the LeBlancs added to your gaming license," Doyle told her with a smile.

Big Shirley snatched the pen and let it hover over the dotted signature line for a moment. Time seemed to slow down, and so did my breathing. Jean had tons of businesses, but I had never cared to have my hands in any of them. But the Blues? I was going to be all over it like white on rice.

Finally, Big Shirley's pen touched the paper, and she started to put her signature in ink. I was so enthralled with her signing the agreement that I jumped terribly hard when the office door burst open.

"Momma, don't sign those papers!"

Big Shirley's son rushed into the room, followed by that crooked-ass Sheriff Clay.

"Marquis! What in the world?" Big Shirley said.

We all were looking at the newcomers in confusion as Marquis ran over and grabbed the papers out of his mother's hands. "Don't sign those papers."

"And why the hell not?" Jean asked, sounding as annoyed as I felt. "I've lived up to my end of our arrangement. Saint's out of the picture for good."

"No, sir, Saint's on the streets," Sheriff Clay said flatly. "He made bail a half hour ago."

"Saint doesn't have a lawyer good enough or money to pull off something like that, and he for damn sure isn't making a million-dollar bail. How the hell does that happen?"

"I don't know, but if Saint is free, then I'm not signing shit," Big Shirley said, snatching the papers back and ripping them in half before tossing them in our direction. "The deal's off."

"You can't do this," I shouted, leaning across the desk to get in her face.

"The hell I can't! Now, if you'll excuse me, I have to make some arrangements. My son's life is still in jeopardy with that madman on the loose."

I turned to Jean, who just sat there looking stupid as he tried to put all the pieces together. I didn't know the connection between Saint and Marquis, but I would bet my last dollar that it had something to do with Antoinette. And if it did, then Marquis for sure was in danger. Now I understood how Jean had weaseled into the deal for the Blues. He'd traded Saint for it. I felt a quiver of fear in my bones. He'd known Saint much longer than me. If he could throw him under the bus just for a business deal, what would he do to me if he found out what I'd done?

"Wait. What about my floor manager job?" I asked once I recognized just how far south the meeting had gone.

"That's no longer on the table."

"We'll talk about it when we get home," Jean finally said.

"But —"

"I said when we get home!" he snapped at me angrily.

"Fine. This is just another empty promise you've made."

I jumped to my feet in a flash of anger, glaring at him as I stormed out of the office. I could feel the temper tantrum swelling up inside of me with each step I took back down the stairs. No manager position, no office, and no ten percent. Nothing. All the happiness I had felt when I woke up that morning wasn't just fading. It was long gone.

I exited the building and walked straight to my car, fuming. Just as I slammed my door and was about to pull off, the passenger door opened. I whipped my head around to curse out my husband but found myself face-to-face with Curtis.

"Don't look at me. Drive," he said when he got in. We were out of that parking lot in a flash.

Chapter 69
Big Shirley

Don't ask me how I got through the rest of the day after the meeting with Jean, but somehow, I'd made it through *and* retained complete ownership of the Blues. However, knowing that Saint was somewhere on the loose, roaming free, made me deeply uneasy. I knew Saint's type. He was like a snake in the grass. You wouldn't see him until he struck, which was why we had to be ready. I never thought I'd say it, but I was glad Nee Nee and her brood were still around to lend a hand. Curtis had volunteered to hunt Saint down using his bounty-hunting skills, and I'd promised him twenty grand if he brought that bastard in. Dead or alive, I didn't care. Marquis hated it, but until it all simmered down, I was sending his ass down to Houston in the morning with Lauryn as his babysitter this time.

Sheriff Clay had a 24-hour deputy patrolling the property, and under no circumstances was anyone associated with Saint, Jean, or the Crescent Boys allowed on the property. The jury was still out on how Jean would react to things not going his way, so better safe than sorry. I also made sure there were armed guards covering the perimeter of my home.

Speaking of my house, I needed to check on Marquis. I pulled out my phone and called him.

"Everything okay, Momma?"

"Yes. I just wanted to hear your voice and make sure you were all right."

"You still at the Blues?"

"Yep. Getting ready to turn off the lights on the trees. I'm waiting for Floyd to get back from having dinner at the witch's house."

"Momma, will you stop calling her that? She's not a witch, and Floyd really likes her. She's the first woman he's liked since Aunt Carol ran off."

"Well, then Floyd should spend time with her instead of doing a hit and run. I don't know why he won't just let me drive myself home from work."

"Because the easiest way to get to me is through you," he said wisely. "If Saint can't get me, then you're the number one next choice. Hell, if I gotta go to Houston, then at least you can let Floyd drive you to and from work."

"You're right," I conceded.

"Look, if you're bored, Aunt Nee Nee and I can come keep you company."

I was worried about him, but it touched me to hear that he felt just as protective of me. "I love you, son, but I'm all right. It's a slow night. I can wait for Floyd."

"OK, Momma. Love you too."

We disconnected, and I stepped out of my office to check on things. As I walked past the guard at my door, I remembered what Saint had done to big-ass Dice with just his fists. Maybe I should add a few more guards, I thought. Saint was just one man, but when someone had that much anger inside him, you could never be too careful.

"If everyone is out, y'all can lock up, Freddy."

"Yes, ma'am."

I did a quick tour through the quiet hallway where our offices were and then found my way back to mine. There wasn't much work to do, so I figured I could catch up on my guilty pleasure, reality TV, while I waited for Floyd. I got comfortable at my desk and turned on my laptop.

I'd only gotten about thirty minutes into the show when I heard a thud outside my office. It sounded like it had come from down the hall, near Floyd's office. If he was back already, he must have been flying on the interstate, which I wouldn't have put past him.

"Dammit, Floyd, what are you doing? They were just about to throw blows!" I got up to see what he'd dropped.

Down the hallway, the door to Floyd's office was closed. "Floyd?" I called out as I opened his door. There was nothing but a dark room. Slowly, I reached my hand to the light switch and held my breath as I flipped it. I exhaled when the room lit up and I saw it was empty. Turning out the lights and shutting the door again, I shrugged it off and went back to my office.

When I got closer to the open door, the hairs on the back of my neck stood up. Something was off. I could have sworn that I had left the show playing on my laptop, but now there was just silence. I told myself that maybe the show had just ended, but when I stepped foot inside, I knew that wasn't the case. I almost jumped out of my shoes when I saw Saint sitting at my desk, his devilish eyes boring holes in me.

"H–How the hell did you get past security?" I could barely stammer.

"You talking about those punk-ass rent-a-cops you hired, or that old-ass deputy in the parking lot?" Saint let out a hearty laugh. "Not that it really matters. They're all dead anyway."

He turned my laptop to face me. I gasped when I saw the live footage of the entrance surveillance cameras. The guards were there, but they were on the ground in pools of their own blood. I couldn't understand how I hadn't heard the shots — until Saint pointed his gun at my head. The silencer screwed on it would ensure that nobody heard it when he shot me either.

I looked around the office for something to defend myself with, but I'd never be able to reach any of the guns I had stashed in there. My best bet was to use the gift of gab.

"What do you want, Saint?"

"Ain't it obvious? The way you beefed up security here and at your house. I'm here to kill your son."

"He's not here."

"I know, but it would be too much work chasing him all over Louisiana, so I figured, why not make him come to me? If you haven't caught on yet, you're the bait."

My stomach did a flip. "Marquis isn't stupid. He's not going to fall for a trap. He'll bring Floyd and his cousins, and they will kill your ass."

"They can try, but I ain't stupid either. I got a plan." He stood up and grabbed my arm. "Let's go."

"She ain't going nowhere." A familiar voice shocked the hell out of me.

"Floyd, he's got a gun!" I shouted.

Saint let me go and aimed at my brother, but Floyd was too quick. He knocked the weapon out of Saint's hand, and the two of them began fighting like wild men. I dove out of the way because they were all over the office.

Floyd dodged a right hook from Saint and then landed one of his own. "Motherfucka, you trying to kidnap my sister?"

Saint might have been stronger, but my brother had MMA training experience. He landed another blow that sent Saint staggering to the ground. Floyd got behind him. As Saint tried to get back to his feet, Floyd placed a strong arm around his neck and squeezed so hard that Saint probably thought it was a boa constrictor that had hold of him.

Saint's hands shot to Floyd's arm as he tried to pry himself loose, but it was clear that my brother was getting the better of him. Flailing around, Saint tried desperately to grasp anything he could reach. Just as

Floyd was about to put Saint to sleep, I heard a small *pfft,* and my brother froze. His eyes widened, and he loosened his hold. Saint slipped out of his grip and stumbled away, rubbing his neck and gasping for air.

Floyd took a few wobbly steps before he fell to the ground.

"Floyd!" I got up to run to him, but something I saw made me stumble backward. I shook my head as if I might clear away the hallucination; but the vision was all too real. I was staring into the eyes of a lunatic. Gabriel was standing in the doorway with a wide grin, holding Saint's gun in one hand and a bouquet of flowers in the other.

"Honey, I'm home!" he shouted.

I went to swing at him, but by then, Saint was on his feet and had grabbed me. I fought against him, but he was just too strong. He put my arms behind my back and used something that felt like zip ties to bind my wrists.

"You!" I spat at Gabriel. "It was *you* who bailed him out, wasn't it?"

"Guilty as charged. What else was I gonna do with a half a million dollars lying around? I mean, I offered it to you, and you pretty much gave me your ass to kiss."

"That's about the only thing I'd let you kiss, you sick psycho."

I lunged at him, and Saint yanked me back.

"You stay right fucking there!" Gabriel shouted, turning the gun on me. He stood triumphantly over Floyd, who was writhing in pain on the ground. "Not so tough now, huh? Maybe I should put you out of your misery like the dog you are."

"No, please . . ." My voice was barely above a whisper as I watched the life slowly leaving my brother's body.

Gabriel turned to Saint and said, "See, that's what I'm talking about. The woman's my weakness. That's why I'm willing to give her one more chance. She just needs to be broken."

"I'm not an animal."

"I didn't say you were. However, I think we can bring your spice level down a notch. I didn't expect to meet such formidable opposition, so I hired Saint here to help me accomplish my goal. Oh, and I'm sorry about your son, but with him out of the way, you'll have more time to focus on me."

"You sick bastard!" I lurched at him, but Saint had a firm hold.

Gabriel chuckled and looked at Saint. "Let's go. You never know when someone is going to see your handiwork at the front door."

When Saint started pulling me, I fought like hell, trying to stay there with Floyd. Even after the ferocious fight, however, Saint still had some strength left. The last thing I saw as he dragged me out of my office was my brother's weak hand reaching for me before it fell to the ground.

Chapter 70
Marquis

I felt an uneasiness in my stomach as I pulled past the deputy's car at the Blues. Not because he didn't wave back at me as he sat in there with his lights on, but mostly because of the call I'd just had with Curtis that sent me over there. I'd been barricaded in the house with Monique and Aunt Nee Nee, packing for my trip to Houston. Lauryn had gone out to see a friend, but I suspected she was going on a date of some kind, because she left the house looking smoking hot. I gave her a pass because once we left tomorrow morning, she'd be stuck with me for as long as it took for things to cool down.

"What's up, Curt? Did Nevada ever get back to you about that surveillance tape?" I asked when he'd called me.

"Ah, yeah. It wasn't nothing he could do."

Have you ever heard someone tell you something, and it sounded like they had *I'm lying* all in between the lines? Well, that's how Curtis sounded, only he had no reason to lie about anything. I'd only asked him because if our tech-genius cousin Nevada could make the tape clearer, we'd know who murdered Pierre. Depending on who it was, the information might end up being a bargaining chip for us.

"But he did find out who put up Saint's bail."

"Who?" That was something we all wanted to know. The bail was hefty, and Jean had assured us that Saint was strapped for cash, so he wouldn't be able to spring himself. I had half a mind to think Jean tried to two-time us, but I wanted to be sure.

"Don't tell me it was Jean."

"That was my first thought too, but nope, it wasn't him. You remember that creepy dude that was stalking Aunt Shirley? The one Floyd beat up and you got the sheriff on."

"Yeah, yeah." The dude's name came to mind, and I snapped my fingers. "Gabriel."

"Turns out the dude is rich as shit, and he was in the cell next to Saint when he got locked up."

"Get the fuck outta here. That means Momma could be in danger too."

"That's what I was thinking. I tried to call

her, but she ain't answering. I'ma head over to the Blues, but I'm across town. You mind checking up on her?" he asked.

"Dude, that's my momma. Of course I don't mind checking on her. Thanks, cuz. I owe you one."

"You're family. You owe me nothing. It's love."

"Love," I said back, and we disconnected the call.

I got out of the car with the bag of food in my hand and started toward the Blues. The parking lot didn't have many cars in it, which let me know it had been a slower night. As bone-weary as I was, I wasn't even mad at it. After checking on Momma and attending to my duties, I planned to go home and get a much-needed night of good sleep.

I'd only taken a few steps when something moving quickly caught my attention at the corner of my eye. Readying myself for battle, I placed my hand on my waist where my gun was clipped. However, there was no need to draw it, because it was just my uncle's voodoo girlfriend, Ernestine. I was intrigued to see her there because she and Floyd usually kept their stuff away from his place of business.

When she got close to me, she didn't crack a hint of a smile.

"Hey, Ernestine. I —"

"Your uncle left this. I don't know why he will not listen to me!" She was holding up the chicken foot my uncle had been wearing lately.

"Um, in his defense, maybe he just doesn't want to wear it?" It came out as a question because the last thing I wanted to do was upset a priestess.

"It does not matter what he wants. The energy inside this is bound to him." She jerked the chicken foot for emphasis. "He has to wear it."

"Well, how about I stop you by his office and you can give it to him?"

"Please do. Tonight is not a good night. The moon speaks to me."

"O . . . kay. Follow me. His office is upstairs."

We headed to the entrance. She was a stunning woman, and I could see why my uncle put up with her vibes, even the chicken foot, but man, she was creepy. I kept noticing her glance at me, and it gave me an unsettled feeling.

"You have darkness around you, boy," she said. "It's heavy. You need to wear a chicken foot as well I fear."

"I'll pass."

"No. You —" She stopped suddenly and gasped.

We'd made it inside the Blues, and I froze too. We were looking at the same grisly scene. Right there at the front security station were the bodies of our security guards, lying on the ground. Blood was still seeping from the bullet holes in their heads, and there was no question that they were dead. A cold, sweaty feeling overcame me before it turned to pure dread.

"Momma," was all I could manage to say. I dropped the food in my hand and pulled out my gun, rushing into the lobby. I didn't have to go far before I saw what I feared. Momma was being herded down the stairs at gunpoint, and the man holding the gun was Saint. There was another man I didn't recognize, but he was so clean cut and sharp I didn't understand what business he could have with someone like Saint. He had Momma's arm in his hand, aggressively tugging her.

Momma was screaming. "Get off of me! No! No! Let me go! You killed my brother! You killed Floyd!"

Uncle Floyd? Dead? No. Her words would have floored me if I weren't in defense mode.

"Floyd?" Ernestine's sorrowful voice sounded beside me.

"Aye! Let her go!" I shouted toward the stairs.

Upon hearing me belt out my command, Saint trained his eyes on me across the lobby. I didn't have a clear shot at them without hitting Momma, but there was nothing between me and Saint to stop a bullet coming in my direction. He aimed at me and squeezed the trigger.

"Marquis!" Momma's earth-shattering scream pierced my ears.

Instinct kicked in, and I dove out of the way, tackling Ernestine to the ground in the process. We landed behind one of the big plush chairs and ducked down.

I peered around the corner when Saint finally stopped shooting, and I realized why. They were rushing Momma into the main part of the casino, making a break for the back exit, no doubt.

"You stay here," I told Ernestine, but she shook her head defiantly.

"No, I must go to Floyd. You save your mother." She jumped to her feet.

Before I could stop her, she ran away. I leapt to my feet and took off after Momma. The moment I stepped foot into the main part of the casino, Saint opened fire on me again. I ducked behind a slot machine.

"Go get the truck!" Saint snarled to the man he was with.

"Okay. Give her to me, and I'll wait for you to handle your business here," the man said eagerly.

"To hell with that shit. She's my ticket out of here and the only way to be sure you keep your word. Go get the fucking truck!"

The reflection in the mirrored walls gave me a clear view of what was going on. After hesitating for only a second, the clean-cut man turned and ran to the exit. Only Saint, Momma, and I were left. It pained me to see Momma so helpless.

"Let her go, Saint!" I shouted. "Let her fucking go!"

I jumped up and extended my gun. He pulled Momma close to him to prevent me from getting a shot. I moved toward them as he started backing away with an evil grimace on his face.

"Marquis Duncan. Just the man I wanted to see."

"Our beef is between us. She ain't got nothing to do with this shit."

"Nah." Saint gave a small laugh. "I'ma take away everything you love, including your momma."

I frantically looked for an open shot, but

there was none, not without the risk of hurting Momma. Her eyes connected with mine and spoke silently to me before she gave me a small nod. There was something in the gesture that reassured me enough to place my finger on the trigger.

"If my momma was a regular momma, I could see how you'd think killing her would be an easy task. But Big Shirley ain't going out like that."

On my last word, Momma headbutted Saint as hard as she could. It caught him by surprise. When his head snapped back, he dropped his gun and also lost his grip on Momma, so she was able to jump out of the way. I relentlessly squeezed the trigger.

My first bullet caught Saint in the shoulder. Defenseless, he ducked and wove between the tables and machines. I shot at him until my gun clicked, and when it finally did, I went after him.

"Marquis!" Momma's voice stopped me.

I watched angrily as Saint slithered away, but I had more important things to tend to. I went to my mother's aid and pulled out my pocketknife. I used it to cut her restraints, and once her wrists were free, she jumped up and fell into my arms.

"Momma, it's okay. I got you," I said as she sobbed uncontrollably.

"No. No, it's not! My brother. They killed my brother!"

I felt like someone had a tight fist around my heart. My entire life with Uncle Floyd by my side flashed before my eyes, and I choked on my breath. Tears streamed freely down my face as I held onto my Momma tightly.

"They're gonna pay with their lives, Momma. Believe that."

Epilogue

Jean LeBlanc watched his sister-in-law Raven passionately kissing a tall, dark-skinned man on his stoop before entering giddily for what could only be considered a booty call. Jean slammed his fist against the steering wheel of his Rolls Royce and drove away, convinced that Raven had told the truth about not knowing Marie's whereabouts. It had been more than twenty-four hours since Jean and Marie had their plans of owning a piece of Midnight Blues ruined by the news of Saint's release. Marie, embarrassed and angry, abruptly stormed out of the meeting. Unbeknownst to Jean, she hadn't left alone.

It had taken a grief-stricken Jean almost fifteen hours to realize his wife was missing, thanks to the horrific gangland murders the news outlets were referring to as the "Crescent Boys massacre." The slain men were not only his friends and fellow gang members, but they were killed at a property owned by Jean, a coincidence that landed him in front of the Gator Lake Parrish sheriff and the DA for almost four hours.

Meanwhile, the real culprits, Larry Duncan and his trio of psychopaths, partied at an Airbnb in the French Quarter, drinking high-end liquor, eating oysters and gumbo, while divvying up the money, drugs, and cache of weapons they'd stolen from the Clubhouse. The four of them partied all night, until Larry got a call from his wife and learned that his sister-in-law had been attacked and her brother Floyd was in critical condition, hanging on for dear life. When she told him that the attacker was one of the Crescent Boys on a vendetta against Marquis, Larry put the pieces together. Now he was even more convinced that, besides providing some entertainment for his traveling crew, the massacre was well deserved. As for Saint, who had escaped, as well as the man Nee Nee called Jean LeBlanc and some rich weirdo named Gabriel, Larry tucked their names into his memory for a future excursion with his crew.

Saint was still on the loose, but Jace, the only Crescent Boy to survive the massacre, was on a different floor at the same hospital as Floyd. This made it easy for Lauryn to slip between floors to be with family and also support her new boyfriend, Prince, as he sat at his best friend's bedside. Like Jean, he had sworn to kill everyone involved with the massacre, but if that time ever came, would he be able to kill the father of the woman he was quickly falling in love with?

In Floyd's hospital room, the only person missing from the Duncan clan was Lauryn's brother Curtis. He was hot on Saint's heels to avenge his family, while at the same time trying to protect Marie from a secret so big that it put her life in danger.

Pulling into the driveway of his expansive house, Jean stared at the space where his wife's exotic sports car would usually be parked.

"Where are you, woman?" he mumbled, forcing himself to the realization that she really was gone and may never come back. He exited the car slowly, making his way toward the dark, lifeless house. His daughter Simone was staying at a friend's house, upset about the killings and, of course, her mother, who was God knows where, living her life without them.

"Jean, help me."

Jean jumped almost four feet backward when he heard the voice. He pulled out his gun and looked around but saw no one. As he reached the front door keypad, he heard rustling and then a guttural groan. Someone was hiding in the bushes.

"Marie?"

There was no response, and Jean took a few steps closer, his gun ready.

"Marie, honey, is that you?"

"Help me."

Jean tightened his grip on the weapon and stepped close enough to recognize his bloody friend. "Saint?" Jean stood frozen, staring down at the man who had been his closest friend for more than thirty years. The same man he had betrayed in his failed attempt to acquire a piece of the Blues. Now he was lying in the bushes, barely able to move, covered in both new and dried blood and looking homeless. Jean's first instinct was to shoot him because he knew what he'd done to the man, best friend or not. He'd turned his back on him, and eventually, those chickens would come home to roost. Better to get rid of the problem now than have to deal with it later.

"Help me, please," his old friend groaned.

Staring down the barrel of his gun, Jean took a long, hard breath. He'd done shit the grimy way, and look what it had gotten him: his wife gone, his dope and a huge chunk of money gone, and twenty of his best soldiers dead by some unknown enemy. Karma was a motherfucker, and in the last two days, it had kicked the shit out of him. Well, that stopped right here, he decided, and put away his weapon.

"Hold on, bro. I'ma help you." He bent down and picked Saint up, and together they went into the house.

ABOUT THE AUTHORS

Carl Weber is the *New York Times* bestselling author of more than twenty novels and short stories. He graduated from Virginia State University with a bachelor's degree in accounting and has an MBA in marketing from the University of Virginia. A lifelong reader, Weber wanted to write stories about ordinary people who have crazy things happening in their lives. Now, when he's not connecting with readers through his books, Weber is finding new talent for his own publishing company, Urban Books. His latest venture is Urban Books Media, a production company that produces television series based on his bestselling Family Business and Black Hamptons series.

C. N. Phillips was born and raised in Omaha, Nebraska. She fell in love with books at the age of eight, but kept her writing a secret. It wasn't until she became a single mother that she decided to pursue her dream of becoming an author. She is most known for her gritty series The Last Kings and has now joined Carl Weber's publishing house, Urban Books.

The employees of Thorndike Press hope you have enjoyed this Large Print book. All our Thorndike Large Print titles are designed for easy reading, and all our books are made to last. Other Thorndike Press Large Print books are available at your library, through selected bookstores, or directly from us.

For information about titles, please call:
(800) 223-1244

or visit our website at:
gale.com/thorndike